A Dangerous Man

An Ellen Parker Novel

A Dangerous Man

An Ellen Parker Novel

Steven M. Silver

Dedication

For Elisa; she was the inspiration for Ellen.

Foreword and Acknowledgments

There is a Butler County in Ohio now and back in 1994. The Sheriff's Office has been in business since 1803. While many good people have served as Sheriffs and Deputies, none are portrayed in this work of fiction.

The information on methamphetamine in the United States, including the success of the counter-culture's rejection of it and its resurgence, as well as the involvement of outlaw motorcycle gangs, is taken from history. Currently it is a major and growing problem, with much of its production having moved from domestic labs to the Mexican cartels.

A number of people have provided information which I have felt free to use or distort to make the story work. These people include, alphabetically, Susan Rogers, PhD, trauma treatment expert and feline behavior adviser (no one is an expert in that field); Jean Silver, Harley-Davidson expert and rural terrain authority; Jim Silver, weapon systems expert and noted merry-go-round historian; John Silver, justifiable search authority whose saddle bags have never been examined. Thanks, guys.

A special thanks goes to Eric Strehl. He helped find foul, evil typos.

Butler County, Ohio
Spring, 1994

Chapter 1

Later, after the killings were over, Ellen would look back at the end of the hearing as the beginning of things.

Having to go to the hearings, to sit in the Hamilton, Ohio, courtroom, was awful – Ellen used the word and understood it in a way she never had before. Going was her father's idea. He said if the family came, there was less chance of "them getting away with it." Well, Ellen sighed silently to herself, the family had come and sat in the courtroom for three days and they were still getting away with it.

During the proceedings, after the first hour or so, her mother would let her leave, though her father frowned every time Ellen did. Waiting out in the hall, reading the old magazines in the waiting area, or sitting on the courthouse steps doing nothing in the Ohio sun, all of these things were better than sitting and watching the proceedings and hearing about Eileen.

By now, though, all the magazines were read, including the six-year old National Geographic. Ellen even had read the single Sports Illustrated, every word, and now knew about Emmitt Smith and football – maybe she could use some of it to impress her father while he watched his Sunday games next fall.

Probably not. He knew she really didn't like football. But Emmitt Smith had a nice smile. She understood her father would not appreciate her saying so. Ellen pictured the scene: the game is on, Emmitt Smith runs for a touchdown, and, from her chair to one side, she says, "You know, he has a really nice smile." Her father blinks at her as if she just said that Martians were at the door collecting for the United Way.

Ellen smiled at the thought. She was a thin, white girl of thirteen, with falcon-brown eyes that sparkled when she smiled. Her light brown hair almost touched her collar and the bangs almost hid her expressive eyebrows; when she studied a problem, they moved like semaphore flags. Her thin lips tended to settle into a natural smile, given the chance.

She wore a skirt, blouse and sweater her mother chose. Ellen judged them "All right," her term for the unavoidably accepted, but would have preferred jeans. Still, she kind of liked the sweater and that morning had

1

said so to her mother. For reasons Ellen did not understand, her mother had smiled as if she had won something important. The sweater had a woven pattern in its dark blue that seemed naturally to draw her eyes when she sat idly, like now. Then she heard noise down the hall.

The courtroom doors opened and Ellen stood to one side, against the wall, waiting for her parents. A crowd of reporters swarmed about the people coming out. Shouted questions echoed in the lofty hall and the high tech shoes of people carrying television cameras and cables squeaked in a rhythm reminding her of a basketball game and that reminded her of Sports Illustrated and Emmitt Smith's smile but her own quickly faded as she watched the crowd of people coming up the hall.

The first swirl of people was mostly observers, reporters, and friends of the defendants. The male friends, marked almost universally by long hair and beards or mustaches, had made an effort to clean up their appearances from the first time she saw them in the courthouse. Today only a few were in denim and black leather; most had found or bought jackets and wore ties strung around flannel shirts. The women with them likewise were trying to look less imposing. Gone were the black tank tops and sprayed-on jeans. Most were in slacks but a few actually wore dresses. They still had the cold, hard look around their eyes that she first thought only the reporters had.

Ellen saw the lawyers, the prosecutors and defense lawyers looking more alike than different, emerge next and take turns talking before a battery of microphones already set up on spindly stands. She could not hear what they said and she wondered if anyone could. The words, whatever they were, appeared to be unimportant as reporters shouted over each other's questions and the responses. What did seem important was time. She saw the sharp glare of the television lights switched on and off for each speaker for almost identical seconds.

As the last lawyer responded to the last question, the white lights faded out and the media crowd turned back toward the tall, dark doors of the courtroom as others emerged. She saw for instant her father, blinking owlishly in the glare of the now reborn lights. Then the crowd of reporters, turning and moving like a school of fish, hid him and the others. Unprotected by the microphones, the electronic equipment and news people almost assaulted them; in the blur of motion, it was hard to tell where one group ended and the other began.

2

As the crowd swept by, Ellen realized her plan to meet her parents in the hall was not going to work. She could not penetrate the feeding frenzy of the reporters. She glimpsed her mother, her hand pressed across her eyes as if she was the guilty one trying to avoid being seen, and her uncle Michael, his arm tight around her shoulders, either to protect her or to support himself. In front of them was her father, driving a wedge through the crowd. She heard his angry, repeated, "No comment," and then they were gone.

None of the reporters looked at Ellen and she had sudden flash of disappointment and a desire to announce herself. She smiled at the silliness of the idea, letting them all pass and stayed against the wall.

As the boiling mass of people made their way down the hall to the main entrance, she realized she hadn't seen her grandfather and she looked back toward the courtroom. Just emerging from the hearing were the defendants.

It was always hard to look at them. Seeing their images on television was easier. Her memory of the glimpses she had in the courthouse was never steady, like a reflection in a pond that someone dropped a rock in. They tended, except one of the five, to long hair. By the time the hearing began some had gotten haircuts and all had their beards and mustaches at least slightly trimmed.

One was in a regular suit, complete with vest – that was the one with the shortest hair and a clean-shaven face. Jack Baker was his name. Their leader. The other four wore slacks and sport jackets.

Bob Baker, Jack's brother, was short, powerfully built, and had dark hair pulled back in a tight ponytail and a mustache that looked a little Chinese. Dave Hollingsworth was fat with reddish-brown hair and a loud voice. Nick Christopher came next, with a thin goatee and sharp eyes that seemed to look everywhere. The last was Johnny Larson, who looked a lot younger than the others. He would look up and smile when someone said something and then, when no one was looking at him, would drop his head. He had troubled eyes.

The other four pulled off their ties as they approached, laughing and talking loud. Several of the hard-eyed women were with them, clinging like remoras. No one took much notice of Ellen as they passed, except Jack Baker, whose blank gaze locked onto her and then swept on, disregarding her as nothing worth considering, like a Great White shark she saw on the Discovery Channel.

Defendant, she thought, the word sounding strange in its reality after so many years of hearing it on television shows. He was the defendant.

He killed Eileen.

Her thoughts skidded away from the phrase, as if it was too hard-edged to be held in her mind, too likely to wound her as she held it. She looked back at the women.

For the first time, she realized a strange thing about the women's eyes. The cold, hard look she associated with them was there; it snapped on each time one of them glanced at her in passing. When they looked back at their men, holding onto their arms so tightly she saw their knuckles whiten, some coldness faded and was replaced with, what? Was it sadness? Then they were gone and she was still looking for Grandpa Tom.

The doors opened again. She saw his long, jacketed arm on the handle, holding the thick door open for two older women who seemed engrossed in their conversation and taking no notice of him. He followed them out and edged around them to stride toward her.

Ellen loved her grandfather, so much so that sometimes she felt guilty that she did not love her father, his son, as much. She had enough self-awareness to know it was partly because Grandpa Tom never had to provide her with any of the restrictions her father did. On the other hand, she knew the old man worked to earn her love.

He was a little under average height – all three of his sons, including her father, were at least two inches taller. But he carried himself so erectly he always seemed taller than most other men. His lined face, the color of deeply stained pine from forty years of farming, was thin and crowned by thinning white hair he wore cut short and parted. Bushy eyebrows and a thick, white mustache under an American Indian nose tended to hide his expression most of the time, though when he smiled widely all the lines around his face and eyes would deepen and spread in unison as if trying to signal his pleasure.

There was no smile on his face as he approached. Tom's golden brown eyes, very similar to hers, were hooded and dark and did not seem to be watching his hands as he pulled sunglasses out of a case. He was almost upon her when he glanced up and saw her.

For a moment, she saw something scary in his eyes as they glared out from beneath those thick brows, as if he was angry with her. In fact, she had never seen him angry and could not imagine what he was like if he ever was. Then, like a door slamming shut the entrance to a private room, the look was gone and it was just Grandpa Tom again. He made a grimace, an effort at a smile she realized was for her benefit, and reached for her arm as he slipped the sunglasses on.

They walked together silently down the now deserted hall and when they reached the main doors he reached in front of her and held them open for her until she was through. It was an automatic gesture on his part and it marked him as a member of a vanishing generation. Ellen knew no boys her age who held a door for a girl.

They stepped out into the late afternoon Ohio sun. Below them on the sidewalk, the reporters managed to get several defendants to stop and talk. She couldn't make out their words but it was obvious they were enjoying themselves. As she stood with her eyes blinking, adjusting to the light, her grandfather slipped off his tie and carefully folded it. While he put it into his brown jacket pocket, she noticed that his eyes, partially shrouded behind the sunglasses, never left the laughing men.

Ellen took his hand and smiled up at him, trying to distract him. Tom squeezed her hand, smiled briefly, and then led her down the steps and away from the county courthouse. They walked east, the sun at their backs, toward the public parking lot. She couldn't think of anything to say and her grandfather seemed content with silence for the moment, so she said nothing.

Ellen knew her grandfather was given to silences. Several years ago, she had discovered they could be enjoyable times. Regularly her family visited him at his farm, sometimes allowing her to spend the weekend alone with him, and always let her stay several weeks during the summer. She liked that best, though her parents increasingly resisted the idea. Nonetheless, in part because her parents were going to be away for vacation, still in place was their traditional deal of letting her spend a large portion of the summer on the farm as a reward for good grades.

There were no smiles from him as they got into his late model car, what he called his "town car" and used far less frequently than his ten year old pickup truck. They left Hamilton in silence, the last of the rush hour traffic only mildly distracting.

Driving back to Grandpa Tom's farm they passed an occasional cluster of white frame houses, isolated islands of habitation scattered haphazardly along the road cutting through the farmland. Some had municipal signs identifying them by name and usually a volunteer firehouse with a large air raid siren on a gray wooden tower would repeat the name in black letters over the open doors. She glimpsed red and lime green vehicles back in the shadows of the bays and occasionally one or two people would be out front and they would wave back if she would. Today she didn't.

Today was different. Special, but not in a good way. When her cousin Eileen was killed ("murdered" was a word she still did not automatically use though the death had taken place three months ago) Ellen felt the pain of the loss as only a young girl can feel her first death. Eileen had been six months older almost to the day.

And now I am getting older and she never will, Ellen thought as the cultivated land sped across her vision. They had been close when younger, less so as the six month difference in their years became significant; Eileen, just older enough to suddenly divert to different friends in school and different interests. She was, after all, first to thirteen. A teenager. That meant something. Ellen was not sure what, but it did make for a difference and, among children, that was enough for a separation.

Ellen had the very mature thought that there would have come a time when the gap in their ages would again become meaningless and they would be closer together again. Now that was gone. Ellen and Eileen. The combination was broken.

The tears were over, mostly. There was a deep sorrow that seemed covered over by a layer that grew thicker every week, for which she was grateful. Ellen found that she remembered the good times with Eileen more easily without her death intruding.

Her death... Her uncle and his wife almost collapsed in their sorrow for their daughter. Uncle Michael and Aunt Dolores had always been on the periphery of her awareness – she saw them through Eileen's lenses. Now they seemed to fade even further, grief-ravaged figures part of a tear blurred background, misty and gray. While the rest of the family gathered at her grandfather's farm during the last part of the hearing, Michael and Dolores stayed at their home in the development on the edge of Middletown. She had not seen them to talk to except perhaps twice – she wasn't sure – since the funeral. Uncle Mike came to the hearing's last day but, as Ellen saw before her mother released her, he sat in grim silence as the judge gave her ruling.

Her grandfather's farm had once been the center of the family. Holidays, birthdays, her aunts, uncles and cousins all gathered about, with her grandparents quietly overseeing the crowd and organizing things.

Sometime back, there was a slow and gradual change and the gatherings stopped.

Ellen realized the farm ceased to be the family center when her grandmother died six years ago. Grandmom was the one, she now suddenly understood in one of those flashes of adult understanding she was encountering more often these days, to serve as the focus. Grandfather, the quiet man driving the car, was what? Distant?

No, that was too harsh. But there was something about him that was, well, private, not easily shared. He did not push himself onto his children, though if they chose to come, as her father and her Aunt Catherine had during the hearing, they were always welcome.

Another flash. Grandpa Tom loved her. This private man had a special place for her, perhaps more, perhaps different, than for his other grandchildren. Though she had never seen him slight any of them, she knew that for reasons unknown he had singled her out for some special affection. Perhaps because she was comfortable with silence.

While working with him on the farm on some task or other there would come periods in which neither would say anything for several hours. Every so often their eyes would meet and a smile would be exchanged. She didn't really enjoy farm work, but she gladly did it in exchange for those smiles of love.

It was in silence that they traveled down the roads that all ran in straight lines; farm roads, built around the plowed land settled centuries before, not through it.

The sky clouded up and she thought it would rain but none fell until they arrived. The temperature dropped and the heater was blowing warm air at her from various vents as they slowly went down the gravel driveway that branched off the county road.

They parked the car between the two story white framed house and the barn on its earthen rise just as the rain began, starting with slow, heavy drops. As she got out, she saw the farm's big, black cat emerge from the swinging pet panel in the door of the work shed attached to the barn and amble down sloping drive toward them. She waved but the cat, who occasionally condescended to answer to the name of Redbone, decided to ignore her. Punishment for being gone, probably. Ellen thought Redbone was cool.

By the time they got to the back door the rain picked up in intensity. Grandpa Tom got to the door before her and held it open as she quickly went inside. Looking over her shoulder, she saw Redbone, half-hidden by the weaving, gray curtains of rain, race through his door into the shed.

Her parents had parked in front of the house. Her mother was on the telephone, talking in her special quiet voice that told her she was talking to Aunt Dolores. Probably about the hearing. Uncle Mike had left them in town to go back to his wife and little Michael.

Her father was talking with his sister Catherine. Aunt Janey was there, but she was silent, busying herself with moving various things in the kitchen around. Janey's husband, Bill Tebault, was coaching the regional junior high school wrestling team presently and she knew the plan was for him to join them for dinner. He would bring Bill, Jr., who was a nice guy but something of a nerd – computers and stuff – and Louise, who was younger than her and tended to be very childish. It probably would be boring unless there was something good on TV.

Her mother looked up and greeted her with a smile that faded quickly as she bowed over the telephone. Her father, caught up in his angry conversation with Aunt Catherine, did not appear to notice her or her grandfather.

Her father seemed to spend much of his time angry. Not just about Eileen's death; that just brought his rage into momentary focus. He was almost continuously angry. His rage simmered, at best bubbling just below the surface. It seemed to be about nothing and everything. There was always someone, some thing, so continuously irritating him that it was clear to Ellen that his anger was a steady part of him. He never allowed it to splash on her, not directly. He never yelled at her and never struck her. He just, well, disappeared. That's how she thought of it. When he was angry, he pulled away from her until he was a small dot on the horizon.

He worked hard and by all standards was very successful – a girl at school once teased her for being rich – but he never seemed to think he was. When you listened to him, and Ellen found she did so less and less, what you heard was his frustration at missed opportunities, real estate opponents, balky clients, whomever, and all seemed to be conspiring to cheat him, defeat him. She didn't know why he saw the world that way but didn't believe things were always like that.

There was something happening between her parents. Ellen wasn't supposed to know, but she did. The words, angry from him, weeping from her, in the other rooms of her home were never clear and always ceased when she entered. They would sit in silence, not looking at one another, holding as still as people defusing a bomb, and she never knew what to do, what to say. Her parents made her feel helpless, in the way of a runaway hurricane that promised only sorrow. Maybe they were all caught out in the path of an oncoming storm.

Aunt Janey was just the opposite. She had calm about her, as if acceptance of life and what it offered was a skill which could be learned but which Janey, like a superb athlete, was born with. She was "solid," the word she heard one of the adults use years ago. Ellen wasn't sure what that meant, exactly. She had thought it meant stupid but knew that was not the truth. It had something to do with Aunt Janey's strength. When Bill Junior cut open his forearm with a broken bottle while the kids were playing in the vacant lot next to his house, everyone seemed to panic, everyone except Aunt Janey.

Ellen still had the picture of Aunt Janey coming out of her house, a dishtowel in hand. Ellen's father was first out in response to her screaming run to the back door but he disregarded her words and ran out to see for himself what was going on. So there he was, holding onto Bill Junior's arm, vainly trying to stop the bright, flowing blood with his hands, a look of horror on his face.

Aunt Janey had heard her. She didn't seem to run, but she got to Bill Junior almost as fast as her father. She wrapped the bleeding arm quickly and then slipped his belt off his now sodden jeans and used it to make a tourniquet. Then she scooped her son up and went immediately to the car in the driveway closest to the street. It was Ellen's family car and, while her father tried to hold all the children back for some reason, her mother ran quickly to it, pulling her keys out of her purse as she came. It was the first time Ellen heard their car actually squeal its tires, something she thought only happened on TV, and never something she thought her mother capable of.

Was that what they meant by "solid," that a person was good in emergencies? She wasn't sure but it had something to do with it.

Aunt Catherine was different. Square-faced Catherine had eyes that always seemed somewhere else, like she could see over the horizon. Kind of like a dreamer, but there was something real hard in Catherine, too, something of Aunt Janey. She wasn't married and Ellen knew that meant something. In past years, there had been discussions among the family adults about her lack of marriage, lack of prospects for marriage. It was a subject no one brought up any more, at least not while Ellen was around. She was beginning to realize there were advantages to being younger.

Her mother hung up the telephone and said something to her father. He grimaced and shook his head. Her mother looked back at her, blinking her eyes clear, and she offered a small smile that Ellen returned. Her mother walked into the kitchen and Ellen followed.

She helped her grandfather chop vegetables to go with the pot roast her mother was getting ready to put in the oven. And a smile and a wink from the silent man made everything feel all right, in spite of what everything really   was.

Chapter 2

Ellen was a good girl, a good granddaughter, Thomas Luther Parker thought, separating the word into its parts, considering it. It was strange, damned strange, to think he had grandchildren, even after all these years. He shook his head as he chopped a carrot into perfect, equally sized pieces. That must mean he was old.

Don't feel old, Tom told himself, and then grinned behind his mustache, remembering morning stiffness and moving a little more carefully around the farm machinery.

Can't jump out of the way as fast as I used to, that's true. Counting on thinking to do what I used to rely on muscle and reflex for. That's what being sixty-some does to you.

He finished the carrot and pushed the neat pieces into the pile of cut vegetables he and Ellen were building. She put them into a bowl to add to the pot roast later. Tom slipped her another smile and took their knives over to the sink and washed them. After drying them, he placed them in their drawer and then carefully folded the dishtowel and draped it on its wire rack. He glanced out the kitchen window and saw that the sudden storm was quietly ending, leaving only drops on the glass that slowly descended and leaving soon vanished trails.

Spontaneously, Ellen's mother came over and gave him a hug, which he returned gently, though not without a flash of embarrassment. She said something about the hearing being an outrage and he nodded, watching as she and Ellen went about the business of fixing dinner. After a few minutes, he stepped into the hallway that led to the living room.

He heard his son Charles talking to Catherine. He was still venting steam about the hearing results. Well, it wasn't right. Tom paused in the hallway and looked at the pictures his wife, Sarah Ann, and daughters had put up almost a decade before. He had added a few since then, but most of the additions were by her hands. There were their children at various ages, and their children, and some of her, damn few of him, and his favorite of her.

She stood on the front porch, framed by the door, smiling in the afternoon sun of a summer long since forgotten. Her hair was brown and long, not the white it was later, and her arms were folded. He couldn't remember how it was that day but he always thought her expression said that she was waiting and waiting for him. He liked the thought.

Sarah Ann, I wish you were waiting for me now. I surely do.

Over to one side was a group picture of their boys and girls. His finger traced a path to each young face and his thoughts followed.

This was a bad time for Mikey, the oldest, worse for him than for any of the rest. Tom wished again there was some magic he could work which let him reach out and protect his children and their children from all the bad there was in the world. *No way to do that, of course. Michael had always been a little more sensitive than the others; maybe being first does that to you.*

Jane, the youngest, was solid, reliable, maybe the most levelheaded of his children. She seemed happy with Bill and he was glad for her. Between his quiet and her seriousness there were times while she grew up when he wondered if she knew he loved her. But a few years back when she and Bill had gotten into some trouble with one another she came to him and talked to him about it and he had helped.

Mostly by knowing when to keep my mouth shut and letting her figure it out herself.

And when it was done and she got up to drive home, to her home, not here, not any more, she hugged him with a fierceness that pushed away all his worry about whether or not she knew what he felt for her.

His finger traced a line to the next figure in the group. James. Next to youngest. *Maybe the wild card in the deck. Something of a free spirit when he was younger. Thought for a while he would try to drop out of school but he hung in there and now was, where?, somewhere in the Middle East using his MBA to supervise the building of various big money projects.*

Catherine, next to oldest. He nodded. There was a time when he thought Cathy turned his world completely upside down, when she had come home from college for Thanksgiving of her junior year, and the night before leaving sat in the kitchen with him and her mother and let out her big secret. He hadn't known what to think, what to say, and could only look at Sarah Ann.

That probably kept him from really messing things up. Her eyes never left her daughter's face and he saw the concern. Concern? But what Catherine was saying was crazy, was maybe even sick, was...

Was hurting her, Tom saw as he followed Sarah Ann's gaze. The pain was what Sarah was responding to, the tears in her daughter's eyes as she struggled to deal with something so huge that she was afraid it would cut the lines to her family. Once he understood that, the rest was easy. Catherine was his daughter, had always been, would always be, and everything else was just details. He reached out his hand and covered her folded ones resting on the table. He let Sarah Ann do the talking – he almost always did – but Cathy gripped his hand that night with strength most men didn't have.

He nodded again. Cathy had done them all proud, putting herself through graduate school, getting that teaching job at Miami U. Teaching psychology, of all things, but it was Doctor Catherine Parker, and he felt a rush of pride every time he used the title. He hadn't told her he saved every copy she gave Sarah and him of every publication of hers, even though he couldn't always follow her research.

There was still that thing, of course, and it was, for him, still a very hard chew. Didn't know that he would ever be totally at peace with it but he was determined that she would never fear again that she might lose her father.

Then Ellen's father, Charles. He shook his head. Somewhere along the line Charles had gotten a big piece of brains but a small piece of humor. You had to hand it to him, though. He had become the most successful real estate agent and developer in the area. But the boy didn't seem to know how to relax. He blamed himself for part of that.

Not exactly a barrel of laughs myself.

Here were Eileen and Ellen. Splashing in one of those plastic inflatable wading pools. Another a few years later when they were trying to wash Sarah's big mongrel dog Smitty, the dog patiently putting up with what appeared to be about a quart of shampoo. There was a separate one of Ellen, a formal picture, black and white, which he didn't much care for.

Up above the pictures of the girls there was a large glass covered frame with a half dozen pictures of his parents, frozen in formal clothes in fading brown tones, and his brother and sister. Ruth was gone, but brother Richard retired from John Deere after close to forty years, outlived two wives, and was living in Arizona. Meant to get out there and see him. He had a boy in Indiana, a couple of hours away, name of John, John Wesley Parker.

He blinked and looked on the other side of the hall. Here was John Wesley, a picture almost thirty years old of a young Marine officer staring sternly into the camera while wearing dress blues, gleaming gold bars on his shoulders, American flag out of focus in the background. Now he had been a definite wild card. He knew Richard talked with him and their mother quite a bit about Johnny, trying to figure out what to do with him after he came back from his war. Tom didn't think he had helped much, at least didn't have words that helped. Johnny spent a lot of time on the farm and Tom remembered the young man's nightmares.

Maybe it helped that Tom had been in Korea, maybe it helped that he hadn't tried to push Johnny into talking, and maybe it helped that, when Johnny finally talked about what had happened, Tom hadn't tried to make it all better, hadn't tried to talk him out of or into something.

All Tom could remember saying was you had to use what you had been through to make something, maybe someone, better. Johnny had thought about that for most of the summer. Then he had gone back to college. Like Catherine, he seemed to have found his focus in school and was another "Doctor," in history, at Indiana University.

There was that streak in the family, he knew, a touch of wildness. Maybe a little of the outlaw. There were stories his mother would hint about his father, stories about his grandfather, nothing ever definite. But James had it, and John Wesley. He stared at the young Marine's face for a while longer and then turned back to the other pictures.

Tom realized he was listening to his son in the living room. Charles' conversation shifted from his anger at the courts and the legal system to his old refrain of selling the farm; "developing it" was the phrase he used. Tom let the words flow past without paying them too much attention. This was old ground, much traveled over, and he wasn't going to retire, whatever that meant besides curling up somewhere and waiting to die, and watch the farm be carved into quarter acre lots for tract housing. He shook his head.

Charles is basically a good man but we should have called him Charley more often.

His attention went back to the pictures. There were so many of them, some individually framed, some grouped in sets, visible through little oval windows. Sarah Ann and Catherine put up some of them, with Eileen and

Ellen helping out during a family gathering years ago, shortly before Sarah Ann's death. They dragged out all the old albums gathering dust in the closets, found the thick stacks of photographs stuck in their Kodak envelopes in the back of kitchen drawers, and opened the chests and boxes hidden deep in the attic.

Relatively few made it up onto the walls; there were too many. And there were almost none of him. He carefully maneuvered during that whole weekend, slipping out the ones of him he found as they were passed around, moving quietly into the kitchen when everyone else was out in the yard playing badminton and taking away those he found of himself. Carefully, he hid them in the olive drab chest in the attic, the one with his name stenciled on it.

Only the ones with his wife and he were spared. Tom wasn't sure why, but it felt wrong to have pictures of himself, alone, standing out for people to stare at. Maybe there was something wrong with that. He shook his head. Sarah Ann always told him that he had trouble finding a middle ground.

You were a wild man back then, she would say when encountering his tendency to go quiet and inconspicuous around others. The "back then" was after the war, Korea, when they met. Now you're a mild man, she would add with that lop-sided smile that had a touch of ruefulness in it that always pulled at his heart, and we've got to get you to be a middle man.

The middle; finding a balance point was hard, harder now that she was gone. He suspected he never would find it, not now. His grief at losing her was also, he knew, grief at losing himself, or at least losing a chance to be more than he was.

Do we ever understand what the total cost of loss is? Tom traced another picture frame, not seeing its contents. A smile played around his lips for a moment, then left. I'm getting too damned profound in my old age. The smile came again and he turned and walked back to the kitchen.

Chapter 3

Catherine joined Ellen and her mother and all three bustled around the kitchen, glad for the distraction of pleasurable work in a place they knew well. The warmth, the familiar sounds and smells, the feel of the tools and bowls, even the slide of the throw rugs on the linoleum underneath their feet, all bound together by the bright glow tinged with yellow of the kitchen lights, these things helped to push back the darkness.

The preparation of the food, changing raw materials into better things worth more than the simple sum of their parts, and the knowing the sustenance and pleasure they would be giving their family was a secret source of happiness they tapped into. Secret, for none of them ever talked about it and would have been embarrassed if anyone ever stated it so baldly. Occasionally an allusion to the secret was made.

"Oh, good, Charles really likes your apple pie, Cathy," Ellen's mother Nan would say, and they would all smile, maybe make a joke. No one would say anything about how good it felt to prepare food that others would enjoy. You weren't supposed to do that, at least not much, Ellen had come to understand. She liked to cook, which was okay to say, but she noticed on some level that when she said she liked to cook for others the conversation subtly shifted onto a different direction like it would when someone said something just a little embarrassing or something that might let the children in on some adult secret.

So, as they worked, they talked about everything except the purpose of the work, of its healing power for everyone, and pretended that cooking was just another chore.

Charles came into the kitchen, impervious to the mood, still fixated on his conversation, or monologue, with Catherine. He glanced around and, not seeing his father, he continued on.

"Cathy, all I'm trying to say is that it's not good for him to be out here alone any more." His arm swept outward, encompassing the farm. He had a tight voice, one that had little of the soft, southern Ohio twang Ellen heard from the others.

"He ought to be in town where it's safer, where we wouldn't have to worry about him. Besides, it's not like he's doing much of the work himself any more. Les Carlisle has rented the pastureland for his dairy herd and he sharecrops the tillable acreage to his other neighbors. For all intents and purposes he's retired."

"Come on, Chuck, he does a lot around here," Catherine said, not looking up from the final touches she was putting on her pie and deliberately using the childhood nickname Ellen knew he didn't like. "Sure, Dad takes it easy compared to when we were growing up, but he still does all the chores around here. Hell, he painted the house by himself. He's paid off the mortgage and now he can do the things he likes to do, like spending time with us, shooting out at the sportsmen's club, and helping his friends. Besides, if he moved off the farm it would break his heart and it would never heal. Losing Mom was bad enough, but at least he had the farm to hold onto. If he lost that he'd roll over and die."

Charles grimaced, though whether at the name or her statement wasn't clear. He paused, his attention diverted by the food in preparation, and spoke almost casually, perhaps not really paying attention to his own words.

"Come on yourself." He opened the oven and sniffed the pot roast. "You know the old man doesn't have much of a heart to break. Hell, I know he was bothered when Mom died, but not by much, and Eileen's death didn't lay a finger on him."

Jane rolled her eyes and looked at the ceiling. She shook her head and glanced at Catherine.

Catherine had her arms folded and stared level eyed at Charles. "Chucky," Ellen knew she was very frustrated with him now, "you don't know what you're talking about." There was anger in her voice that Ellen never heard before.

"She's right; that's unfair. Your father is just very quiet about his feelings," Nan chided her husband. He gave her an arched eyebrow. She seldom disagreed with him and never in public.

As the four adults started talking over one another, only Ellen heard the creak of the floor in the hallway. She looked up and saw the outline of her grandfather standing back from the doorway, dark and silent, his arms hanging loose at his sides. Then he silently turned and walked away.

At the end of the hall, Tom reached into the bedroom and emerged with a jacket. He crossed the hallway and Ellen glimpsed him through the living room doorway as he opened the front door and disappeared outside.

17

A Dangerous Man

He had heard her father's cruel words and Ellen felt sudden anger. She spun to shout at him, to strike at him with words that would hurt him as badly as he hurt his father. She saw that none of the adults were looking at her. They hadn't noticed Grandpa Tom and they weren't noticing her, all caught up in dealing with one another. The moment passed and she found the anger fade away, though part of her wanted to hold onto it.

Ellen washed her hands in the sink and dried them with a paper towel. She caught her mother's eye and motioned towards the front door. Taking the nod as a release, she went into the living room and put on her coat.

Day was gone and the early darkness of late spring hid the countryside. Here and there in the distance, she saw the isolated lights of other farms, the yellow glows of house lights, the starker, metallic white of yard lights. Overhead she saw an occasional star as invisible night scud, the last remnants of the storm, slipped silently past. The storm left the air cool and moist.

Should have grabbed my sweater.

Redbone, having decided that Ellen suffered enough, walked around her ankles and signaled his forgiveness by allowing her to be used as a rubbing tree. She absently bent down in the dark and stroked him.

Ellen did not see her grandfather so she walked down the porch steps and circled the house. As she went around the back, she saw the barn, a dark shape slightly higher than the house, and its attached tool shed showed no lights. She struck off away from the house, following the dirt track that split the wire-fenced fields.

It was so dark she had difficulty seeing the track and made her way primarily guided by the weeds on either side. They could not keep her from stepping into the puddles formed in the ruts from the late afternoon's rain; when she stepped into the third one, she decided that she wasn't going to find her grandfather this way and she turned back.

When Ellen got back to the back of the house, she paused in front of the barn to empty some of the silt she had splashed into her shoes. Balancing with one hand holding onto the pickup truck parked on the sloping ground in front of the barn, she slipped off her shoes and socks. They were soaked through. She shook all the dirt out she could and then stuffed the socks into the shoes. She circled around the house barefoot. It wasn't that cold after all and she didn't feel like trying to put the wet things back on. She just hoped she could get the spare Nikes she had in the upstairs bedroom she used before her father noticed.

Ellen never saw her grandfather standing beside the tool shed, though at one point she was less than a dozen feet away from him. He was aware of her ever since she stepped out onto the front porch and let the storm door slam.

Tom knew Ellen was looking for him but did not want to be disturbed. Now that she was gone he stepped silently back into the shed. He walked easily to the workbench, though he could barely see it. Forty years of use made the room as familiar to him as any could be. The light, ancient odor of a working farm filled the room – fertilizer, wood shavings, old metal, various feeds, and hay. Nearer the bench was the fresher smell of linseed and Hoppe's gun oil.

Resting in a locked steel case, bolted to the wall the tool shed shared with the barn, was a shotgun and a rifle. He planned to clean both the day before but had not. In any case, he didn't leave the guns in the house when any of the grandkids were visiting. As his fingertips lightly traced the shape of the locker doors in the darkness, he chided himself for getting behind in his work.

Well, maybe a little distracted of late.

Tom checked that the lock on the case was secure and then took a moment to straighten a few things. He placed a hammer on its wall rack and then squared his chair to the worktable. An old wool blanket covered the chair seat. He straightened its folds and then paused. He was going to a lot of trouble to find a reason not to go back to the house. He made his way outside and secured the shed door with its heavy padlock; the metallic click as it locked seemed very loud in the night. He paused for a moment, waiting to see if anyone in the house noticed the noise but no one came out. He turned away and walked around the barn.

The ground sloped away from the barn and was soft under foot, though firmer than in the fields. Once in back he sat on an old bench next to the large sliding doors.

Tom sat silently for a while, his hands grasping his upper arms. If there was any one to see and if they could see in the dark, they would have noticed that he was slowly bending over, his body rocking gently as he did so. They would have seen his eyes clench shut, the deep lines around them becoming even more pronounced. They would have heard his breath coming and going through clenched teeth. Finally, they would have seen him shudder as if in fever and then they would have seen him cry.

Little sound came from him. At one point, he pressed a fist against his mouth to muffle the sobs but his breathing came in gasps and was expelled in shudders.

Slowly the outpouring ceased, or rather it changed. The clenched fist, grasped by his other hand as if sharing strength, left his mouth and as his body straightened. His head tilted back for a moment, his shut eyes aimed up into the night. The observer would have seen his eyes slowly open as his head came level and might have noticed the twisting right fist as it ground into the palm of his other hand.

A sensitive observer might have felt a change in the night, as if a cold wave of air from some low spot in the dark suddenly swirled about, dropping the temperature, or as if great power lines were unexpectedly stepped under and now the air was filled with a feeling of electric tension. As the old man stood, his now dry eyes glinted in the darkness. It might have been reflected light from some far off farmhouse or even from the few stars visible through the scattered, low-lying clouds.

He stood still for a moment. Then the night quiet was disturbed when he spoke; though one word, and that through clenched teeth and lips that barely moved, an observer would have heard it in the stillness.

"Eileen."

But there was no one to hear, no one to see, except the dark of the night, and the old man walked back to the house, quietly, alone, and no one   knew.

Chapter 4

Dinner passed more in silence than had its preparation. The reality of the experience of the hearing with its disappointing results finally caught up to them and there was a general sense of exhaustion.

Ellen was unable to follow the details of the charges and the hearing procedures and the rulings on evidence. Eileen was dead and some of the men in the courtroom were responsible. Never mind that she had not been the target of the stray bullet, that it was aimed at someone else. One of them fired the gun and Eileen was dead. It seemed very clear.

The phrase, "probable cause," meant nothing. So what if the police officer who stopped Baker didn't know of the shooting and pulled him and his big motorcycle over because of failing to have his lights on? The police officer was a part–timer who became suspicious of Baker's staring at his latched shut cargo boxes and when opening them found the MAC-10 (she always remembered the name of the gun; her portable computer was a Mac but she didn't call it that any more) that killed Eileen. It was Baker's and his fingerprints were all over it. And, while he was not seen at the shooting, four of his gang were. So they had to go to jail forever. It was very clear to her. What was not clear was why that could not be. Why did a technical error mean that the person who killed Eileen got to go free? That wasn't right.

Ellen wanted to ask the adults around her but sensed no one wanted to talk about the hearing. Besides, during dinner they had her sitting with the other children at the card tables while the adults sat at the main dining table. She hated that; it made her feel like she was only five years old. It wasn't fair.

Her grandfather caught her eye at one point and winked and she felt better. Still, it would be nicer to sit with the adults.

With everyone in the house, it seemed very crowded. It seemed very tedious (she heard her teacher use that word in a conversation with another teacher, looked it up, and adopted it for the week) to put up with everyone. But some time in the evening Bill Junior showed her a game on his portable computer and several hours went by without notice as the two of them descended through a multilevel dungeon, fighting dragons, casting spells, and gathering gold.

Finally, everyone seemed to scatter to the various rooms of the house, snuggling in for the night. Bill Junior and his brother Mike got the living room and unrolled their sleeping bags in obvious enjoyment of the idea of sleeping on the floor. Little Louise was with Jane and Bill in a spare bedroom while Ellen's parents took what had been one of the children's rooms on the second floor. Ellen, too old (when did that happen?) to sleep with the boys in the living room, was allocated a small room called "the sleeper" that took up half of the attic.

She trudged up the stairs, dragging her pillow and blankets with her. At the top of the landing, she turned to the left and opened the door. She grimaced when she realized she had turned into the attic storage area. The only light came from a single bulb in the center of the room that activated by a string hanging from it, too far away for her to bother to turn it on. She turned around and crossed the landing to the sleeper.

This room was much nicer. Part of the roof was raised to allow a window. It had a bench where you could sit and look out towards the back of the farm, not that there was anything to see in the middle of the night. Yellow pine paneled the walls, which she liked because of the dark knots. Her hand found the light switch beside the door and a warm light flashed to life. The bed rested in the far corner, fresh sheets already spread on it. She dropped the pillow on one end and shook the blankets out across it. She smoothed them out and turned on the small lamp on the bed stand.

Ellen paused in front of the low bookshelves next to the door, considering the books resting there but finally decided against picking one. She turned off the light and climbed into bed.

I'll probably fall asleep in a minute.

But her prediction was wrong.

Her mind wandered as she lay in the darkness, hovering here and there on topics, ideas, like a butterfly trying different flowers, never staying with any one thing for very long. She tried to will herself to sleep but it didn't work (it never did but she always tried) and she found herself staring up at the invisible ceiling. Her eyes simply did not want to remain closed. She gave a dramatic sigh, copying without realizing it an actor in a movie she had seen two weeks ago. The glowing numbers of the clock told her it was just after eleven.

I should be a werewolf or a vampire so I could put this time to good use.

Suddenly there was a thin streak of cold light across the sky, visible through the window just long enough to leave an afterimage in her eyes. She threw the covers aside and quickly moved to the window, looking up into the sky, hoping to see another meteor.

Time passed and Ellen tried to pick out the constellations but she had difficulty deciding if she was looking at Orion and began yawning. She felt an almost pleasant tiredness coming over her and turned to go to bed when she saw a dim light from below. She paused.

It lasted only for a few seconds but she could clearly see that it was the cab light of her grandfather's truck. He appeared to be getting into it. The door slowly shut with a soft click and the light went out. There was a pause and then she heard the soft grinding sound of the truck rolling over gravel. The dark shape rolled down the incline in front of the barn and, using its momentum, continued on down the drive around the house, out of her sight.

A few moments later, she dimly heard its engine start; he must not have wanted to wake anyone.

Wondering on the why, focusing on the question, seemed to make her sleepier and she carefully walked back to her bed, yawning the whole way.

Where's he going?

And then she was asleep and asked no more questions in the night.

Chapter 5

Tom glanced in the big outside mirror on the driver's side. No lights came on in the house as he eased into gear. Good. No sense waking up anyone else just because a man can't sleep.

He ran his hand over his face and glanced at the glowing numbers on his wristwatch and shook his head.

Of late, sleep was tough. Either he couldn't fall asleep or he was waking up at odd hours and then lay in the darkness for what felt like two or three weeks. He always prided himself on his ability to sleep.

Could sleep lying on granite in a hurricane at high noon, always could.

He paused and checked both ways on the highway before pulling out.

Of course, it wasn't entirely true. Tom found that as he got older he seemed to sleep less, and, when he found himself unable to sleep, sometimes getting out on the road for a little while seemed to unwind the tension just enough for him to feel sleepy. But most of the time, most of his life, he always seemed to sleep well.

Well, almost always. Had some problems after the war.

His sleep the first year or so after Korea had been rough. That was one of his reasons, *One of my excuses*, he reminded himself, *for the drinking.* Some of it was caused by the thoughts that didn't stop, about the people he knew, some who died, some who lived, and some of it was the dreams. "War dreams," he called them, when he called them anything at all. He believed them to be expected – you go to war, you have bad dreams. He didn't talk about them with anyone.

Anyone except her. Sarah refused to accept his silence beginning on the first night that a nightmare brought him upright in bed. How do you talk about it, he wondered, but she got him to do it. She heard him out, that night and many others, and she got him to talk about the worst parts, which weren't the Chinese bugles in the frozen night, or the screams of the wounded, or the cold silence of the dead, or the hideous sights.

She got him to talk about the awfulness of being a survivor, of the terrible feeling that you had little right to be alive, that somehow you cheated by not dying while others, friends, good men, maybe better men than you, did. That was one of the last things he dared to talk about, when he finally understood he wasn't going to scare her away, when he realized that he was the scared one.

They were sitting on the front porch steps in the warmth of a July evening. The sun was just edging down below the western horizon and a few high clouds were catching its last light in contrast to the darkening sky. High on the porch post beside him a flagpole holder dimly glinted the light off of its new, galvanized surface. It was the Fourth and he wanted to fly a flag but, like every day since leaving the Army, he had not. It just had not seemed right, like he was unworthy.

Sarah found him sitting there in the lengthening shadows, silent, and joined him in the silence. After a while he tried to speak but no words came. She didn't press, just put her hand on his arm.

Finally the words came. Now, decades later, Tom couldn't recall exactly what he said, but he had the memory of the feelings, of the pain and guilt, of not belonging, of not having a right to belong. She heard him out. While his own words faded, he remembered clearly everything she said and did.

She squeezed his arm, persisting past simple reassurance, until he looked at her. She held his eyes with hers and spoke slowly and carefully. Her voice was graced with a southern Ohio twang, a clear sound that he always associated with the word home.

"Tom, you know I've never been in a war and I thank God I never will be. It seems to me that you've been thinking about all this a little backwards. You keep talking about not knowing why you were spared, why you lived while so many good men died, and I guess you feel that there's no meaning and no purpose in it. Maybe you've got it backwards, though, because maybe the reason for being spared isn't found in the war. Maybe a battlefield is just too chancy a place for rhyme or reason, and maybe your being alive only has a little to do with what you did; maybe it has more to do with what God did, or luck, or the Chinese and Koreans. But if you're trying to figure out the purpose of being alive, the real reason and value, then you have to look somewhere else. Maybe the purpose in being a survivor is in what you do with that survival."

Sarah paused and looked over at the setting sun. He saw tears glistening in her eyes. She went on.

"When you got home it seemed to me that all your wildness was about giving up on life, like you didn't figure life mattered. Then we got together and you took a hold of yourself, and I know it was hard, and you

25

changed, and you have my love. You've started living a good life, like the good man you really are. So I think that is what you need to look at when you wonder whether or not you should even be here."

She turned her gaze back to him.

"You haven't used the word; men don't, much. But you loved those guys; they were your family. I reckon they felt the same way about you. Well, if they had been spared and you had been taken, I think you would want them to live as good and happy and full a life as they possibly could and it makes sense to me that they would want you to live that kind of life, too, maybe even for them."

The words came over him like the cascade of a burst dam and poured into his heart. Tom felt his own eyes flood with tears and he looked away, blinking furiously, trying to hide them. Finally, he sighed and stood. He looked down at her intently, nodded, and walked across the porch and into the house.

He stepped back out a moment later, holding a flagpole with a flag loosely wrapped around it. Tom stood next to the post, slid the pole into its holder and then loosened the folds in the flag. His movements were not dramatic but relaxed and casual, as if he did this every day. A small bit of breeze moved the flag slightly and Tom sat beside Sarah again. He said nothing, just smiled and reached out for her hand. Somewhere in the evening they heard the distant echo of a fireworks display.

Now, almost forty years later, he sighed again, feeling the sweet pain of memory. Well, a lot had happened since then, and while there were days in which he found himself looking around feeling a bit surprised at being here, most of the time he felt belonging as natural as a heartbeat.

Tom drove aimlessly in the dark, letting the driving relax him, with no particular destination in mind. He was near the outskirts of Middletown when he saw the open roadhouse. The name was familiar; the restaurant portion of "Buddy's Place" opened early in the fall to serve breakfast to the deer hunters he knew. The tavern part stayed open late on. Stifling a yawn, he decided to stop and get a cup of coffee to stay awake for the drive home.

Idiot. Driving makes you sleepy for sure but you get twenty miles from home, so far that you need to get some caffeine to keep from falling asleep on the drive back!

Shaking his head at his own inattention, Tom eased the pickup across the gravel-filled parking lot. He turned off the engine and got out, still smiling at himself.

As he approached the entrance, he suddenly saw a long row of gleaming motorcycles parked facing the wall of the roadhouse. He stopped, looking at the heavy shapes resting in the dark, each one reflecting the roadhouse lights off metallic paint and polished chrome. He had an urge to leave, to get back in the truck and drive home. He didn't need the coffee now.

Something inside of him moved and his jaw tightened.

Damned if I will...

Tom opened the door and walked in.

Buddy's was a large place, but it seemed smaller than it was since the bar was a rectangular island in the middle. To the left of the door booths lined the walls. To the right were free-standing tables and a small stage, on which he saw a band packing up their gear. They regularly had country and other music here. Beyond the bar were more booths set back in little alcoves against the far wall that shielded the kitchen from sight. It would be closed now.

There were still plenty of people in the place and he saw a couple of waitresses moving about, clearing away dishes from the late diners and delivering drinks and pitchers of beer.

He sat at the bar and soon had a cup of coffee. Tom was about half way through it when he began looking for the men's room. Spotting it off to one side from the kitchen entrance, he made his way to it through the increasing trickle of people leaving.

When he got back, his cup was refilled and so he took a sip while still standing. He heard some men talking loudly to one another behind him, their booted feet heavy on the wooden floor. Someone bumped into him and the hot coffee spilled across his hand.

Tom sucked his breath through clenched teeth and quickly took the cup by its rim in his right hand, putting it down on the bar top while he shook his burned left hand free of the few drops of coffee still on it. He plunged the hand into a glass of ice water, cooling at least his fingers. Then he turned toward the man who bumped into him.

It was a biker, one of four, all clad in bits and pieces of leather. The man was taller than he, heavy with weight, only some of which was fat. He held a half full beer bottle in a large hand and was slowly turning his

27

bearded face towards him, as if only just becoming aware of what he had done. He looked like he was tough enough to take care of himself and his companions were almost as big. They were all at least twenty years younger than him.

It made no difference. Tom felt a surge of rage go through him and he took half a step forward, judging the distance, when the biker spoke.

"Oh, jeez, man, did I do that?" The biker's eyes went wide. "Christ, mister, I'm sorry. Just didn't watch where I was going." In the moment of hearing the words, he knew the man was being sincere, that it really was an accident, and he paused. "Here, let me get you another cup of coffee – hell, should be drinking it myself, this late at night. Mike!" He yelled to the bartender. "Get us another cup of coffee here and another glass of ice water." The big man turned back towards him and held out his hand. "Sorry, again, mister. Okay?"

Tom paused for moment and then took the hand and shook it firmly, the way men do when they are trying to impress one another either with their strength or their sincerity.

"No problem," Tom said, and the big man relaxed, as did the other three men as the potential confrontation faded. As it often is when men meet, there was tension in the air, and he realized it could have become violent very rapidly. "Let me buy you and your friends another round."

The biker grinned. "We'd love to, but we're at our limit now – these were our lasties before we could hit the road," he said, cheerfully waving the bottle.

Tom said, completely deadpan, "Johnny Ringo once shot a man dead for refusing to drink with him. The grand jury refused to indict him." The other men's expressions froze. Tom paused, then grinned to let them know he was only joking, "So let me buy you all a cup of coffee for the road."

The other men smiled, one laughed, and they joined him at the bar.

"So who's this Johnny Ringo?" the big man asked, and Tom talked about the Nineteenth Century gunfighter's life and times.

"You see," Tom said later, the other four men leaning towards him, listening, "in those days if you insulted a man you were expected to be prepared to back it up with your life."

"Damn," the one at the end said, "there must have been a lot of people ending up very dead."

"No, it didn't work out that way." He took a sip from his cup of coffee. "What it did was encourage politeness."

28

Two of the others chuckled.

"But what that meant was that the best gunfighter was in charge, right?" The man at the end was taking the conversation seriously.

"Not always, and never for long," he said. "You see, everyone felt responsible. They didn't always depend on the law to act. There wasn't much of it back then, not always enough to go around."

"Sounds a lot like now," said a biker in a black leather vest.

He nodded. "Maybe so. When the Daltons hit the bank in Coffeeville, Kansas, the first person to get shot was one of their gang holding the getaway horses. An old guy (Hell, he was younger than me!) in a hotel across the street saw what was going on and opened fire. By the time it was over the whole town joined in. All the outlaws were dead or wounded."

"What about 'High Noon'?," the end biker asked, still skeptical.

"Never happened. Hell, that was a movie about our own times."

"That's right," black vest said. "I took a film course while in prelaw and the movie was supposed to be a metaphor about McCarthyism or some damned thing."

Tom raised an eyebrow. The big biker caught it.

"That's right, Jack's a lawyer, a genuine bloodsucker," the big biker said, ignoring black vest's yelp of protest, "and Peter there at the end is a mortgage officer. Merv, here, is a Presbyterian minister and has the unenviable task of keeping us on the straight and narrow at our gatherings. And I'm gonna get a lecture about using our Lord's name in vain." All of them laughed and talked over one another, joking with one another, while Tom looked on and smiled.

"And what about you, Mister Em-Cee?" Peter asked the big biker. "Come on, Joe, do you dare tell him what you do for a living?"

Joe hung his head in mock shame, a gesture belied by his smile. He looked up.

"You've fallen in with bad company, mister," he said. "I may be the worst of the lot. I'm a building contractor. My card." He whipped out a card that Tom took and examined.

Joseph Bernelli and Sons
General Building and Contracting

"We met when I put a bid in on doing an extension to Merv's church. Jack was handling it for the congregation and Pete worked for the bank. Turned out we were all members of the Harley Owner's Group, but different chapters." Tom started to hand the card back, but Joe waved his hand negatively. "Keep it. Who knows? You may want a new barn someday."

The barn I have will outlive me.

"Thanks," Tom said, sliding it into his billfold.

"Hey, catch the time," Merv said, looking at his wristwatch. "We've gotta roll."

They got up, shaking hands with Tom again, and left with their laughter swirling around them like a warm, friendly mist.

Tom turned back to the bar as the gentle rumble of the four motorcycles came into the bar. He listened as the engines thundered louder as their riders shifted into gear and then faded as they left.

Damn, why do I feel sad?

Tom raised his coffee cup to his lips and paused as he heard loud laughter from the other side of the room. There were few people still about as the clock closed in on midnight and he paused, curious. He squinted, looking across the bar. The laughter was coming from one of the tables in an alcove. He only saw the backs of several people. He shrugged and finished his cup.

He was turning to the door when he heard the laughter again, but this time accompanied by a loud voice, full of alcohol, arrogance, and the angry humor of a man used to being a bully. Tom froze in place. He tried to tell himself the voice was unfamiliar, was that of a stranger, only sounded like someone he knew because it was late, or the acoustics of the bar, or something.

No, that was a delaying tactic. The voice was recognizable, though he had never heard it spoken so loud before. Tom turned around and slowly walked around the island of the bar, far enough to see into the booth clearly.

He recognized one of the men from the hearing, Dave Hollingsworth, plus an assortment of women and other men. Now the men wore no suits. Dark stained jeans and Levi vests over leather jackets decorated with black and red patches; "colors," he recalled hearing a police officer call them. On the back of the vests, red on black, in an arc going from shoulder to shoulder, were the words "Steel Riders." Below that was a skull, face on, done in gray with screw heads and seams carefully embroidered to give a fair representation of a metal head. In the lower corner was, again red on black, was a small patch with just the letters "MC" embroidered within it. Under the patches, looking like a rocker, another patch as wide as the Steel Riders one, just said "Ohio."

The man with the loud voice and coarse laugh was Hollingsworth, who had little pig eyes in a fat face. Tom remembered his perpetual, sullen scowl during the hearing, as if some kind of injustice was being visited upon him because he was required to answer for the killing of a child.

One of the men who killed his granddaughter was laughing. Tom started forward automatically, no clear thought in his mind, just the need to stop the laughter, to stop the celebration, for that is what it clearly was.

He took only two steps when someone bumped into him. Tom spun to face the intruder.

It was only another farmer weaving his way to the door, too far gone to realize he had committed any transgression. But for an instant Tom felt the rage surface, felt his face flush, his hands and jaws clench.

Then came the realization that the other man was no threat, was not to blame, was no one at all, and the hot rage faded, though something colder, more dangerous, was left behind. He looked at the small crowd in the alcove.

No one looked back, no one saw him, and no one saw the look in his eyes. Instead, he gathered his breath, and turned deliberately away, his boots thudding solidly on the thick wooden floor.

One of the bikers looked up, briefly, at the sound, but only saw some old fart walking around the bar, headed for the door, nodding to himself as if he had just made a decision about something. The biker thought nothing of it and turned back to the beer and laughter. He almost immediately forgot ever seeing the man.

Somewhere in the room an old clock was chiming the hours. It was midnight.

Chapter 6

Ellen fiddled about in her room when she awoke. It being Saturday and all the family around, someone would be starting a big breakfast. Ordinarily she liked helping prepare it, especially making pancakes, which she finally had mastered, but this morning something was bothering her.

She watched the earth below awaken with the morning. A farm woke up differently than a town. There were birds around before the sun appeared, she knew, but different ones began to sing at different times. She spent some time on the window seat idly brushing her hair. Gazing across the fields, she watched the morning crows arrive and begin talking to one another in short, terse phrases, interrupted now and then by an outraged sparrow who decided they had violated some air defense boundary and pursued them away from the tree line.

Then Ellen remembered the night before. Where had her grandfather gone? She looked and saw that his truck was where it always was, on the inclined ground in front of the barn.

Ellen quickly dressed and went down the stairs two at a time. She was half way down the stairs when she remembered her mother saying that when Grandpa Tom had rare trouble sleeping at night he would go for a ride until he was sleepy. Maybe that's what it was.

She landed at the bottom of the stairs in a controlled crash. Family members were scattered about but mostly were in the kitchen. She gave a hurried good morning to her parents; her father barely looked up from the business section of the morning paper but her mother gave her a kiss on the cheek, which was a little embarrassing in front of the other kids.

She didn't see her grandfather and, grabbing a muffin on the way, went out the back door to see if he was working. It did not occur to her to ask her parents where he was. Ellen learned that mentioning him to her father was to invite some derogatory comment, and so she never initiated referring to him.

The back door screen slapped shut behind her as she stood squinting in the bright morning light. The sky was that clear blue that she liked to call "robin's egg," even though it really wasn't. She called it that because its clarity seemed as alive as the small group of eggs she had seen in a robin's nest the previous year's spring.

With Eileen.

She deliberately made herself pay attention to finding her grandfather, avoiding thoughts of Eileen. She walked over to the barn, throwing a piece of her muffin to the arrogantly strutting Redbone.

Grandpa Tom wasn't around the barn and the tool shed was locked up. She went over to the fence bordering the lane going away from the barn and climbed up on it. Swaying a little, she looked across the rolling farm fields, trying to see him. Disappointed, she climbed down and began to return to the house.

Ellen heard the tractor coming down the drive and she ran around the house. She saw her grandfather atop the big green John Deere tractor. He must have been in the other fields beyond the north side of the house. She waved but he gave no response. Her hand dropped and she felt a sudden pang.

Ellen raised her hand again, and waved once more. The old man, his eyes hidden in the shadows of a faded, Cincinnati Reds baseball cap, seemed not to notice and she felt like her heart would break. But then he saw her and with a smooth movement whipped his hat off and, sweeping his arm wide, bowed to her. He shifted the machine into neutral and gestured to her to come over and she ran to the tractor and, holding onto his outstretched arm, climbed up onto his lap.

He let her steer towards the open doors of the barn, though his hands were close to hers. She loved riding the tractor, loved the growl of its heavy engine and the sway of the machine as it climbed over the ground like some determined bulldog. She even loved the smell of oil and fuel that followed it. Mostly, she loved riding with her grandfather, seeing everything from high up.

Tom eased her down, her two hands clinging to his one, and she did not think it remarkable that the old man could slowly lower her weight with one arm effortlessly, as if she weighed no more than a loaf of bread.

She heard a call from the house and he gently pushed her in the direction of the open doors.

"Time for breakfast," Tom said.

"Already had a muffin," she said in mock protest, already moving toward the house.

"Not enough for a big farm girl like you," he replied as they walked to the house together. "And don't forget to brush your teeth."

"All of them?"

"Just the ones in your mouth."

Breakfast was the usual chaotic affair it always was when there was a large gathering. Stacks of pancakes and muffins lay on broad platters, cooked bacon strips waited inside of folded paper towels, and eggs were shoveled off the frying pan as they were done for those who wanted them. All the grown-ups had coffee cups that they filled while dodging the children wandering around them.

Ellen picked up a plate, added some bacon and pancakes to it, and then picked up a large glass of orange juice. Some people were sitting at the dining table but a few were in the living room, watching something on television. It turned out to be Saturday morning cartoons. Bo-ring. She finally ended up on the front porch.

Aunt Catherine – never Aunt Cathy to her or the other kids – was already on the steps holding a large mug of tea in both hands and gave her a smile as she emerged from the house.

"Needing to get away from mutated turtles?," she asked.

"That stuff is so dumb," Ellen said, sitting in the porch swing. She wondered if she made a mistake, for while her plate was easily controllable on her lap, her glass of orange juice, sitting on the wooden armrest beside her, seemed inclined to be unsteady in the slight swaying motion of the swing. She sat there instead of the steps because her Aunt Catherine was a little intimidating.

Not like her father; Aunt Catherine never seemed to be real angry, and never said anything harsh to Ellen. But there was a something about her that kept her a little distant. Maybe it was remarks she heard her father make about her, things said which her parents assumed she did not understand. She didn't, but she knew that the words used to describe Aunt Catherine were filled with negative judgments, some subtle, like little pieces of glass laying hidden in the yard, cutting as you walked on them. So she was a little afraid of Aunt Catherine.

Or maybe it was just that Aunt Catherine had no children of her own. Ellen related to most adults through their children, so that avenue of approach was cut off.

If Aunt Catherine noticed Ellen's concern she never gave any sign of it that Ellen was aware of. Ellen did not know the smile Catherine gave her was a small treasure, not routinely shared with others in her family.

The ancient conflicts of all families were to be found in Ellen's and the eddies from the savage rapids of past battles still lightly swirled around Catherine. But the river still flowed and Catherine was still with them; there was a streak of mule–hard stubborn in the family, more than one observer had noted, and Catherine's fight, though still echoing, was over. For some wars there are no victories, save survival and a cease-fire.

"So how goes it, Big E?" Catherine's nickname for Ellen was not particularly objectionable, just not understood. Ellen shrugged and looked around.

"Okay, I guess. Glad to get the summer off from school in a couple of weeks."

Catherine raised an eyebrow. "I thought you liked school, E." A statement, not a question. Ellen shrugged again; words came hard with Aunt Catherine.

How to tell her what the past few months were like? Eileen's death had made her the uncomfortable focus of attention of the other students, even of the teachers, who should have, she thought, known better. How many times had she been asked about the killing, about how she was feeling, about how the family was doing? All the attention, all that kind of attention, left her feeling alone.

"Usually," was all Ellen finally said. Catherine nodded and looked out across the fields. Ellen wondered if she understood.

They sat in silence, Ellen slowly eating her breakfast. She was just draining the last of her juice when Catherine spoke again, softly, without looking at her.

"It's been a bad time, E." She paused and watched while a sparrow pursued a blundering crow overhead. "Everyone's been pretty badly hammered by everything, including that damned hearing. People have been a little distracted. Maybe you've noticed." Catherine let the words lay for a moment while Ellen slowly nodded her head in agreement.

"So maybe there've been times when you've needed to talk to someone but it hasn't seemed like anyone's been around. Just want you to know that your Aunt Cath is always here for you, any time." Catherine turned her head and looked her in the eyes. Her own eyes matched her voice and were steady and certain. "Any time at all, Big E."

Ellen wasn't sure, later, how she got into Catherine's arms, but for a moment all the concern and anxiety she had about the woman was gone. Maybe it was the accumulation of things, the awful past months, or maybe it was another one of those flashes of adulthood that she sometimes got. She suddenly saw the ties binding her, if she wished, to her family and this woman.

Aunt Catherine is strong!

The press of the arms felt very good in the summer morning. They said nothing more and sat quietly together for a while. Ellen realized the words of broken glass would no longer mean anything to her.

Later she wandered through the house. Her grandfather was about but seemed distracted, spending some time in the spare bedroom her parents used the previous night but which mostly served as his study with its shelves of books and computer for doing the farm accounts. Occasionally he would emerge to dig through the stack of newspapers next to the living room fireplace or to hunt up the county and local maps scattered in various rooms. He didn't seem to have much time for her but she did catch his eye and got a brief smile from him.

Everybody was gathering up their possessions. They did a quick laundry load with amicable confusion in sorting children's socks afterward. Shortly before lunch, she and her parents were in their car rolling down the long driveway while her father complained about the potholes. Catherine's car was in front of them and the others were already gone.

She looked through the back window, automatically tuning out her father, and watched the farmhouse become more distant. Her grandfather stood on the front porch watching them leave. She realized he had not said goodbye, but then he never did.

Chapter 7

The crickets were quite active. The fireflies had risen with the dark and now, close to midnight, showed no signs of quitting for the night, perhaps feeling obligated to make up for the moon's absence. A warm breeze, an early signal of expected rain, was smoothly and gently pressing across the farm fields and roads of southern Ohio.

Tom's work boots crunched in the gravel as he walked from his house to the tool shed. He pulled a long, dark, Australian windbreaker on as he walked. A black ball cap with a blue logo advertising a local seed distributor covered most of his gray hair. With his jeans, he was a dark figure in the night. From a few yards away, he was hard to see and without the sound of his boots it would have been hard to tell he was there at all. There was no change in his pockets and his key chain lay next to the kitchen sink. The truck's ignition key was in his left pocket, the tool shed padlock key in his right.

The tool shed's bank of flickering fluorescent lights came to life grudgingly. The Remington 12 gauge pump shotgun laid on an old blanket, the cleaning gear he used on it after his family left was all stacked on their shelves. His hands drifted up and down the length of it and then carefully folded the blanket around it. Placing the bundle under one arm, he picked up a box of shotgun shells. He turned and walked out into the night, turning off the lights as he went.

Tom carefully opened the driver's side door of his pickup truck. There was little sound from the well-oiled door. As the overhead light came on, he put the box of shells on the seat and laid the shotgun next to them. He opened the blanket and spread it in the narrow storage space behind the seat.

He opened the box of shells and fed them into the shotgun. He jacked the slide back and forth, chambering a shell. Tom slipped the safety on and, with the chambered round now allowing more space, he pushed one more shell into the weapon. Then he placed the shotgun on the blanket and folded it lightly over. The box of shells went under the seat. He quietly pressed the door closed. He walked back up to the shed door and shut it.

The heavy padlock slipped into place with a double click and then there were no more sounds. Even the crickets had gone silent.

He stood in the night for a moment, pausing, like a stick balanced on the edge of a knife, able to go either way.

Not a damned stick.

He chose and, with only the gleaming stars and fireflies as witnesses, he climbed into the truck and started it.

It was not a long drive and he had memorized the route. The newspapers had not listed any addresses but the names appeared repeatedly in the coverage of the hearing. The telephone book revealed addresses for four of the names and the maps supplemented his knowledge of the east side of the county.

He followed Route 73 east, picking it up in Oxford. Traffic around the college town was moderate. There would be more college kids' cars in the regular school year, but attendance in the summer was still pretty good and Saturday night was Saturday night.

After a half hour, he passed the intersection for the north-bound road which would take you to Buddy's. A few miles later, he was watching for the railroad tracks that ran to the steel processing plants in Middletown. Crossing them, he took the next right. Run down houses hunched sagging in the darkness on either side of him. He counted blocks to himself and then made a slow left at the fourth one. His headlights passed over a street sign and he nodded. It was the right one.

There were few vehicles on the street. Most people preferred to park in their drives. Tom drove slowly, looking to his right. He missed it the first time and circled the block. On his second pass, he saw a number in reflective tape on a mailbox next to the street. He estimated the house he wanted was two more doors down. Almost none of the houses had any interior lights on, but that one did.

Tom drove past it and turned the corner and pulled up to the curb. Switching off the engine, he sat and listened but there was little to hear. Off in the distance he heard a big semi working its way up through its gears, its sound fading as its speed increased. Then there was only the wind. Still he waited.

Finally, he reached up and pushed the cab light lever all the way forward to the off position. He eased open his door and stepped out onto the pavement. His rubber soled work boots made little sound as he reached around and pulled the shotgun free of the blanket. Closing the door quietly, he slipped the shotgun under his windbreaker, putting the butt under his right armpit. Holding it there with his left hand, he put his other hand into the windbreaker's pocket and felt for the flapped opening that gave him access to the gun. He grasped it well in front of the receiver and then released his left hand. As he walked back towards the house, the shotgun was completely hidden.

He walked past the house, looking for a number but couldn't find one. He walked half way down the block before turning around and coming back. Then he noticed the house numbers were all painted, white on black rectangles, on the curbs in front of the houses.

It was hard to make out most of the house numbers but the interior lights of the house gave enough light for him to be sure. He turned up the sidewalk and was halfway up it when he saw a glint of metal at the head of the driveway, in front of a large dark car. He watched the house for a moment, pausing, and then he walked across the yard to the driveway.

The glint was the chrome of a motorcycle. He looked at the two vehicles. Were there other people in the house? He looked around. The street was still deserted, though as dark as the shadows were he doubted if anyone on the sidewalk could see him.

Most of the house's lights seemed to be coming from the rooms in the rear. Carefully Tom stepped around the corner of the house into the back yard. He made out the dark shapes of things scattered distantly in the yard but could not identify them. Nonetheless, the place had a trashy appearance. Pale yellow light shone from an open backdoor.

The first window he encountered was dark. He heard music. He pressed close to the wall and slowly approached the door. Getting next to it, he waited a moment, listening. The music seemed to be coming from a cheap radio. From time to time, he heard someone mutter something and the snap of a playing card.

Tom squatted down, smoothly sliding the shotgun out as he did. He then very quickly chanced a look through the door, using only one eye at the bottom corner of the screen.

His brief glimpse showed him a single man, big, clad in jeans and an extra-large t-shirt his fat threatened to spill through. He had his back to the door, sitting at a table. A bottle of beer was to his right. A partial deck of cards was in his left hand. He seemed to be playing solitaire. Carefully, Tom backed away from the doorway.

He made his way to the front of the house where it was darker. For anyone inside to see him, they would have to open the door, unlike in back where he would be fully in the light as the man turned around. Tom needed time to be sure it was the right man.

He put the shotgun back under his windbreaker and gripped it as before. Then he reached out with his left and knocked on the door. Tom waited and second and then knocked again. He heard the man yell something and waited, stepping back from the door.

A light over the door came on and he heard someone fumbling with a lock while complaining about the lateness of the night.

So much for hiding in the dark.

The door opened wide and the man stood before him. He was probably muscular under his layers of fat for his shoulders were broad but his large gut was spilling out from underneath a dirty t-shirt.

"What do you want?" he asked, his left hand on the door, his right carefully kept behind him.

His small eyes had dark circles under them and his hair was lying over his forehead in messy clumps as if smeared with engine oil. He smelled bad from too much beer, cigarettes, and soured sweat.

He didn't look at all like he had during the hearing, wearing his suit, shined shoes, neat and clean, and not even as he had at Buddy's. But there was no mistaking him. The squinty eyes, the reddish beard, the layers of fat, the hulking, arrogant air of a man who expected to always have his way, for he always had.

"Dave Hollingsworth?" Tom asked, just to be sure.

"Yeah. So?"

He loosened his grip on the shotgun while raising his arm rapidly. This had the effect of throwing the weapon forward as it came up so his right hand, sliding and supporting the shotgun, met the handgrip at the instant it was level. His left hand reached the slide at the same second. Hollingsworth stood frozen in that instant, able only to widen his eyes. As the shotgun's safety thumbed off with a soft, metallic click, his right arm started to move, but it was too late.

The blast echoed for a moment in the street. A dog a few streets over began barking. Then the silence returned.

Bracing the butt of the shotgun against his hip, Tom placed his right hand over the receiver and worked the pump with his left. The hot, spent shell was ejected into his hand and he put it in the windbreaker's pocket. He slid the pump forward, chambering another round.

The second blast echoed just as long and the distant dog became more insistent. A light came on inside a house down the street.

Tom turned away, slipping the shotgun back under the windbreaker. Walking quickly across the yard but not running, he was around the corner in a moment. As he stowed the gun in the truck he looked around. No other houses showed any responses. As he started the truck, he finally noticed how few street lights were working, a bit of luck.

He eased carefully into gear and drove away, keeping his speed down. In a few minutes, he was back on route 73, west bound. He kept his window down but heard no sirens.

The light in the house went out, though the dog barked on in the dark for a few minutes more, still irritated by the interruption of its sleep. Then it   was   quiet   again.

Chapter 8

"Deputy Jeffers, this is Special Agent Peter Santiago."

Butler County Deputy Sheriff Jim "JJ" Jeffers looked up from the file he was reading. He was a tall man, well over six feet, with thick dark hair and a large nose that might have been Roman or American Indian, depending on one's politics of the moment. A perpetual five o'clock shadow plagued him, though he often shaved twice a day. A wide mouth over a prominent chin might have made him handsome, but his eyes, small, dark, and always in what looked like the squint of a man too vain to wear glasses, which he didn't need, subtracted from his appeal. In his early thirties, his face was deeply tanned from many hours in a patrol car and lined around his mouth, lines that seemed to multiply when he smiled, which was often.

He rose to his feet and extended his hand automatically. The FBI man shook it, also automatically, and muttered the usual pleasantries and then was gone, taken away by the DEA agent doing the introductions to the members of the task force.

Jeffers lowered himself back into his chair and resumed reading the file. This was his second month with the special joint drug task force and, as usual, he had little to do except read the files.

This was not to say that the other members of the task force treated him badly. To the contrary, he was made very welcome. At first, it was the usual political skill displayed by federal cops when working with locals, and Jeffers was the primary liaison officer for the various state and local law enforcement agencies. Beyond political considerations, by his third week on the task force, growing recognition of his personal and professional abilities resulted in an increasing acceptance.

Jeffers attended every training opportunity in his eight years as a deputy, including several courses offered by the FBI and the DEA. He also earned a master's in criminology while working full time and had a squeaky clean reputation on a force sometimes tarnished by political patronage allegations, something the intelligence groups of the federal agencies undoubtedly knew.

What opened the door for him with the others on the task force, at least as far as it had gone, was not just the review of his credentials but an afternoon they spent on the state police firing range. During his third week on the task force, there was a review of captured criminal weapons. The task force leader, a gray haired DEA agent named Carl Davidson, put the meeting together as a way of building team cohesion. One thing nearly all cops liked was guns, and they had a mess of them to play with, all seized in a recent raid by an ATF team working the Ohio and Kentucky border.

They set up some targets on the pistol and hundred yard rifle ranges of the Ohio Highway Patrol in Columbus and began plinking. They were using various guns, including some Israeli Desert Eagle handguns and Uzi submachine guns, a few Italian Beretta nine millimeter pistols, a Spanish Star automatic pistol, several American Colt and Smith and Wesson Magnum revolvers, three Chinese AK-47 semiautomatic rifles, several American military M16s, and a long barreled M1A, complete with telescopic sights, from Springfield Arms, an American manufacturer. The drug dealers the weapons were taken from were apparently a nondiscriminatory group and strongly supportive of the Second Amendment of the United States Constitution.

There were several good shots in the group, but it soon became clear there were four who were really good, three federal agents and Jeffers. On the pistol range he was beaten, though not by much, by one of the FBI shooters, a former Quantico instructor who used a .357 like she was wearing it and handled the Magnum-sized Desert Eagle with a casual grace that had the others envious.

Her name was Karen Deevers. She was a white woman of about average height with blondish-brown hair cut short enough that she used a hair style which might have been referred to as "Treat It With Contempt." It framed a face that was pleasant to look at, JJ decided, though not stunning. She had an easy smile and eyes that seemed to check out everything.

On the rifle range, Jeffers had the edge. At a hundred yards it was very close, with the four top shooters almost identical in their accuracy. Gentle jokes were made and a series of small wagers appeared as they backed up to the two hundred yard range. Jeffers' edge grew slightly. They took it out to the five hundred yard range and, passing the M1A back and forth, each tried to shoot the tightest possible group.

Jeffers walked away with the competition at that range. A group of holes in the target no more than five inches across would have been considered good shooting. Most of the others were able to come in under that, with the best slightly less than four inches across. They let him shoot last, expecting him to do well. His group of five shots was well under three and a half inches, which had the former instructor whistling in admiration and several agents shaking their heads.

But what led them to at least provisionally accept Jeffers was not his accuracy nor his beating them. Most of the men could just as easily ended up resenting him for his performance. What allowed them to admire him was his self-deprecating manner. Without overdoing it – an equally fatal error among men – he made a point of acknowledging the shooting of the others and down played his own skills.

He congratulated Deevers, who out shot him on the pistol range, and asked intelligent questions about the Desert Eagle pistols, which he never handled before, and listened attentively to the explanations. This lack of condescension towards the woman agent, who had worked her way to her position and was sensitive to being regarded as a token, won her respect and the other women on the task force took their cue from her.

He had that quality men instinctively admire: competence coupled with an ability to laugh at himself. A stranger in the group would have known immediately that Jeffers was accepted by the gentle joking he received and returned, something men only do and permit with other men they regard as their peers.

By the time the afternoon drew to a close and they retired to a nearby Italian restaurant for pizzas and beer, he was regarded with respect and considered a relative equal.

This opinion was cemented over the following weeks as he showed a willingness to take on any job he was given with reasonable enthusiasm and an ability to get it done competently.

It was true, nonetheless, that the jobs thus far were small ones and he was a little tired of being on the periphery of the investigation.

The women, being cops, shared much of the orientation of the men of the task force, in that they respected his abilities and willingness to work with the team. They also quietly noted his lack of jokes about sex and women, which some of the others engaged in. While they laughed or at least smiled at the jibes they considered part of the dues paying process, they privately, almost unconsciously, assigned him their individual labels reserved for what, if articulated, they would have called a "good man."

His input during the briefing sessions was mostly providing local intelligence centering on the target of the task force. They were after the traffic in methamphetamine, speed, which ran through the Cincinnati-Dayton–Indianapolis crescent. From Dayton it went through Columbus and arced up to Cleveland and east to Pittsburgh, with some indications it was making its way to Philadelphia, New York, and Baltimore. From Indianapolis it went up to Chicago and out through the Midwestern states. DEA intelligence thought it was getting down to Oklahoma City and maybe Austin and maybe as far west as Denver and Phoenix.

Over the previous thirty years the federal antidrug efforts had focused primarily on the major imported drugs of addiction, first heroin from the Golden Triangle of Southeast Asia and Turkey, and then all-powerful cocaine from South America. The domestic trade in American manufactured illegal drugs was of only peripheral interest as the battle with the high profile drugs was waged without great success.

That home grown trade steadily grew, opposed primarily by local law enforcement, which was to say opposition to it was accidental. A bust of a cocaine dealer might also include other substances, but that was initially rare. Somewhere in Washington, however, a computer program compiled the daily, weekly, monthly, and yearly statistics, and at some point it was noticed that the number of arrests involving speed was growing.

Speed was a drug with a unique history. It had been around for many years, initially used in WW II by Allied pilots, panzer crews, and others, and then by long haul truckers and others needing to stay awake for long periods of time. Then during the flowering of the Sixties the counterculture discovered the fun of intravenous injection of methamphetamine. The warning statements from various institutional figures were ignored; after all, they had lied about Vietnam, hadn't they?

Mainlined speed tore through the flower children like a windblown prairie fire. This was different than grass or acid and people died. The various traditional authorities preached, warned, admonished, and cajoled, all of which probably served to encourage the drug's use.

Then some knowledgeable people within the counterculture – doctors in Haight-Ashbury, premed and chemistry grad students – recognized what was happening and a grassroots effort sprang up to get the word out. Cooperating with everyone from alternative comic book artists to rock and

45

roll magazines to drug hotlines, they began to get out the fact that there was no such thing as an old speed freak. It culminated in a legendary radio commercial by Frank Zappa, which began with, "Hi. Wanna die?"

They turned back the tide of use. Within two years, it was almost impossible to find anyone still using the drug.

Then the counterculture graduated and went to Wall Street, Ms. magazine, and Apple Computer, and the lesson was forgotten; Americans were never particularly interested in history, including their own. Meth came back, largely carried in the saddle bags of outlaw motorcycle gangs needing a boost to make a run and then, inevitably, to make money.

Like cocaine, methamphetamine produced a rush, a high, a feeling of great energy, power, and a sense of mastery. Like cocaine it could be sniffed, smoked, or injected, so it, too, had its little rituals of use that allowed one to feel that one was doing something special. Unlike cocaine it didn't have to be imported, being manufactured from initially easily purchased components using equipment no more complex than that found in a typical undergraduate chemistry lab, often less. And unlike cocaine, there was no bad press associated with it and its consumers remained ignorant of all the counterculture education.

With a lack of press coverage, there was little direct law enforcement effort to interdict its use. Occasional labs were discovered and busted, but usually in error – the cops were after crack cocaine labs and, tracking down shipments of lab equipment to unusual addresses, typically thought they were onto something else. Most were disappointed with their finds and prosecution was often perfunctory.

After all, there were much bigger fish to fry.

Traditional organized crime, highly invested in heroin and cocaine, largely overlooked the trade in speed. The newer criminal groups, as new immigrants usually do, emulated the success of the more established groups and likewise focused on the traditional moneymakers and continued to target the cities as the primary revenue generators.

Speed went a different path. It had always been big among the outlaw motorcycle gangs, who used it on their cross-country runs. Not wanting to be unnecessarily dependent upon the established pharmaceutical industry, they began to build their own labs in the late Fifties. Not exactly a part of the hippy culture, the bikers missed the anti-speed education efforts.

Their manufacturing and distribution might have remained primarily internal except for the limited success of the federal efforts against cocaine. The massive interdiction effort drove the price up and incidentally increased crime by forcing addicts to steal more to generate more cash. As this happened speed became more attractive.

It's high was not as much fun as coke's, but it had several things going for it over cocaine besides a lower per high cost, always an important consideration among those considering the substance abuse life style. First, it ran on an entirely separate distribution network than either cocaine or heroin, thus lowering the probability of an unfortunate encounter with a representative of the law enforcement establishment. Second, in the absence of anyone speaking to the contrary, it was viewed as not as dangerous as cocaine or its extremely big brother crack. Third, it was cheaper (it always pays to repeat things to people using speed as their ability to concentrate, focus, and retain information is usually impaired).

Methamphetamine benefitted from the traditional American virtue of looking to make things better. "Crystal meth" became the new name for the form of methamphetamine and it required the use of precursor chemicals that were remarkably easy to obtain. One such chemical, ephedrine, was a common ingredient in over the counter cold medication. For small "kitchen labs," techniques for getting the ephedrine from the medication were developed and highly successful, though also highly inflammatory. For larger industrial production, a relative handful of companies – several located in India – produced ephedrine by the ton for legitimate pharmaceutical companies in the United States and, as they discovered, for illegitimate drug manufacturers in Mexico and the United States. Other ingredients, such as solvents, ether, and anhydrous ammonia, a common fertilizer, were readily available.

Unlike the long forgotten truckers, who used speed in pill form, and even the bikers, who tended to snort it, the new generation of meth heads injected or more commonly smoked the drug, as they did with crack. As with crack cocaine, smoking greatly enhanced the drug's impact. This resulted in extremely rapid addiction, a factor greatly appreciated by suppliers. The downside was, of course, that, just as in the Sixties, there was no such thing as an old speed freak. Suppression of appetite led to malnutrition and, as a special added attraction, there was the variable of methamphetamine induced psychosis, complete with paranoid ideation and auditory and visual hallucinations. From a psychiatric point of view, it was interesting that none of the drug users who progressed to that point had anything approaching enjoyable hallucinations. All seemed to have found an accelerated downward escalator to whatever private hell their minds happen to be carrying around. In the midst of their madness, such people were capable of torturing their own babies to death.

And some did.

Methamphetamine production and distribution began to experience an accelerating growth curve. As the supply increased, thanks to the move to industrial-level production, the number of addicts increased. Once addicted, crystal meth users had one of the lowest recovery rates of any addicted group. Discontinuing the drug, a heavy user might experience symptoms similar to those of psychosis for up to a year after becoming clean – few waited that long, so, for as long as they lived, they supplied the manufacturers with a very stable and growing consumer base.

By the late 1980s, the outlaw motorcycle gangs had become, simply stated, organized crime enterprises. Resistance to their emergence from the older crime organizations was disrupted by, first, the new and typically very violent groups that fought for the heroin and cocaine supply systems – their battles served as a distraction. Second, the efforts of the FBI, freed of the shackles of J. Edgar Hoover's blindness to the reality of organized crime, had paid off with the destruction of Mafia and similar empires that had existed for half a century.

The outlaws were, by definition, mobile and the major gangs had chapters through all of North America above the Rio Grande and several went international in the Nineties. Besides their mobility, the gangs had going for them the fact that the outlaw motorcycle groups attracted and recruited disaffected, semiliterate, young white men with a desperate need to belong. Hell's Angels, Pagans, Warlocks, Steel Riders, and all the other members of the horde prided themselves on their brotherhood.

Wise people did not laugh when they heard the expression, for in the latter half of the Twentieth Century, in the richest nation in the history of the world, the need to feel that one belonged to something, to someone, was perhaps the only need not met. In payment for gaining a sense of belonging, the outlaws would often kill, die, or suffer imprisonment, and gladly; moving drugs around presented no moral qualms and getting caught was regarded simply as the righteous dues one paid for acceptance into the brotherhood.

Their success attracted attention in the fashion of checks and balances, as to be expected in a free enterprise system. The various surviving organized and semi-organized criminal institutions, in spite of their problems, noticed the traffic and its associated cash flow opportunities. New markets were developed, accelerated by the use of speed by smoking.

In some cases, these institutions tried to expand into the markets built by the bikers; bloody clashes, the price of doing business, resulted. But the easier way, and a way favored after the years of fighting with other groups and pursuit by the FBI, used the bikers as suppliers for their own closed but surviving markets, chiefly the smaller cities. In turn, the bikers' apparently insatiable need for firearms was met through the criminal supply and distribution network.

Also attracted to their success were the various federal agencies that paid for the computer programs into which all the arrest data poured. They would have denied it, but there was a threshold that had to be passed before federal law enforcement would get involved. Sometimes it was a dollar amount, sometimes it was simply the raw publicity associated with a particular crime.

The trade in speed slowly edged across several of these thresholds. The money involved, while still relatively small when compared to heroin and cocaine, was large and getting larger.

Local "kitchen" production of methamphetamine by users, dependent upon relatively crude materials and readily available ephedrine, soared in and around major population centers, paralleled closely by the gang-run "industrial" labs. In 1993, the year before the joint task force and JJ met, the DEA seized 180 speed labs in southern California alone and no one believed any real dent in the California production was made.

Several horrendous crimes committed by people in a speed-generated psychotic state also caused a blip in the statistics. Naturally, the public attention generated by media accounts of these crimes also generated a certain amount of pressure.

And, of course, there was still the outlaw biker manufacture and distribution system. Media attention towards the outlaws went through periodic cycles (few subjects held the media's attention long enough to be understood) and was currently on the upswing, perhaps due to the soaring popularity of Harley-Davidson motorcycles. Even when the city-based speed labs were attacked, there were always those of the outlaws, often operating outside of the cities, that drug dealers could fall back on. Finally, the gangs, in an era of increasing scrutiny of firearms and their procurement, were identified as major players in the field of automatic weapons. Rather than any one single reason, attention converged on the outlaw biker methamphetamine trade from several directions.

Hence, the current task force's activities. There had been high hopes for the prosecution of Jack Baker and his four followers. Indictment for the death of the little girl might have provided a lever to use on one or the other of the group of five. These hopes faded when the defense learned of the manner of the discovery of the semiautomatic pistol, one of the crude MAC-10 series, which fired the bullet killing Eileen Parker.

Jack was running north on a state route, away from the shootout. Ironically, no one from either of the two motorcycle gangs was injured during their gunfight in front of the small bar. Bullets sprayed in all directions with a fair lack of discrimination – most modern biker outlaws had no military service and learned to aim from movies; while they looked cool, their accuracy was severely impaired. None of those involved were aware that one wayward round crossed a four lane highway and sliced into the parking lot of the large shopping mall to their west, striking Eileen Parker in the head and killing her before her body touched the pavement.

A local, part-time police officer, Jim Piotrowski, saw Baker's motorcycle speeding north a half hour later and, being a rider himself and wanting a closer look at the radically modified black and chrome machine, followed for a short distance. His radio was tuned only to his local dispatcher and he did not hear the county's relay of the highway patrol alert for the fleeing suspects. It would turn out his dispatcher, a retired schoolteacher, had excused herself from her console to make one of her periodic visits to the bathroom and she did not hear the call from the county.

Thus, when Piotrowski turned on his flashers to pull Baker over, it was only because he finally noticed that Baker's brake light appeared to be out. His subsequent search of the bike's bags, in which he discovered the MAC-10, was performed because Piotrowski noticed Baker's eyes shift towards them several times, as if measuring distances and time.

Opening the closed bags was deemed a violation of Baker's constitutional rights during the hearing, leaving many people upset, including Piotrowski, whose drinking increased dramatically. The other four bikers charged as having participated in the firefight were picked up by other officers but their identification was shaky, based primarily on eye witnesses. Everyone understood that the gun was the key and without it the case would collapse.

It did; the charges were dismissed and the weapon was returned, since it turned out that Baker's possession of it was legal. The defense lawyers' statements to the media as the hearing broke up celebrated the triumph of the civil liberties guaranteed by the Constitution. No one bothered to make a heavy handed, ironical enquiry as to the whereabouts of Eileen Parker's constitutional rights in the proceedings, in part because she was in the ground for a little over three months by that time.

Jeffers sighed and put the papers he read carefully back into their folder and initialed beside his name on a routing slip stapled to the folder's cover. His name was at the bottom, as was customary, and he walked the folder over to the group's secretary, Anne, for filing.

She smiled and made a joke about it being close to closing time. He was glancing at his watch when Davidson called to him and motioned towards the small room used for conferences.

The room was too small for the thirty-person unit and several of the latecomers had to stand. Davidson gave them a moment to arrange themselves as best they could and then held up his hand for silence.

"We just received word that Dave Hollingsworth was murdered last night," Davidson said. There was a flurry of voices. Someone whistled in surprise and the woman next to Jeffers muttered "Holy shit!" Davidson's hand went back up.

"The Middletown police are handling it. What we have I'll distribute, but, to summarize, it looks like someone walked up to his front door at maybe two in the morning and blew him away with a shotgun at extremely close range. One round in the gut, about three inches below the sternum, and a second in the head. Double-ought buckshot so close that the wadding was in him. Whoever did it put the second round into his face while standing over him. Someone wanted him to be dead a lot. No empties were recovered, and they have no witnesses." Davidson paused and consulted his notes.

"Hollingsworth had a girlfriend sleeping it off in a back bedroom, but she's claiming she slept through it. If you're ready for this, the body was discovered by a newspaper deliverer shortly after dawn. She was slinging a paper into the driveway of the house next to Hollingsworth's and saw his feet sticking out the open front door. The next-door neighbors, by the way, are claiming they didn't hear a thing. It is surmised that the neighbors were afraid of Hollingsworth's compatriots who apparently visited him frequently to crash and assumed this was some sort of family squabble."

"Last tidbit: Hollingsworth had a nine millimeter Beretta next to his hand, round in the chamber, safety off, but didn't fire a round – the clip was still full. Whoever it was, they were very fast, very slick, very professional. Middletown cops think it was someone he knew because of the proximity thing and because of the girlfriend's silence. Maybe another member of the gang. Maybe it was over the girlfriend." Davidson looked up from his papers.

"I'd like Steve Johnson, Mike Krulak, and Karen Deevers to cover our liaison with Middletown PD. See if you can't get a crack at the girlfriend," he looked back at his notes, "a Patricia Ann Pierelli." Heads nodded and notes were scrawled as he continued. "George, you and Peter see if we can find out if this is any kind of inter-gang thing. Remember he was one of the five involved in that shootout with the Dragons. We thought everything had chilled between them but maybe the second round has just begun now that the court case is dead." His smile was ironic. "Perhaps they were disappointed with the course of justice." His smile faded, his expression becoming serious.

"Now Middletown PD is a little sensitive, folks, so let's be careful about stepping on toes. JJ," he looked at Jeffers, "I'll want you to give a general briefing to their people of all relevant information. I think it will go better if you do it. Go along with Steve. You talk to the cops while the others talk to the girlfriend and get a look at whatever evidence they have."

Jeffers nodded like the others and understood what Davidson meant by "relevant information" – nothing that might compromise the task force's own investigation or publicize its existence. He was expected, as he had in several less important contacts in the past two months, to introduce the feds and help preserve their cover.

They were walking a hazy line with the various law enforcement agencies in the county. The County Sheriff's Office, of which JJ was a member, obviously knew of the existence of the task force and what it was after, at least in general terms. The other agencies were kept at a distance. Some knew there was a task force, a few did not, but the target of the task force, the methamphetamine trade, was held at a very low profile.

The concern was, of course, two-fold. On the one hand, no one wanted leaks, accidental or intentional, which might warn their potential prey. On the other, there was always the fear that another group of cops might jump on the case and steal their thunder.

JJ was aware of this. Johnson, Krulak, and Deevers were FBI, not DEA, so a direct connection with drugs would not be made. Jeffers guessed the feds would use a civil rights cover to mask their true purpose, as in Eileen Parker's civil rights possibly were violated when a nine millimeter bullet ripped a tunnel through her brain in front of her mother while, on the other side of the highway, representatives of two gangs brought their negotiations and her life to an abrupt end.

Other assignments were handed out but for the most part the unit members went back to their previous tasks. Jeffers huddled with the three feds and, as expected, Steve Johnson, the senior agent, worked up their cover story around some sort of civil rights investigation. JJ made a telephone call to the Chief of Detectives for Middletown, who he knew, and set up a meeting for the following morning.

By the time he finished his call, most everyone was leaving, the working day ending. A few continued to work, gathering information from various data bases, preparing reports, checking through files, and there would be a duty officer present twenty-four hours a day. Jeffers retrieved his .45 automatic from his desk and slipped it into its holster slightly to the rear of his right side. He made sure his coat was not snagged on it and locked his desk.

The parking lot of the building the task force used – it was seized during the collapse of a local savings and loan – had only a few vehicles in it when he got into his Toyota. He didn't allow himself to think about his second-string status nor to curse aloud until he was well on the road driving   home

Chapter 9

Tom sat on the back steps, a cup of coffee cooling in the morning light beside him. He idly scratched Redbone's ears as the big cat leaned into his legs. His gaze kept going back to the pickup, now back in its place in front of the barn. The shotgun was still behind the seat.

He was thinking carefully, like a man who thinks a wasp may have crawled into his clothes, trying to see if there was anything next to his skin that might sting him.

The drive home after the killing was uneventful. After undressing to his boxer shorts, he lay on his bed just for a moment before going under the covers; "resting his eyes," he called it, waiting for the tug of sleep to come. He fell asleep before he ever slipped between the sheets.

When he awoke, he was into his morning routine before he remembered what he had done.

Operating on damned autopilot.

Tom's hand paused, the shaving razor held over his face, and for a moment he stared into his own eyes, trying to see what was changed inside the figure in the mirror. But he saw nothing.

He went about his chores while part of his mind watched himself, looking for something to be different.

I just killed a man. I ought to feel something about it.

There was nothing. No guilt, no remorse, nothing like that. Some small sense of satisfaction drifted about, like a buoy on a calm sea, tethered to something deeper down.

He didn't want to follow that tether too far down, not at first. Tom suspected it led to a part of him he would prefer to believe was all cleaned out and done away with many years ago. But the more his mind worked, the clearer it became. Something deep inside, something dark within his own abyss, a thing of rage and violence, was stirring.

It was, of course, the part of him he worked so hard to leave behind for Sarah. Now he was beginning to realize maybe nothing was left behind. Walled up, buried, maybe, but it was still there.

Steven M. Silver

Tom sighed and scooped up Redbone as he stood. The cat tolerated it for a moment and then decided it had better things to do and twisted itself out of his grasp to drop to the ground. He picked up his cup and walked to the truck.

Maybe the problem was in thinking too much. Was he trying to make himself feel bad because he didn't feel bad? Isn't that how people made themselves crazy? He grinned at his self-analysis.

He opened the truck door quietly and slid the blanket wrapped shotgun from behind the seat. He put his cup on top of the cab to free a hand. The door closed with a muffled click as he leaned into it.

The tool shed lock opened easily and he soon had the shotgun broken down for cleaning. His hands moved with practiced agility over the weapon. He enjoyed administering to tools, cleaning and repairing them, readying them for their next use.

Next use?

Tom paused as he was reassembling the gun. He had not thought beyond Hollingsworth, the big, laughing, arrogant man in the roadhouse, the obscene figure celebrating his liberation from justice. Deciding the biker had to die had felt as natural as throwing a light switch and everything he had done was almost automatic.

But now he began to think. Did he intend to kill the others responsible for Eileen's death?

Aren't you a little old for the avenging angel bit?

And who was he to decide whether or not revenge had to be taken?

Who do I have to be?

Maybe it was time to back off, let it go. He had drawn blood, partial payment, for Eileen's death. Killing all of them, even if he could, would always be only partial payment. It would not bring her back nor would it ease her family's sorrow.

Tom secured the shotgun into the gun rack and locked up the locker and then the shed. He retrieved his cup from the top of the truck and walked back towards the house.

Besides, it was a long time since he was a soldier. That was a thing for young men. Old men don't fight wars, he reminded himself, they just start them. They certainly don't end them.

Who says?

The rest of the day went quickly. Around noon, his neighbor, Les Carlisle, drove over to talk about running his cows on some of Tom's

55

pasture acres, an arrangement they had for several years. Les hung around for a while, making a pitch for volunteering for the local Fire Police, the people who assisted the volunteer firefighters with traffic control. Mostly it meant standing around with a reflective vest on and directing cars and trucks around at three in the morning. Tom said he would think about it and was grateful that Les didn't throw in some line about how it would be something he could do even at his age.

Some Red Cross workers used that line with him and he stopped donating blood for the better part of a year.

Tom heated some of the leftovers from the family gathering and ate while watching the news. The coverage of Hollingsworth's death was fairly perfunctory and didn't say much. He didn't know if that was good or bad and realized that the police were now looking for him.

At least, they were looking for someone. He had taken precautions but really had not given a damn if anyone had seen him or not. Tom pushed his plate back and stared blankly at the screen for a moment while he thought about what it might mean if he was arrested for the killing.

He needed, he decided, to stop and think. To consider what came next.

Deep in the darkness, something moved, something dangerous, and its movement sent electric vibrations, faint for the moment, through his nerves. What he wasn't sure of, or didn't want to be sure of, was whether it   was   fear   or   anticipation

Chapter 10

Middletown sucked, of course. JJ knew the reception they were going to get would be cold – the city cops thought of themselves as representing the only civilization in the county. All other police were hicks and rent-a-cops, especially the county Sheriff's Office.

The Middletown detectives managed to have their entire conversation with the three Federal agents and ignored their attempts to bring JJ into the dialogue.

JJ worked on keeping his composure, promising himself he could curse as loud as he wanted once he was in his car and out of this place, a tactic he developed in dealing with the various slights he had to endure in his current position.

In spite of their rudeness, the Middletown cops had zip. No witnesses, lots of suspects, but, as yet, no hard leads. They tended to lean towards the possibility of a hit by the Steel Rider's most immediate enemies, the Dragons, but there wasn't anything to back that up.

JJ found interviewing the girl friend, Patricia Ann Pierelli, a lot like talking to a wall, if you could think of a particularly stupid wall. It was clear that she wasn't withholding information. Indeed, her vacant expression suggested she had no information on much of anything, such as her name or current whereabouts. JJ and Steve exchanged expressions. Patricia Ann's emaciated figure, only vaguely focused eyes, and wandering speech made it clear she was into drugs a long time.

Of course, "long" was relative. While her gaunt face and stringy hair made her look like she was in her forties – and very beat up forties – the folder in front of JJ stated that she was still some days short of her twenty-third birthday.

JJ and the feds went through the procedures anyway, exchanged what information they could with the locals, promised they would let the others know if they found anything relevant, shook hands all the way around, and then got out by lunch time.

They sat in a diner waiting for their lunches and traded impressions over ice tea and coffee. Steve Johnson, the senior agent, looked like a television caricature of a CPA and had an accountant's sharp memory and eye for detail, which compensated for the fact that he was one of the poorest shots JJ had seen carrying a badge. Johnson sat back and let the others discuss what little they had. When it was clear they had exhausted their contributions, he leaned forward with his hands folded in front of his chin.

"So what we have is a professional style killing of a major member of the Steel Riders occurring shortly after a pretrial hearing in which the victim and four fellow perps got off on a technicality." His hands opened, his fingers framing his jaw. "There is a possibility it had something to do with the girlfriend of the victim in that some months ago she apparently was the property of another member of the gang. That possibility has not been fully explored." He flipped open a notepad. "Middletown PD is trying to check that out, but their intel on the Riders is not great." He looked up at JJ. "They didn't say, but it sounded like most of what they did have on the Riders came from the Butler County Sheriff's Office." JJ nodded, remembering that the information sharing had been, at times, one way.

"Additional suspects include members of the Dragons organization," Johnson went on, putting his notebook away, "primarily for two reasons. First, their conflict with the Steel Riders over control of the speed trade in the Dayton-Cincy area has not been resolved. Second, in their recent shoot-out with the Riders, both sides came off looking inept, even ridiculous. It is not a good thing in their business to appear clumsy. So maybe they have the motives, but we have nothing tying them to this particular killing."

He paused while the waitress brought their food. He let everyone get settled again before proceeding.

"The nature of the killing suggests either a very good professional or someone the victim knew."

"Or a stranger he didn't regard as a threat." Karen Deevers interjected. In response to a questioning eyebrow, she continued, glancing at her own notepad. "There was a peephole in the door. Hollingsworth could see whoever was at the door. Maybe he looked, saw a stranger so he kept his gun handy but the person he saw wasn't of a type that he would regard as a threat."

"You mean didn't look like a biker," JJ said.

"Right, or at least didn't look like a threat, so maybe not a man, maybe a woman..."

"That might mean a Dragon shooter, but a woman. Some of those ladies can get a little rough..." Mike Krulak interrupted.

"Yes," Karen replied while taking a quick bite of her salad, "or a man he didn't see as a threat, somebody looking a little wimpy, maybe."

"Or working hard to look that way," Krulak added.

"Or a man he wouldn't view as an assassin," JJ added, "like a cop."

The rest of the group fell silent, thinking on the possibility.

"Okay, we've got nothing from anyone suggesting they saw a cop, but the silence might be about that. On the other hand, the cop thing might be good camouflage. A possibility." The tone of his voice made it clear that Johnson regarded it as a long shot but at least he was considering it.

"Any other possibilities?" There was silence for a moment. Finally, Karen spoke up.

"Well, there's always the family."

"What family?" Krulak asked around his cheeseburger. "You talking about mafia or maybe Colombians?"

She shook her head negatively. "Not really, though if it was a pro he may have been a loaner from the Dragons' connections in Columbus and we know some of them are affiliated with the Chicago crime families. No, what I had more in mind was maybe the little girl's family." She flipped her notepad back. "Eileen Parker, the one killed in the pseudo-shootout at the OK Corral."

Steve shrugged. "It's a maybe, though I would think that a family member would have gone after the actual shooter that nailed her, Jack Baker." Karen nodded in agreement. He took a bite from his sandwich and then licked the mustard off his fingers. "But that does open up an interesting question. If we go with the Dragon scenario, why didn't they hit Baker, why didn't they go for the bastard at the top?"

"Hollingsworth was number three among the Riders," JJ pointed out. "We've always identified him as muscle, a sergeant at arms type, definitely not part of the brain trust. Very reliable, etcetera, sort of a two-legged guard dog. But maybe he was a more central figure than we thought, someone worth killing if you wanted to mess with the Riders' business activities or their security."

"Maybe; if so, if he had his hand in more than we credit him with, then the focus rolls on the Dragons a little tighter. We need to check him out a little deeper. Nice idea, JJ." He waved his sandwich. "On the other hand, if he wasn't higher than we thought, that takes the focus towards something personal. Checking JJ's scenario will help either case."

JJ bit into his sandwich, letting nothing show but pleased with the praise. He knew the others accepted him but also knew no one really regarded him as a major player on the team. Sort of a family member in the way that a slightly retarded brother might be accepted. Patted on the head and given something simple to do while the other adults have real conversations. So JJ didn't throw out as many ideas as the others, feeling that he could not afford to be wrong in their eyes. He found himself treasuring the acknowledgments of his work when they came.

JJ grinned around a sip of iced tea. He wouldn't be cursing on his way home   tonight

Chapter 11

Tom walked slowly from the house towards the tool shed. Redbone was circling among his feet, as cats do, forcing him to move carefully. He remembered Sarah saying once that cats were from another planet, one where they were the ruling species, and they had never gotten the word that humans ruled the Earth.

Redbone certainly was some sort of alien creature, he decided. Either that or simply insane. He shook his head. The cat seemed incapable of realizing that it could get hurt by those size ten work boots. Maybe that was what it was; cats lacked imagination.

Redbone paused, his ears erect, looking at something beyond the barn, or maybe nothing at all, or maybe just some cat hallucination. Then he leapt off, racing down the lane. Tom shook his head, suspecting that Redbone had seen nothing but felt obligated to act as if there was something actually there.

That settles it: the cat's gone insane.

Tom opened the shed door and stepped into the dark interior. His hand found the light switch without thinking.

Against the narrow wall to his left hung various tools, extension cords, and several pairs of work gloves. A small window, a single steel bar mounted on the inside blocking entry, showed blue sky. His workbench butted up against the opposite wall. The wall shared with the barn had numerous irregular shelves on which sat in semi-organized array containers of nails and screws, several red or black toolboxes of different sizes, some power tools, and an old car battery. Tom turned to the bench.

Underneath the bench were two large wooden boxes, both locked, in which he stored his rifle cartridge reloading equipment. Tom pushed aside an old wooden chair, opened them and placed their contents on the bench.

First came a set of scales in its own small wooden box. Tom carefully opened the box and placed the scales to one side. Then he brought up a plastic bag of empty rifle cartridge cases. The brass chinked as he placed the bag on the bench. Various small tools came next, which he precisely laid in front of him. Several green boxes of Speer bullets came next, along with two thin plastic boxes for holding loaded cartridges. A case trimmer and a powder measure came next. Finally, he brought up a large mechanical hand press and placed it into a steel mount already screwed into the bench top. He worked the lever handle a couple of times after tightening the loader down, carefully examining the alignment.

Tom eased into the large, heavy chair. He took several handfuls of the brass cases and laid them on the table. He handled each one in turn, carefully inspecting it for any imperfections. He tossed several into a large rubber trashcan in the corner of the shed. He took the inspected cases and checked them for weight variance – he hadn't expected any significant differences among these Norma cases and there weren't. He examined his sample for their flash hole diameters with a wire size drill bit and found that all were at .082 of an inch or less, again as he expected.

Tom used a small Sinclair neck wall thickness gage on each case, looking to see if any were unusually thick. Again, there were no problems.

His hands were almost independent of him as he picked up each case and inserted and turned a primer pocket uniformer, stopping to remove any brass chips, and returning to the task until he felt that metal was no longer being cut. He then used his deburring tool to remove any metal left around the cartridge's flash hole during the manufacturing process.

Tom did this with every cartridge case, losing himself in the work of preparing them for loading. As each case was completed, he would carefully place it into a wooden board into which holes were drilled just for the purpose of holding rifle cartridges. With each one, he felt a small sense of satisfaction.

He had been hand loading rifle and pistol cartridges for years. The boxes under the table contained gear for almost every caliber known, though in recent years had narrowed his focus down to the one rifle he still owned, a Remington 700 Varmint Special in .308 caliber with a variable Leupold telescopic sight and a Harris bipod.

The precise, handcrafting skills of reloading were only part of what attracted him. Yes, the meticulous nature of the work, even the careful written record keeping, he found enjoyable as it forced him to concentrate, to exert discipline over himself, though he would not have looked so introspectively to see that part of the experience.

The shooting of these carefully prepared cartridges was the other part, the part that he was aware of. He liked the challenge of working to fire smaller and smaller groups with what he referred to in an unconsciously old-fashioned way as his "long rifle." The accepted standard was a moment of angle, an "MOA," a variation in a group of one inch at one hundred yards, which translated into an ever-expanding circle of one additional inch for each additional hundred yards. None of that metric nonsense on an American rifle range.

On a bad day, Tom would shoot three quarters MOA; on a good day using his own hand loaded ammunition he would bring home groups of less than one half MOA. Tacked to the wall over the bench was a page-sized target with a tight group of five overlapping holes, all within a circle of just a shade over one quarter of an inch. It was dated and signed by several other shooters who were present when it happened.

Tom remembered the occasion with a little embarrassment and pleasure, mixed together. A regular at the local sportsmen's club, he typically would come to the rifle range in the early morning when the air was stiller than in the afternoon. Usually he was alone at the 100-yard benchrest range but this morning there were several others. They were older men sipping coffee from a shared thermos and talking quietly. Tom knew one by sight and nodded to him. He mounted three targets. One he used just to warm up, pausing after each round to peer through the Leupold to confirm where his round went and to enter the information in a small folder.

Then Tom had gotten serious, using five rounds he hand loaded several weeks before. He would align the crosshairs in the center of the target, watching them rise and fall slightly with his breathing. Unlike the other shooters, he was using the bipod mounted on his rifle as opposed to resting the entire weight of the rifle on a padded benchrest device. While slightly less stable, it was part of his personal challenge to see how well he did with the bipod. That was closer to the real world of trying to shoot real varmints, though he could not remember the last time he fired on an animal, varmint or otherwise. Later on, he would use a rest to get bullet data, but he regarded that almost as cheating and not really about his skill as a shooter but as a hand loader.

Tom took a breath, let it slowly out, and squeezed the trigger. He did this five more times. The bullets made a tight little group in the second target, about two thirds MOA. He noticed at some point that the other three men had stopped shooting and were watching his targets through their range telescopes.

Then Tom used the rounds he loaded the night before. Similar to the others in almost every respect, he had used a new electronic scale to segregate the bullets by weight variations. These rounds all used bullets matched out to several decimal places.

There were shooters who measured their groups using three rounds; Tom always counted five because it was a greater challenge. After he finished shooting, they all walked down to retrieve his targets; the other shooters weren't interested in their own, they wanted to see Tom's.

"Jesus," someone said quietly. Tom felt a little embarrassed as he received the low voiced congratulations from the others. One of them had a caliper and offered to do a quick measurement of the bullet spread.

After careful checking, the man shook his head and announced, "Nine thirty-seconds Moment of fucking Angle."

"Jesus," someone said quietly again. "Off a bipod."

Then Tom let himself feel the pleasure, compounded when he showed the others his rifle and talked with them about hand loading. Pleasure in the shooting, yes, but pleasure in the respect he received from the other men as they stood around the benches, sipping coffee in the cool of the morning.

That was the thing that he found deep satisfaction in, the respect of others, especially of other men.

Tom continued working, turning and reaming the necks on some of the cartridges before inserting CCI match quality primers. Then came the loading of powder and the bullet, a Speer hollowpoint boattail round, arguably the most accurate bullet made in .30 caliber. Each completed round was placed in one of the plastic cases. He put a yellow sticky label on each case when it was full, noting the date. He filled in an entry in a logbook with all the technical data of the ammunition. He then carefully cleaned up and stored all the equipment into the two boxes.

Tom sat back in his chair, staring at the bench. Part of coming into the shed and working was about not thinking, but there was no real way to keep his thoughts from returning to the questions he was wrestling with since the killing of Dave Hollingsworth, questions about the other four Steel Riders.

Does this go on?

Eileen was dead. Would killing the men responsible bring her back?

No.

So it is just about revenge?

Yes. No. Not only.

What else?

It would keep the bastards from ever doing it again.

Isn't that the law's job?

Had their chance; blew it.

Do you really think you can hunt down and kill four more men?

Yes. The response was as certain, cold, and hard as a rock.

And not get caught?

There was no answer.

What about the rest of the family, what about Ellen? What will it do to them if you get yourself killed or even just arrested?

He paused, thinking, seeing something coming clear, like landfall from behind a veil of fog.

It's about the family, it's about Ellen. It's about keeping them away from my family, everybody's families, everybody's Ellen; stopping them before they do it again. Otherwise...

What?

Otherwise I wouldn't be able to respect myself.

The questioning was over, like the finishing of a book so thoroughly read you know you will never lift its cover again. Tom nodded to himself, switched off the light, and stepped out into the daylight.

Chapter 12

Ellen found herself balancing two points of view as the days rolled into June. Of course there was the anticipation of school ending, after making up the extra days lost to a particularly severe winter, and the fun of summer. She would be able to stay out at her grandfather's farm for the whole summer, a reward for a particularly good year's worth of grades.

And, of course, it was a way to keep her supervised while her parents took several weeks off on vacation. They had a time-share condo down on the Gulf coast they went to each summer for about a month. Florida in the middle of summer; Ellen shook her head. Her father spent most of the time chasing down various real estate deals, but at least her mother got some time off.

Maybe the two of them would get a chance to work out whatever was going on between them. Ellen hoped they would, the same way a sailor, seeing distant dark clouds flashing lightning almost too faint to hear, might hope the storm would dissipate before it swept over him.

Ellen found it a little weird to admit she would miss, of all things, school. In her early years, she found school fun and a great place to play with her friends, but otherwise not very interesting. She was unaware of the conferences between her parents and her teachers that resulted in her quiet transfer to an entirely unofficial and illegal education track between her third and fourth grades.

The school principal and a small core of teachers were well aware that most schools were being reduced to the level of the lowest common denominator of their enrolled students. Since placing children by ability was declared illegal by the courts, the so-called "tracking" system of education was officially abandoned. This meant, of course, that teachers had far more heterogeneous classes than ever before. Some teachers solved the problem by teaching to the middle, which meant the kids at the lower end of the scale couldn't keep up and the kids at the upper end became bored.

Very quietly, the principal and her core of teachers set up a system of identifying the most intelligent students and placing them with teachers who were prepared to give these kids more work and more challenges.

Knowing that the courts, parents, teachers' union, and half a dozen other watchdogs, many self-appointed, were watching every move made by the school, though few seemed particularly concerned with how well the children were doing, the principal made sure that all the external signs which such groups used to measure fairness, equal education, and all the other issues which crowded out actual learning, were provided. Hours of instruction, student to computer ratios, teacher to student ratios, racial proportions, and so on, all met the various standards that the various groups devised.

The end result was a rebirth of a program for what had been called "gifted" children, and Ellen was a beneficiary. Now faced with real challenges in her classes, she suddenly took an interest in school. The promised reward of being able to spend a portion of the summer at her grandfather's farm in return for high grades probably was unneeded. Nonetheless, she agreed to the bargain quickly and spent six weeks of each of the last two summers on the farm. This year, thanks to the scheduling of her parents' trip, it would be almost the entire summer.

Even the confusion of gathering up her stuff and packing, a process clearly irritating her father, was fun. Ellen enjoyed deciding what clothes she would take along, though she knew her jeans would receive priority. She allowed her mother to over-pack, something she seemed to need to do whenever anyone in the family went on a trip.

Ellen slipped in a paperback book and double-checked for her bathroom stuff. With as long as her hair was, she found that she needed both combs and brushes and over the past year began using her mother's conditioner, which seemed to quell the threat of rats' nests in her hair.

Using both hands, she managed to carry the heavy suitcase down the stairs to the front door. Her father was waiting impatiently there (she had never seen him wait patiently anywhere for anyone) and his frown only deepened when she remembered her portable computer and ran back up the stairs.

The beat-up old Apple PowerBook 160 was adorned with various decals and stickers, breaking up its somber dark gray exterior. She slipped it into a bag made for the purpose, which already held utility programs on carefully labeled disks, along with a number of blanks. She checked a pocket to ensure the double-ended telephone line was in its place, along with an extension cord for the electrical adapter and then quickly zipped everything up.

Though impatient herself to be off, Ellen permitted herself to be hugged by her mother before climbing into their station wagon. She had not finished buckling in when her father let off the brake and rolled the car down the driveway. They bounced a little as they hit the street of the housing development, one her father had a big hand in, and then they were off.

The morning sun was still low in the sky but it promised heavy heat for later in the day. The fields they passed looked like they could use some rain; the plants seemed to sag a little under the bright sky, as if flinching from what the day would bring. They passed the occasional farmer but she didn't wave. Her father didn't like it when she did and she didn't want to spoil her anticipation by feeling his irritation.

They passed the bar, what her grandfather called a roadhouse, which was about half way to the farm. She had seen a movie of the same name with this young guy who all the girls said was really cool so she said so, too, even though she had actually liked more the young guy's older partner who had this mustache that looked just like Grandpa Tom's. She always thought it dumb that they killed him off in the movie.

The roadhouse had one of those yellow signs with small wheels out front and in large plastic letters they were advertising a band called "Finally Balanced," which was a cool name.

Ellen found that deciding what was cool and what was not was a great puzzle and she committed a number of social blunders with the other girls at school by declaring something cool when it was not. After some study, she figured out a mathematical way of determining it, which seemed to clear up the enigma. When with a group of girls, if two in a row referred to something as cool, then it probably was. If one of the girls was popular, a category that tended to remain stable through the school year after September, then it was definitely cool.

So when with her friends she tended not to describe anything as cool until she had a chance to do some counting. In the months she used this technique she had made no mistakes.

However, she still did not know what cool really was, so she practiced identifying things as being cool or not, but was careful not to mention her judgments aloud.

For example, Ellen decided that volcanoes, horses, and all the guys in Bon Jovi were cool, but that Mr. Simpson, the assistant principal, was not. This despite the fact that all her peers refused to acknowledge anything like schoolwork, such as volcanoes and geology, were cool. They all thought Bon Jovi used to be cool and never paid any attention to farm animals of any kind. Many of the girls were from farms so everyone had to work hard at pretending they weren't and work very hard pretending they were from "the street," which no one really understood but was a phrase they heard on MTV a lot. Further, they loved passing around rumors about the assistant principal that hinted at some kind of exciting but possibly forbidden activities involving some of the women teachers.

Ellen decided that her grandfather was cool, her father most assuredly was not, and her mother was probably not, which made her sad.

Grandpa Tom, a watering can in his hand, was next to the house when they came down the drive. She waved and was out of the car almost before it came to a stop. As he approached, she dipped in a courtesy, something she had seen on television and practiced privately for the past three weeks.

Tom paused for a moment and she thought that for some reason he was not glad to see her but the moment passed and he picked her up for a hug. Then she was dragging her suitcase and computer bag out of the car.

Her father reached over her and grasped the bags and lifted them free. He put them down beside her and then turned to her.

"You have a good time," he said, his hands gently squeezing her shoulders. "Be careful; listen to your grandfather." Then he hugged her and gave her a kiss on the cheek. Ellen barely overcame her surprise in time to hug him back before he released her, waved at Grandpa Tom, and then was in the car, turning around. He was gone before the dust from their arrival settled.

Well, maybe even uncool people can be cool sometimes.

Chapter 13

JJ sat before the computer monitor quietly rippling his fingertips across his lips. He was updating himself on the task force's progress by reading through the reports of the various teams and came to the conclusion that they were all going nowhere.

The murder of Hollingsworth was a temporary distraction. Primarily a matter for the Middletown police, it still had not shed any light on their primary responsibility, which, he reminded himself, was breaking up the amphetamine traffic that they were still convinced originated somewhere in the local area.

In the three weeks since Hollingsworth bit the big one, there was little to suggest they had any real leads on the illegal traffic. There was a moment of hope that the killing might be part of a resurgence of warfare between the Riders and their bitter rivals, the Dragons, but both sides kept their heads down.

Which was too bad, really, JJ thought. *We could afford to lose a few more of the bastards.*

An outbreak of gang war between the outlaws might provide the task force with opportunities to break open a few leads, true enough. But JJ was concerned with more than the task force accomplishing its mission.

He would never admit to it, not to the other members of the task force – especially not to them – nor to any other cops he knew, but he felt personally insulted that these people were operating in his county. Despite all the education, all the sophisticated training, all the traveling, JJ secretly knew he was that rare creature, a person of a place.

He was an Ohioan, a Buckeye, and Butler County was his home, and these bastards were shitting in it. He took it personally and he wanted them stopped.

But the task force, which he originally joined with hopeful enthusiasm, was not succeeding. Somewhere in the county was a major speed lab, probably up some farm road, maybe in a warehouse, maybe in a basement, and they were having no luck tracking it down.

The latest reports from the agents trying to link the delivery of equipment and chemical supplies were discouraging. They had not expected to find direct shipments of the lab gear from the manufacturers to a nicely identified site somewhere in the county. The equipment needed could largely be improvised, if necessary, and frequently was.

On a large scale, the chemicals were not as readily available and a number of the task force teams were culling every source imaginable, trying to find a trail that would lead to Butler County. Thus far, they had turned up exactly nothing.

The fear was that the gang was using layered cutouts. Have the stuff from different manufacturers sent to different receivers, who in turn would forward it to various other cutouts, and then, sooner or later, on to someone who collected it and delivered it to the Steel Rider's lab.

The main ingredient, ephedrine, was tracked fairly closely when manufactured in the United States. The problem was that it was also manufactured in Mexico, Europe, and Asia, and there were few oversights on production in many of those places. Indeed, the task force members were well aware that a great deal of legally manufactured American ephedrine was legally exported to other countries only to find its way through a series of cutouts back into the States.

JJ glanced over at the large bulletin board that lined most of one wall of the office. One of the agents had posted the yearly national statistics of the results of the methamphetamine trade. In some cities speed was accounting for up to a third of all the people in drug abuse programs. Since 1990, emergency room admissions for speed-related problems, such as amphetamine psychosis or cardiac collapse, were up almost a hundred percent and deaths were up by fifty percent.

JJ shook his head. He knew it was in every high school and many of the elementary schools in the county. The girls liked it because it helped them lose weight in their pursuit of the perfect body they saw portrayed in the magazines. The boys liked it because it eliminated fear and made them feel up for anything. All of them liked it because it was cheap at two dollars a line and the high lasted for six or seven hours, at least until the body became acclimatized to it. Then it took more. A lot more.

Six months before joining the task force he was involved in a bust of a small dealer operating on the periphery of Miami University. He turned out to have even smaller dealers working for him who he promptly turned over to the law, undoubtedly as a result of discovering a previously unsuspected vein of civic virtue. One of the subdealers was a 15-year old girl who supplied her friends in school. She would set up in the girls' restroom and the others would snort a line right off the edge of the porcelain sink.

This little girl with the angelic face and baby blues was making close to $100 a week. Out of a restroom. Not even trying to sell anything more than lines.

JJ stretched, hearing the joints in his shoulders pop. He was a little stiff today; last night was the first summer game for his softball team and he had a few dues to pay for overexerting himself. He sighed, switched the terminal off and turned to his desk.

The task force members were mostly gone, carrying out various assignments. Besides himself, only three others were around. One was busy clacking away at his keyboard, trying to get his report entered so he could go home early and get a jump on the weekend. The other two, one of which was the duty officer, were mulling over a mass of papers spread over a tabletop, talking quietly, sipping coffee, and occasionally rearranging the pages.

JJ reached down and slid open a desk drawer. Inside was a map of Butler County, laminated in clear plastic. He looked around and unfolded it across his desk. He pulled a felt tipped pen from a jar and considered the map.

The map represented his own approach to finding the drug lab. While the other members of the task force were following the lead of the DEA and trying to find the routes of the needed imported supplies and equipment, he had taken the approach of, If I were a speed lab, where would I be?

The task force knew that a lab could be quite small. Some manufacturers even set up operations in vans and campers, which allowed outstanding mobility. They could take an order, drive off to an isolated spot, make the goods, and return to consummate the deal. Manufacturers were generally getting around $6,000 a pound, so affording the mobility was not a problem.

But the Steel Riders were moving a lot more than the odd pound, though that was probably how they started and DEA intel made it clear they didn't pass up any sales, no matter how small. It was also clear that within the past ten months the Riders had become known across the Midwest as major suppliers providing a consistently high quality product.

They could provide on demand, which suggested inventory and continuous manufacture.

The high quality was the key. Intercepted speed deliveries in Dayton, Columbus, Cincinnati, Cleveland, Chicago, Indianapolis, and numerous other cities, showed a rapidly increasing proportion of the drug coming from, as chemical analysis proved, the same source. The map of the Midwest on the same bulletin board was dotted with color-coded pins indicating locations and frequencies of busts of speed produced by the same lab.

Careful work and some luck identified the Steel Riders as the source. Even knowing that did not reveal the location of the lab. The task force spent three months in Dayton before deciding the trail there was cold. But they had an undercover source within the Dragons and he provided them with the information that the Riders had put the lab somewhere south of Dayton, down in Butler County. The process of elimination corroborated this intelligence, but there still was no proof.

With the murder charges dropped, the task force was hoping to find the lab and use it as the basis for busting the Riders, but the gang's security was tight. There was no word on the street giving any suggestion as to where it might be. Arresting street-level dealers had yet to result in a roll over leading to more than a low level Rider, and of the four of them busted thus far, exactly none had cooperated.

Indeed, charges against one Rider were dropped when the dealer who fingered him suddenly reversed himself and took the five to ten the county prosecutor held over his head. It might have had something to do with the mysterious burning of his trailer out on State 732 and a number of late night telephone calls his common law wife had gotten afterwards.

JJ sighed. If they were going to find the lab, he suspected it would happen because they went out and tracked it down themselves rather than have it revealed to them. He pushed the county contour map flat and studied it.

Using various colored pens, he identified what he considered were the highest probable areas. He excluded in black the towns and cities of the county. First, because the police in those areas would be more familiar with them and, second, because when he started this project he had in mind places that he could get to. That left the rural and wooded areas of the county.

Which was a hell of a lot of land. If he hadn't known that before starting his independent project, he knew it now.

The nature of such labs was that their users would want them to be out of sight. This suggested a place in some woods, or in a shallow valley, or something similar. The map's own green shading indicated where the woods were supposed to be at the time the map was made, but he knew that the wooded areas could change from year to year as land was either cleared for farming or given up.

He had spent some time on the roads, double-checking the map. JJ seriously doubted the lab would be in sight of a road, so a yellow pen marked areas that you could see from your car. He had gone out on some of the roads to see if his estimates were correct and was gratified to find they were.

Figuring that a lab likewise wouldn't be built in a position where it would be seen by a neighbor resulted in shading large areas in orange. He knew farmers would always notice what was happening on land next to theirs and any local people, like the Steel Riders, would be careful to avoid doing something sure to arouse comment.

With all the shading, there were still large areas in which the lab could be. There were parts of the county that had grown over into dense forest and there were plenty of places where the rolling Ohio hills kept prying eyes away. Some of those farm boys counted on that when they grew their own cash crops of marijuana. The introduction of aerial photography had taken care of a lot of that, though some still tried to plant their crops in between rows of corn.

JJ raised an eyebrow. Aerial photography might be useful for his problem, but he didn't have enough to go to Carl Davidson and ask for that kind of imaging to be done, much less the infrared scanning which might tell him about the levels of activity in the buildings. There was no way the county budget could be stretched for this long shot; he was going to have to play this one like Sherlock Holmes.

He peered closely at the survey map. Little black squares marked the sites of individual buildings. Again, the indicators weren't always accurate. Some farm buildings were torn down, new barns were built every so often, and so on, but if the bad guys were making use of, say, an older building, out in the middle of nowhere, it might be on the map.

He was still studying the map, jotting down the locations of buildings in the unshaded, unseen areas, when the others left for the day.

Chapter 14

Tom waited until Ellen went to bed before going into his own bedroom and retrieving his notes. He had begun to fill in a spiral notebook with information on the Steel Riders after making his decision to kill the remaining four defendants, drawing on his memory and the newspapers he saved – though he had not had a specific purpose at the time – covering the apprehension and legal proceedings of the five.

He sat in the kitchen, a cup of coffee cooling beside him, and hunched over the notebook opened on the table. Each page consisted of his notes, summarizing whatever he had been able to put together on each one.

Turning the pages, he came to one headed "David Hollingsworth." Other than the name, the page was blank. There was no need to transcribe anything, since its subject was dead. Nonetheless, he felt that it was important in some way to have at least one page devoted to the first one, the laugher, the one who lit the fuse.

Tom grimaced and flipped to the front of the notebook. The name at the top was Jack Baker. He ran down the notes, already familiar to him. Leader of the Steel Riders for three years. No street address noted in any article, though there was reference to him living somewhere near Hamilton. Tom noted his physical characteristics, mostly based on his own observations.

The man was tall, six feet in his bare feet, though Tom noticed at the hearing his tendency to cowboy boots made him look even taller. The police photograph published in the newspaper articles showed him with dark, stringy, shoulder length hair and a goatee, but during the hearings he was clean-shaven with his hair cut short.

Baker was slim, but gave an impression of strength. He had an athlete's stride. Tom still remembered the hard click of the man's boots as he strode in triumph down the aisle of the courtroom, headed for the door, headed for freedom.

Black hair, black eyes. Tom had looked into the man's eyes, though at a distance, trying to read them, but had seen nothing. It was almost as if they didn't reflect light.

Well, he was going to have to find Mr. Baker. He flipped to the back of the notebook where he had written extraneous information. One newspaper sidebar piece on the Steel Riders traced their history. Apparently, they had been around for well over two decades and, though initially based in the Cincinnati area, moved the center of their organization up to Butler County during the past several years. The dying steel town of Middletown and the stagnant city of Hamilton with its paper mills and county seat provided young men for the organization, otherwise cast adrift in the collapsing economies of the rust belt.

He noted the names of several bars where the Riders tended to congregate. This could be a place to start looking for Baker, but it did not promise fast results.

Taking a sip of coffee, he flipped back to the front of the notebook. By chance he found himself at the page headed "John Larson."

He scanned down the page, looking through his brief notes. Yes, here it was. Larson's address, culled from the telephone book. A street address he was unfamiliar with, but he could find it with a little searching. He leaned back in his chair, thinking.

He remembered Larson as a short, young man, nervous during the hearing, always moving in his chair. Shaggy blond hair, a little soft looking. While the others stood and shook hands and pounded each other on the back when the judge dismissed the charges, he remained sitting, shuddering with relief.

Mr. Larson was a bit on the shaky side, it appeared. Maybe he could talk with him, persuade him to give a little information, such as Jack Baker's home address.

Tom sat for some time, occasionally sipping at the cooling coffee, looking at nothing at all. If anyone had been in the room they might have wondered on the slight, tight smile on his face, wondered at what he thought.

And if anyone looked close, they might have wondered on the deep fire burning in his eyes, and wondered at what he hated.

Chapter 15

On the scale of such things, Johnny Larson would not be labeled a truly evil man. Stone cold stupid, sure, the gods sitting in judgment would have universally agreed to that, but evil presupposes sufficient moral sophistication to know the difference between right and wrong.

Johnny Larson, in the words of one of his Steel Rider brothers, didn't know the difference between spit and piss and would try to do both into the wind unless you turned him around. If this was an exaggeration, it was only slightly so.

What Johnny mostly was, was scared.

He had been scared all his life, it seemed. His earliest memory was of trying to find a closet to hide in when he saw the headlights of his father's car lance into the living room of his family's poor white trash trailer home just south of Covington, Kentucky, which lay across the river from Cincinnati. His father, a man soured on his own sense of failure and filled with the kind of rage that filters down the generations like links on a chain, would come staggering into the house looking for someone to beat on, someone he could feel bigger than. Johnny would hide and then pray that his father would find someone else to savage. Sometimes it worked, though he still had dreams from which he awoke with his younger sister's screams echoing in his ears.

She never learned to hide.

In the midst of his fear and despair, there was a chance for a turning point, though he never recognized it. Johnny had a talent, totally unexpected, for numbers, and for a moment there was a teacher in high school who had seen this hidden ability, like a deep buried vein of gold, and who wanted to use it as a lifeline for Johnny to pull himself out of the quicksand of pain his family had become. Johnny responded to the attention, to the concern, with an almost dog-like devotion.

But then had come the worst beating of them all, one that started in the trailer, and then spilled out onto the yard, and up the narrow lane to the county road. Kicked, punched, hit repeatedly with a length of board until it began to break up, he was very close to dying. Unlike in the movies, a severe physical beating is not something you can stand up from and shrug off. Internal damage in the form of ruptured organs, burst blood vessels, broken bones, and torn internal structures can kill.

Why his father was delivering a beating this particular time was a complete unknown to Johnny. He never did learn the why.

Johnny staggered, fell, and crawled to his feet again and again, struggling to get down the fifty yards of drive from their house to the main road. When he got to the intersection, and without thinking clearly, he turned toward the hard, packed dirt parking lot of the small bar his father visited frequently. Johnny fell and was on all fours when his father caught up to him and began kicking him. While drunk enough that his aim and timing were poor, Johnny's father was connecting well enough to break three of Johnny's ribs before he rolled among the vehicles parked in front of the bar.

He had a glimpse through the eye which was still open of a large, black rubber tire, flashes of light from the sun reflecting off chrome, and what appeared to be coins hanging in star-studded space. It made no sense and Johnny didn't have the time to consider it further. He tried to roll to one side, his bloody face becoming covered with dirt as he did, but there was another vehicle in the way and for some reason he couldn't get under it.

What he thought were stars hanging in space were conchos on the side of black leather saddlebags hung over the back of a black and chrome Harley-Davidson Softail. It, and the four other Harleys parked with it, had little in the way of customized chrome features, fancy painted details, radios, stereos, or any of the other items favored by Yuppies. It was simply a low-riding piece of steel reflecting the sometimes excessive savage beauty of the country that built it and the muscular build of its rider who was just emerging from the bar with his companions.

The five, all Steel Riders, had stopped at the bar for a beer or five after completing a run to Tennessee to attend a friend's wedding. As they came blinking out into the sunlight they saw Johnny's father, the splintered board raised above his head, swaying towards the bikes, between two of which they also saw a small, t-shirted figure sprawled in the summer-warmed dirt of the parking lot.

They didn't talk it over. As one, they surged forward and proceeded to beat the holy hell out of Johnny's father. It should be noted that one did so because he thought Johnny's father might damage the bikes. Another because the others did. The third because he liked to fight and cheerfully would have leapt into Hell to kick the shit out of Satan if he could have found Perdition's portals. The last two, including the Softail rider, went after Johnny's father because what they saw him doing violated their sense of justice. They didn't think it right that a full-grown man was beating the piss out of what looked to be just a kid.

No one lives without a moral code and the Steel Riders were no exception, albeit they had one which most might regard as extremely rough-hewn. Never mind that, if they had come out and thought that same kid was messing with their bikes, they might have booted him down the county road a mile or two. As it was, Johnny's father was getting a demonstration of its applied practicality, though he was not in a position to appreciate the moral expression in any detail.

When they finished with him, they lifted him and tossed him face first into the big, green trash dumpster next to the bar. Johnny's father voiced no complaints and, indeed, even had he been conscious and coherent – something he would not be for another twenty-four hours – he would have expressed heartfelt gratitude for the opportunity to fall in among the offal of a back road bar as an alternative to continued discourse with the Riders.

The bikers strode back to their bikes to find that Johnny had managed to get to his feet and, weaving in the slight breeze, was blinking at them through one eye.

"Hey, kid," the Softail rider said through a blond beard which looked like something Leif Ericson might have worn, "you can go on home now. That bastard's not gonna bother you for a while." His sharp blue eyes studied the bloodied youngster.

Johnny stood silent for a moment, focusing on the leather and Levi clad men in front of him. They were, with one exception, bearded, and all had long hair of varying hues. All wore dusty boots. Three had on shades. They looked like tough sons of bitches, which was as accurate a description of them as Johnny could come up with and, considering the circumstances, wasn't totally inaccurate. He swallowed, twice, and spoke through bloody lips.

"Where is he?" He paused and spat out some bloody saliva, most of which dribbled down his chin and stained his filthy t-shirt. His hands raised in small fists.

The gang members looked at him for a moment as he barely stood in the summer sun, blood dripping off him from half a dozen places. A couple of the bikers chuckled. One of them, the tall biker without a beard and who liked to fight, spoke.

"Shit, kid! Don't you know when you're ahead?" With that, they all started laughing. For a moment, Johnny stood uncomprehending, thinking they were making fun of him and then realized it was all right. He tried to laugh but could do little better than a croak, which the Riders found hilarious. Their sense of humor was as rough as their sense of justice.

They scooped him up and half carried him into the bar where they administered heavy-handed first aid, which included some techniques not found in the manuals of the American National Red Cross. After his third beer, Johnny, certainly underage by any applicable state or county law, could not have cared less. He never had anyone fight for him, never had anyone tend to his wounds, and at that moment would have licked the dirt off the Riders' boots.

An hour later the one with the Viking beard, roughly inspecting the bandages they had put across Johnny's face with a hand about twice the size of Johnny's, decided that the kid might live.

"Where you going, kid?" he asked.

Johnny blinked for a moment, his eye semaphoring his fear.

"I got no place to go, mister; I want to go with you guys." It was the first brave thing Johnny had done in his life.

The Viking laughed and slammed the tabletop with his hand so hard the empty beer bottles bounced off and fell to the floor. No one seemed to notice. The tall one leaned over the table and studied Johnny, then turned toward one of the riders who was leaning against the bar lighting a cigar.

"Hey, Tommy, your sister still got that spare room?"

Tommy nodded in the affirmative and that was it. Fifteen minutes later, Johnny was on the back of one of the outlaw's bikes, holding on for dear life while the wind and the engines thundered in his ears. From that moment, his life's devotion was to the Steel Riders.

He learned to be a mechanic to the big bikes and found that his talent for numbers translated into a knack for manipulating motors. When they finally made him a member of the Steel Riders a year later in a ceremony which included threatening him with a .44 Magnum, it was as if he found a family denied to him during the previous 17 years of his life. He did everything they asked of him.

But the fear was never gone. There was the continual anxiety, just below the surface, that one day he would wake up and it would all be gone and he would be back in the grip of his father, who he never saw again after that bloody day.

There was fear in being a Rider, too, far more immediate. Johnny was afraid when they had confrontations with the law or other gangs or citizens. He was afraid when he was smuggling drugs or covering someone who was going to make a sale. But he always did what he had to do in spite of his fear.

Then came the shooting of the little girl. Jack Baker had just gone ballistic in the face of the Dragons and pulled the MAC-10 and starting spraying bullets in all directions.

Johnny was never involved in a killing before. There was violence, sure. Once he helped break the legs of a guy who tried to rip off a Rider in a drug deal. He almost vomited but swung the crowbar with all his might; he could still hear the crunch of the kneecaps going. But killing was another thing, especially of a little girl. Johnny saw her picture in the newspaper almost every day. She looked a lot like his little sister, the one who never learned to hide.

The one he left behind.

All through the legal proceedings, Johnny waited to be punished and when it didn't happen he didn't feel the elation of the others but, weirdly enough, guilt, like he was somehow cheating at something.

While confused about what he felt, there was one thing that became clearer all during the hearings and since. He had to leave the Steel Riders. He couldn't be involved in anything that might hurt little girls.

Especially little girls that look like Meggy.

Very quietly he prepared to leave, to get away. In making the decision, he put a great deal at risk. One did not resign from the Steel Riders. If they were in a good mood, they would come over to your house, beat the hell out of you and then take your bike. If they were in a bad mood, they would kill you.

With the death of Dave Hollingsworth the Riders were in a very, very bad mood. Johnny, like the others, figured the Dragons for it and knew there would have to be bloody retaliation. Johnny didn't want to have anything to do with any more killing. That much was clear to him.

He packed what he could into a T-Bag that he was going to strap onto the back of his own black and chrome Harley and he was going to take off. He had a cousin near Memphis and a couple of telephone calls resulted in a tentative, and temporary, welcome extended. Johnny figured to pull out tonight, in the dark, so no one could see.

Johnny glanced out the window to check the weather. It was cloudy all day but now that night had fallen, as near as he could tell, things were clearing up. He looked down into the parking lot; his small apartment had a good view, situated as it was over the garage where he worked. There was no one in the washed out orange of the streetlight and little traffic on the street. Across the way, the big grocery store with its prairie of a parking lot was open and would be all night, but there were few cars in its lot. Outside of the old pickup parked near the street, most of the vehicles were huddled around the front of the store like travelers trying to get the heat from a fire.

Johnny had thought about it a lot and decided to leave his colors behind. He laid the black leather vest with its embroidered patches carefully on the bed. Sooner or later they would find it. He shrugged. He hoped they would understand, but he knew the code.

Johnny paused, checking everything a last time. He grimaced and went to the small table beside his bed. He opened the drawer and took out a nine millimeter Beretta automatic pistol. He checked that it was loaded and shoved it into the front of his pants like that cool guy did in the movie "Lethal Weapon." He grabbed a spare loaded clip and slipped it into a jean pocket. He picked up the T-Bag – its straps for securing it to his motorcycle flopped around his legs as he hefted it. Now he was ready.

Turning off the light, Johnny closed the door softly and paused, waiting for his eyes to adjust to the dark. He could barely make out the wooden steps running down the outside wall of the garage; they were a pisser when it rained but tonight was fine. He stepped down carefully, using both hands to carry the T-Bag.

His bike was under the stairs, double chained to them and to the pipes going to the gas meter. He rigged the T-Bag to the sissy bar and the rear of the seat. He bent over to unlock the chains when he heard the voice.

"Going somewhere?" it asked.

Johnny didn't recognize it. It was just a whisper, cold and hard. Fear rolled over him like an icy wave. All he could figure was somehow they had learned of his plans and were here to stop him. He thought he could get the drop on them and then still get away. It was desperate reasoning and it was totally wrong.

Tom had parked an hour earlier in the grocery store parking lot and then walked around, looking for ways to get to Johnny's apartment. He settled on an alley that came off a side street parallel to the main road. Then he went back to the truck and, carefully looking around, put on his long raincoat and slipped the shotgun underneath it.

Using the dark as best he could, Tom made his way to the stairs where he found the Harley. He saw the apartment's lights above him. He thought for a few moments, considering. The lights were still on up above, so maybe what he would do is wait for maybe an hour and then go on up. Maybe Mr. Larson would be asleep by then. If so, he was in for the ultimate in rude awakenings.

Tom was surprised, then, twenty minutes later, when the lights went out in the rooms above and he heard the apartment door open. He backed into the shadows, away from the motorcycle. The figure carried a large bag, which he quickly attached to the bike.

Tom didn't know who it was but assumed it was probably Larson. Nonetheless, he had to be sure. He had a small penlight in a pocket and he gripped it in his left hand, his right holding the shotgun under the raincoat.

When he spoke, he did not expect the reaction he got. The figure froze, bent over the bike, and then spun on him. He punched on the penlight.

It was Larson, pulling at something in his pants. For a second Tom didn't understand what he saw, and then he realized Johnny was going for a gun. His reflexes kicked in. He swung the shotgun up and squeezed the trigger before his left hand was able to provide support.

Johnny clawed at the pistol but it wouldn't come free. In his panic, he didn't realize it was snagged on his pants and to free it he would have to push it down, turn it slightly, and then pull it out. All he did was try to pull harder. When the penlight came on, he yanked the Beretta even harder. With his finger on the trigger of the double-action pistol and a round already chambered, Johnny was about to shoot himself in the thigh when the shotgun fired.

Johnny didn't hear the blast. He saw a blinding flash of light, like an electric ball of flame, and simultaneously felt a blow to the front of his body as if several people at once hit the entire length of his torso with baseball bats.

Johnny folded over on himself. His balance upset, he fell forward, striking the parking lot pavement with his head. He found it very strange that he didn't feel the impact of his fall but before he wondered very long the pain came.

The pain grew rapidly. For an instant there wasn't any, just the sense of a heavy impact and the worst feeling of his breath knocked out of him he had ever encountered. Johnny knew he was shot and thought for a second that it wasn't so bad. Then the pain washed into him like liquid lava poured from an endless container. It wasn't just on his skin, on the outside; that the terrible burning was felt, no question, but it was inside, too, and spreading, going deeper.

His body convulsed and Johnny felt an overwhelming urge to vomit as everything inside of him seemed to be a burning liquid. In that perception he wasn't far wrong.

The pellets from the twelve gauge, each about the size of a .32 caliber bullet, had taken him just below the heart. They had little chance to spread after leaving the shotgun's muzzle and struck in a circular mass about three inches across. Several veered once in his body and encountered organs of varying densities and, of course, bones.

When a solid object goes through a less solid object, it produces cavitation. Like a ship's propeller moving through water, a hole in the less solid object is formed by the action of movement. It takes a while for the less solid object, be it water or human tissue, to fill in the hole.

A bullet produces two types of cavitation. The first is stretch cavitation. This is the hole left by the passage of the slug that the body tissue collapses into. Stretch cavitation, which can result in a great deal of damage to anything it runs through, by its nature is slower to disable or kill since the surrounding body tissue collapses the hollow tube and presses against itself. This slows the rate of blood loss. Johnny's nine millimeter pistol was an excellent choice for producing stretch cavitation, as its relatively high velocity bullets typically produced long, thin tubes through people. It usually takes several such hits to put someone down.

The other kind of cavitation, called crush cavitation, is the kind that stops people quickly. It refers to holes caused by the crushing of body tissue; when such holes are large, the collapse by the now compressed body tissue will not completely fill it. This permits the freer loss of body fluids, most importantly blood. The larger the crush cavity, the sooner shock, unconsciousness and, ultimately, death set in.

At close range, a shotgun produces relatively poor stretch cavitation but excellent crush cavitation. What Johnny experienced was the massive outpouring of blood that caused his blood pressure to drop like a rock. Noticing the loss of blood pressure, his brain signaled his heart to beat ever faster, which served only to dump blood out the massive cavity now existing in his lower chest. Blood movement slowed, depriving his brain of oxygen. In only a few seconds he was incapable of organized movement. In far less than a minute insufficient blood was available for his brain to remain conscious and he passed out. His bowels and bladder opened. As the brain fell into unconsciousness, that portion of it governing the heart lost its coherency, and the heart, which up to then had been working furiously trying to maintain pressure in a system that was wide open to the outside world, spastically shut down.

By the time Tom probed Johnny's throat for a pulse, Johnny was clinically dead, though it would be several more minutes before all his brain cells finally failed. In the meantime, he experienced rapidly distorting dreams, which became a vision of a great, bright light as the visual centers starved for oxygen, and an all-encompassing darkness.

Then Johnny was dead.

Tom rolled him over and looked into his half opened eyes. He moved Johnny's right hand aside, careful not to touch any of his blood. He saw the Beretta.

"Damn it," he whispered, the only words that would be spoken over Johnny Larson's body.

Looking around, Tom saw no one. There were no sirens, but he didn't want to wait around to find out if there would be any. Using his light to avoid the rivulet of blood that was making its way towards a drain, he carefully walked to the street. There was no traffic and he crossed to the store's parking lot.

He put the shotgun behind the seat and took off his raincoat. Folding it up, it followed the shotgun. The truck started on the first try and he slowly drove to an exit from the lot to the street, one away from the streetlights. He pulled out, switching on his lights as he went. When he got to the main highway, about a quarter of a mile from the cooling body of Johnny Larson, he saw a police car, its emergency lights on but its siren off, race by in the opposite direction.

He flipped his turn signal, looked both ways, and made his turn. He was home less than thirty minutes later.

Chapter 16

Ellen sat by the window in the dark of the night watching her grandfather's truck slowly come down the lane. It's lights were out, but the rear brake lights occasionally flared and backlit the vehicle. Why he wasn't using his headlights was a mystery. For the moment, it did not occur to Ellen that her grandfather was trying not to be noticed.

She had awakened earlier, needing to go to the bathroom – too much cider while watching reruns of Mystery Science Theater 3000. Her grandfather seemed a little preoccupied, though he grinned at some of the jokes made by Joel and the 'bots.

For a while, after going to the bathroom, she lay in the dark, not thinking about anything, content to let sleep come back to her. Then she heard the gravel crunching beneath the truck's wheels.

She knew of her grandfather's late night rides; he sometimes took one just before going to bed when he had a long day to help him relax a little. Still, they were rare and he never tried to come back without being seen.

That's what it is. He's sneaking back with his lights off. He doesn't want to be seen.

She paused for a moment, considering.

He doesn't want to be seen by me.

She was still puzzling on this mystery when she fell asleep twenty minutes   later.

Chapter 17

Carl Davidson, twelve-year veteran of the Drug Enforcement Agency and head of the task force operating in Butler County, motioned to JJ to join him after the group briefing on the killing of Johnny Larson. JJ had gotten the call from the Middletown cops and, in turn, passed on the information at the morning brief.

The reaction among the task force members was almost universally to point the finger at the Dragons. There were three reasons.

First, of course, gangs like the Dragons could not afford to be perceived as weak, and it was inconceivable that they would not retaliate for the shoot-out where Jack Baker violated what was supposed to be a flag of truce. Second, their internal psychology demanded they strike back. Further, Johnny Larson, like Hollingsworth, was one of the Riders involved in the violation, thus making for a sort of murderous logic. The third reason was based on information the Middletown police did not have.

The task force had a man inside the Dragons, code named "Johnny Ringo." He managed to pass the word that the decision may finally have been made to retaliate for the shoot-out. Ringo thought the Dragons were gathering their people to take out a large number of the Riders, and soon.

Upon getting Ringo's report and news of Larson's death, the task force members agreed that the expected war between the two motorcycle gangs was now officially underway, with the score Dragons two, Steel Riders zero.

And if a war broke out, they might be able to move in among the survivors and get people to testify in exchange for, what?, safety, revenge, whatever. The point was some of the minnows in both gangs might try to hide from the sharks and provide the task force with its chance to get the intelligence needed to shut down the drug trafficking.

As Davidson repeatedly reminded everyone, the drug business, not the murders, was their responsibility. He wanted convictions, he wanted the lab and he wanted both. Thus far, they had neither.

Davidson motioned to a chair in his office that JJ took tentatively. Davidson buried his nose in a handkerchief; he seemed to always suffer from an allergy. After sneezing hard enough to cause the overhead lights to sway he sighed, wiped his nose, and put the handkerchief away.

"There's something about all this that doesn't quite fit," Davidson said, blinking his eyes owlishly. "If the Dragons are going to war, why would they bother to hit this Larson, who everyone says was a nobody?" He opened a file and studied it for a moment. "Been with the gang only a few years, worked a day job as a mechanic, implicated in a few things, maybe was a courier for moving drugs, but hardly a key figure. The Dragons aren't stupid; why hit him, and so long after hitting the other one, and maybe alert everyone as to what's coming?" He looked at JJ.

JJ was puzzled as well. These were the same questions that floated inside him during the briefing. He had not voiced his doubts then, not wanting to say anything until he had the answers. Davidson was looking at him calmly, with his big owl eyes, patiently waiting. On the spot, JJ realized Davidson wanted to hear from him specifically.

"Well, maybe some Dragon jumped the gun, or wanted to get in the first licks to prove himself to the others." JJ paused for a moment. Davidson did not fill in the silence, so he continued.

"Or maybe it's like Agent Deevers suggested. Maybe it wasn't a Dragon," he said, taking a leap as he warmed to the question. "I mean, the killings are what we've been expecting, and what every other cop in the tri-county area has been expecting. 'Johnny Ringo' is saying the Dragons are probably going to move, but maybe we've overlooked something important. The first killing, Hollingsworth, took place before the Dragons reached a decision, according to Ringo. This second one comes after the decision, all right, but it's a low guy on the totem pole, not one of the brain trust, and it happens in a way that is sure to put the Riders on their toes. From that point of view it doesn't make any sense."

JJ fell silent, a little concerned. The sequence of the deaths and the Dragon's decision did not fit well to him but he had not felt comfortable voicing this contrary point of view in front of the feds. Now he had. Davidson smiled.

"That's right; as a part of a coherent opening move on the part of the Dragons it doesn't hold together well. Not at all well. What are the other possibilities, besides someone being over eager on the Dragons' side?"

JJ thought for a moment.

"There are two areas we have not explored and that the Middletown cops aren't going into, either, since they figure both killings were the work of the Dragons." JJ paused, gathering the words.

"First, maybe there's something internal going on the in the Steel Riders. Something that has nothing to do with the situation with the Dragons, maybe, but in any case somebody may be attempting to take over or change the direction of things. Remember one of the ideas we had about Hollingsworth was that he was wasted by someone pissed off about the girl. Maybe it's about that kind of thing, or maybe something in the leadership. An argument about money, maybe." Davidson was nodding. "Jack Baker has been ruthless in taking over the Rider leadership and there are rumors he's had at least two rivals killed. Maybe one of the survivors has decided to take out his allies."

"The second thing is one that was only slightly examined by the Middletown cops, but they don't seem to be pushing too hard on it. Maybe it's not about the Dragons or the Riders' internal politics. Maybe it's someone from the outside, not affiliated with the Dragons, who has their own agenda. Remember Eileen Parker was killed by Jack Baker during that blow-up with the Dragons."

"He wasn't alone," Davidson said.

"Right, he was with four other Riders. All five were a part of her death, then. Two of them have now been killed. That leaves three, though why someone interested in revenge wouldn't start with Baker, who actually pulled the trigger, I don't know. In any case, we know the Middletown detectives had done only a brief check for alibis among the Parker family. Might be something there."

Davidson nodded again. "Any other agendas that might be in play?"

JJ grimaced. "The problem with bastards like the Riders is there can be all kinds of reasons people might have for hating them. Drug deals, past killings, whatever. Someone may be using this time period for a little payback." Davidson leaned back in his chair, looking at the ceiling. His hands pushed back his thinning hair while he thought.

"I think there might be something in what you're saying," Davidson finally said, and JJ felt a small surge of satisfaction. "If there's some kind of power struggle going on inside the Steel Riders we may have the same opportunities for breaking things open we would have with a war. Deevers and Johnson can look into that." He folded his hands in front of him and looked at JJ over them. "I'm going to put some people on that second idea, that an outside party with another agenda based on past interaction with the Riders is in the game. I don't think there's much to it, but we should check it out, and at least rule it out, especially if the locals are going to pass on it." He shook his head and started groping for his handkerchief again. "I hate loose ends."

Davidson blew his nose and looked at JJ. "I want you to do a work-up to brief the entire team on the final possibility, that maybe some member of the Parker family is involved. Gather up the intel we have already. Go out and get some more if you need it."

Davidson paused to wipe his nose and put his handkerchief away. He shook his head. "Hell, JJ, I know this isn't going to go anywhere but we've got to clear it from the table. You're the man for it, being local; you looking around won't draw any attention to the task force. In any case, I'd like you to have a package ready for presentation by no later than Friday AM briefing. We'll start with it."

JJ sat still for a moment. His heart picked up a few beats. Yes, it was a small assignment and not one he could reasonably expect to lead anywhere, but it was his, and he was operating independently. It was his chance to stand out, to be recognized. He nodded.

"Okay, boss, I'll get on it." JJ got up and left the office.

Once back at his desk JJ made himself sit quietly for a few moments, marshalling his thoughts. He tried to keep from thinking about how much it meant to him to be recognized by these people, to be thought of as more than just a "local." He was careful, cautious (he would not have said afraid) about what he said and did in front of the others, determined not to appear the clown, determined to win their respect.

Up to now, all he had been was a "go-fer," the member on the task force not for competence or skill but for politeness, a sop to the locals. While he was personally accepted, he had not really been called on to demonstrate his capabilities. Now he had his chance to show something to them. If he did a good job on this there would be more. He knew how Davidson worked. He made the best possible use of his talent and this was JJ's chance to show Davidson what he had.

JJ glanced down at his desktop. The map he was working on, trying to figure where the drug lab might be, lay beneath his hands. He opened up a drawer and carefully put it in. There would be time for this later. Now he had a mission. He turned his chair towards the computer terminal and keyboard and began punching in his enquiries.

First he needed to get some background information on the Parkers. Then he would double-check their alibis. He wanted to do a complete job and he only had the four days until Friday.

Chapter 18

Tom walked with Ellen, a morning cup of coffee in his hands, while Redbone sat on the backdoor steps and watched them. Ellen had a small pair of binoculars and a bird book. He had promised to show her where he thought a red-tailed hawk had nested earlier in the spring and she wanted to see it.

As they walked down the lane, Ellen would occasionally start tracking some bird, peering intently through her binoculars, and then feverishly flip through her copy of Roger Tory Peterson to try to identify the bird while she still held it in memory. Tom was a little surprised at the variety of birds she had thus far identified. He had worked this farm since he left the army, forty years before, and the only birds he could identify for sure were three: turkey buzzards, red-tailed hawks, and everything else. Well, there were a few ducks and rarer geese, sure, with "Vs" that set his heart racing in the fall, maybe more each year, but it was like he had lived around these animals for so long they had faded into the background.

Listening to Ellen talking excitedly about birds was like being introduced to strangers who lived next door but had never been quite seen. She named each bird and then talked about it, where it came from, where it went to, what it ate, and so on. Tom shook his head. There was a lot you overlooked being a farmer.

His mind kept drifting back to the killing of the previous night. He was past being angry with himself. There was nothing gained in that. Bad preparation led to his being taken by surprise. That left him unable to question Larson and get the information he needed on Jack Baker.

He stopped and blew on his coffee before taking a sip. Should have gotten more information about Larson before moving on him.

Better recon of the area, he thought, using a phrase from forty years ago, *that's what I needed. Too much of a hurry. Need to stop and think.*

He watched as Ellen ran ahead to climb up the remains of an old gate in order to get a better view over the fields. Could he keep on without in some way arousing her suspicions? She was smart and observant, though he doubted that she had any reason to be suspicious of him.

He would have to be more careful with her. Maybe a little misdirection, have some plausible answers ready, but make sure she had no reason to become concerned. The whole point of all this was Ellen, after all, and he had to keep her from being hurt.

Ellen gave a shout from her perch on the gate and pointed up over the trees. Tom looked and saw a climbing red-tail. He nodded to her.

"That's the one. Hold still, now, and just watch."

She nodded back and turned back to the low flying hawk, raising her binoculars to see. The hawk, less than a hundred yards away, flapped once and then dipped a wing, turning towards them.

Silent as a good death, the raptor, the morning sun causing its underside to glow almost white and picking fire in its reddish-brown back and wings, glided towards them.

Ellen was watching through her glasses and then jerked them away from her eyes as if not wanting anything to get between her and the hawk. It swooped right over her, almost within arm's reach, and for a moment Tom looked into its fierce eye and thought he was looking in a mirror.

I understand you, one said to the other, though which to which was unclear in Tom's mind.

Ellen whooped with joy as the hawk flew away. She was filled with excitement, overjoyed at seeing the winged ferocity so close. Tom smiled and listened to her excitement while part of him held onto that fierce eye.

Chapter 19

JJ was on the road, a place he had spent a great deal of his adult life. Secretly, he enjoyed driving. There was the rhythm of the road, of course, the sheer fun of rolling down the roads and back lanes of the county, the view of which never bored him.

What he enjoyed most was driving one of the sheriff's patrol cars. It wasn't that they were particularly good cars to drive; while they had the standard General Motors cop package, the county Pontiacs were really more suited for high speed pursuit on long stretches of interstate, which was not in the patrol area of the sheriff.

He just liked being identified as a cop and the car was... What was the word his ex-wife used? Oh, yes, dramatic. She said he liked to make dramatic entrances.

Okay, sure, he liked the uniform, he liked the cars, and he knew how to put on the cop look that got you respect or at least compliance whenever you entered the scene. But it was more than that.

For JJ, just having the appearance was not enough. He needed to live up to what the display, the dramatic entrance, was all about. Look good, be good, one of his instructors said, and JJ bought it. Like many other men in his country in the final quarter of the Twentieth Century, he was confused by what was expected of him, what was not, and who he was supposed to be. Being a cop cut through all the crap and gave him a purpose and a value, especially being a good cop.

A "good cop;" the phrase was the understated accolade made by one cop about another, and it was the goal he worked for, every day of his life. He received awards for his academic work, plaques for community service, even decorations for valor; all of that was part of the job. What counted most to him was hearing that another cop called him a "good cop." There it was, all the recognition a man could ask for. Unequivocal, honest, direct, and given by someone in a position to know.

What else could you want?

JJ slowed the unmarked cruiser to a stop at a crossroads and checked in both directions before rolling forward again. He was on a back lane, one of the many rural delivery roads identified only by a county number. In this part of the county, roads tended to go fairly straight, north-south, east-west, until they ran into someone's farm, at which pointed they would take a ninety degree turn and follow the property line until they resumed their original direction. In Ohio, the farms were here before the roads and the civil engineers tended to remember that.

JJ passed the Parker farm and a quarter of a mile later turned onto yet another narrow and straight road.

He watched for the small cluster of buildings, usually close to the road, which marked the residence and barns for each farm. Tree lines divided the fields as windbreaks and occasionally there would be a wooded lot, sometimes fairly large. Dairy cows spread across fenced fields crossed by well-worn paths the cows took when they returned to the barn in the late afternoon.

Up ahead by the side of the road was a small island of mailboxes. There was a reddish brown one, very large, marked with the box and rural delivery number. Fastened to an old milk can weighed down with sand, a green steel garden stake was hammered into the earth beside it and was festooned with several different plastic boxes for receiving various newspapers. He glanced at the clipboard beside him and slowed down.

The house was well off the road, which was a little unusual, as the further away from the road the house and its outbuildings were, the more farmland not available for use. This kind of layout was more common in the hilly portions of the county. He turned onto the lane that ran arrow-straight to the house. This would be the O'Bryant farm.

He stopped the Pontiac behind a fairly new, blue Ford F250 pickup, its bed holding two large bales of hay. In front of it was a much older Oldsmobile.

As JJ got out of his car, instinctively straightening his tie as he did, the front door of the white house opened and two men emerged. While they were separated in age by several decades – the older was in his late sixties, maybe older – they were clearly related, having the same look about the eyes, the same prominent chin, and, when they looked at him, the same frown.

He pulled his identification from his coat pocket and opened it for their examination.

"Butler County Deputy Sheriff James Jeffers, Mr. O'Bryant," he said, addressing the older man. He nodded at the younger who looked at his father quizzically.

"What can I do for you, Mr. Jeffers?" the older man asked, squinting at JJ.

"Mr. O'Bryant, I'd like to ask you a few questions concerning an investigation we have underway." He paused and the older man took the hint and turned to his son.

"It's okay, Bobby. Go ahead. Give me a call tonight." He made a waving gesture with his hand.

His son grinned. "Okay, dad, but if I gotta go your bail, I hope they take plastic." He nodded to JJ and walked down to the pickup.

"Well, come on in, deputy, and let's see what I can do for you." The farmer led the way into the house.

They sat in the living room. The furniture was old and looked like it had originally come from Sears. The room had the vague feel that suggested that a woman was not around. JJ refused O'Bryant's offer of a cup of coffee and waited until he returned with his own.

"Now, what's this about?"

"Mr. O'Bryant, you've probably heard about the killings of those motorcycle gang members over in Middletown."

"Oh, yes," O'Bryant said, nodding his head, "I saw it on the news last night. And it's been in all the papers."

"Well, part of the details of an investigation like this is that we have to gather all the information on everyone who might in any way be involved. For example, one part of this thing we have to check out is the fact that both of the men who were killed were probably involved in the killing of Eileen Parker."

"I remember," the farmer said, his eyes narrowing. "Little girl hit by a stray shot. Those sonsabitches got off on a technicality, didn't they?"

"That's right, they did." JJ leaned back and rearranged his clipboard, trying to carefully choose his words. "So there's the outside possibility that someone in her family could be considered..."

"A suspect?" The old man grimaced. "If they did, more power to them, I'd say. Bunch of sonsabitches go around, killing little girls, ought to be dead." His eyes, dark, bored into JJ's.

"Well, I'm not arguing with you," JJ said cautiously. "While I was doing this little check I talked with some of the people in the county who know the Parker family. Been confirming alibis, getting a little background, that sort of thing. Just getting them off the table." JJ tried to make it sound very routine, which it was, and make O'Bryant step away from his apparent anger so he would be cooperative.

"Everything looks fine, nothing unusual, I just need some background on some of the people in the family. I was talking to Reverend Donner and he helped out a lot and suggested I might talk to you about Tom Parker."

Donner was the pastor of the local Methodist church, which was the church of the Parkers and O'Bryants. JJ figured mentioning the reverend might get his foot a little further in the door. He was not expecting O'Bryant's reaction.

O'Bryant threw back his head and burst into short, sharp laughter. JJ just stared for a moment, and watched as O'Bryant then quickly ceased his laughter and leaned towards him, his elbows on his knees, his face showing nothing but anger.

"Donner expects too damned much. I know what he's doing, oh, sure. He figures putting me in this position will force me to be objective about that sonuvabitch Tom Parker. Well, he's just flat wrong. I got nothing to say about him." With that he folded his arms and leaned back on the couch, his face wrinkled around a massive frown.

JJ noticed he was not asked to leave and decided to do a little fishing.

"Mr. O'Bryant, I'd really appreciate any help you could provide. I'm not looking for someone to attack or defend Tom Parker. I just want the facts about him, about what kind of man he is."

"I'll tell you what kind of man he is," O'Bryant said angrily, leaning forward and jabbing at the air with a finger. "He's a back-stabbing sonuvabitch, that's the kind of man he is. You can't trust him. Not at all." He fell silent and there was a small look of fear about him, which JJ thought might signal that he was beginning to think he was saying too much.

JJ just looked at him, waiting, leaving the silence open, hoping it would draw O'Bryant out. It did.

"All right, I'll tell you what happened. It was after that Korean thing, the police action thing. Parker had been in the service during it. He hadn't been anyone before the war but afterward, when he got out, he was a real troublemaker. Run-ins with the law, all kinds of stuff. Bad reputation. Then he takes up with Sarah Ann Terrence. Well, she and I had an understanding and I could tell he was no good for her. I tried to talk to her but she didn't understand someone like Tom Parker. Couldn't see what he was. Just like a woman." He shook his head, remembering.

"Women," he said, much softer, staring out the window. He was silent for a minute before continuing.

"Anyway, that Tom Parker decides I'm interfering so he comes around and threatens me. Just like that, like he was the king of the county or something. No one did anything about it so I said good riddance to Miss Terrence."

JJ spent several more minutes questioning O'Bryant but the old man didn't add anything else of value. After a while he left. O'Bryant didn't see him to the door but just sat on his couch and stared out the window, not looking at anything except, maybe, remembered images from four decades before.

JJ drove back to Oxford and the Oxford Methodist Church. He was lucky and the Reverend Donner was in the parsonage next to it.

Donner, the newly elected pastor of the church, shook his head at JJ's edited description of his conversation with O'Bryant.

"I'm sorry, Deputy Jeffers, I really wasn't aware of any bad blood between the two of them." He smiled slightly. "I'm afraid I'm not totally aware of a lot of the old history of my parishioners. I thought that, since they were almost neighbors and about the same age, Robert O'Bryant would be able to give you a good picture of Thomas Parker." He shrugged and took a sip from his cup of coffee. JJ's sat cooling in front of him.

"As I told you earlier, Tom Parker has a good reputation here in the church, though he was much more active when his wife was alive. Her funeral was one of the first services I performed when I came on board."

"How did Mr. Parker handle his wife's death?" JJ asked.

"Oh, well, he seemed to do fine," the minister said, "but you can't go by outward appearances with these folks, especially the older men. You know, raised by different standards, big boys don't cry, that sort of thing. He handled it well, I thought. The children, it was hard on some of them, you could tell, but Tom was a rock. At least, that's all he would let anyone see." Donner rubbed his hands together and looked over at JJ.

"Do you recall Michael Clanton, died last year, last spring?"

JJ thought for a moment and then nodded. "He was a suicide, over near the state line."

"Yes, that's the one," Donner said, nodding. "Had gone deep into debt, had a new combine, took it out into the fields too soon, got bogged down.

Tried to pull it free with his tractor. Thing tore in half, totally destroyed. Drove his tractor back to the barn, shut it down, went into the house, and used his shotgun on himself."

JJ nodded. The department handled it, what there was to handle, and he had seen some of the paperwork go by.

"Thing was," Donner continued, "Clanton had been on the short end of the stick for the past two years. Bank had been giving him all kinds of extensions, he was on the edge of going under during all that time, wife left him to go live with a daughter in Dayton when he started abusing her, had come close during the winter to killing himself. Talked to some kids working at the Oxford Community Counseling Center. They got him past the crisis but he didn't make use of any of the follow-up counseling they tried to set up for him." He took a swallow of coffee.

"Point is, all this was going on, and no one knew. Not his kids, not his friends, no one in his church, no one. I talked with his minister, Pete Kilby, runs the Episcopalian church here in town. Totally stunned, as was the whole congregation. No one had an inkling that he was on the edge."

"Different generation," Donner said, shaking his head. "Like I said, born in the Depression, children during the Second World War, teenagers during Korea. Bred differently, not better or worse, but different, than our generation." Donner paused, thinking and considering his words. "Tom Parker's like that, I think. Whatever is going on with him is something he would just naturally keep close to the chest. No heart on the sleeve or anything like that."

JJ glanced at his watch. It was still early in the day and his curiosity was aroused.

"I don't suppose there's anyone else you could point me to who might be able to help me fill in a little more background on Mr. Parker?"

"Well, of course, as I said earlier, you should talk with him directly. I'm not real comfortable with him getting the idea someone was going behind his back." The minister was frowning.

JJ held up a hand. "Don't worry, I'm planning on doing just exactly that. I just want to be sure I have a good sense of the man before I talk to him so I don't sound like a complete fool." He smiled his most disarming smile. The reverend bought it.

"The other people I would suggest are Charley and Peggy Johnston. They're retired now. Peggy has a bad hip and doesn't get out much. They have a house in that development on 73 just east of town. Charley was big in business here in town, had a couple of restaurants, owned some apartments the students from Miami used, town council, that sort of thing. Peggy ran her own business, art supply store right off the square. Her daughter and son-in-law have it now. They knew Tom and Sarah back in the old days, I think, from what I remember at the funeral. They were longtime friends, though more of her than him." He paused for a moment and studied his coffee cup, then looked at JJ, concern on his face.

"You don't really think Tom is in any real trouble, do you?"

JJ realized the minister was concerned not just for the sake of Tom Parker but his own role of contributing to the gathering of information about him. JJ shook his head in the negative.

"No one suspects Mr. Parker of anything. We just have to cross all the T's and dot all the I's. All we're trying to do is narrow the field by eliminating as many people as possible." He gave the reverend his best smile again as he got to his feet.

As JJ started the cruiser's engine, he glanced at the dashboard clock and decided he didn't have enough time to call on the Johnstons before swinging by the task force headquarters to check out for the day. He could get to them tomorrow. There were a couple of requests he had made over the computer that he expected replies to by now and it might be useful to have that information before coming back to talk to the Johnstons.

Boss hates loose ends, he reminded himself. Time to tie this one down tight and move on.

Chapter 20

Ellen was troubled. There was something going on with Grandpa Tom and she didn't know what it was. Several nights a week, he went out, and sometimes during the day, driving his old truck. He always had a reason during daylight, always took the time to tell her what he was leaving for, and sometimes it was like he was trying to convince her.

He never referred to the night rides. Ellen knew about his long drives when he couldn't sleep, though she had never seen much of it herself before this summer. She would have just shrugged it off except his trips during the day seemed odd, funny, like something was going on.

In the past, he would just have told her he was going out, maybe ask if she wanted him to get anything for her, or even invite her along. Now that seemed to change. He almost never invited her and always took the time to explain what he was up to.

Grandpa Tom reminded her a little of one of her cousins, one of the boys, when he did something that he wasn't supposed to and was trying to build his alibi.

Is this something all boys do?

Like today. Here it was, late in the afternoon, and he wasn't back. He left right after lunch, saying he needed to run over to Middletown to the John Deere dealer and see if a part had come in. He hadn't looked her in the eye as he got his jacket and left.

She worked on her PowerBook, trying to write song lyrics to the tune of some popular songs, but it failed to distract her for very long. Redbone rubbed against her leg to be let out so she put the computer to sleep almost gratefully and went out.

The wind was picking up, coming in out of the northwest. Great rolling clouds, looking like gray cotton balls, hurried by overhead. Off on the horizon great anvil-headed thunderstorms were rising, darkening the afternoon sun. Sudden bursts of birds flying to wherever they thought was safe signaled that a hard storm was coming.

Deciding that being outside was a dumb idea in the long run, Ellen went indoors again. There was nothing on the television this early in the day except some kind of talk show on virtually every channel, so she headed up to her attic room to get a book she was laboring to get through.

At the top of the stairs, Ellen turned and entered the room, only to discover she had absentmindedly turned in the wrong direction and was in the storage room. She was about to reverse her course but paused.

There was a lot of real junk up here, she noticed, including old cardboard containers, some dusty furniture, a set of bookshelves, and a large, dark green wooden box. There was black lettering on the box.

She never spent any time in the storage room. Ellen wouldn't admit that when she was younger she was afraid of the room because of its darkness. Even now she felt a twinge of the younger child's fear and it was because of that, to show herself she wasn't the child that she had been, as much as curiosity about the green box, that she stayed.

The letters said "Parker, Thomas L." in a neat stencil centered on the top of the box. Beneath the name was a row of numbers, which she ignored. Above the name, also in black, was an emblem of a parachute with some kind of wreath around it.

The top was a lid that had a latch on the outside, but no lock. The room was becoming dimmer with the approaching storm so she reached up for the string going to the light and gave it a pull. The yellow light revealed the box to be stoutly built with metal handles on either end.

It was obviously her Grandpa Tom's. Ellen looked at it for several minutes, absently chewing at her lower lip. She knew she wasn't supposed to invade peoples' privacy and all that. At the same time, she was curious and a little angry and hurt about Grandpa Tom leaving her, doing something without her. The hurt, again something she would not have admitted, led her to kneel and raise the lid.

In the distance thunder rolled, but almost gently, as if trying out its strength, preparing itself for the hammering to come. She glanced up at the distant rumble and then, brushing her hair out of her eyes, bent down to the chest.

Ellen found that it contained the paper trail of a life, or, to be more precise, two lives. Grandpa Tom and Grandma Sarah were both found here.

There were picture albums with yellow photographs held in place by their corners to heavy dark paper. Pictures of Tom and Sarah, her parents and their brothers and sisters as children, of the farm, of people she didn't know, of cars, with Tom as a young man leaning against them with his arms folded, squinting in the Ohio sun, or Sarah at the wheel, smiling as if she was about to drive away.

There were envelopes of papers, mortgages, titles to vehicles, a marriage certificate, a baptismal record, then another. Letters from a bank. Letters from her father in college. It was like an archaeological dig on The Discovery Channel.

Near the bottom was another old photo album. She pulled it out. It was a light blue and someone had precisely lettered on it "Thomas Parker" in darker blue enamel, though the letters were slightly chipped.

She carefully opened it. On the first page was taped a letter. The tape was all yellow and the paper was from a pad with very faint blue lines. The letter was written in careful but elegant longhand in black ink.

"Dear Thomas," it began. "I have kept these things from these past years because I thought you would, one day, need to look back at where you have been and know how far you have come. You know I have loved you from the first. Do you know I have always been proud of you?"

The letter was signed "With all my love, Sarah Ann" and was dated "Christmas, 1960." Carefully, Ellen turned the page.

The first two pages were collections of clippings carefully taped in place. They were about Tom in the army. One was a short note about a "local boy" enlisting. There was another in the same stilted style about a "local boy" completing basic training and yet another about the same boy earning his paratrooper wings.

Grandpa Tom was a paratrooper? One of the boys at school had a father who was a paratrooper in Desert Storm. He was always bragging about how tough paratroopers were and his father drove a car with a military emblem in the back window.

Ellen turned the page and there was a blurry newspaper picture of Tom in uniform with a flag in the background. The caption referred to being decorated. He looked very young but you could tell it was him. There as a glossy photograph of a serious looking Tom in khakis having a medal being pinned on him by some army guy. There was another newspaper clipping talking about him getting some medals, a Silver Star and a Purple Heart. She turned the page.

Another clipping about another medal. And a clipping saying Tom was on his way home after being wounded. A picture of him visited by a relative at an army hospital in California. The page opposite was very different, though. Nothing about the army.

A single newspaper clipping, carefully positioned in the middle of the page, reported that a Thomas Parker had been arraigned on charges of assault and carrying a concealed weapon.

Grandpa Tom was arrested? The idea seemed impossible. There was nothing else in the clipping to indicate what was the result of the hearing. She turned the page.

On this page there were two more clippings, both also about Grandpa Tom and the law. In one it reported he had his license suspended for drunken driving, apparently one of many offenses. The second was a hearing for a charge of assault on a Robert O'Bryant. Charges were dropped when O'Bryant refused to testify.

What was that all about?

On the page opposite, in strange counterpoint, was a wedding invitation card. She opened it and found it was for Thomas L. Parker and Sarah Ann Terrence. On the next page, there was a newspaper account of the wedding, with most of the attention paid to her grandmother.

Only she wasn't a grandmother then. She wasn't even a mother!

Apparently the Terrence family was fairly well known or something because the reporter wrote a lot about her and her family. Tom was barely mentioned. The two of them were in the picture at the top, though, and Tom had his first mustache.

The rest of the album had pictures of Ellen's father as a newborn. It was strange to see her father as a baby. He looked a little cute.

Well, all babies do.

She shook her head as she closed the book. So Grandpa Tom had gotten into trouble some way back then. She started to put the book back when she noticed several folders with heavy covers and small, rectangular boxes at the bottom. She pulled them out and opened them.

The folders held military citations. She began reading, skimming through them quickly:

For conspicuous gallantry...while engaged in the defense of a position crucial to...attacked by enemy forces...outnumbered heavily...with disregard for his own safety...exposing himself repeatedly to heavy and accurate enemy automatic weapons fire...refusing medical attention for his wounds while...responsible for the defeat of the enemy attack.

And another:

Steven M. Silver

As the senior noncommissioned officer present...his platoon attacked by a battalion...personally conducted a rearguard action enabling his unit to successfully withdraw with its wounded...attacking an enemy machinegun position, killing all five enemy soldiers in savage hand-to-hand combat, he then turned the captured weapon on the Chinese Communist forces maneuvering...continued fighting though wounded by numerous mortar fragments...highest traditions of the United States Army.

The small boxes held medals, one in each. But the bright ribbons and metal devices did not make as much an impression on her as the phrases from the citation. *Savage hand-to-hand combat.* She had an image of Grandpa Tom killing someone like in a karate movie, with his bare hands, but she knew that wasn't how wars were fought.

Soldiers shot each other, or threw grenades, she thought as she returned all the papers and albums to the chest. As she lowered a pile in, they slid out of her hands and there was a sudden loud metallic thud as they struck something in the back corner of the box. She moved the albums and looked in the dark corner.

It was hard to see but Ellen's groping hands found something made of metal and she pulled it free.

It was a knife in a metal scabbard, held in place by a strip of thick, greening canvas with metal hooks near its top. It was military. She unsnapped the strap around the handle of the knife and pulled it free.

It came out of the scabbard with the hiss of metal on metal, like an angry snake. The hand guard between the handle and the black, single edged blade was pierced, obviously for a rifle muzzle. It was a bayonet. The blade itself was long, as long as her forearm. It was lightly dusted with rust but when she touched the edge it still was sharp, so sharp it was as if the metal wanted to bite her thumb. She started to put it back when she saw something on the back of the blade, something that caught the weak light.

Ellen looked closely. On the back of the blade, someone had cut thin lines, five in all. She stared for a moment, wondering, then her eyes grew large and she shoved the blade into the scabbard and threw it into the chest.

The rest of the debris was in the chest and she was running down the stairs in only a few heartbeats. Ellen didn't notice that the thunder was much   closer.

105

Chapter 21

JJ got back to the task force headquarters later than he anticipated. Prior to leaving, he had dropped off the names and Social Security numbers of the Parker family males with the secretary and requested she send them to National Criminal Information Center to see if any of them popped up. His selection of the males was, in part, stereotypical thinking on his part but also a recognition that when a family member sought violent revenge it was almost always a man.

The secretary, Anne Dwyer, wore her hair bleached to the iridescent side of white and up in a style the Iroquois would have admired and which was doubly impressive on a woman now in her fifties. She was sharp, with a twinkle in her eyes and a ready smile and had more than once saved one of the task force member's butts by finding some misplaced document or file.

She looked at the list and then at JJ.

"We already have the NCIC readout on most of these folks, JJ," she said.

"Okay," he replied, "I figured the locals had run them, but I didn't know we had a copy."

Anne smiled. "No copy; the boss ran his own search." She raised her eyebrows at JJ's rolling of eyes as he clutched his chest in mock shock. "But you do have a couple of names who weren't on his list. I'll run them through NCIC. Do you want to do NCISR as well?"

JJ thought for a moment. NCISR was the local network between police departments. In the case of Ohio, it was quite thorough and had links to some of the adjacent state law enforcement agencies or, in a few cases, their counties. Like NCIC, all that was needed was a name and a social security number.

"Sure, go ahead. I don't think any of these folks are going to show up as criminals or fugitives. But there's one more place we might try, now that I'm thinking it a bit further. How about St. Louis?"

"Military records? Sure, we're plugged in, though the response won't be as fast as NCIC or NCISR. They have to do a lot of visual searching. And they lost a chunk of records to a big fire there back in the Seventies."

"Let's go ahead and do it anyway. I'm guessing that if someone from the Parker clan is taking shots at Steel Riders he's got some familiarity with guns, maybe courtesy of Uncle Sam."

Anne had smiled and turned to her terminal as JJ left.

Now he was back from talking with Reverend Donner; Anne had left for the day and only a handful of people covering late paperwork and the duty officer were still in the office. He rubbed his short hair and went to his desk.

JJ was delighted to find a folder with a yellow stickie on it.

"ALL DONE!" it announced. It was Anne's handwriting. On the bottom, in very small letters, "(except the stuff from St. Louis...)" Well, he didn't expect the military record people to respond that fast.

He flipped it open and went through the printouts. There was very little to read. Occasional driving citations were about all that had ever been recorded on any of the Parker men. Likewise, Bill Tebault, Jane Parker's husband, apparently led a life devoid of sin, or at least illegalities.

He sighed as he flipped through the pages and then stopped, his eyes narrowing, as he got to the last page.

"Subject: Parker, Thomas Luther" it began, and then small font type filled half the page. JJ read through it, silently pursing his lips.

Listed by date, and all from the Fifties, was a string of offenses apparently related to excessive drinking, including driving under the influence, speeding, and so forth, as well as a number of misdemeanor fighting incidents, usually with the charges dropped when restitution was provided.

And an arrest for assault. Against Robert O'Bryant. JJ raised an eyebrow. It wasn't just threatening. Old man O'Bryant apparently didn't want to admit someone had beaten the holy hell out of him, at least to the extent felony charges were filed. The entry gave few details except the notation of when the charges were dropped. Probably O'Bryant had decided against testifying and that knocked the bottom out of the case. JJ snorted. It had happened to him enough times in the past to be a fairly familiar song.

It had been local, here in Butler County, but JJ knew there was nothing in the files going back this far. He double-checked the date. 1955. Forty years ago. Ancient history. Meaningless now. What was that expression he came across in that novel, when they wanted to refer to someone who was old? Yes, he remembered.

Long in the tooth.

Tom Parker was a little long in the tooth for the kind of thing happening to the Steel Riders. But if all this had gone down forty years ago, back when he was a dangerous man, it might be a different story.

JJ slipped the papers back into the folder. What he needed now was the info from St. Louis. Not that he expected anything to come out of it, he just wanted to be able to make a complete brief on Friday and it would be good to be able to say that none of the Parkers had any previous experience in the business of killing people.

JJ stretched and looked at the clock. Time to go home and decide which microwave dinner he would serve himself tonight. He made a mental note to meet the Johnstons tomorrow and see what additional insight they might have. With some luck and an efficient clerk at the National Personnel Records Center in St. Louis, he might have the last piece for his Friday briefing by close of business tomorrow, with another whole day left to tidy up any loose ends.

He was putting his key in the ignition of his car when the phrase came back to his mind and he smiled to himself as he drove away.

Long   in   the   tooth.

Chapter 22

As JJ sat with his legs up and let a made for TV movie help him feel sleepy enough to go to bed, Tom Parker, binoculars pressed to his eyes, was puzzled. He felt like a man at an intricate ballet in which he had been assured every move had a meaning but, nonetheless, still was completely baffled as to what it all meant.

Making the decision to slow down was the right one, he was sure of that. He had to find Jack Baker so he had carefully plotted his move.

Reconnaissance was obviously called for. There were three remaining names on his list. Jack Baker, of course, whose location was an unknown. His brother Bob, who the newspapers referred to as a "warlord," whatever the hell that meant. The papers indicated he lived in the county, but a check of the telephone book revealed a long list of "R" and "Robert" Bakers. Hard to tell which was him. And Nicholas Christopher. Of the three, Mr. Christopher was the easiest to find and track.

As reported in the newspaper, Christopher worked at the Tail Gunners Lodge, one of the bars used as a regular hangout by the Steel Riders. It was no major feat to locate him. He worked days, a little before lunch until six and parked his GMC pickup out back, out of the way of the customers.

Christopher was an easy man to spot. He was tall, slightly over six feet, with reddish blond hair and a dark brown goatee. He often emerged from his apartment in the evening, would take his motorcycle out of his garage (the GMC slept at the curb), and go out for the night. Usually he went right back to Tail Gunners but occasionally to another of the Rider hangouts. Tom followed him at a distance and, once it was clear where Christopher was going to stay, Tom would go home, easing down the drive with his lights off to avoid waking up Ellen.

He did that for almost two weeks, going out three and sometimes four times a week. But now the pattern had changed and Tom didn't understand why.

Christopher still went home from work but when he emerged it was to use the GMC. Tom shadowed him four more times and each time the biker went nowhere near the bars frequented by the Steel Riders. In fact, he kept going to a place totally unexpected.

Tom squinted again through the binoculars and then lowered them, rubbing his chin. He was parked in the lot of an all-night Big Boy; there were lots of cars and trucks coming and going and he doubted that his somewhat battered pickup was unique enough for anyone to take notice. Less than a quarter of a mile away, next to a Marathon gas station, was a bar set back off the main road.

The "Mail Boxx," as its neon proclaimed, was not just any oddly titled saloon sitting on the county line near the interstate connecting Dayton and Cincinnati. According to his research in the newspapers, corroborated by the brassy roaring of Harleys with straight pipes, this particular place was the local chapter headquarters of the Dragons.

What the hell was a Steel Rider doing here?

Tom saw Christopher's GMC in the lot, off to one side, away from the Harleys parked in a row near the front entrance. He waited for Christopher to emerge.

There was a pattern to all this. Christopher would arrive early, close to seven. He would park in the same place, off to one side from the main entrance and always in front. Around eight or so, the Dragons started showing up. By nine there would by ten or twelve bikes out front, sometimes accompanied by a couple of four wheel drive vehicles. At nine thirty, Tom glanced at his watch and nodded, Christopher would come out and go to his truck.

There he was. Almost to the minute. Tom watched through the binoculars as Christopher climbed into his truck. And now he will wait.

Around ten thirty, sometimes later, the Dragons would leave the bar, get on their bikes or in their vehicles, and roar off down the street, passing the Big Boy and disappear down the road. A few minutes later, Christopher would start his truck and drive off in the other direction and go home. That would be it.

Tonight was no different. Christopher seemed content to stay in his truck with only the occasional flare of a lighter revealing his presence. The Dragons came out almost an hour later. Several talked together briefly then they rode off. Tom watched as the dust in the dirt parking lot settled. The GMC's lights came on and then swung around and Christopher was on his way home. Tom shook his head and reached to start his own truck but paused. He had figured it out.

The bastard's doing to them what I'm doing to him.

Tom drove home with a grim smile. He didn't need to follow Christopher any more. He already knew where he was going. The next time they met there was a good chance he would be waiting on Mr. Christopher and, with a little luck, maybe one or two of the others in his notebook.

The Steel Riders were planning a little party for the Dragons. Wonder how they'd feel about an uninvited guest dropping in?

Chapter 23

When your world changes, when what you thought was reality turns out to be a fantasy, what do you do? Lucky people have someone whose hand they can grasp when the darkness heaves around them. Ellen had always had Grandpa Tom.

But her picture of Tom, she believed, was wrong or, at least, changing. With the distancing of her parents, like ships at war over some night horizon giving off flashes difficult to interpret, she came to rely on her grandfather to be a steadying influence, the person she would come to, even when she couldn't talk about her troubles. There was often sanctuary in his silence.

The photo album in the attic, the medals, the marked bayonet, all these things had shaken her, and perhaps Ellen would have let them pass and be quickly forgotten, because, like most children, she learned early on there were things over which she had no control and had to let go on by. But the attic was only one of three things that turned things upside down and made it impossible to pretend nothing was different.

The second was Grandpa Tom's strange trips away from the farm. He always had a reason, always had an excuse. Needed to get something for the truck, to check out a sale, run an undefined errand. He only occasionally invited her to go with him and never at night.

She felt like they were people on two separate life rafts, adrift without paddles, each caught in a different current, slowly moving away from one another by forces neither could control.

The third thing was on the kitchen table in front of her, spread open like some obscene flower, and it terrified her.

Grandpa Tom was off on one of his late afternoon errands, as he had done several times over the past two weeks. She had watched him drive away from the front porch, feeling hurt, abandoned, and angry.

She had walked around back with nowhere in particular as her destination. The low sun had reflected a sparkle off the front of the tool shed and she wandered over to it out of curiosity and a desire to find something to do and stop thinking about her grandfather leaving her.

The reflected light had come from the padlock holding the door. She had idly slapped at it and was surprised when it slipped open.

Ellen knew the rules laid down years before. None of the children were allowed in the shed; that's where the particularly dangerous tools were kept and, of course, Grandpa Tom's guns when the kids were visiting.

She had never seen the guns but everyone knew about them and that Grandpa Tom was supposed to be some kind of great shot. Unlike some of her cousins, she had never been interested in seeing them. She remembered a heavy-duty spanking Eileen's brother Mikey got for trying to get into the shed just last year.

Ellen was hurt and angry and, being a child, curious, a dangerous combination. So she lifted the heavy lock off the clasp – doing it quickly before she thought about it too long, which is how a child deals with issues of conscience – and swung the door open.

Though initially exciting in a nervous sort of way, the shed was actually pretty boring. There were some locked chests under a big worktable and a bunch of tools (*more bor-ring!*) hanging on or stacked against the walls. A tall metal cabinet, with yet another padlock, painted green like the gym lockers at school, stood next to the worktable and against the wall. She assumed that was where the guns were.

On the table there were a couple of manuals for reloading ammunition that weren't entertaining at all. She was about to leave when she saw the spiral notebook in the corner, under a fat and funny sized three-ring binder with the name "Speer" on it. The notebook looked like the kind she used for school so she reached across and pulled it free.

It lay before her now, open. Part of Ellen was trying to find a way, as children will, to take back the act so that she would never know what she had seen. But there was no way to undo seeing the clippings and notes carefully entered into the notebook.

Grandpa Tom had collected information on the five men involved in killing Eileen. She saw their newspaper pictures taped over neat notes entered in his hand, listing residences, job locations, and other bits of information culled from the papers and telephone books.

There was Jack Baker, the man with the cold eyes, and his brother Bob, and Nick Christopher with the funny beard, and Dave Hollingsworth, who was as big as a bear, and Johnny Larson who actually looked kind of cute in a Fox TV kind of way.

Over the pictures of Hollingsworth and Larson large X's were drawn with a thick, black, felt tip pen. Ellen immediately remembered the etched lines on the back of the bayonet.

Grandpa Tom likes to keep score.

She slapped the book shut and closed her eyes. Maybe if she kept them closed long enough, or squeezed them hard enough, all of this would go away. But it didn't happen.

Grandpa Tom killed people.

The man of quiet strength, of gentleness to her troubled heart, was murdering people. She shook her head. But Grandpa Tom couldn't do anything wrong, he just couldn't. And there lay the problem.

She needed someone to talk to, someone to help her understand, to explain it all away, to make things right again. She couldn't go to her father or her mother. Her mother wouldn't know what to do and whatever her father decided to do would be the wrong thing.

Besides, how could she? When they were down at their condo, outside of the occasional postcard, most of her contact with her parents was through email messages left on her CompuServe account. The only way she knew they had come back was when she began to get weekly telephone calls. They were perfunctory when initiated by her father. He seemed to have nothing to say and no idea what to ask her about. Her mother's were longer, but there was a tension in them, as if there was something she wanted to say to her daughter but could not.

Her cousins were too young; she knew she needed an adult. Not Eileen's parents, Uncle Mike and Aunt Dolores. They were good people but they had been through too much as it was. Aunt Jane was someone who tended to relate to her through her children, and her husband Bill was further away.

There was Aunt Catherine, who she had always regarded as cool and distant until this summer. Maybe it weighed in her favor that Ellen's father had spoken cuttingly of her when he thought the children were out of earshot.

Maybe Ellen could talk to her to relieve herself of the heavy weight she felt pressing down, as if knowledge itself had substance, and this knowledge was made of granite.

But if she did speak to Catherine, would she not be putting Grandpa Tom in danger? What if Catherine went to the police, even to protect him from himself?

And, even more scary, what if she confronted him with the knowledge? What would he think of her, Ellen? Wouldn't he regard it as a betrayal? Suppose she was wrong, suppose nothing was going on as she thought?

Maybe she was jumping to conclusions; adults always told her to avoid doing that, even before she knew what it meant and could only imagine leaping like in a game of hopscotch to the last chapter of one of her favorite books.

She began to grasp that possibility, that she was interpreting the information all wrong, as a lifeline out of the terrible morass she felt she was sinking into.

After all, I'm just a kid, what do I know?

Maybe there was some simple explanation for everything. Heck, it would be all right with her if it was a complex explanation, just as long as it wasn't that Grandpa Tom was killing people.

Accepting the idea of being in error was infinitely preferable to the alternative and she was smiling by the time she carefully returned the notebook to its place and locked up the shed. She was positively glowing with relief, so thoroughly was she grasping to that lifeline, by the time Tom   came   home.

Chapter 24

Rain smeared the Ohio countryside to a uniform dull gray as JJ drove to meet the Johnstons. It was one of those continuous rains of low but steady intensity that promised to hang around awhile. The county could use some, he thought, though it would be good not to overdo it. The problem with farmers was there was always too much or too little rain for them, never a happy medium. He glanced at the fields passing by on either side.

Soybeans on one side, low to the ground, and corn on the other, both marching off towards the edge of sight on the rolling hills. He still had his boyhood eye for judging corn, trained from summers working on his uncle's farm for college money, and it looked like this would be a good crop, though it was still early to make the call.

Of course, that was a problem, too. If everyone had a good year, then the prices went down. On the other hand, if it was a bad year, then the price was high but a farmer had less to sell. JJ shook his head and grinned, thinking that deciding to go into law enforcement was a better decision than becoming a farmer.

Crime doesn't pay, but the hours are good.

He caught 73 east of Oxford and turned onto it, heading to the development where the Johnstons lived. Ohio 73 in this part of the county was one of those Ohio roads laid out by a civil engineer whose access to drawing instruments was pretty much limited to a straight edged ruler. It was laid right across hill, valley and stream with no nonsense about compromising with the contour lines or following the old Indian trails.

JJ almost missed the entrance to the development as it was located just after the crest of a hill and he hadn't spotted the landmarks he saw when leaving Oxford yesterday. He stopped more abruptly then he liked and hung a left through a drive flanked by two short columns made of brick.

The Johnston house was a low-slung ranch house looking like every other ranch house ever built in the last half century in America. Their name was pasted in reflecting letters on a large, farm-style mailbox next to the curb. JJ parked and walked through the rain to the front door.

Charley Johnston was a short man with a ready smile beneath wavy, white hair. His grip when he shook hands was firm. He gave the impression of a man used to being in charge. His wife, sitting in a wheelchair, was gray haired and a bit thin, but she had a ready smile as well and JJ suspected the two of them had done a certain amount of merging of their personalities over the decades.

After the introductions and greetings and the obligatory offer of coffee, which JJ accepted with gratitude as a way of chasing the gray of the day out of his bones, they both sat and studied him with calm appraisal. He had the feeling there was little they missed and felt sorry for any salesmen who had the job of trying to get them to buy something they didn't need.

"I assume Reverend Donner has talked with you," JJ began, looking back and forth at the couple.

"Oh, yes, deputy," Charley nodded. "He called yesterday and said you might be by. He said you were looking for some background information on Sarah Ann's husband Tom."

JJ remembered Donner saying that the Johnstons were originally friends of Sarah Ann Terrence before she married Tom Parker.

"Well, actually," he said, "I'm interested in any information about the Parkers that I can get. You see, we have to investigate the deaths of several men..."

"You mean those bikers." A voice flat, cold, and as low as a slab of marble on a grave, Peggy Johnston looked at JJ with eyes that lost all their humor.

"Right, those people. Naturally, in a situation like this we try to clear out any loose ends, touch all the bases, cross all the t's," JJ felt like he was beginning to babble under the sharp gaze of the two and pulled himself up. "None of the Parkers are under investigation. Most have alibis and so forth. What we're looking to do is to get a picture of them, so we have a better understanding of them." He glanced at his notebook, open to a blank page, as if consulting notes.

"I've pulled down the job of working up our information on Mr. Thomas Parker," he said, making it sound like it was an inconsequential and burdensome task which no one was taking too seriously, which was close to the mark. "Just about everyone I've talked to has said he's a fine, upstanding man, good neighbor, dependable, that sort of thing. There's just a small thing that I'd like to get some clarity on. Reverend Donner suggested you might be able to fill in the blanks for me." With the mention of Donner, the Johnstons visibly relaxed.

"Well, what can we tell you, Deputy Jeffers?" Charley shrugged. "We've known Tom since he took up with Sarah Ann, who we knew ever since school." JJ took this to mean at least high school and probably grade school; they were of the generation, and maybe the last one, which stayed in one place their whole lives and formed friendships that endured for the better part of a century.

"The thing that I'm trying to get straight on," JJ said, leaning forward, his elbows on his knees, "is what happened between him and Robert O'Bryant. I got the impression there were some bad feelings there." He gave them his best disarming smile, sensing he was walking into a potential minefield.

They didn't buy the smile. Charley and Peggy looked at each other for a moment, communicating in silence, and then they turned towards him again.

Maybe they're aliens and use telepathy with one another.

"I assume you've been over Tom's record with the law," Charley said slowly, placing each word down like a rock used to cross a stream and wanting to be careful about falling in.

JJ nodded a half lie. The detailed records were long since gone and only the brief, single line summaries in the printout he reviewed remained but he decided not to mention that.

"Well, it's a little misleading," Charley said, speaking a little more naturally, a small smile coming to his lips. "Tom got into a few scrapes after the war but it was never anything serious, just a young fellow blowing off some steam from Korea. Local law people understood, knew he came from a good family, knew he just needed a chance to settle down, that he would be all right, given time. There were a fair number of boys coming back like that and not too long before from the big war." Charley was smiling broadly now and Peggy nodded in corroboration, a friendly and sincere smile on her face.

Man, they are good!

"Now Tom was a couple of years behind us in high school, same class as Sarah Ann," Charley continued. "Her family and mine were pretty close. Our fathers had worked together, put some business things together, both on the church board, Masons, that kind of thing. We lived one block over from them on South Poplar in Oxford." He looked at Peggy, who had turned her face to him in perfect synchronization. "Peggy and I started dating in high school, junior year, and got married right after graduation. Sarah Ann was maid of honor."

"Sarah Ann didn't really have a boyfriend in school," Peggy said, taking up the narrative, "though she went out on a couple of dates. She was a little progressive for her time, a little independent. There's a streak of strong will, some would call it, that runs in her family and she wasn't ready to settle down. So after graduation she got a job in town clerking in one of Charley's father's stores for a while and then started taking courses part time from the university." Charley nodded and began talking.

"In the meantime, Tom enlisted in the Army. The war in Korea had just begun to heat up. We didn't know him personally, though he played baseball in high school and we knew him by sight. His people were farmers here in the county and over in Indiana. When the war was over he came home." Charley put his coffee cup on the end table beside his chair.

"He was a little unsettled. I guess he'd been through a lot, though he never said, then or later, after we got to know him. You know about some of his wildness." He looked up at JJ. "It was just exuberance. Anyway, he met Sarah Ann where she was working and tried to get her to go out with him. About all she would do is have lunch with him. Sarah said later she though he was like a river whose depth you couldn't be sure of, so she had to feel her way carefully." He shrugged his shoulders.

"We all thought she was making a big mistake, to be quite truthful. Tom was getting a bad reputation, what with the drinking and the fighting. We tried to talk her out it, but she was attracted to him, maybe because of his wildness." He looked out the window for a moment, remembered sorrow briefly touch his face. "There's no doubt Tom saw the quality in her. She was pretty enough, but she had substance, what we used to call character, and I got the impression he was trying to get a hold on that as a way of pulling himself back from wherever he had been." He turned back to JJ, the smile returning.

"Sarah Ann made Tom toe the line, set up some rules and boundaries, and damned if he didn't go along with it. It was hard to believe it was the same man. He went back to his father's farm, it's his now, and began working it, which was good because the old man was ailing from an injury with a combine. He settled down, went to AA, one of the first chapters in the county, started taking his mother to church, which he continued to do until she died in, when was it?," he looked at Peggy. "Sixty-two?" Peggy nodded and he continued.

"They got married in 1955, had five beautiful babies, and that was about it. Tom's been a solid fixture in the county ever since."

JJ nodded in the silence and made of show of consulting his notebook. *They're waiting to see if I've bought it.*

"Did you know much about his Army service?" *Might as well start slow.*

Charley and Peggy shook their heads in unison.

"Not really," Charley said. "There were the things in the local newspaper, of course, about him getting a couple of medals during the war, but we had a lot of boys from the county in Korea. It wasn't unusual."

JJ nodded again, still studying the blank page. Time to go for the live one.

"And this thing with O'Bryant," he said, raising his eyes to look at them (*I didn't forget, folks*), "what was all that about?"

For a moment, there was just silence and the level stares of the Johnstons. JJ didn't look away and finally Charley spoke.

"How much of this is on the record?"

Bingo!

"Look, Mr. Johnston, the statute of limitations on anything that might have taken place forty years ago has long since expired. No one is going to get in trouble for anything they did 'way back then." He paused to let that half-truth sink in and then threw his next pitch low and inside. "I've already got a statement from Mr. O'Bryant and I just want to get another point of view."

Charley and Peggy exchanged another of their alien communications on a frequency JJ couldn't hear and then turned back to him.

"What happened," Charley said without further preamble, "was Bobby O'Bryant was sweet on Sarah Ann, though she wasn't at all interested in him."

"He was," Peggy added, "a spoiled little brat most of his life and couldn't get the idea that he couldn't have everything he wanted. Raised too much by his mother, I think."

Charley nodded in agreement. "He was very used to having his own way, that's for sure. Hasn't changed all that much over the years, to be honest. Anyway, he was in pursuit of Sarah, but she wasn't having any.

He wouldn't admit it to himself or anyone else. Used to brag to the other guys that she was coming around, talk about her in a way that implied that she was loose with him." He shook his head. "He was really hurting her reputation among people who didn't know her well. In the meantime, she began to see more of Tom."

Peggy smiled fiercely and stabbed the air with a finger. "When Bobby heard about that he was fit to be tied. He just couldn't take the idea that a woman would be interested in someone else and not him. So he pursued Sarah Ann even harder, what you might call nowadays stalking her. She showed me letters he sent her, notes he slipped under the door at the store she worked. He even tried to enroll in her classes. Finally, she decided to have it out with him. Tom and her had announced their engagement and she wanted him to knock it off." Peggy fell silent. Charley reached out and took her hand.

"We were at home the night she was going to straighten out Bobby. It was well after dark and we heard a knock at the door. It was Sarah. She was beat up pretty bad. The bastard had tried to rape her but she managed to hit him with an ashtray and get away. All she could do was blame herself for agreeing to go to his apartment." He shook his head.

"We got her patched up and then I had Peggy take her home. What happened next was my doing, in large measure." He looked up at JJ. "While they were walking to Sarah's apartment, I got in the car and drove out to Tom Parker's. I told him what happened. I told Tom because I knew I couldn't do anything about Bobby O'Bryant myself, as tempted as I was to try. Bobby would have taken me with one hand tied behind his back. Going to the police was out of the question because of what it would do to Sarah Ann's reputation in those days. But I figured that between Tom and I we could bring him down a peg or two."

"We were on the porch. Remember the whole thing like it was yesterday. Tom didn't say a lot, asked if Sarah was really all right, and then went into the house. I heard him tell his folks he had to go with me into town to take care of a couple of things and came out wearing a windbreaker."

"He sat beside me in the car, silent, the whole drive back to Oxford. When we got to Bobby's, I started to get out but he reached across and closed my door and told me to stay put. I started to protest; hell, I thought Bobby had a good chance of whipping both of us. But Tom was having none of it. He looked at me in the dark of the front seat of that car, and I swear I saw something burning in those eyes, even in the dark, and said in a voice as cold and dangerous as a diamondback, 'Stay here.'" Charley wasn't smiling.

"At that point, I began to worry about Bobby O'Bryant. I thought Tom was intending to kill him. But I stayed in the car. Tom went to Bobby's apartment door and knocked on it. The place isn't there anymore but it was set back from the street, single story, with doors for each of the four apartments at ground level. Bobby's door was right in front. I saw it plain enough. It opened a little and then started to close. I guess Bobby saw who it was."

"He didn't get it closed. Tom hauled off and kicked it as hard as any mule could. It flew open into the apartment and he dived in after it. I couldn't see what was going on inside except for a brief glimpse of the two of them and then the next thing was O'Bryant came flying backwards out the doorway, and Tom came right after him."

"O'Bryant was down but Tom wouldn't let him up, none of this Marquess of Queensberry stuff. Every time Bobby would get on all fours, Tom would kick him in the ribs like he was trying to make a field goal. Or Tom would almost crouch beside him and, as Bobby started to get up, would hit him with his fist so hard I thought that bones had to be breaking, if not Bobby's, then in Tom's hand. He even used the edge of his open hand on Bobby, something I'd never seen before but I guess Tom had learned in Korea." Charley shook his head slowly.

"He beat that man all over the yard. I could see Bobby's face was a bloody mess, though most of the damage was going into his body. It was the most savage thing I ever saw in my life, before or since. Somewhere during it, I realized that Tom could have killed Bobby at any point and was deliberately not. He wanted to hurt Bobby and he was doing a hell of a job of it." His eyes were still looking at JJ but were out of focus, like he was seeing a remembered image.

"They ended up on the sidewalk not ten feet from where I sat, frozen. Bobby was on his back, all but unconscious. Tom was standing over him, his feet on either side of him, looking down at him with a face that had no expression at all. He reminded me of a doctor looking at a patient. His right hand went behind him, I couldn't see where, but when it came around he had the biggest handgun I'd ever seen. It was one of those service automatics, a .45 caliber Colt, a brute of a thing. He jacked the slide and I saw Bobby's eyes open wide. Then he reached down, grabbed

Bobby by his hair and pulled him upward. I think I stopped breathing at that point. Tom brought that big pistol and put it in Bobby's eye and just held it there for what seemed like three days." Charley rubbed his face a hand.

"I figured Bobby for a dead man and myself an accomplice to a murder. Then I heard Tom. He said, in that low, dangerous voice he had used on me, that if Bobby ever went near Sarah Ann again he would kill him. I believed him, as sure as anything I'd ever read in the Good Book; I knew I was hearing a prophecy that was written in stone. Bobby believed it too, I think. Then Tom let go of his hair and Bobby's head bounced off the sidewalk. Tom did something to the gun and put it in the back of his pants and walked on back to the car. He got in, looked at me, and said, politely, that he would like to go see how Sarah Ann was doing." He shook his head. "I was shaking like a leaf, but I got us there in record time."

"Peggy was still there with her. All he did was talk to her a few moments alone, give her a hug, and then, polite as hell, asked me for a ride home. I gave it to him. He didn't say a word all the way to the farm until he got out. Then he came over to my side and held out his hand. I took it and he just said thanks. I drove home."

"That was just about it. Bobby tried to sic the law on Tom but that didn't go anywhere, thanks in part to my and Sarah's fathers having a word with the chief."

JJ sat in the silence, thinking. Charley and Peggy were looking at one another with a range of feelings running across their faces. It was obvious to him that they were concerned that they might have said too much.

They were acting like it all happened yesterday, JJ realized. It was forty years ago. What was a man in his twenties was now a man more than sixty years old. Sure, he had been pretty damned rough back than – and JJ found that he really didn't blame him for beating the hell out of O'Bryant – but the issue was, how did he figure into the equation today?

The whole thing of a family member doing some kind of revenge thing, playing out a vigilante fantasy, was the least likely possibility for the deaths. He figured that when that kind of thing happened, it was usually immediate or not at all.

On the other hand, it did give him a flavor for the family. If Tom Parker was that kind of man, even that far in the past, wasn't it at least possible that he had passed on some of those values to one of his kids? Maybe someone in the Parker family was carrying on in what they thought was a family tradition. He shook his head. But none of the sons were likely candidates. Unlike Tom, none had military backgrounds that he was aware of, though he still awaited information from St. Louis, nor had any evidence of familiarity either with weapons or violence surfaced.

JJ spent several minutes more talking with the Johnstons, mostly ensuring that they knew of no other or more recent violence in Tom Parker's history. His questions about the sons brought the expected negative responses.

"Oh, no, Deputy Jeffers," Peggy insisted. "The boys were never in trouble, not of any kind. Tom and Sarah Ann were good parents who loved their children and believed in discipline. They all did well in school and so did the girls, for that matter."

"Well," Charley said, hesitating, "Young Jimmy had some trouble in school. Just a lack of application, I think. He was a little shaky there for a while. Began to hang around with a bit of a hippie crowd. But he was able to pull himself together and graduate. And Tom and Sarah Ann were there for him all the way. When he wanted to go to college, they supported him the whole time. He pulled down that graduate scholarship in civil engineering and you'd have thought Tom had done it, he was so proud of the boy. James is in," he looked at Peggy, raising his eyebrows, and she nodded back, "Kuwait, I think, helping them with some kind of big building project at their university."

JJ took it all in; none of it looked at all promising. He already knew James Parker was out of the country. It didn't look like Tom's past violence was anything that was inherited by any of the others.

After a while JJ made his goodbyes and walked out to the car. The Thursday morning rain was slowing down and the gray overcast was becoming lumpy. Maybe the day would clear up after all. As he drove back to the task force headquarters, he mentally outlined his brief for the next day.

He still needed the responses about military records; he had dumped in everyone in the Parker family, thanks to Anne's urging. There was just an outside chance they would get the information back today. He would like to have it to at least reference during the brief. It would tie another of those loose ends Carl Davidson hated.

If it went real well maybe he would get a slice of the pie that was a little bigger, maybe something that was going somewhere, instead of just

touching bases in the rain, which, despite his expectations, was picking up
in   intensity.

Chapter 25

Tom and Ellen spent the Thursday daylight hours, such as they were, in a kind of dance, circling around one another, observing the conventions, but both aware the other was at least distracted and both aware they did not wish to inquire too closely of the other.

Ellen liked the rain while at the farm, much more than when she was at home. When she was younger she would go down to the small creek that ran through the fields and with the other kids make dams or sail paper boats down the now rushing water. She didn't do that anymore; it was one of those things that seemed "childish," even when the adults were doing them.

She worked hard at trying to feel that everything was all right. Her effort to convince herself that she had made some kind of mistake in judgment was successful, but only in part. After all, she told herself, the notebook might just be an example of Grandpa Tom's meticulous – that was her new word of the week – record keeping. He did the same thing with his reloading hobby, and favorite recipes, and there was a three shelved cabinet in the living room almost filled with binders holding old farm records. Out in the barn were notebooks detailing the maintenance records of every piece of farm equipment he ever owned.

Her father had tried to get him to use a computer and he had finally bought a Macintosh IIsi several years ago. He had spent two months studying computers, making detailed comparison notes, visiting dealers in two different towns, even interviewing her about them, before buying one. Her father was contemptuous of his choice.

"Hell, it's a Macintosh, for crissake! It's a toy, point and click." He stood there, she remembered, with his arms folded, looking at it and shaking his head. "It costs too much compared to a PC."

Her Grandpa had reached over to the machine's keyboard and pressed a key. A chime sounded from the light gray box of the CPU and the monitor began to flicker to life.

"PCs are cheaper," Grandpa Tom conceded, "but when you figure in how long it takes to learn the machine and how long it takes to tweak it to a level of productivity to make its use worthwhile, the Mac comes out 'way ahead."

"That might be right for people who don't want to really learn their machines," her father responded, "but there are a lot of programs you can get for business not available for the Mac."

Tom slid the mouse on its pad and double clicked an icon on the screen, causing a spreadsheet to blossom.

"All the top names of everything I need make a Mac version," Tom replied, studying the columns and rows. "I set this thing up and had it running in less than 30 minutes with only a little help," he said, throwing a wink towards Ellen. "Any machine that can make up for my illiteracy can't be all bad."

Tom still gathered his information in notebooks, on paper, but he religiously entered it into the computer each week and then would print out his pages of summarized data. He had resisted getting a modem for several months. "Who would I go online with?" he had asked her. "And anyone I want to talk to is already here," an explanation which had pleased her.

Nonetheless, Tom kept talking to her about it and finally did get one, after she showed him a list of the subjects one could find information about on CompuServe. But his resistance fit, too. If he didn't need it, he didn't bother with it. No need to be nerdy about it or try to show off.

So maybe the notebook with the information on the Steel Riders who killed Eileen was just, well, like a scrapbook, just his way of following the hearing, of keeping a record.

Souvenirs?

So she settled it, partially, in her mind. But it was always there, out on the edge of her thinking, like some distant dark body orbiting the sun, and who knew what it might kick loose out there in the darkness, to come plunging inward? Some planet-killing comet, maybe. Better to leave it alone.

Tom saw that she was trying to be extra cheerful, which was usually a good indicator that Ellen was disturbed about something. In the past, it usually meant her parents were fighting again, but he knew she hadn't had a call from them in the past week, which was not unusual while they were vacationing.

He considered the possibility that she was unhappy about his comings and goings but thought he had successfully explained his absences. In case he hadn't, he thought he had a way to deal with the situation. They were in the kitchen, cleaning up the dishes from lunch.

"Well, I've got to go out tonight," he said, handing Ellen a plate to dry. He saw the flash of disappointment on her face before she could look away.

That's it.

He cleared his throat. "Seems to me these past few weeks my errands have gotten really out of hand, people wanting me here and there for all kinds of things." He washed a small bowl and handed it to her. She studied the bowl as she dried it like it was a rare gem, carefully not looking up at him. "And I figure if I hang around here any time at all somebody from the church or the post or someplace or other will try and get a hold of me for something or other. So I need your help." He paused, waiting, and was rewarded with her looking up at him, with a touch of a question on her face, and a little hope as well, and that hurt.

"What I figure is, no one can ask me to do anything if they can't get in touch with me. Figure that makes sense?" he asked her. She nodded. "So let's you and me escape for a couple of days." Tom lowered his voice in a conspiratorial whisper. "Let's take the weekend off and go on down to the river and see what kind of trouble we can get into."

A smile blossomed on Ellen's face like one of those time-lapse movies of a flower she liked to watch on the Discovery Channel. She turned back to drying the same bowl, which he figured was going to lose its glaze before she was done.

"I figure we can cut out Saturday morning, say, stay overnight somewhere along the river, and then come back Sunday."

"Sounds like a plan," she said, using a phrase she had heard on some sitcom. "I'll bring the binoculars and my bird books and pad..."

She was off and running, now, and Tom nodded silently to himself. It would be good for her to get around a bit, she'd always liked the big Ohio River, and after tonight he would stand back a bit and decide what would be his next step.

As for tonight, he would gamble that the Steel Riders were going to strike the Dragons. If they did, he would be there as well and the opportunities that possibility offered were very inviting. If there was an ambush, which he suspected was behind Nick Christopher's stalking of their hang-out, then there was a damned good chance Jack Baker would be there. Even if it was just another spy trip for Christopher, Tom planned to be there with his long rifle and settle at least of one of them.

The more the merrier, of course, and he smiled as he scrubbed some spoons.

Chapter 26

JJ took longer than expected to get back to headquarters. The rain had gotten downright mean tempered for a while there and forced him to slow down. Then he had come across a good fender-bender that required calling it in and standing by until one of the uniformed deputies showed up. He hung around while the volunteer firefighters made an appearance and then waved to the other deputy and eased back out onto the road.

The rain gentled down some by the time he pulled into the parking lot, but there was nothing about it that suggested it had any intention of quitting any time soon.

He remembered as a boy putting up relatives from near Springfield who had to go for high ground when the Mad River swelled over its banks. It was rains like this that seemed to do it, he recalled.

Of course, the Army Corps of Engineers had gone in there and put in dams and dug channels and raised the embankments and all, so now whole new areas seemed to flood out each spring. He shook his head as he jogged from the car. Mother Nature sure has a poor sense of humor.

Anne waved to him as he shrugged off his raincoat. He nodded back and walked over to her desk.

"What's up, Anne of a Thousand Days?"

"Did she make it a thousand days?" she asked. "Dealing with a king must be a lot easier than with representatives of our nation's law enforcement community."

"Ouch," JJ said, clutching his chest, "you've broken my heart."

"I don't know about that, but I think I've just increased your workload." She handed over a pair of folders. "Here are the records from St. Louis. They can really move when they want to."

Thanking her, JJ had one of the files open and studied it well before getting to his desk.

As he expected, Thomas Parker had served in the Army during the Korean War. Enlisted, volunteered to be a paratrooper, was in the Fifth Rangers, made sergeant, couple of medals, couple of Purple Hearts, nothing too bad, apparently, honorable discharge. He went through it quickly. The service record was simply a listing of assignments, training, qualifications, awards, disciplinary actions (there were none in Tom's file), promotions, that sort of thing. A small box recorded awards and decorations but gave no details.

He flipped the file to one side. No surprises there. He opened the second one, the only other name from the list of Parker family members to have served in the military.

John Wesley Parker had served in the United States Marine Corps from February, 1968, to February, 1972, according to the first page, which was a copy of his DD-214, his discharge form. He scanned down it quickly. A DD-214 wasn't always complete, but John Parker's service record was attached and he would go through it in detail.

The 214 was interesting. An Honorable Discharge, and left with the rank of O3, Captain. There didn't seem to be any way of telling if he had any problems. He scanned down the page. Twelve months, twenty days overseas time.

A large rectangle held a bunch of abbreviations, only some of which could he identify. "PH" was probably Purple Heart, but what were CAR, VSM (Vietnam Service Medal?), VCM, PUC (Presidential Unit Citation?), and a bunch of others.

JJ turned the page and read through the service record. John Wesley Parker had completed college at the time of his enlistment. Had done well on a series of tests whose initials were totally obscure. JJ flipped the page. He wasn't sure Anne had stapled them in the right sequence, but this next one apparently listed his unit assignments, with many of them listing grades for conduct and military proficiency.

It took a little reading but he was able to decipher the notations. He had gone to Quantico for something called PLC (G) and TBS and went to Fort Benning. Fort Benning? Wasn't that an Army base? Wasn't there very long, just a few weeks. And then off to a Navy base in California. Well, sure, weren't Marines sentries for the Navy? But it didn't look like he was an MP or the Marine equivalent. Some sort of training thing there as well.

Then FMF WESPAC. Vietnam. All right, what unit? First Force Troops. What was that? Did his whole tour with them, and then back to the United States, Camp Pendleton.

JJ looked around. Steve Johnson, the FBI agent who had been with him in Middletown, was an ex-Marine. JJ had seen the small gold eagle, globe and anchor emblem in his suit lapel. Steve was over next to the bulletin board, putting up a couple of intelligence summaries. He waited until the agent turned around and waved. Steve walked over.

"What's up, JJ?" The tall man asked, sitting on the corner of JJ's desk.

"I got the military service record of a Parker, one John Wesley, nephew of Thomas Luther. Looks like he's an ex-Marine. I figured you could translate his record into English." He handed the folder over.

"That's Marine veteran to you, cowboy," Steve said, grinning. "Once one, always one." He flipped the folder open. "Well, well, what have we here? Our boy was an officer. PLC." He looked at JJ. "That's cool, that's like ROTC except they don't do anything during the school year, just during the summer. Think of going to boot camp twice, a year apart, six weeks at a time. I heard they would lose 50% of their candidates just in the time interval between PLC sessions." He bent back over the folder. "Purple Heart, National Defense Service Medal, Vietnam Campaign Medal, Vietnam Service Medal with star, Expert qualification, rifle and pistol, must have liked guns, Bronze Star with combat 'V,' Navy Unit Commendation, Presidential Unit Citation, and did The Basic School, what else?"

"Let's see..." He flipped to the next page.

"Pretty good qualifications scores, college, ah, yeah, nothing out of line here." He turned the page. "Went to Camp Lejeune as a platoon commander, sent over to Benning, probably for jump school. Must have been real gung-ho. Yeah, here it is; jump qualified. Then out to squid school. And then First Force troops rear in Okinawa and then Vietnam. The guy was with First Force Recon." He looked at JJ. "I joined the Corps in '78, but I remember those guys who were in Force Reconnaissance, Force Recon, those who were still in. Bad mothers. Hard core among the hard core. 'Swift, Silent, Deadly', was their motto, and some of them really were." His finger went down the page.

"His basic MOS was infantry, small unit commander, no surprise. Then some cross and additional training. Lots of courses from MCI and MCS." He looked up again. "Those are Marine Corps extension courses or schools."

"So he's in Vietnam as a brown bar, makes First Lieutenant while he's there, blam, makes Captain a few months later, which is unusual for Marines in that their promotion line is usually slower than for, say, the Army. But this was during the war and Marine L-Ts get eaten up pretty quick." He turned the page.

"Awards and decorations; the guy was in combat. Got dinged once – Purple Heart. From the date it looks like he was returned to the field fairly quickly. CAR means 'Combat Action Ribbon'. Just means he was in ground combat, sort of like the Army's CIB, Combat Infantryman's Badge. Bronze Star, but a combat one; no, two of them, and, see, it's not on his 214, some clerk didn't transcribe it, but a Silver Star, too. The guy was in combat and handled it pretty well, it looks like. May explain his rapid promotion to Captain." He turned to the last page.

"Bunch of military operations, some of which I've heard of from reading about the war. Looks like he was in the thick of things. No fitness reports included."

"I'm guessing," Steve said, "but I would think he was pretty good at what he did. Decorated, promoted. But this is a little odd. You figure a guy like this is on the fast track, but you can see his last two assignments stateside were, first, as an instructor back at The Basic School. Had to be sharp to pull that down. But his second one is OIC of the Marine Guard at Naval Air Station Lakehurst, New Jersey. Now that's nowheresville. I would guess he screwed up in some monumental way down at Quantico and, rather than court-martial his butt, they bounced him up to overseeing the walking wounded who were guarding the blimp base. Definitely the signal his career was over." He shook his head. "I don't know, maybe he was too intense for the training command, maybe something else. You'd hear stories about some of the combat vets taking things too far when trying to train the newbies, or maybe he just plunked some general's wife. Who knows?" He flipped the folder shut and handed it back. "So what's all this in honor of?"

JJ took the folder and paused.

"I was trying to see if there was a case for one of the Parkers maybe playing vigilante. Old Tom Parker might have been a contender if all this had gone down twenty years ago, but John Wesley, he'd be about 48, 49 now. I got the report from the Franklin, Indiana, cops. They can't account for his whereabouts at the time of the killings of either Hollingsworth or Larson, though they've only done a cursory check." He turned the folder around on his desk idly. "If there's anyone in the family looking to get some revenge for Eileen Parker, he looks like the leading candidate."

"Working up your brief for tomorrow?" Steve asked, smiling. "Well, it's good to cover all the bases and his name ought to be in the pot. He's got kind of a prime background and it ought to be simple enough to do a good check and see if there's something the Franklin boys have missed." He stretched his arms and scratched his head.

"I like the age, too. Our stats show the vigilante thing is usually done by males between 30 and 45; he's close enough. I'd like him better if he was a little closer to the girl, relative-wise. It's usually an immediate relative. Maybe he had a special relationship we aren't aware of. The timing's lousy. Most vigilantes react pretty quick, or nothing seems to happen. But the familiarity with guns and violence is real strong, though contrary to popular mythology the vigilante usually is not a combat vet. Don't know why. Maybe we just don't have a large enough of a sample to generalize. Maybe combat vets have had enough war and don't go looking for more." He scratched his head again. "But those 'Nam vets have a reputation. Do you really like him for this, JJ?"

There it was, the question. What were his instincts saying? He shrugged; nothing but silence in that quarter.

"I don't have any kind of feel for him, Steve. I threw his name into the St. Louis check as kind of a last minute deal. Nothing else ties him in, so I guess I'm saying, no, I don't think he's in it. But we ought to have him checked out. I think it's a Dragon thing and I'm betting a full scale war is about to break out between the two gangs."

Steve smiled sardonically. "Forget it, deputy dawg." He gestured toward the window with his thumb. "No one's going to war in this weather. You can't ride a cycle in the rain." He slid off the desk and walked back to bulletin board.

JJ turned in his chair and looked out at the rain. Well, he was going to be presenting the boss with one more loose end: John Wesley Parker. He shook his head. If a war is coming he hoped it would be a quick and violent one for both sides.

The   coming   night   would   prove   him   half-right.

Chapter 27

It was night, but Tom found himself looking upward anyway. The rain had largely stopped, but a drifting mist still faded in and out.

He looked through his binoculars from his position on the same side of the highway as the Mail Boxx. Tom had been in position in the trees on the other side of the Marathon gas station since nine. While the station's interior light was on, the exterior lights went off when they closed at 10 PM.

Tom saw Christopher's truck; Tom was directly behind it and estimated the range to be about 250 yards. The GMC was in its usual position, off to the left of the entrance, parked facing the lot. A small trash dumpster squatted next to it, bordering the road, but he could see over it easily. As near as he could tell, there was no one in the truck.

While he could see a couple of motorcycles glinting chrome in front of the bar, there were fewer than on other evenings. On the other hand, there were two pickups and a Cherokee in positions usually occupied by the Harleys. Maybe it was too wet to ride a motorcycle.

Two other vehicles in the front parking lot had attracted his attention. Located almost directly across from the bar's entrance was a dark van, a hulking shape taller than the cars parked around it. It parked facing the bar. The interesting thing was there were at least two men in it but they had not come out, content to remain in their seats and apparently wait.

The second vehicle was a pickup, a big Ford F-250, with a cap. It was beyond the van, in the corner near where the parking lot ended. Like the van, it parked facing the bar. He had seen the light of a match or lighter in the passenger's position. Again, no one had emerged in the past hour.

Tom's own truck was behind him, waiting on the dirt road that branched off the highway and curved into the woods behind the gas station. While a fence ran between the trees and the highway, there was no gate across the opening for the road. He had driven past the entrance twice before the traffic was light enough for him to pull in without being seen. He had gone into the trees far enough that his truck was hidden.

Then it was a slow walk from the truck to the edge of the trees. He had taken his time to find his position, which turned out to be an old, lightning-shattered tree, its trunk now sprawled on the ground. He was checking now to see if the person leaving the bar was Christopher.

No.

Tom put the binoculars to one side and lifted his rifle up. He reached out to the Harris bipod and swung its legs out with quiet clicks. He carefully lowered the rifle to the tree trunk. There was a slight slope to the tree and he adjusted the length of one of the legs to level the rifle.

The Remington was familiar to his touch and his movements were smooth and accurate. He flipped up the plastic covers covering the Leupold variable telescopic sight and peered through. He laid the crosshairs on the wide exterior mirror on the driver's side of the GMC, allowed himself to relax, and then closed his eyes. When he reopened them, he saw that the mirror was no longer dead center. He didn't move the rifle. Instead, he shifted his body until the crosshairs were back on target. He repeated the process, always adjusting his body, which laid the rifle on target with little need to strain against the natural inclination of his body.

There were five rounds in the rifle, one already chambered. All were matched hand loads. The rifle was sighted in using rounds from the same hand loaded group from the 200-yard range of the Sportsmen's Club. The difference between the range distance and here was negligible and he easily compensated for it.

Now that the rifle was set up, Tom monitored the scene through the telescopic sight and let the binoculars stay where they were. He was concerned that the drifting mist might cloud the glass but it seemed to be lessening.

There was a small flood of light across the parking lot. Someone was coming out. He moved the rifle slightly to pick up the emerging figure. It was Christopher. He let the crosshairs follow him, resting lightly in the upper half of the dark blob of his head.

Christopher stopped once, looking around, and then continued to the GMC. He opened the door but instead of getting in he reached inside and turned off the light. Then he pulled something out. He kept it low, next to his body, and just stood in the darkness, facing the bar. At the same time, the doors of the van and Ford opened and men stepped out. Tom noted that their interior lights stayed off, just like the GMC's.

Here it comes.

Two men came from the Ford. There were at least three from the van, maybe more he couldn't see. They were all careful to keep their hands hidden. When the bar door opened with a sudden flash of light, they all turned towards Christopher, who made a quick wave of his hand and everyone acted like they were deep in conversation.

A pair of women, their laughter barely audible to Tom, walked with their backs to him, heading for their vehicle parked on the other side of the Mail Boxx.

Tom considered what he had seen. When the other men had looked towards Christopher, one next to the Ford had looked like Jack Baker. It was just a glimpse, but Tom thought it was possible that the one he wanted more than the others might finally have come out of hiding. Did he want to go for him or stay with Christopher?

The decision was taken out of his hands. Light flared across the parking lot again. He picked up the figures coming out the door. Six men and he had a brief glimpse of long hair and beards. He swung slightly to get Christopher back in his sight. This time there was no wave. He took a slight step away from the GMC and now Tom saw he was holding a gun.

Tom reached up with his thumb and slipped the safety off. He settled the crosshairs in the middle of Christopher's skull. The Remington 700 Varmint Special had little noticeable slack in the trigger but what there was he had taken up. He was gently squeezing the trigger when all hell broke loose in the parking lot.

While the ambush was well planned, set up so the Dragons were in a crossfire, the men conducting it were not professionals. Virtually simultaneously, they opened up with a variety of handguns and automatic weapons. Christopher, who had seen many a movie but had never fired on anyone for real, had thrown up his own pistol with both arms fully extended and dropped to an exaggerated crouch, which took him below Tom's sight.

As Tom lowered the rifle to pick up his target again, he saw multiple flashes of light and hear the firecracker-like popping as the other Riders sprayed the Dragons. They were shooting with everything they had, squeezing off rounds as fast as their pistols would cycle or holding back the triggers of their Uzis or AKs or whatever bullet-hose they were using.

This resulted in two phenomena, only one of which Tom was aware of. The part he didn't see was that of most of the bullets missing, fortunately impacting the cinder block front of the bar. A few went high, with several going through the narrow windows holding neon advertisements for various beers. Their sudden intrusion into the bar with the concurrent yammering of the guns, led the patrons to throw themselves to the floor, which saved several from injury as some of the heavier caliber bullets from the two AK-47s ripped through the cinder block wall and imbedded themselves in a series of electronic poker machines on the other side of the room.

The part he was aware of was the Riders' lack of fire discipline. This meant they all fired all their guns as fast as they could, with the result that they ran out of ammunition almost simultaneously. There was a sudden and, to a certain extent for the Riders, embarrassing silence while they fumbled in the dark trying to reload. None of them had practiced this, even in daylight. Tom heard a loud "Fuck!," made louder by the silence.

Christopher stood upright and reached into his tight jeans, apparently trying to retrieve another clip. Tom gently raised his sights to the middle of the man's head again, took a breath, and slowly let it out. Christopher was sliding in the clip when the Remington fired.

In the silence, any shot would have been startling. But the .308 caliber rifle spoke with a sudden, abrupt, slamming sound which was a quantum level, even from more than 200 yards away, above the various pistols and automatic weapons used by the Riders.

Through his sight, Tom saw Christopher convulse and drop like a wet dishrag. Low brush hid the body once it fell to the parking lot.

He swung the sights up, looking for the Rider he thought might be Jack Baker. His right hand raised the bolt handle but he moved it to the rear with the back of his hand, which allowed him to catch the empty, hot brass cartridge case as it ejected. He put the case into his raincoat pocket and reached up to close the bolt.

The lull caused by the Riders' ammunition depletion and their surprise at hearing the roar of the rifle seemed to result in a raising of the dead. Lacking any sort of discipline, the individual Riders had concentrated their fire on the first two men out of the bar, which had resulted in both men being hit, one fatally. The next two men dived for the parking lot asphalt between the motorcycles while the last two ran a few more steps before dropping behind the Cherokee. After the crack of the Remington and with the momentary pause in the Riders' assault, one of them pulled out his own pistol and returned fire, shooting almost blindly towards the dark shapes around him.

The two men crouching behind the Harleys were unarmed and clambered to their feet and dashed back towards the bar entrance. It was the wrong thing to do.

In the dark, the Riders were not sure what the rifle shot signified. Their sight was dazzled by their own weapons' muzzle blasts and none saw Christopher collapse. By the time the two Dragons made their run for safety, their guns were reloaded and the fear they felt when their fire was inaccurately returned only served to urge them to repeat their previous behavior of firing as fast as possible.

There were eight Riders firing and almost all of them scored at least one hit on the two running figures. Most of their rounds went behind them but it was enough. One fell in an awkward sprawl in between the bikes and rapidly bled to death. The other, already dead with a head wound, nonetheless ran two more strides before falling spastically.

The Dragon crouching behind the man with the gun decided to run the other way and the remaining ammunition in the Riders' weapons was expended in his approximate direction. He was hit in the leg but ran on, unaware of it. Other rounds punched holes in the cycles and vehicles and in the shooter, killing him, and, as their fire indiscriminately sprayed back and forth, striking the three already dead Dragons and the wounded one. Hit five more times, he moved from the category of wounded to dead.

Tom was uncertain about his target. He saw a man in the position occupied by the Rider he thought was Jack Baker, but in the darkness, he couldn't be sure. He played with the idea for a second of dropping the figure anyway, but the thought was cast aside. There were only five who were on his list, and he didn't want to kill anyone who wasn't on it.

That wouldn't be right.

Slipping the safety on, he then reached up and closed the covers of the telescopic sight. He reached down for the binoculars and put them in his pocket. Backing away from the fallen tree, he folded up the bipod. The shooting had stopped and he heard at least one powerful engine roaring into life.

Tom moved carefully but quickly through the dark, slightly crouched. The rifle was cradled in his right arm while his left hand held the warm muzzle, forming a wedge less likely to snag on something in the night. He came out onto the dirt road half a dozen yards in front of his truck.

Must have curved a little to the right.

Tom hurried down the road to the pickup. He slipped the long rifle into the space behind the seat and covered it with a blanket. The truck started and he backed down the lane. He saw the lights of several vehicles speed past, moving away from the bar. Maybe the Riders were leaving.

He didn't turn on his headlights until he was on the highway, heading away from the Mail Boxx. He turned off on 73 and followed it to Oxford. He saw no police, save one Oxford police car setting up a speed trap at the bottom of the hill just outside of town.

The lights were out in his house when he came up the drive. Figuring Ellen was asleep, he took the opportunity to take the rifle, still wrapped in the blanket, out of the truck and put it in the shed. He dropped the blanket and slipped the Remington into its cabinet. He took a moment to open his notebook to Christopher's page. Using a black marking pen, he crossed the page with a large "X" and then put the notebook back.

It never occurred to Tom he might have missed.

He double-checked all the locks on his way out.

Redbone sat on the backstairs, watching him as he walked up in the dark. He stopped to scratch the big cat's ears. Up above, the sky was finally clearing and he saw faintly shrouded stars. He watched them fade in and out for a while before going inside.

Up above him, silently watching in the dark, sat Ellen at her window. Grandpa Tom had given her a reason for this trip and had said he might be late coming back from the Legion meeting.

But   what   had   he   carried   into   the   shed?

Chapter 28

JJ got the word through his beeper as he was going over his notes for the Friday briefing. Letterman droned on in the background; he found it easier to work when there was some sound in his bachelor apartment but not something that he might be tempted to actually listen to, like music.

He glanced at the LCD screen on the top of the device and started punching numbers in his telephone.

"Deputy Sheriff James Jeffers returning..." he started, but a voice quickly interrupted. He listened in silence for a few seconds and then let out a low, soft, "Damn."

Within five minutes, JJ was taking the stairs two at a time headed for the parking lot. As he drove away, he pulled the blue strobe light out from under his seat and plugged it into the cigarette lighter receptacle. He shoved it onto the dashboard and drove as fast as the wet roads would allow.

The highway in front of the Mail Boxx was blocked off with traffic detoured down side roads. JJ showed his identification and passed through. He saw more than a dozen marked police cars, their red and blue lights throbbing in the dark, and a row of ambulances. There were people everywhere, most in some police uniform or other.

The Mail Boxx was not in a township and so fell into the jurisdiction of the county sheriff's office, which explained the rapidity of the call to him.

There were plenty of deputies about, but neighboring towns had responded to the call as well and so had the Highway Patrol. The Staties were taking over the roadblocks, freeing up the locals who were returning, slowly, to their patrols.

JJ parked on the opposite side of the highway from the bar and left his flasher on. He walked across the road, past the ambulance crews who were standing together and talking quietly, and ducked under the yellow tape someone had enthusiastically and unnecessarily strung across the driveway. He shook his head; they'd have to pull it down to get the ambulances in.

Rescue lights gave the scene a stark, blue-white appearance. There was the occasional flash of light from a forensic photographer and he saw small clusters of technicians on their hands and knees at various points around the parking lot, carefully examining the ground.

A small group of cops, almost all in civilian clothes, stood in the center of the lot, facing the entrance. He recognized them as members of the Sheriff's Office. Bob Phillips, the department's lead homicide investigator and the man who had JJ called, was in the center. He was a balding, heavyset man in his late fifties.

JJ stood on the edge of the group and caught his eye. Phillips nodded and continued giving orders to the others. After a minute, he was free and stepped over to JJ.

"Hell of a night," he said, extending his hand. JJ took it.

"Thanks for letting me know, Bob. What's the situation?"

Phillips shook his head. "I've never seen anything like it. This was a full-scale ambush delivered by the Steel Riders. We've got six dead, one wounded. The wounded guy is a Dragon named Peter Taylor and that's about all he told us before we sent him off to the ER. Took a hit in the leg; doesn't look serious." Phillips paused and looked JJ in the eyes.

"JJ, is there anything you can tell me about this? That task force thing with the feds, does it figure in on this?"

"Bob, I think there's a connection. I can't say too much at this point" – Phillips snorted – "but we're working on the Riders involvement in the drug business."

"So what else is new?" Phillips said bitingly. "I know that, I've been briefed. By you. Listen, JJ. Remember that when the feds leave you've got to come back to work in Butler County, so don't jerk us around."

"No, Bob," JJ said quietly. "Anything I got that pertains to this you'll see. I just got to get clearance from the boss. First thing in the morning you'll get our package on what we think is going down between the Riders and Dragons."

Phillips said nothing for a moment, just looked down at his shoes.

"Ah, hell, JJ. Must be the weather. Sets my arthritis off and I get cranky. Come on and I'll show you what we think happened so far." He took JJ by the elbow and walked towards the bar entrance.

"OK, we've got two down here," Phillips said, gesturing with his free hand. "Looks like they were coming out of the bar when they were hit.

Lots of lead flying." He pointed at the front wall and JJ saw the numerous bullet holes in the cinder block and narrow glass windows.

One body was of a young man with a scraggly beard. His long hair was tied at the back of his head with what looked like a strip of leather. He was wearing a Levi jacket and jeans. He was on his stomach, his head to one side, and his eyes were half-open, as if he was casually studying the asphalt. A bullet hole was just above his eye and looked black in the rescue lights. The second was an older man with a thick, heavy beard but was as bald as Phillips. He lay against the wall, his arms and legs at awkward angles. He wore a t-shirt under an open leather jacket. It was sodden with blood from a half dozen holes but you could still make out a cartoon character who was saying, "Don't have a cow, man."

Good advice.

"There are three more over here," Phillips said, walking towards the Cherokee and Harleys, all of which showed bullet holes. He pointed at a figure stretched out in between the bikes and the bar, just a yard short of the two dead in front of the door.

"This guy took a clean one right in front of his ear. Must have dropped him right where he stood." The man had one arm stretched parallel to the wall while the other was partially under him. He was wearing glasses in steel frames that had survived his fall in better condition than he had. He wore a leather jacket and leather trousers were tucked into heavy, cavalry-style boots.

"We found a gun with this one," he gestured towards a dark figure on the ground, partially hidden in the shadows behind the Cherokee. "This other one was shot all to hell."

The one shot to hell was lying between the bikes and was easy to see. He had a thick mustache and long but well maintained hair. His mouth was open. He was the only one wearing Dragon colors, sewn on a leather vest he wore over a red sweatshirt. The sweatshirt hid none of his wounds. He was hit in the legs, stomach, right arm, and throat. A pool of blood as wide and long as he was, spread from him to under the Harleys.

"The wounded one was around the corner here. We found him in back, hiding inside a trash can, bleeding like a pig." Phillips smiled grimly. "I think he was very happy to see the cops arrive."

"I can give you a preliminary ID on a couple of these people," JJ said. "This one in the colors is Daniel Parr, local chapter treasurer, basically their money man. I don't know the guy with the pony-tail or the guy with

143

the leather fetish, but Baldy is Charles Danson, who is another one of their officers, sergeant at arms, I think." He pulled a pocket flashlight out of his jacket and shined it on the dead man behind the Cherokee.

It illuminated a man with part of his cheek gone and a hole where his left eye had been. There was remarkably little blood obscuring his features, which were handsome in a windblown sort of way.

"And this is Peter Powers, nothing less than president of the local chapter of the Dragons. This is the guy who was sent down from Columbus to organize a Dragon chapter here and use it as the base to challenge the Steel Riders in their own territory."

"I don't think he's going to do much more organizing." Phillips said with a slight smile. "Do you have anything on the wounded guy, Peter Taylor?"

JJ shook his head in the negative. "I don't know the name but I'll see what we have. And if you can get me something on the other guy I'll add him to the list."

"Right, we'll pass that on in a bit. We're letting the photo and forensic guys do their thing before opening them up. Just want to get them tagged and then they'll be bagged."

JJ looked around. "Did I lose count? Didn't you say there were six dead?"

"The other one is over there, next to that pickup. I think he was one of the guys pulling the ambush." JJ followed Phillips over the GMC.

Christopher lay sprawled, partially in the shadow of the truck. JJ flicked on his light and wished he hadn't. A large piece of the front of the biker's face was missing, beginning just above the eyes. A vaguely circular portion of his skull had blown out, taking with it a fair sized portion of his brains. JJ saw the white of the inside of his skull before he clicked off his light.

"That's a very big hole," he said quietly, working to keep his stomach calm.

"You noticed that, huh?" Phillips was silent for a moment. "The nine the Dragon shooter used was carrying straight ball ammo. No Hydra-Shocks, no Silvertips, not even wadcutters. One other thing. The entrance wound is in the base of his skull. This happy camper took one from behind."

JJ looked towards the bar entrance. "Another Dragon, one who got away? This guy turns away, looks down at something, and gets popped?" The doubt was in his voice as he mentally calculated distance and angles.

"Don't think so. He's a Steel Rider, right?"

"Nicholas Christopher," JJ said, nodding.

"So he's throwing lead like mad," Phillips said, "just like the rest of these bastards. There were at least two other groups, by the way. One opposite the entrance, the other over in the corner of the lot." JJ saw technicians gathered around both spots. "We've got lots of empties laying in both places, mostly nine millimeter but some casings from at least one AK-47. Anyway, my point is that the only cases we've seen so far from anywhere else are around the Dragon shooter, and they're all nines."

Both men looked at the Marathon station, illuminated only by a security light inside its glass. Beyond, the darkness hid everything.

"Dragons had a man over there, caught this one when he looked down to reload, is what I think," Phillips said. "Couldn't get the others because the GMC was blocking him out, or maybe the other parked cars."

JJ nodded. Made sense. But something was gnawing at him.

"Like I said, this one is Nicholas Christopher," JJ said. "He's a Steel Rider, all right. He was in the original shootout the Riders and Dragons had last January. Where that little girl was killed."

Phillips softly whistled. "What goes around, comes around. So he comes back to finish the job and this time his luck runs out when somebody shows up unexpectedly behind him. That's a little spooky."

JJ smiled grimly in response. "It gets spookier. There were five Dragons at that meeting. Three of them are laying over there: Powers, Danson, and Parr. One of the others is in jail as we speak on DUI charges and the fifth is in the hospital. Wrapped his bike around several trees two nights ago. Now, get this." He paused for effect. "There were five Riders at that gunfight. This guy makes the third of them to get killed."

"Those two the Middletown cops are investigating, Hollingsworth and Larson, they were in that."

JJ shook his head in the affirmative.

"So the Dragons were picking them off, one at a time. But the Riders had enough and decided to settle things once and for all by killing the leadership." Phillips delivered the hypothesis slowly and both men stood in silence, considering the possibility. Finally JJ spoke.

"I think a lot of the people on the task force will buy that."

Phillips looked at him. "But you're not so sure."

"It's not that," JJ said. "No doubt in my mind that the Riders did this in retaliation for the two they lost. It's this shooting of Christopher." He looked down at the body. "Seems a little off, somehow."

"You may be right," Phillips said easily. "We're going to be up all night on this. I'll get a prelim to you tomorrow morning, say around nine. Think you'll have a package for us by then?"

"No sweat." Then he remembered. "No, wait, I've got to give a briefing tomorrow morning at nine. OK if I run it over to you at noon?"

"Sure, that's fine. I'll still get the prelim to you by nine." He grinned. "What're friends for?"

JJ returned the smile to the older cop. "Thanks, Bob."

They shook hands and JJ made his way back to his car. It took a few minutes for his eyes to lose the dazzle from the lights. Then he started up and did a U-turn. Once past the roadblock he turned off the blue strobe and rolled down the window to let some air in.

The picture of Christopher's shattered head kept coming into view. It was going to be another of those nights, he could tell. JJ sighed. Part of the job. He had never gotten used to it, not really. Something always got past the walls, past the defenses you built if you were going to remain functional. Without them, you'd have a sudden attack of sanity and go find an entirely different line of work.

As the highway slid behind him his mind kept pulling at the Christopher image. Past the blood and brains and bits of skull bone, past the horror, there was something else, a dark thing heaving around in the darkness, almost in sight.

Something   is   a   little   off.

Chapter 29

Bob Phillips was better than his word. The preliminary summary arrived at eight o'clock, hand carried by one of the county deputies. JJ, returning to his desk from the coffee pot the task force had running 24 hours a day, only had a chance to wave to the deputy and shout a quick "Hey!" as the man was leaving the building. The deputy, Chris Warrington, a man JJ had worked with on a stolen car ring, turned at the door and waved back.

"Gotta go, JJ!" he yelled down the hall, the door held half open. "Got some stuff for you from Phillips – gave it to your secretary."

JJ pointed at his cup of coffee, making an offer, but Warrington only shook his head in the negative before stepping through the doors and hurrying to his marked car, sitting near the glass doors.

Suspect they're just a little busy just now.

JJ caught Anne's eye as he entered the office area and she held out a manila folder as he passed. He nodded his thanks and stepped to his desk.

The shootings at the Mail Boxx were the prime topic of conversation among the task force members. Almost all of them heard something about it on their motel radios – cops are almost continuous listeners of news radio stations – and they passed bits of information to one another as they met for breakfast in the restaurant next to the Holiday Inn most of them stayed at.

Several agents saw the delivery to JJ but avoided asking him questions as he pawed through the prelim and studied it. He had a serious look eventually compounded by a frown as he got to the last several pages.

Carl Davidson, his face half hidden by a handkerchief, walked up to JJ's desk a little before nine.

"The Sheriff's office gave me a call last night," Davidson said, pausing to wipe his nose and stuff the handkerchief away. "They said Robert Phillips was handling the case and he had requested we be notified. They said you'd get a preliminary summary of what's happened and you would pass it on." JJ looked up, nodding in response.

"Yeah, boss, just delivered a little while ago." He shuffled the papers together and started to hand them to Davidson, who held up his hand.

"No, hold onto them. Go ahead and make it part of your brief to the whole team. You can drop them off with me afterward. I'll get Anne to make some reference copies for anyone who needs to go over the info in detail. Got a question for you, though." He paused, and looked around the room, ensuring they weren't being overheard.

"This Robert Phillips, the one heading up the investigation. Is he any good?"

JJ looked at the papers on his desk, organizing his words carefully. He knew that one of the things the feds used the local liaison for was insight, and sometimes more, of the local law enforcement services. While he appreciated Davidson's need for information, he also felt strong loyalties to his own people. As Phillips had pointed out, long after the feds left he would be living and working here.

"Bobby Phillips is pretty sharp," he began. "He's been our homicide chief investigator for five years. I don't think he's lost a case that he's turned over to the prosecutors. He is very thorough, which is probably his strongest point. He doesn't miss anything and stays up on all the technology and research. Knows people well. Not a hunch man, not a guy to go on his gut instincts."

"'Just the facts, ma'am,' sort?" Davidson said, slightly smiling.

JJ nodded. "Exactly. Which is probably why the department has one of the highest arrest rates for homicides for all Ohio counties." JJ paused before continuing.

"On the other hand, you've got to remember that most of the killing that goes on around here is relatively straight forward. We don't get much in the way of gang killings, drive-by shootings, or St. Valentine's Day massacres, like last night. The other thing is, the Sheriff's Office intelligence on the main motorcycle gangs operating in our area, the Steel Riders and, in the southern end of the county, the Warlocks, is pretty thin. On the Dragons, it's almost nonexistent. Until the arrival of the task force, most of what we got was the monthly summaries from Columbus," he said, referring to the update organized by the state. "And their stuff was mostly gotten from us. Zero plus zero equals zero."

"Okay, thanks," Davidson said. "Is there anything we can do to help them?"

JJ was careful to keep his expression neutral. "Well, I think giving them our working summary on the Dragons and Steel Riders, especially the Riders stuff, would help out. It's all in the computer; we can easily protect our source in the Dragons and delete anything critical concerning the drug investigation."

"Such as it is," Davidson interjected. "Yeah, tell Anne what you want, take a look at it, and if it's okay, get a printout for me to review. I'll sign-off on it and you can take it over to Phillips. Now," he said, straightening up and looking at his wristwatch, "I've got just enough time to get a cup of coffee before team meeting begins." He walked away, leaving JJ feeling pleased.

It was good to hear Davidson volunteer to send the information to Phillips; it took some of the load off JJ in asking for it. Far too often, the various police departments got into turf wars and vital information, the pawn in the game, never got to the people who could use it. He knew it happened among the federal agencies and had run into it as a problem between state and federal investigators. Hell, even within the confines of Butler County it happened, especially among those jurisdictions whose heads were elected or whose budgets were in jeopardy. There was always the temptation to hold onto some information that might lead to a spectacular arrest and generate favorable publicity. It was the real world, after all.

JJ shook his head and gathered up his files. Davidson was an upfront guy. He hadn't liked being put on the spot and asked about Phillips. On the other hand, he figured Davidson would do what he could to aid the locals' investigation. It evened out.

The briefing was in the too small conference room opposite the large room used by most of the task force for office space. Down the hall, conveniently located, was the small room which served as a lunchroom with their 24-hour coffee machine. Several other offices were located off the hall as well, including the private one for Davidson and one for his FBI liaison, who was at the Cincinnati field office today.

Almost all the rest of the task force, close to 30 officers, were present. JJ was the only nonfederal cop; the state had three representatives from the Attorney General's office but they maintained their contact via email and telephone.

Davidson called the meeting to order and asked for a summary of the effort to track down the movement of chemicals, especially ephedrine, into the county. Karen Deevers got up and briefly outlined what they had.

Which was not much. One promising lead coming out of a pharmaceutical manufacturing company with a branch in Cincinnati had gone belly up on them when it turned out that the people involved in the illegal diverting of some of their company's goods were selling various prescription medications, none of which was ephedrine. Nothing had moved in mass bulk; the employees were taking drugs off the packaging lines a bottle or two at a time, nothing more, and resetting the mechanical counters with an unbent paperclip.

All this was known to the task force beforehand; the company's closed circuit television monitors caught the thefts and the management went directly to the police. It was hoped they were into something bigger, though the company steadfastly maintained their records showed no missing amounts of ephedrine. However, when the three employees were arrested, each tried to outdo the others in cutting a deal. They gave away every piece of information they had, but when asked about ephedrine they went blank. Davidson thanked Deevers for the summary. He looked out across the group, some of whom were forced to stand along the walls.

"We've hoped there was a single, fixed-site methamphetamine lab used by the Steel Riders," he noted. "Chemical analysis of speed picked up in several locations suggested that several months ago and is still indicating a single source. Finding a single lab, even one large enough to support the kind of poundage being put out by the Riders, is tough. We know that small labs have even been set up in the backs of Chevy vans and in bathrooms in other places. It wouldn't surprise me to find that the Riders are using a Winnebago and keep it on the run." He paused and looked around.

"Hell, they would have to keep moving to avoid the smell. But frankly, I doubt they're doing the mobile lab routine because the amount of production wouldn't be nearly enough for what we think is the demand."

"In any case, we'll keep slogging down that particular road as long as we can. Now most of you have gotten the word about what happened last night to some Dragons. I've asked Deputy Sheriff Jeffers to fill us in with a summary prepared by the lead investigating officer, Deputy Sheriff Robert Phillips." As JJ made his way forward through the crowd, Davidson continued. "As soon as he gives us that information, I've asked him to give us a briefing on some of the Parker family. I wanted to rule them out as a possible source of the hits on the Riders which took place prior to last night so as to narrow the field for sure onto the Dragons."

JJ stood beside Davidson, who nodded and moved away from the podium. JJ began with a summary of the shootings from the night before.

Basically, there was very little to add over what he was told by Phillips personally. The numbers were more thorough; they now had counts of the empty casings, organized by calibers and location, which suggested seven shooters in the ambush. There was some information from the patrons. Several identified Christopher, the only KIA Rider, as leaving the bar moments – there was disagreement just exactly how long – before the Dragons.

All the Dragons were now identified. In addition to Powers, Parr, and Danson, all dead, and Taylor, slightly wounded, they could now identify Vincent Morgan – noteworthy the previous evening for his ponytail and bullet hole just above his eye – and Fred Applegate – noteworthy for his fondness for leather riding apparel and bullet hole behind his ear.

JJ filled in the team using the information he had culled from their central database. Taylor had no police record, something of a distinction among the Dragons, but their inside source identified him as fairly active in the purchasing and sale of weapons without the formality of a federal license. Morgan was one of the troops, a new member from the local area. Applegate had a serious police record and had already served time for assault with intent. He was believed to have participated in two murders on behalf of the Dragons in the past.

"I don't think we're going too far out on a limb here when I say it seems clear the Dragons were having a meeting about taking some violent action against the Riders. Applegate has been in Columbus up until this past week, and tying him in with Taylor, their prime weapons supplier, would make it seem that they were getting ready to hit someone."

"What about Morgan?" Davidson asked from one side.

"I think Morgan was the local gun dog," JJ replied. Seeing Davidson's look of puzzlement, he continued. "When you go hunting, it helps to have a gun dog along to point out the game." Davidson nodded.

"There's just one oddity here," JJ said, picking up his briefing. "Nicholas Christopher, a Steel Rider, was found at the scene dead from a gunshot wound to the head. He was, as I mentioned, the man who probably scouted the Mail Boxx; he may have organized the ambush as well. In any case, he was shot from behind. Ballistics is putting it together but at this stage it looks like a large caliber rifle, something in the .30-caliber range. There were a couple of odd things about this shooting. He was hit from behind, indicating a shooter not in the ambush's kill zone. There's the size of the weapon, not your standard gang-banger favorite. And then there's the fact that the shooter only fired once."

JJ stepped away from the podium to a dry marker easel and quickly sketched out the area of the ambush and the front of the bar with a blue marker. He drew in the gas station and the wooded area to the northeast of the Mail Boxx in green.

"Here's where Christopher was hit. It was originally thought that the shooter was in the parking lot of the gas station, maybe serving as lookout, maybe whatever. However, the angles suggested that the shooter was actually further away, over here in the woods. Just before sending this report over, they found the shooter's location. He was about here, along the tree line." He made a circle with a red marker. He then drew an angle extending from the front of the bar to the circle to the front of the bar's parking lot. "As you can see, from this position the shooter would have been able to see just about the entire parking lot. Blocks to his vision included the gas pumps and Christopher's pickup truck. From the locations of the empty casings from the assailants' guns, it seems clear that most, if not all, of the Riders would have been in his sights. Because of his location and the darkness it is doubtful any of them would have seen him other than the muzzle flash." He paused.

"So the question remains. Why didn't the shooter continue to come to the aid of his brother Dragons? Why did he stop at one Rider?"

There was a low buzz of conversation from the team. JJ held up his hand. They quieted down. "The Sheriff's investigating team is proceeding on the assumption that the shooter panicked, that he got off one shot and then fled the scene. All available witness testimony, and here we're mostly talking about Taylor, though a couple of the people in the bar thought they heard a rifle firing in addition to all the automatic weapons and pistols, suggests that there was only the one shot."

He walked back to the board. "If this guy panicked, then it was a strange sort of panic, because he hit his target in the head at 246 yards, two feet, in the dark, on a rainy night. He also stopped to police his brass. He then walked out of the woods to a vehicle they think was located on a brush covered road another twenty yards further back."

JJ shook his head. "It doesn't make much sense to me. If it was a Dragon sentry, wouldn't it have been more logical to have someone outside the bar, in the parking lot, maybe with an automatic weapon, an Uzi, keeping an eye on people coming and going? Whoever was in the woods apparently had no way of communicating anything he saw in the parking lot, because he didn't. The Dragons were cut to pieces and had no idea what was waiting for them. And there's just no way he could not have seen the Riders gather."

"One last thing to add," Davidson said. "As JJ pointed out, Christopher apparently was killed by a large caliber rifle round. This is not what we expect to see in the hands of folks like these. But what it rings for me is a bell about how those other two Riders were killed. Remember that Hollingsworth and Larson were killed by shotgun, again not a weapon we've seen a lot in recent years from these people except incidentally. They prefer to have a lot more firepower available." There were several nodding heads while he folded his arms and fell silent, studying JJ's crude drawing.

"But whatever was going on, keep focused on the drugs. That's our target. We'll let the locals worry about all of this unless someone can figure a way it aids us in busting the Riders' lab and distribution system. Remember, if this is the outbreak of a major war, we may have opportunities to break into the Riders and get one or the other of them to roll over." Davidson made a gesture with his hand and JJ took it as a signal to continue.

"Right. Okay, let me take a quick look at the possibility that the killings of the three Riders was not done by the Dragons. Peter," he raised his voice and looked at the FBI agent near the back of the room standing near the light switches, "if you can drop the lights."

As the room dimmed, he flipped the switch on an overhead projector and laid on it his first transparency. It was a picture of Eileen Parker.

"This is Eileen Parker, the little girl killed during the original shootout between the Dragons and Steel Riders, now almost six months ago. What I was interested in was the possibility that the killing of the three Riders was due to her death, instead of the Dragons starting a war. Because of our interest in the possibilities coming out of a war between the two gangs, it was important to be sure, or at least as sure as we could be, as to who was doing the killing."

One at a time, he laid transparencies on the glowing machine. Each was a different adult in the Parker family. For each one JJ gave basic information and what had been learned as to the individual's alibi. Failing an alibi, he would refer to the probability of the man engaging in revenge killing.

He pointed out that the style and timing of the killings, coming so long after Eileen's death, were not typical of the more spontaneous revenge motivated killings with which they were familiar. He laid his next to last transparency on the projector.

It was Thomas Parker. He gave them some of the background information he had on the older man and then ran through his military history. He saw a couple of the others nod as they listened to the recitation of his decorations. He paused for a moment.

"So what about someone who would have the patience to come after these people later, who wouldn't be operating from passion, someone who would be cool and calculating? As you know, that almost never happens. It is so rare that the FBI Behavioral Science folks are very careful to say their profile of such an individual is almost certainly incomplete. What they do have is what you would expect: the individual almost certainly would be a male, probably higher than average intelligence, most likely familiar with weapons, and probably a veteran. Maybe a combat vet, but maybe not." He looked up in the dim light, his face illuminated from below.

"The kicker here is that they guess that this type of person takes action far more often than they know and does so successfully, meaning he is not caught, which is one of the reasons they don't have much in the way of data." He paused again, studying the picture. Someone in the group said something. He looked up; it was Karen Deevers. He raised his eyebrows in question.

"I was just remembering," the FBI agent said, "the story of Wyatt Earp, the real one, not the movie version. After his brothers were shot up, there's a six week period in Earp's life no one can account for, and he never did. But several of the remaining members of the gang he and his brothers fought at the OK Corral were killed, including Johnny Ringo, no relation to our Johnny, who was found shot dead lying against a cactus, scalped." There was a low whistle from the back of the room and Steve Johnson made a Western fast draw gesture and grinned. Deevers smiled back.

She picked up the thread of her thoughts. "Well, what JJ is describing is something you might expect from someone with an old fashioned sense of family and that sort of thing. Tom Parker, from his description, was at one time a very dangerous man. If he were twenty or thirty years younger, I'd say I liked him for this business, at least to the point where I'd want him checked out."

Now JJ smiled. He slipped Tom's picture off the machine and replaced it with his last transparency.

"Allow me to introduce John Wesley Parker, who is, in Agent Deever's phrase, a 'very dangerous man.'" He gave the information he had on John Wesley and took the time to go over his combat record and service qualifications. He saw several agents leaning forward, studying the face on the screen.

"And the good news, I'm afraid, is that Mr. John Parker has no alibi for the first two killings. I don't know about last night. But the Franklin, Indiana, cops did a low profile check on him for me and there's nothing he has to account for his whereabouts. Zip."

Davidson shook his head. "Damn, JJ, I hope you're wrong. But be sure to include all this in the package we give Phillips. Nice job." He turned to the group. "Does anyone have any questions for..."

He was interrupted by the watch officer entering the room and waving to him as the lights flickered to life. Davidson quickly made his way to the back of the room and stepped into the hallway with the officer. After a moment he returned, a tight smile on his face.

"Well, I don't know who killed our three Riders, but it may be academic," he said while walking to the front of the room. He turned and faced the group. "We just got word. Late last night, apparently within a half hour of the ambush at the Mail Boxx, three Dragons were gunned down in Dayton." There was a murmur of voices, that fell silent as he raised his hand.

"It gets worse. The Columbus headquarters of the Dragons was also hit. Five were killed, three wounded. The building in which the killings took place was then firebombed. One assailant was killed. He was Theodore Murphy, a Steel Rider in good standing." He paused and looked around the room.

"Ladies and gentlemen, if it hasn't been ended by this preemptive strike, we have our gang war."

Chapter 30

The thing about the Ohio River, for Ellen, was it seemed strong. You looked at it sliding past, the surface so smooth, and its effortless movement was like the muscle of some Olympic athlete. There was power in its depth, in its darkness, and she found she could sit and watch it without ever getting bored.

The movement, that never ending smooth flow, was almost hypnotic. It was never the same, but it was always the same.

On the other side was Kentucky (she always called it "Cain-Tuck-Ee" in her mind since she heard it pronounced that way in a movie that was really cool). From the Ohio side, Cain-Tuck-Ee looked green and dark and, with only a little imagination, she could see settlers or even Indians moving through the forests, and she could see herself joining them.

It would have been a very good thing, Ellen decided, skipping a stone across the river's ripples, if you had someone like Grandpa Tom along with you when you went into Cain-Tuck-Ee. She saw him as some kind of mountain man, a man making his way across the hills and valleys of unexplored territories.

He sat on the bluff above her, eating an apple she had bought at the farmer's stand back down the road, and reading a book. He seemed to be enjoying taking the day off. Ellen didn't think he did that very often; at least, he didn't seem to when she was around.

Then she remembered his disappearances from the farm during the past few weeks. Ellen deliberately turned her mind away from the thought. After all, that was just her misunderstanding, her mistake, and she wasn't going to think about it anymore.

She walked along the water's edge, studying the stones beneath her feet. It was hard to find good skippers. Most of the rocks smoothed into fat ovals by the Ohio's endless caresses. They'd be great for a slingshot, she decided, but as skippers they were pretty useless.

She had gone further than she realized when she came across the five high school boys. You could tell right away they were assholes, she would decide later, using a word of her father's which she saved for particularly deserving boys, because they were smoking and trying to act like it was something very casual.

Naturally, being boys, they said some things, most of which she couldn't make out. Boys were required by boy law to tease girls, she had discovered years before. That's about as far as it would have gone, except for maybe then becoming friendly. Boys have a weird way of saying hello. Except they were also assholes.

"Hey, girl, where you going?" One of them yelled, a little louder than the others, half mocking in his tone.

"Yo, sweet thing," another took up the call, "why don't you come over here and say hello?"

Ellen said nothing, just looked out over the water and kept walking back, hoping that by ignoring them they would leave her alone. There was a moment when they might have let her go without incident, maybe if there was something else going on that they were interested in, but there wasn't, and her effort to ignore them, they decided, was disrespectful.

"Hey, girl," said the first one again, a trace of anger in his tone, "don't you walk away from us." But she kept walking, avoiding eye contact, not sure of what else to do.

One of them cast his cigarette aside in a high arc with a flick of his finger and sauntered towards her. That's when she realized how far she had gone from her grandfather. Then the second one walked towards her, then a third, and that's when she began to feel afraid.

One of the three turned back towards the two remaining behind and said something to them. Whatever he said got him the finger but he kept coming toward Ellen.

Ellen walked towards where she had last seen her grandfather, but then the first boy blocked her path. The second got on the other side of her. They didn't touch her, they just kept getting in the way, making smart remarks, but the meanness was increasing and she was becoming more afraid. The third boy joined them, forming a semicircle around her with the river at her back.

"I know what you want, little girl," the first said with a smirk. "Why not just hang around and get some of it?"

"Yeah, little cheeks," the second added, raising his arms to block her from escaping, "we got everything you need."

The third didn't say anything, just kept moving towards her, licking his lips as if he was thirsty, his eyes dark.

It was like watching a fire grow. Their faces, originally amused, became taunting, then angry, as if she had done something to provoke them. They started grabbing at her, at first in a clumsy way designed to scare her. The whole thing was getting dangerous and what was scary was she didn't know why, other than they were boys and she was a girl, and that wasn't fair. In her fear and confusion, tears came and she felt embarrassed for it.

They tightened their circle, moving closer, and her heels were lapped by the river. She saw they would drive her into the water unless she let them grab her and, for a moment, she thought about throwing herself into it just to get them to stop but then something happened deep inside of her.

I will not go into the river, not for them, not for anyone.

And while still choking back her sobs, with one hand wiping the tears from her face, Ellen reached down with the other and picked up a rock. The solid cold of her fear was washed away with the heat from anger and she stood erect, her arm back, her hand tight on the stone. The three boys stopped, looking at her like she was something they had not seen before, something they were uncertain of.

"Which one of you bastards," she said through clenched teeth, borrowing again one of her father's favorite words, "wants to go to the dentist first?"

Ellen held herself as tightly as the rock, determined not to let them see her shake or cry again.

The boys were surprised, then confused, then embarrassed. They made rude jokes and laughed.

"C'mon, bitch, put it down."

"Yeah, cunt, chill. No one's going to hurt you."

But they backed off.

She didn't lower her arm until they had turned and, with a few more asshole remarks, walked back to their friends. She heard one, the one who had flipped the finger, laugh at them. Then she went back the way she had come, not hurrying, not looking back.

And not dropping the rock.

Ellen walked back upstream, the sun and the Ohio wind drying what remained of the tears on her cheeks. To one side, up on the bluff, Tom watched as she strode past, heading to where she had left him.

Tom had followed when she had gone out of sight and saw her confrontation with the boys. He started down the bluff to intervene when he saw her reach down for the rock and then stopped himself, pausing to see what the boys' reactions might be.

He couldn't make out what she said, but he caught the tone and he saw the boys' belligerence evaporate into the air. The boys backed off, saying things over their shoulders to her. Tom stepped back carefully so she wouldn't see him.

It was important, he thought, to allow her to have her victories on her terms. He hurried back to where she had left him.

He met her coming up the bluff. He motioned over his shoulder, back towards the parked truck.

"Just checking on the truck," he said. "Have a good walk?"

She nodded. "It was alright," she said, standing erect as she got to the top of the bluff.

And he felt a slight sorrow as he saw her standing there, seeing a little of her childhood being dropped on the riverbank, flowing away from her as if carried by the Ohio.

Ah, damn, does it have to happen?

He looked at her, watching her as Ellen turned and looked back at the river, the wind flicking her hair slightly, and he had an image of what she would look like as a full-grown woman, and the sorrow faded. He was left with a sense of pride and gratitude. The pride, of course, was in her as a part of him. The gratitude was for the glimpse of what he might not ever live to see.

Then she grinned, and it was Ellen the little girl, and she started to lean back, getting ready to throw her stone towards the river. He reached up and took her hand as she cocked her arm back. She looked at him in surprise.

"Not a bad rock," he said, taking it from her and acting like he was studying it, "but not a great rock." He gestured to one side. "Why don't you see if you can find a great rock to throw at the mighty Ohio. Otherwise," he said, winking, "it might not even realize you were calling on it."

She laughed, her old stone forgotten, and searched and found a bigger rock, one so large that it barely made the river when she threw it, though it produced a satisfying column of water when it splashed. She didn't notice him pocket her stone (that's how he would always think of it: *her* stone) nor, later, did she see when he slipped it behind the driver's seat as they got   ready   to   drive   away.

Chapter 31

Over the weekend things were something of a blur for JJ. Davidson put most of the task force personnel on the road. Working with the Dayton and Columbus police and the various federal agents, they tried to see if any of the pieces of the apparent war could add to the picture they were building of the drug trade.

That meant almost everyone else was gone while JJ covered things in the office. He got verbal reports and files sent via computer modem, organized them, and make sure it was all properly filed.

The advantage of being stuck at home, he saw, was that only he and Davidson were in a position to get a sense of what was happening on the large scale. It also gave JJ time to work on his own project.

The big picture soon began to look like something out of a Warner Brothers' cartoon. Basically, what they saw were the Dragons putting on a Road Runner imitation, while the role of Wile E. Coyote was replaced by a particularly humorless wolf.

The Dragons were pulling out of southern Ohio. Panic-stricken flight marked the exodus of some of them. The Columbus reports showed some were leaving so fast they left their motorcycles behind. Clearly, the Dragons felt that other blows were coming and just as clearly they felt helpless to head it off.

"Johnny Ringo," the informant the DEA was running in the Dragons was, in his words, "going with the flow." To do otherwise would be conspicuous, of course, but the undercover agent was close to panic himself when he snatched a moment at a rest stop on I-70 to call in. As far as he could tell, everyone was retreating back to Cleveland and Buffalo, the cities of origin for the Dragons, or were burrowing into the Ohio soil deep enough that it would take professional badgers to get them out.

Badgers?, JJ thought as he heard the agent's brief stab at humor. *We don' need no stinkin' badgers...*

Well, it was understandable. This was Steel Rider turf. Between active members, associates, in-actives, and various degrees of hangers-on, the total Rider count in Ohio was well in excess of three hundred. Figure about half that in Indiana and half again in Kentucky, plus outposts in West Virginia and Pennsylvania and scattered chapters in Illinois, Wisconsin, Michigan, Arkansas, and God only knew where else, all meant you were looking at one hell of a lot of people.

With someone like Jack Baker in charge, there was no telling where the bloodletting would end. JJ shook his head as he reviewed Baker's file. It would have been real nice if whoever got Christopher, Larson, and Hollingsworth had decided to start with good old Jack.

Maybe they wanted to and just couldn't find him?

JJ remembered a presentation by a psychologist at a hostage negotiation team training he had taken with the Pennsylvania troopers. The shrink covered the psychology of the various kinds of people who end up behind a barricade and was giving suggestions as to what to listen to and how to respond. Despite JJ's aversion to such things – his contact with mental health professionals in court was almost entirely negative, with the shrinks being mouths for hire to get perps off – he found the information interesting. Then one of the negotiators-in-training asked about dealing with a sociopath.

The shrink stroked his bald head, cleaned his glasses, and then looked the officer in the eye.

"Put a round through his medulla oblongata and drop him like a bad habit."

The psychologist went on to say a lot more about how to talk with those kinds of people, the Jack Baker kind, but his one-liner was not the kind of response one usually got at these formal trainings, though it was much appreciated by the troops. JJ heard the remark miffed the brass – it was said to be "inappropriate" – and never invited the psychologist back to Hershey Barracks.

That was the kind of man Jack Baker was. He simply had no sense of right or wrong and only his own needs mattered. One of those needs was to be in control and the way in which he could best demonstrate that control to himself was by hurting others. If it hadn't been for his success in generating lots of cash for the Riders it was highly likely that someone within his own gang would have put a round through his head some time ago.

Money, as they say, changes everything.

JJ smiled grimly to himself as he entered the names of the Dragon dead on the list they were maintaining on a bulletin board. The Riders had concentrated on the leadership. They had paid attention to the Gulf War; cut off the head of the snake first and then kill it.

Over the weekend the killing continued, but at a much slower pace, almost incidentally. There were few Dragons around by Sunday who hadn't gotten the word and either taken off or gone underground. Only the slow learners were still walking around. A few of these were picked off – by Sunday night the total was four more dead and four wounded, in addition to the three city massacre which started everything with such a flourish.

The Rider leadership, Jack Baker in particular, was making a big show of being in plain view over the weekend. Davidson figured that's how it would be. After the initial ambush the follow-up killings would be conducted by lower echelon Riders anxious to prove their mettle (JJ shook his head with a smile; Davidson had used a word like *mettle* with a straight face) and get a few personal scores settled.

The Riders lost two themselves; a Dragon had turned out to be a cooler hand with a gun than either of the two overeager pups who had jumped him in Fairborn, outside of Dayton.

Live and learn.

As the weekend ended, JJ sat in his chair, his feet up on his desk, his hands behind his head. He had gotten only a little sleep in the preceding two days, but the tiredness was more than balanced by knowing he did a good job and did it under Davidson's careful eye. He reached over and pulled his porcelain coffee cup to him but it was empty.

JJ frowned and got to his feet to get a fresh cup. As he did so he noticed the file folder he had used for the briefing on Friday morning – God, was it really 60 hours ago? – and idly picked it up. He walked down the hall to the break room and used it to tap a beat on his hip in time with a Waylon Jennings song he liked.

He slid the folder on the countertop as he filled his cup. When he finished he reached for the folder and noticed that some of the transparencies had started to slide out.

Slick little bastards.

JJ put down his cup and started straightening everything out, picking up the slides as a group and tapping their edges on the counter together. He paused, looking at the overlapping images. Something weird...

JJ dropped transparencies from the set, one at a time, studying the remaining ones as he held them together and looked at the overlapping images.

Finally, he was just holding two of them. Their scale was similar, something he had done intentionally for the presentation. But there was something else.

He kept looking at the image. The two faces were different. One's ears were bigger, the other had a more pronounced jaw, one had a mustache. Hair, cheekbones, teeth, often close – they were, after all, from the same family – but almost all the features were different.

What was the same were the eyes. Overlapping the eyes they appeared to be virtually identical. He used his hand to cover the faces below the eyes. You couldn't read any expression in them. They were open, observing, you got the impression they didn't miss much, but they gave nothing away, like there was something they held back.

He separated the two transparencies and looked down at the images of Thomas Luther Parker and John Wesley Parker. The faces looked silently back at him. Inside his mind came a growing realization, a grasping comprehension of the truth, based on nothing and everything, like religious faith. Call it a hunch, intuition or blind in the wind dumb ass guess, but JJ was suddenly convinced he knew, and he felt his pulse quicken.

It was one of you, wasn't it?, who laid behind that tree in the dark, in the rain, and calmly put a bullet through Christopher's head at two hundred and forty-six yards and two feet.

The pictures remained silent, not mocking, just not saying.

You did Larson and you did Hollingsworth and you did all of them because they had a hand in the killing of Eileen Parker. That's why you didn't nail anyone else at the Mail Boxx – they weren't on your list.

The pictures still said nothing as JJ stared into their eyes, trying to see something.

And next you'll go after the Baker brothers.

JJ shook his head. He had no proof, nothing solid, just what he knew of the personalities of the two, and even that was limited. But he had no doubt.

There   was   more   killing   coming.

Chapter 32

Ellen had doubts about whether cats were really Earth creatures. After she and Grandpa Tom returned to the farm on Sunday afternoon, she tried to organize Redbone's feeding.

She did not leave too much food in his bowl when they left Saturday morning since he would stay closer to the house if he was looking for something to eat. Nonetheless, he spurned her offers of both dry and wet cat food and was now acting like he had never met her before.

Ellen saw him sitting on top of Tom's truck as they arrived, idly flipping his tail back and forth. She thought he was probably glad to see them but, upon reconsideration, she suspected he was actually contemplating his revenge.

Redbone stood by, licking his paws, ignoring her offerings of food. When she called him by name, he turned away suddenly as if something interesting had just taken place off in the distance. When she approached, he bounded off, head and ears erect, intent on chasing a bird, perhaps, which a mere human (particularly one who would go off and leave a marvelous cat – just ask him! – behind) was incapable of perceiving.

Ellen shook her head in exasperation. Cats were supposed to be cool, but there were days when she thought they were just about the dumbest creatures around. She shrugged and went back into the house, rejected cat treats in her hand as a token of Redbone's contempt.

Tom was looking in the refrigerator as she returned.

"Any success in getting him to eat?" he asked as he shuffled through the containers on the shelves.

"No. He didn't want anything to eat, including the tuna. He wouldn't even take a treat." She showed the fish-shaped biscuits she still held. "Is there any possibility that Redbone is insane?"

Tom looked inside a plastic bowl and grimaced.

"I think most people find cats difficult to deal with because they act so human," Tom replied. He closed the refrigerator door and opened the freezer. "They're selfish, stuck up, stubborn, and limited in intelligence. Like a lot of people, when you think about it. Since we have so much trouble dealing with one another, it's not much of a surprise we have problems with cats." He removed several frozen packages wrapped in plastic and handed them to Ellen.

"Put these in a pan and let some warm water run on them. I'm going to make us some chili tonight."

"Great!" She took the frozen meat to the sink and rummaged in the storage drawer under the stove, looking for a pan of the right size. "How about if I make some garlic bread to go with it?"

Tom nodded his approval and then returned to his theme.

"Dogs, now, are a different case." He opened a cabinet and took out a bag of onions. "We relate well to dogs because they're different from most folks. They're intelligent, friendly, loyal, curious about new things, and very patient with their friends. Damned few people around who are like that. I think we sometimes keep them near us just to remind us how we're supposed to be." He examined the onions and selected two medium sized ones.

Ellen thought he might be right. It seemed to her that, at least among the girls she knew in school, there were few who were initially friendly. Girl law said you had to be distant at first until you determined whether the other person was cool enough to be a friend. And loyalty was something that didn't seem to apply, if the approval of others was involved.

Prior to their trip, she had baked two loaves of bread, mostly because she knew her grandfather liked it. One went on the trip with them and vanished right after they found a farmer's roadside stand selling fresh preserves and jams. The strawberry, she remembered, was particularly good.

She took the second loaf and set it up for the oven. While she used plenty of garlic powder, she was light on the salt; she knew her grandfather was on a low sodium diet. When she was finished, she put the loaf in the refrigerator. Tom was busy "slicing and dicing," as he liked to refer to his forays into cooking, so, after prodding the still semi-frozen beef sitting in the pan of warm water, she decided to go outside and see if a reconciliation with Redbone was possible.

The black cat was not around, but little nibbles had been taken out of both the dry and wet cat food in his bowl. Ellen smiled and walked over to the barn, suspecting he was hiding there and watching her.

The barn held the day's warmth but was dark now that the sun approached the horizon. Ellen stepped in and waited for a moment as her eyes adjusted. The barn was big, much bigger than it had to be nowadays since Tom did so little actual farming himself. Its broad plank floor, the boards dark with age, supported little other than the green John Deere tractor and a few pieces of equipment, most of which were carefully stored under tarps. An old hay wagon was to one side and she check that out first, since Redbone tended to perch on it to watch the comings and goings of the various small animals in residence. He wasn't there, or anywhere else in the barn.

Ellen decided to look around the outside. When she stepped out the back, she caught a glimpse of something small and black slipping around the corner. She pursued after the cat and got to the corner of the barn just in time to see him race around the next corner. She dashed after him.

When she turned the corner, the cat had vanished.

Is this how it happened to Alice?

Ellen checked around the work shed while trying to keep an eye on the cat's food bowl on the back steps but Redbone was declining to be interviewed. She looked in the shed window, suspecting the cat might have gone in through his little swinging panel in the door but if he had he was hiding.

Elvis has left the building.

She walked on back to the house. She wasn't worried; Redbone was an old farm cat and frequently spent the good weather nights outside. She had never succeeded in talking her grandfather into keeping him indoors to protect the birds, though she had never seen evidence that he had jumped many of them.

Dead voles and mice, on the other hand, showed up on the house steps with regularity. Ellen still remembered when, as a little girl, she had gone outside barefoot one morning only to step on the corpse of something very small, furry, and, for lack of a better word, rubbery. She had really freaked out, she knew, but that was a long time ago, back when she was a kid of only seven.

When she went through the kitchen, Tom was mixing his spices, which he like to measure out onto a plate and then add all at once to the beans and tomato sauce. The beef, finely diced, was frying and a small hill of chopped onions waited. Her grandfather was a very precise, meticulous cook, who, though he had been making the same style of chili for maybe a zillion years, still followed his hand lettered notes in the three-ring binder labeled "Recipes."

She flopped onto a soft chair in the living room and keyed the television into life. Outside, the sun had almost disappeared but the sky was still fairly bright. She channel-surfed for several minutes before settling on a Cincinnati station rolling into its local news broadcast.

Cincinnati had the worst chili in the world, she decided. Not at all like her grandfather's. Nonetheless, there was a chain of restaurants specializing in Cincinnati-style chili on spaghetti, with and without cheese or onions, and they were slowly spreading north. She shook her head. What kind of people would like chili flavored with cinnamon?

Ellen suddenly heard the television.

"...With the gang war raging across Ohio this weekend, Middletown police still have made no arrests in the ambush murders of the Dragon motorcycle gang members at a local bar Thursday night. A member of a rival gang was also killed, but police refuse comment as to any leads they might be..."

The pictures on the screen showed the usual images associated with announcements of violent crime: large men, mostly white, some in police uniform, some not, but still looking like cops, behind stretched yellow tape conferred with one another while yellow and orange blankets covered undefined shapes on the ground. The background shifted – apparently, people were killed in a bunch of different places, some in front of bars, some in alleys, some on streets, but the foreground was almost always the same. As the announcer finished, a series of pictures of men, captioned with their names, flashed on the screen over the films of the murder scenes. Apparently, these were the victims.

Nicholas Christopher.

She knew that name; the face was the one the newspapers used during the hearing, which was at least a little like what he looked like in real life.

Had looked like. He was dead.

That made three.

His name, along with a taped picture taken from a newspaper, was also to be found in a spiral notebook in her grandfather's work shed.

Ellen looked towards the kitchen from where her grandfather's cooking sounds were quietly coming. They had been together ever since his return Thursday night. They hadn't read a paper or listened to the news all weekend. She got up quietly and walked out the front door.

She walked quickly around the house, headed for the work shed. She kept watch over her shoulder as she approached the small building but she didn't see her grandfather in any of the kitchen windows. The heavy lock was in place this time and securely fastened. A squeak at her feet attracted her attention.

It was the pet door, swinging as Redbone emerged. The cat strolled in a semicircle to Ellen's feet and rubbed himself against her ankles, evidently forgiving her for her sins. But she was too impatient to pay any attention to the cat. She gave him an absentminded caress as she turned back to the house and half ran to the back door.

She dashed up the stairs and swung open the kitchen door.

"Grandpa Tom," she called, "I've found Redbone but he ran into the work shed. Can you unlock it so I can get him fed?"

Tom looked up from his cooking, a spoon posed in front of his mouth, a look of mild surprise on his face.

"Well, Ellen," Tom said, "You know he tends to sleep in there; that's why I put the panel in. He's alright there."

"But he hasn't eaten anything I've tried to give him since we got back and I'm afraid he's angry with me so I want to make up with him." For the first time in her life that she could remember, Ellen was lying to her grandfather and she was concentrating as hard as she could on appearing believable.

Her agitation at attempting a falsehood was seen by Tom as the seriousness of her concern.

She's a sensitive girl.

Tom shrugged and put the spoon down. He felt around in his pocket and pulled out his keys. He singled one out and handed it over to Ellen.

"Try a few cat treats," he said. "He's a sucker for the goldfish." He winked at her nervous smile. She snatched the keys and ran from the kitchen. He shook his head at her concern and turned back to the chili. He was glad to see that she took to the big cat, of course. It was important that she respect animals. But she seemed to worry too much sometimes. Well, with age she'd learn that a cat is going to do what a cat is going to do. He smiled to himself as he sampled the chili again.

Ellen had to try twice before she got the key into the lock but she was finally successful. The security light shining from near the top of the barn and through the window only partially illuminated the inside of the shed. She felt with her hand and found the switch.

The notebook was where it had been before and she had a sudden sense of relief, believing that it had not been touched. She pulled it free and quickly leafed through it.

The page devoted to Nicholas Christopher had a large, thick X drawn through it.

There was only one time her grandfather was able to get into the shed and that was when he arrived late Thursday night, the night of the killings. He knew then that Christopher was dead and she could only see one way that could be.

Ellen put the notebook back, turned off the light, and carefully locked up. The walk back to the house was slow. She felt like some enormous weight pressed down on her head and shoulders. Each step up the backstairs was like moving through thick oil.

As she opened the door, Redbone appeared from behind her and scooted through the doorway. Her grandfather looked up.

"Well, you talked him into it," Tom said, smiling slightly. "I figured he was going to take a while before forgiving us for taking off. You must be," he said with a mock serious tone, "blessed with a golden tongue worthy of a politician."

Ellen forced a smile and shrugged and was glad he turned back to his chili quickly. She paused in the doorway, taking a second.

I can't let him know I know, and I've got to figure out what to do.

For the second time that weekend, she reached inside herself and found the strength needed to do what she figured had to be done.

But even as she joined her grandfather in preparing supper, her mind was roiling with the realization.

Grandpa Tom is killing people.

And   what   would   she   do   about   it?

Chapter 33

Davidson sent JJ home as soon as some of the task force agents returned late Sunday. When he left, the mood was hopeful that something would break but there were no arrests, despite the widespread violence.

The DEA agent turned over command to one of the returning agents, making a small joke about getting more sleep driving to Dayton and back then he and JJ had gotten all weekend, and walked out to the parking lot with JJ.

"I got a feeling," he said.

"Maybe it's gas," JJ replied, stifling a yawn as he started to stretch his arms wide.

Davidson grinned in the darkness. "Maybe so; that's the last time we order pizza from a place named after an Irishman." He walked JJ to his car.

"But all we need is one Rider to get picked up who's gotten involved in any of these hits. We could lever that into the lead we need."

JJ unhooked his keys from the hook on his belt and clumsily found the ones for his car among the dozen or so. He turned towards Davidson.

"If one is caught, if he's got a case over him, if the locals let us at him, if he knows anything, and if we can get him to cooperate...it still feels like a long shot to me."

"Long shot?" Davidson snorted in derision. "It's damned near intercontinental." He blew his nose. "But we haven't had much luck tracking the chemicals and we haven't gotten any of the few mules we've picked up transporting to roll over. And in this place," he gestured out towards the night-hidden rural landscape, "they could have a hundred labs set up and we would never run across them unless we walked every square foot shoulder to shoulder."

"Hell, boss," JJ said, finally sliding the right key into the door lock, "we could use the exercise."

Davidson grinned and shoved his handkerchief into a back pocket.

"Take it easy driving home, JJ," he said, turning away. He stopped and turned back as JJ slid behind the wheel, the door still open. "By the way, you did some good work in that briefing. This whole weekend, for that matter. Glad you were on board."

He turned away before JJ said anything. JJ looked at the retreating back of the heavyset federal agent for a moment.

"Thanks, boss."

Now it was Monday morning and JJ slowly emerged from the same car. The lot was almost full; most of the task force agents must be back already. He was glad Davidson had told him to come in later than usual but it was hard for him to stay away even two additional hours. He still felt tired but contemplation of his first cup of coffee from the communal urn steeled him.

As he opened the glass door, he felt electricity in the air. Cops gave off vibes and the ones last night were depressing, reflecting the lack of a break.

This was entirely different. JJ knew the feeling. You picked it up even when it wasn't about your case. When someone else had finally scored a breakthrough on a tough one, every cop in the place seemed to vibrate with the excitement, like tuning forks sensitive to the same frequency. It was in the air of the task force.

JJ stuck his head in the big office area, waved to Anne and then went down the hall to the lunch room. He had learned within weeks of becoming a cop that the best way to learn what was going on was to get next to the coffee machine.

There were several agents standing around, sipping at their coffee and talking quietly. He poured himself a cup and nodded to the others, acting nonchalant. He had also learned that if you came right out and asked, you tended to get misdirected.

Karen Deevers was one of the agents. Her short, trim figure reminded JJ of an athlete. Her hair, which seemed to have difficulty deciding whether it was reddish brown or blondish brown in the office lights, was vaguely straight – or at least straighter than when he first noticed it – and was still worn in the short style he saw when they were shooting together that he would have described as, "Stay the hell out of my eyes."

She had left her jacket at her desk and JJ noticed that she was carrying two pistols, one in a side holster, canted forward for a fast draw, and looked to be an FBI-issue ten millimeter automatic. In the small of her back was a Paraordnance .45 caliber automatic, one of those that held a dozen rounds. He noticed it was carried cocked and locked. Apparently, the lady liked guns.

She caught him studying her and smiled at him but didn't say anything. He grinned to cover his embarrassment and found a reason to turn away.

OK, you've gawked the women. Now, how about getting to work?

He walked back to his desk, feeling a little silly. What the hell was going on with him that now he was suddenly getting stirrings of interest in another cop, interest which was not entirely professional?

As he got to his desk, Davidson appeared in the doorway and hooked a finger at him. Still gripping his coffee cup, he went over to him.

"Get a good night's sleep?" Davidson walked down the hallway and JJ followed.

"Yep, just what the doctor ordered."

At his office door, the DEA agent turned and smiled. "I hope so. I think you're going to need it."

Davidson sat behind his desk and motioned JJ to one of the chairs in front of it. This indicated, JJ knew from past experience, that something official was about to come down.

"Deputy Jeffers," Davidson began, his voice clear and precise, the title further underscoring the official-business atmosphere, "the task force has come into information suggesting the location of a criminal enterprise. In your capacity as Butler County liaison, we would like you to request the mobilization of the Butler County Sheriff's Office SWAT Team as soon as possible."

Then he sat silent for a moment and just looked at JJ, who saw the merriment in his eyes. Finally, JJ could control himself no longer.

"For God's sake, Carl, what do you have?"

Davidson folded both hands in front of him as if about to pray. His face lit up around a smile Alice's Cheshire Cat would have been proud of.

"Yesterday morning Dayton PD walked right into three Steel Riders ambushing a Dragon and a civilian. When the dust settled, the Dragon was dead, the civilian was WIA and on her way to the hospital, and Dayton PD had blown away two of the Riders. The third," he paused for dramatic effect, "surrendered. They held onto him for twelve hours before letting any of the feds know." He made a brushing movement with his hand, choosing to ignore the possible slight. "No autopsy, no foul. The thing is, they have this guy abso-fuckin'-lutely cold. Not only did two of Dayton's finest see him put a bullet into the prone body of the decedent, they managed to have their traffic video camera running as they drove up onto the scene. They got the dumb bastard on tape."

JJ was smiling by now, caught up in Davidson's excitement, and started to speak but the federal agent held up a hand.

"It gets better." He paused again, obviously savoring the moment. "So they call us, our guys go on over, and they encounter an assistant DA who's very interested in looking good to the feds and he is nothing but cooperation itself. He goes in and tells the guy that if he cooperates he won't go for murder one. The Rider is shell shocked. They've shown him the tape, they got two cops as eye witnesses, he's seen their statements, and he saw his two partners get blown away in front of him. His lawyer is a public defender, not one of the shills for the Riders, so he's urging a deal and not trying to protect the organization." He rubbed his hands together. "So he's going to plead to a lesser penalty and he's given us what we want."

"JJ, how'd you like to bust a methamphetamine lab?"

Chapter 34

Ellen awoke from a restless night with a sense of dread. She lay in bed, reluctant to leave its security and face the day. All her efforts to direct her thoughts to something else failed, which made her feel even more miserable.

The problem seemed unsolvable. If her grandfather was killing people (she kept jerking her thoughts away from the word "murder"), and she no longer could find a way to hide from that reality, then...

Then what?

Ever since Ellen became aware of the nature of her own father, her perpetually angry and unapproachable father, and that of her caring but withdrawn mother, she had relied on her grandfather as her source of security, a sense that there was something she could depend on.

Ellen knew other kids who came from families like hers, intact officially but actually made up of loose shards which happened to be rattling around in the same box. And the kids of the single parent families, the two parent working families, the "blended" families, all the descriptions for the shattered nature of, what?, what seemed to be most of a generation's families.

It left children without roots and she saw the results of that every day. Kids were willing to do anything to belong, and what the other kids did became their touchstone. If the other kids were doing drugs or having sex or engaged in that broad phrase, "getting into trouble," then so be it.

The kids who couldn't or wouldn't or weren't allowed in, who weren't able to join by paying such dues, often were the isolated ones, the ones in class staring blankly out the window with nowhere to go and no one to go to.

Only a few were able to rise above the wreckage of their families and find something, someone, else to hold onto because there was often nothing. Ellen knew her own sense of despair – though she would not have used the word – was held off by the firm grip of her grandfather's hand. With that gift of security, she had not retreated from the world.

Instead, she was like an explorer charting new areas who could always return to a base camp. Her willingness to get involved at school, to push herself in her studies, to try new activities, to counter the pressures of the other kids, and, most importantly, to overcome the sickness of heart at not having her parents as close as she wanted and needed was all due to having one adult in her life who unconditionally loved her and could communicate that love on a frequency she could hear.

Ellen knew Grandpa Tom was more than support for her. That was the problem. She knew he still loved her. But he was also her guide.

Everything seems to just be crap except Grandpa Tom.

That was the critical point for her. In a time of trumpeted moral ambiguities, he was a constant. He offered no exceptions, no excuses; he did what was right, every time, or so it had always seemed to her.

Her father played loose with right and wrong, she knew, reducing everything to a battle between himself and "them." In his life as war, the ends always justified the means. She had seen his delight at finding some way to use the law, to bend the point of a contract, to twist things to his own advantage, and had also seen her mother's embarrassed smile and turning away of eyes after giving her a glance of shame.

It seemed that everything she heard about at school, on television, from her friends, reinforced the idea that there was no right or wrong, that everything was made of soft clay.

Some of her schoolteachers seemed unwilling or unable to take a stand, to simply say that something was wrong to do. Indeed, they seemed to become nervous approaching such issues, as if afraid of violating some law themselves. Instead, they tried to adopt some middle course that never took a moral position. Ellen and her friends interpreted that as a lack of a moral position; in effect, to children's ears, an encouragement to do whatever they wanted.

The world around her offered no better stability. In the brief offerings of what passed for news, she had the sense that the soap operas had drifted into the nightly news broadcasts. What was supposed to be serious was offered with the same trappings as MTV. The people on the news, the politicians, the leaders, were, even to her eyes, clearly engaged in games involving their own advancement. While they used the language, none were really interested in doing what was right.

Among her friends, for the most part, the ongoing lessons taught by school, family, and the world were readily absorbed, even embraced, as an excuse for license. As children, even teenagers, they were not yet acquainted with the reality of outcomes. The world seemed designed to protect them from consequences and also seemed to encourage actions whose goal was nothing more complex than their own gratification.

Ellen had friends who stole from their own families even though they were provided with everything. She had friends who routinely lied to their parents even when the lying gained them nothing. These things were done in order to do them, as if the actions themselves offered a counterpoint to the moral chaos around them.

And they did. By engaging in such behavior and worse, a child could belong, could be a part of the subfamily of other children growing up without roots, without adults to relate to. It was not accidental that children were quick to tell one another of such deeds. These were their entry fees, their identity cards, to join the group.

Ellen knew that there were other kids whose lives were on firm paths, who had parents, or even that rare teacher, or some adult, who gave them a sense of direction, but they seemed to be the minority.

Certainly, outside of her grandfather, there were few adults in her life who had done this for her.

Grandpa Tom never sat down with her and preached a set of commandments, though if he had she would have listened. He reserved his words and used them sparingly, which increased their value to her. Instead, he taught by example. He did not lie, or cheat, or steal, yes, but much the same could be said of other adults she knew, like her teachers, like her mother. But there was more.

He offered lessons by what he did, not just by what he avoided. When she was troubled, he was there. When a neighbor needed a hand, he was there. When a job on the farm had to be done, he did it the best way he could. She saw his behavior and it legitimized his words.

She still remembered, from several years ago, when she got in trouble at school. She and some other girls had stolen another girl's backpack and found her lunch money in it. When the theft was discovered, her parents were called in.

Her mother was embarrassed and silent, saying nothing. Her father scolded her for doing something that required him to interrupt his workday and for being stupid. Not wrong, stupid. She had been only nine but she understood the difference.

Two weeks later her grandfather was over at her house for dinner, something that never happened any more. Her father mentioned the incident over dinner, phrasing it in the context of his embarrassment, his frustration with the school authorities that they couldn't handle something so insignificant.

Her grandfather looked at her across the table. When her father paused in his rant, Grandpa Tom quietly asked if she had apologized.

Her eyes widened with surprise and she turned towards her father and made a brief apology for his inconvenience. Her grandfather shook his head.

"That's fine, but who did you really hurt in all this?"

She looked at him in confusion. They hadn't hurt anyone, not really.

"If your things had been stolen, how would you have felt?"

It was the first time anyone had introduced the idea of empathy to her, at least in terms of the consequences of her actions. It was a simple, small moment with no grandiose speeches. Nonetheless, Ellen knew she would remember those words for the rest of her life.

She apologized to the girl whose backpack she had stolen and returned her share of the money, and then some, from her own allowance. The other girl was surprised and then wary; no one did that kind of thing.

When she told Grandpa Tom the next time they met he just nodded his head and looked her in the eye.

"Good girl."

Simple words, softly spoken, and she felt like she received every prize, every treasure in the world.

But now she had to confront, to question, her grandfather's behavior, and she never had to do so before. She never imagined that she would ever have to.

Killing people was the worst thing she could think of. On her scale of things, it went so far beyond the stealing of a backpack as to be out of sight. She had difficulty imagining people killing Eileen and tried to fit it into the category of accidents, though the law had treated it differently.

What Grandpa Tom was doing was not an accident. She had seen the notebook. He planned this. He was, and she remembered the bayonet with its thin lines, keeping score.

She was afraid, but not because she thought he might do something bad to her or even that he would be caught. That thought did not occur to her.

Ellen was afraid because the one adult in her life who she felt would do no wrong was doing the worst wrong she could imagine.

It was as if, while climbing up a steep, slippery slope, she discovered the boulder she had paused on to rest and gather her strength was not firmly in the ground and was sliding free with her still sitting on it. What she knew, what she thought she knew, was changing, and she didn't know what to do about it.

Ellen pulled on her jeans and a sweatshirt. Outside, the day was opening up and looked to be full of sunlight and rolling white clouds.

She needed, she decided, to talk to someone about this. But who? Obviously, none of her friends. They wouldn't be able to keep something like this a secret and, in any case, she didn't believe they would be able to help her deal with it.

Her parents? She toyed with the idea again for a moment, batting it around in her mind like Redbone did with the occasional toys she brought him. No, that wouldn't go anywhere, she decided. Her father would just get angry – which was pretty much a constant, anyway – and her mother would probably be solicitous but little else.

Ellen needed things explained, to have her world back on its proper tilt. She thought about going to Grandpa Tom and found she was too afraid, though she could not say of what. The thought What if he can't explain? came floating to the surface. She hurried her mind on.

Were there any other adults who might understand, might be able to help, and would keep the secret?

The face of her Aunt Catherine came into focus. There was that moment on the porch when she discovered the woman was not so scary and cared about her. She had also gotten a sense of something, maybe from the porch, maybe from what she had overheard about Catherine, something about her compassion and, very importantly, her strength.

Catherine, she decided, could keep a secret. Ellen decided, as she slipped on her Nikes, that she would call Aunt Catherine.

The making of the decision to talk to someone, like adopting the idea she was wrong she had earlier, allowed the tension she was carrying to ease. It was like the morning sky brightened a bit more, or at least she could see it now. She went down the steps two at a time.

Chapter 35

For an August morning, it was cool, but JJ felt the beginning of the heat and humidity which would gradually lay across the countryside like a heavy, glowing blanket of ever increasing density. No breeze came in through his car's open windows. More clearly felt than the heat was the growing tension.

Beside him, Davidson had taken off his coat and loosened his tie. A hand held portable radio lay on the seat between them.

Their car was positioned nose first in a large square of woods. To their immediate left was another car holding four task force agents. Beyond, and out of sight, was their target. They had been waiting for almost two hours.

Most of that time was spent waiting for the SWAT team to assemble. Unlike in the movies, being a SWAT team member was not a full time position, at least not in Butler County. All the deputies on the team had other assignments and were called in as the need dictated. It took the better part of an hour to contact everyone, get them equipped, and fully briefed.

The rest of the time was spent as the team, clad in military-style camouflage fatigues, slowly took up position around the suspected speed lab.

JJ glanced down at the map attached to the car's radio clipboard. The lab apparently was in one of several outbuildings making up a farm listed as belonging to a Donald Jones. The Sheriff's Office had nothing on him and NCIC and other computer-based checks were still in progress. Located in the western edge of the county, close to the Indiana border, the farm was set in an area with wooded plots and heavy tree lines; observation from the road was pretty well blocked. It fit in nicely with JJ's map project, he noticed, and grinned to himself.

It would have been nice…

About two miles away the task force team that would enter the farm waited in two unmarked vans provided from the government pool of confiscated vehicles. The SWAT team's job was to secure the perimeter and serve as back-up; they were not going to go in kicking down doors.

The Ohio Highway Patrol had a chopper available but it stayed well out of sight to the east. Likewise, an ambulance with paramedics was in the same parking lot as the task force vans.

The radio hissed to life.

"Five is green."

That was the last of the SWAT units to get into position.

"Boss, everything is green." The SWAT commander confirmed what they were hearing.

"Roger that," Davidson replied, lifting the radio to his mouth. "Break, break, Steve, do you copy everything is green?"

"Roger, boss, we are rolling," came the slightly weaker response. JJ could picture the two vans rolling out of the mini-mall parking lot, the ambulance following as far as the turn off from the main road to the dirt track leading to the farm buildings. He switched on the car's ignition and backed out of their hiding place, looking over his shoulder. He heard Davidson calling in the helicopter to an orbiting position as he maneuvered. The other car waited until he was on the road and then followed.

They arrived at the mailbox swing-off on the other side of the road from the farm lane just before the entrance team did. They watched as the two vans pulled onto the lane and sped down it as fast as safety would permit. The ambulance parked in front of JJ's vehicle while the two marked cars gingerly picked their way onto the shoulder on either side of the lane entrance.

Tactical command was with Steve Johnson in the first van; Davidson didn't like to armchair quarterback his people when they were up against it. They heard Steve double-checking with the SWAT commander, hidden in the woods beyond the farm, as the vans disappeared for a moment behind their own dust clouds.

JJ got out the car and raised a pair of binoculars. He could just see through the trees glimpses of the main house, a large barn with faded, peeling paint, and several large equipment buildings. One had a sagging roof. As he tried to scan the area, he saw no movement but it was hard to get that kind of detail through the blocking trees. From what he saw, the farm itself looked pretty damned raggedy-assed. Buildings needed paint, the main house had some loose shingles on its roof, there was an abandoned truck off to one side with weeds growing up around it, and the yard and immediate area needed mowing.

The vans entered his field of view. He saw the agents, all carrying guns and clad in black, spilling out of the vans as they slid to a halt. Several raced up to the main house, taking the steps three at a time. Most of them headed for the other structures.

The lab was believed to be in a building directly behind the barn and that's where most people were headed. He turned towards Davidson, who was studying the map and listening to the agents call back terse numbers, indicating which building they were checking, and the single word, "Clear!" Each call seemed to take away some of the tension which floated in the air.

Davidson looked up just as Steve's voice came up. "Boss, area secure. We have entrance. Lab is secure. Come on down."

"Roger, copy. Break, break, perimeter team leader, you are cleared to move your team forward."

They heard the acknowledgment of the SWAT commander and his orders to bring his team in from their hiding positions to form a closer circle around the buildings.

"Let's go," Davidson said, and JJ got the car rolling. As he turned into the lane with the other task force car close behind, the two Sheriff's cars took up position to block off the lane, their lights now flashing.

The land dipped downward slightly for a brief distance, as if diving underneath the enclosing trees. As they approached the front of the house, it rose again and Davidson pointed to one side. JJ snatched a look as he tried to steer through the ruts and saw a green-painted box attached low on a tree.

"Alarm system," Davidson observed as JJ braked the car to an abrupt halt.

The SWAT team members were in sight now, formed in a loose circle around the farmhouse and the outbuildings. The task force agents who made the building entries mostly stood in front of their various targets. JJ saw the farm had not received the kind of ongoing maintenance you would expect. The place was neglected and, for someone raised around farms and had affection for them, was depressing to look at.

He and Davidson got out of the car. Davidson took the radio and they heard the agents tersely talking back and forth to one another as they explored the area.

Steve Johnson, wearing a black uniform made bulky by the bullet resistant vest over it, walked up to them while slinging his H and K submachine gun over one shoulder. He had a gas mask pushed up on his forehead.

"Looks like no one's home except in the lab, where we found three." He pulled the mask free and wiped the sweat off his brow. "Apparently they've had a failure in their ventilation system and the rest of their people went out to get parts to get it fixed. I guess they won't be coming back any time soon." He gestured with his thumb towards the house. "The house was just used as sleeping quarters, but we'll do a thorough exam as soon as we finish with the lab. What I'd like to do is have all nonessential people stay well clear until it's properly ventilated." He shook his head in disbelief. "Those jerks had gone ahead and kept working even with the ventilation system shut down. They just propped the door open with a chair."

JJ and Davidson looked at each other as they followed Steve to the lab. Large methamphetamine labs, because of the chemicals used in processing, especially ether, could literally be bombs. JJ knew from the literature that such places typically were well ventilated, sometimes even out in the open, though he had never seen one for real.

They followed Steve up a drive running between the main house and barn. It was badly rutted from erosion. JJ kicked at a jutting rock, sending it bouncing ahead. Another thing these assholes weren't taking care of.

The ground rose as they came abreast of the house and he saw it continued to gently climb into a brush and woods covered hill.

The first thing JJ noticed was the smell. He couldn't put his finger on what it was; certainly ether was involved, but there was something else – a lot else! – as well. It was strong and got stronger as they approached the lab itself, which looked like it was constructed in a large chicken coop, about seventy feet long. Single-storied with a canted roof, it had the same degree of neglect as the other farm buildings. At one end he saw a door open, held in place by an ancient kitchen chair. Taped to the inside of the door was a hand-lettered sign that said:

Don't Smoke In Here, Asshole!!!!

JJ was reminded of the smell of a hospital crossed with the worst chemical spill he could remember. He couldn't imagine working in there without adequate ventilation.

They took Steve's advice and didn't attempt to enter. Several task force agents clustered in the doorway, taking notes on what they saw. JJ noticed they didn't use their electronic flash-equipped cameras. Was the danger of explosion that great?

Off to one side stood the three lab workers, their wrists handcuffed behind their backs. Davidson walked up behind the agents interrogating them for a moment while JJ studied the three.

They were remarkably alike. As JJ studied the three, he would have believed Auschwitz had come to Ohio. It was not just they were thin; they were malnourished. Their eyes were red rimmed, their hair, generally worn long, was listless and dry, all the life sucked out of it. They seemed to sway slightly while talking, as if there was a breeze present that only they could feel. He saw sores on their skin, like they hadn't bathed in several weeks, an observation corroborated by adolescent-like pimples on their faces and necks.

JJ knew prolonged working in such labs could be devastating to health but this was the first time he had seen such people. He felt an urge to take a shower, as if their filth was contagious. Davidson turned away to meet another agent and JJ was glad to follow.

He didn't catch what the agent said but saw he was pointing out beyond the lab and Davidson immediately went striding off. As they turned the corner of the lab JJ saw a large concrete slab, maybe six feet by six feet, on which sat an industrial sized air conditioner.

The slab's crisp edges testified to its newness. The metal of the air conditioner was likewise shiny and new. A panel on top was thrown back, probably from an earlier attempt to fix it. He saw a galvanized metal tube, maybe a foot wide, going from it directly into the wall of the lab. A similar tube emerged from the other side but then made a right-angled turn into the earth, which seemed a more than a little odd.

To one side were two, large wooden pallets, each loaded with flat cardboard boxes of varying sizes. Steel ribbons held the loads in place. As he passed, he saw they were labeled as the components of an aluminum garden shed. Probably they were planning to cover the air conditioner.

Up ahead Davidson and the agent stopped and were talking with one of the SWAT team members who cradled a long barreled rifle with a telescopic sight in his arm like a back-country hunter. The officer turned and the other two followed with JJ close behind. Davidson used the radio to report his whereabouts.

The ground continued to rise slowly as they encountered low brush, mostly of thorn-armed berry bushes.

JJ saw the thin path the SWAT sniper followed into the low wall of brush. At first he thought it was an animal trail but he saw quickly it was entirely too straight. As he started into the bushes, he had to pause to unhook a thorn in his pant leg. He looked back towards the lab. Oddly, the straight path aimed directly at the lab; in fact, right at the air conditioner.

As they went deeper, trees appeared, though few were of any real size. The berry bushes quickly fell behind them, for which JJ and his thin pants were grateful. The heat was held by the foliage and JJ saw the sweat soaking through the back of Davidson's shirt.

Suddenly there was a barn in front of them, or rather the remains of one. Long since abandoned, its black painted wood walls had begun to collapse from rot and the weight of vines. Near one end, a silo, made of cinder block, still stood. Another SWAT team member, this one carrying an H and K similar to that of the federal agents, stood by an open, small metal door near the base of the silo.

Davidson handed the radio to JJ and then dropped to his knees and stuck his head inside the door. He could have wiggled on through if he wanted, but a quick examination was all he needed, He backed out and, dusting off his pants as he got up, told JJ to take a look.

It was lighter inside the silo than he expected. The silo roof was partially torn away. Natural decay caused some of it, but the rest was clearly the work of people, judging by the new boards hammered into place. The opening allowed the high sun in. What caught his eye was a metal air duct, similar in composition and size to the ones he had seen attached to the lab air conditioner, running up the inside of the silo wall. At the top of the silo, covered by a portion of the intact roof but otherwise open to the air, was a rotating ventilation cover. The ducting itself was attached to the cinder blacks by aluminum straps, each securely riveted in place. He carefully backed out.

"What they did was run the exhaust pipe all the way out here in a shallow trench," Davidson said, explaining the trail they followed. "They not only wanted to get the fumes as far away from the lab as possible, they wanted to get the stench away as well. After all, there was always the possibility of someone making a wrong delivery and driving up here."

They walked back out of the woods.

"I've seen speed labs in towns where they ran ventilation ducts from the basement all the way up onto the roof of a tenement building. You see a lot of that near Miami and in LA."

JJ nodded. "What about those guys? They looked totally messed up." One of the SWAT team gave a soft, "Amen."

"That's typical," Davidson replied, working his way around the thorns of a blackberry bush. "They'll use masks sometimes because of the chemicals involved in processing, but remember that they're making methamphetamine in an atmosphere saturated with ether. It gets absorbed one way or the other. Appetites tend to fall off, they fatigue quickly, and generally fall apart. Stop taking care of themselves."

They emerged into the sunlight and walked down the gentle slope towards the lab.

"We busted one lab in LA. It was being run by Mexicans. They didn't ever let their people out, they slept in the lab, ate there. Hell, half of them didn't realize they'd been arrested for two days." He shook his head. "The processing doesn't take a lot of smarts. It's pretty repetitious. So once you teach them, all you have to do is back off, supply them, take away the product, and pay them, if you want."

By now they were near the front of the lab. No one had ventured in yet.

"How long do you think it will take before it's safe?" JJ asked, looking towards the open doorway.

Davidson gave a small laugh. "It'll never be safe, not perfectly, until all the chemicals are removed. Ether is highly volatile and I figure these guys have tended to disregard most OSHA guidelines for the handling of HAZMAT."

They walked on back to their car. "The first lab I was ever called in to investigate was one that had blown up by accident. The locals thought it was just a conventional fire until they found a guy stumbling around the street, totally in shock. He had third degree burns over fifty per cent of his body. He was blown through a wall by the explosion. We found his imprint in the wallboard – looked like something out of a Roadrunner cartoon. You could even see his fingers." He shook his head. "Incredible. Anyway, once he could talk, he said that he wasn't sure but he thought a spark had gone off in a ventilation fan. Scratch one speed lab. And the building it was in. And most of the surrounding block."

When they returned to the car, they heard a weak call over the portable radio, asking for their location. Davidson responded but had to repeat himself before he was heard. He looked at the radio.

"I think the batteries are beginning to fade," he said, frowning.

"I got new spares in the glove compartment," JJ told him.

Davidson nodded and sat down on the passenger seat while he made the exchange. "I got to get one of those Motorola rechargeable radios." JJ heard the snap of the radio case closing.

"What do you want me to do with these empties?" Davidson asked.

"Just stick'em back in the glove compartment; I'll take care of them later."

Davidson got back out of the car and laid the radio on the roof and looked over at JJ.

"This is good work, one of the first payoffs we've gotten from the war. Maybe this marks the turning point," Davidson said.

JJ was about to reply when he saw Steve jogging towards them. They turned towards him as he arrived. His look was grim.

"Boss, we got some word I think you ought to hear. One of the suspects we have says this is not the main lab. He said they've got so much business that their big lab couldn't handle it all, so this was a satellite. He also said he heard that others were going to be set up."

"Shit," JJ said.

"Where's the main lab?" Davidson asked.

"That's the bad news," Steve replied. "None of them claim to know. They were brought in to work in this lab from one down in Kentucky that accidentally burned down. They never saw the other one. Maybe one of the others who we didn't get knows, but these guys are saying they don't have a clue. He says they have a lot of product done, bagged, and just sitting in there, waiting for pickup."

"Well, let's see what they say after we've had a chance to work on them a bit," Davidson said. Steve nodded and jogged back to the lab.

"What do you think?" JJ asked.

Davidson sighed and swept his hand over his bald head. "I have a feeling that they're telling the truth. I mean, why would they know? Bad security to spread that kind of information around." He looked at JJ. "Still, not a bad day's work and we may get some good leads out of this place once we take it apart." He tightened his tie and reached into the car for his coat.

"Let's go find the SWAT commander; I want to thank him for his team's work." He pulled the coat on as they walked. "And then let's see if we can't nail the rest of these bastards."

Chapter 36

Ellen tried to put off the call to Aunt Catherine by finding things to keep herself busy. She curled up with her PowerBook to work on a paper she was writing for the Chess Club that she was supposed to present when school resumed next month. It worked a little, but after Grandpa Tom got out the tractor and trailer to go work on some fencing her ability to distract herself began to weaken.

Her first efforts to call met with no success. She had a small moment of panic when she suddenly realized she didn't know Catherine's number, but there was a red directory beside the telephone in the living room and Catherine Parker was easy to find.

She encountered an answering machine the first three times she called but left no message, too nervous to say anything, a little grateful at the excuse not to.

The chess paper sat on the computer's display, going nowhere. The more she stared at it, the more it became undecipherable hieroglyphics. She quit her word processor and tried to get into a game but that, too, could not hold her attention. She sat passively as aliens blew her little spaceship into a fireball three times in a row and a message across the screen proclaimed it was the end.

Who cares?

Grandpa Tom came back briefly for lunch. It was a quiet meal as they sat and ate sandwiches made of leftover roast. He spread a newspaper beside his plate and she concentrated on her sandwich as if it held some vital clue to the meaning of life. They said little, which was not unusual, until the end of the meal.

"What's on your agenda for today?" Tom asked.

"Oh, nothing," Ellen replied. "Been trying to work on this stupid paper for Chess Club," she said with a touch more anger and frustration than she had meant to let out. Tom raised an eyebrow.

"Well, hang in there with it. You'll get it done." He got up and cleared the table, putting the plates in the sink.

"I've got about an hour or two more to do. When I get back, you want to run into town with me? There's something I need to get."

"Sure," she said, trying to keep her face neutral. "That'd be fine. What do you need to get?"

"Oh, just some stuff," he said, walking towards the backdoor. He turned and winked. "Maybe a surprise." He stepped outside as Redbone vaulted in, just clearing his tail before the screened door swung shut.

Ordinarily, Ellen would have been intrigued, but all she felt was anxiety. The overwhelming problem of her grandfather and what to do seemed to be filling up all her thoughts.

She walked back into the living room as she heard the tractor driving off. She punched in Catherine's numbers. It rang twice and then a woman's voice came on.

"Hello?" Ellen could tell it wasn't Catherine. For a second, she thought about hanging up, but her desperation kept her hand on the receiver.

"Hello," she replied. "Is Catherine Parker there?"

"No," the strange woman's voice said. "She's having a brown-bag committee meeting at school. She'll be back in an hour. Would you like to call her back?" The woman had a nice voice, very calm.

"Could she call me when she gets home? I'm Ellen Parker and I'm at my grandfather's house. Could you tell her it's very, very important?" She heard her own need creeping into her voice and she felt embarrassed.

"Yes, I'll let her know. Are you all right?" The woman apparently could hear her anxiety as well.

"Yes, I'm fine, I just need to talk to Aunt Catherine as soon as possible, please."

"All right, I'll be sure she gets your message." The woman paused for a moment. "I'm Terri, by the way; that's with an 'I'. I'm," there was another pause, "a good friend of your aunt's. If there's anything I can do..." Her voice trailed off.

"No, it's OK, thank you. Just let Aunt Catherine know I called. Goodbye." She hung up, her hand trembling. She didn't understand why but she felt like she wanted to cry.

189

Chapter 37

Catherine suffered through the committee meeting with what she considered good grace. It was awkward having such a meeting during the summer sessions but she understood the need to get some things rolling before the regular semester began. Unfortunately, this meant the handful of faculty still around in August made decisions that effected everyone.

The real problem with such meetings was, of course, that they ever took place. University faculty tended to be talkative. Some of them were known to never use one word where they could fit in seven. As statistically improbable as it was, the extreme garrulous fringe of the school's instructors seemed to make up the majority of the fifteen or so attending the meeting.

Catherine demolished the fruit she brought, chewing her way through two apples in an effort to keep herself from giving voice to her frustration. It was clear to her the more inconsequential the point under discussion, the more people had to say and, indeed, the more people wanted to say something.

Her department chair flashed her a smile and slightly shook her head as some nontenured member of the Physics Department droned on into greater obscurity than his immediate predecessor, who Catherine thought had climbed new heights of inconsequentiality.

Finally, it was over. She swept her notepads into her bag, pushed a stray hair out of her face, and stood to leave. There was a thesis proposal back in her office she had to review and this would be a good time to get it done. She turned to the door when one of her department's graduate students came through it.

"Dr. Parker, Mrs. Simmons asked me to get this message to you." The male grad student was slightly out of breath but smiled at Catherine's thanks. He left as Catherine unfolded the yellow message form. It was carefully filled out; Mrs. Simmons, the department secretary, was meticulous.

Date/Time: 8/11/95 12:51 PM
To: Dr. C. Parker

From: Terri Stoneroad
Wants you to: (the box next to CALL BACK was checked)
Message: Ellen called. Wants you to call back. Seems important.

Catherine frowned slightly, wondering what was going on. Terri was not given to exaggeration. In fact, she tended to be a bit understated. She folded the note, stuffed it into her book bag and walked quickly outside, heading for her office.

Catherine thoroughly enjoyed teaching and, to only a slightly lesser extent, writing. She preferred the campus in the summer, though not because of the fewer people. During the summer there was less of the academic business and politics going on and she found it difficult to involve herself in such things.

Summer also brought with it a slightly more informal atmosphere. Students were more likely to approach and were more approachable. The pressure seemed to be off, or at least less, and it was possible to do more real teaching.

The frustrating thing about teaching, especially at the graduate level, was the state of fear most students seemed to live in. Grades were the primary focus and actual learning and comprehension was, for many, a distant second. She remembered the first time a graduate student came into her office to plead her case for a higher grade and ended up crying, describing herself as a failure. The student had gotten a "B." She shook her head.

Her own graduate school experience was not so long ago that she couldn't empathize. She noticed that when two graduate students got together there was a noticeable tension in the air. If there were three, you could recharge batteries with it. If there were four, Geiger counters three buildings away began to flicker. Any more than four and you had a core meltdown and people would run screaming from the room.

It hadn't been that way with her, she knew. Where other students got anxious, she got angry. When she encountered the real world of graduate education, with its artificial hurdles justified only by tradition ("We did it, so you have to as well"), as well as indifferent, sometimes irrational, and even, sometimes, sadistic faculty, she made a conscious decision that no one was going to make her quit.

Catherine used her anger as fuel, as a source of energy to stay disciplined, to make herself do whatever was necessary to get it done. She lived by the grad school credo, "Get it done, get it in, get it approved, and get out."

It worked and worked well. Not only had she finished her degree in near record time, her dissertation proved to be publishable in several parts and became the springboard to her hiring. Indeed, when she thought back on the experience, she felt that fifty per cent of it was just busy work, twenty per cent was personally damaging, and thirty per cent resulted in professional growth; satisfying numbers, as she knew many who reported severe differences in the proportions.

Her second floor office was fortunate. In terms of her seniority, she was relatively new but the Department of Psychology had its quarters in an older building whose faculty offices tended to be, especially when compared to the broom closets of the newer buildings, spacious. She had two windows overlooking the back of the building with as fine a view of the loading dock as you could hope for.

On the right of her desk, an old wooden one she salvaged from basement storage, sat her computer terminal and keyboard. The cursor blinked patiently and dimly in the lower right hand corner of the monitor screen with no mail indicator. She had another computer, a self-contained one not hooked up to outside lines, on a rolling table behind her. To her left was her telephone, its broad face acned with over a dozen buttons, only some of which had she figured out in the past three weeks since its installation.

Catherine had set up the speed dial buttons successfully; she picked up the receiver and fingered the one for her grandfather. She heard it ring several times and then Ellen answered.

"Hello?," came the young girl's voice.

"Ellen? This is Catherine." There was silence and Catherine thought the connection was lost.

"Aunt Catherine," Ellen said. For a moment, that was the only response.

"Ellen, is everything OK?" More silence, Catherine thought she heard Ellen sniffling.

"No," she finally said. "Everything is all wrong." With that, Ellen began crying.

"Ellen, you can talk to me. It's all right," Catherine said, trying to keep the panic out of her own voice, "I'm here and you can talk to me." She began repeating words and phrases of reassurance, trying to get Ellen to calm down, trying to find out what was wrong. She had to struggle to push down her own demon thoughts that came erupting from the darker corners of her mind.

Has she been hurt? Is Dad all right? Has someone hurt her? Has she been..?

She clamped down hard on that last one. Ellen needed her attention and her own ghosts would remain buried.

Finally, the young girl quieted down. Catherine kept talking, helping her to become calmer.

"Ellen, what's happened, what's going on, honey?"

She heard Ellen sniff and then inhale, as if gathering her strength.

"Aunt Catherine, could I see you and talk to you? It's really, really important." The tension grew in her voice.

"No problem, Big E. I'd be very happy to get together with you. Do you want me to come out to the farm or..."

"No, no, I'll get Grandpa Tom to bring me in to see you. Where are you going to be?"

Catherine thought quickly.

"Would you like to meet me at my house or here on campus? We could go out for a coke or something..."

"Your office; I've been there before. That'll be fine." She heard Ellen taking a deep breath and letting it out. She was calmer. "Grandpa is out fixing a fence but should be back in a half hour or so. Is that OK?"

"That's fine, E. I've got a little paperwork to do so I'll just wait for you." She paused. "Are you OK now?"

"Yes, I'm all right. Thank you, Aunt Catherine." She paused. "Goodbye."

"Goodbye, Ellen," Catherine replied, but didn't hang up until after Ellen did.

She stared at the telephone for a few minutes, wondering about the call. Feeling her own tension beginning to climb as she began to consider the possibilities, she deliberately forced herself to turn to the thesis proposal lying on her desk.

She would just have to wait, she told herself, and then she would learn what was wrong. Whatever it was, she would make sure Ellen got the help she needed.

No   matter   what.

Chapter 38

Tom swung the tractor towards the barn, the trailer carrying the remains of the fence mending tools and material raising a small rooster tail of dust as he travelled down the lane. He turned before the barn, nosing the tractor in beside his car, and then slipped the gears into reverse. Backing up and turning, he carefully passed through the wide doors.

A swing of the wheel allowed him to back the trailer against one wall before stopping. He jumped down and unlocked the hitch. There was a time when he wouldn't have bothered to go through this little dance across the barn floor with the tractor. He would have just backed in, unhitched the trailer, and then pushed it into place with his own strength. He smiled to himself as he climbed back into the tractor seat.

Learned to bless internal combustion over the years.

Tom moved the tractor into its parking position and shut it down. He did a quick walk around, listening to the ticking of the metal as the engine cooled. Satisfied that there was nothing amiss, he went back to the trailer, gathered up the tools and stowed them. Some stayed in the barn but a number went into the work shed.

He double-checked the door lock and then walked to the house, pulling off his heavy work gloves as he bent to give Redbone a scratch behind the ears.

Ellen was in the living room, her computer resting on her lap. She smiled as he entered and he felt a small feeling of relief. She had seemed distracted since their trip down to the river and he feared she still was bothered by her run-in with the boys.

Probably should have done something about it.

Or maybe not. It was damned hard trying to be sure about what a child needed. He didn't have Sarah's unerring knack for knowing what ought to be done and what ought not to be done. And it was sometimes harder for him when it came to the girl children than for the boys. At least with the boys he could imagine he understood what they were dealing with, what they needed.

But Ellen was smiling so maybe he had guessed right after all.

"How's the paper going?" he asked. Tom never had the patience for chess when he was younger. Ellen, on the other hand, showed an early interest and talent for the game. He tried to learn the game in recent years so he could play with her. He knew he wasn't very good, tending to narrow his focus too much and lose the big picture. Nonetheless, Ellen was patient and explained the concepts to him in a way he couldn't get from any of the books or even the chess tutor on his Macintosh.

"Pretty well. Are we still going into town?"

"Yep. I have to swing by Fred's and pick up a few things."

"Oh, good. Aunt Catherine called and I said I'd drop by and see her at her office, 'cause I knew we were going into town. Is that OK?"

Surprised, Tom replied. "Sure. Was it anything special she called about?"

"No," Ellen said, her eyes on the laptop's screen, "She just wanted to chat. I just thought I'd swing by and see her, if that's OK."

Tom thought for a moment. Actually, this wasn't a bad idea. There was a surprise he planned for Ellen and this would help it along.

"Sounds like a good idea. Been awhile since you two got together. If you're all set, we can hit the road as soon as I wash up and change my shirt."

Ellen flashed him a smile and he went to get cleaned up. Yes, this would actually work out fine. She wouldn't have any inkling as to what he was up to.

He   was   planning   to   get   Ellen   a   gun.

Chapter 39

JJ leafed through the pages of reports the task force already had generated from the raid on the lab. Slowly they were removing material from the lab. In the meantime, detailed searches of the other buildings proceeded.

Chased by the growing heat, Davidson and he had returned to the office. Davidson made a preliminary call to the agencies in Washington. Likewise, JJ had let the Sheriff's Office know what happened. They would relay his information to the various police departments throughout the county as well as pass the report on up to Columbus.

The first report said it all: lab was fully operational but had not managed to export any of its product. The raid hit it just before their first scheduled pickup. There were stacks of sealed plastic bags that would never make it to the street. JJ smiled as he remembered one of the red-eyed workers complaining about the cops' timing.

"You work your ass off getting everything set up and then it all turns to shit."

Probably should have told him that could be the motto of most cops, too.

They must have gone into production even while building the place. One of their intelligence guestimates thought the Riders might have problems with cash flow after the loss of the Kentucky lab and were trying to get production up to pay for the expansion into Ohio.

Ain't capitalism a bitch?

JJ felt a savage satisfaction at the seizure of the lab, tempered only by the fact that he was not personally responsible for taking it down. One less pile of maggots in his county. He turned the pages of the reports the search teams were sending in, looking for items he might need to include in his prelim.

Most of the buildings yielded nothing of interest thus far. The main house was basically a large crash pad. Sleeping bags supplemented the beds, the kitchen was a mess, but showed that at least a half dozen people were routinely eating there. That meant that there were at least three residents of that establishment they had not caught.

Well, they were still working on the three they did catch and Davidson was pretty hopeful of getting a lot more from them. JJ thought his hope was on fairly solid ground, given the cooperation they already had provided. He smiled. Davidson really got into the hunt; he hadn't seen the federal agent so excited since he joined the task force.

Karen Deevers sent in a long list of the weapons and ammunition found in the main house with a smaller list of the ones found in the lab. Only one revolver, a Smith and Wesson .357 Magnum. The remaining ten handguns were all automatics of various makes, nearly all nine millimeters.

Two Uzis capable of fully automatic fire were also found, a never fired Winchester pump shotgun in 12-gauge with its department store tag still attached, a MAC-10, modified to be fully automatic, a double-barreled shotgun with the barrels cut off just forward of the stock and the stock cut down and carved into a pistol grip, likewise in 12 gauge. Three Chinese-made AKs. A flare pistol.

What the hell for? In case they went down at sea?

JJ shook his head. These folks seemed to like guns, all right. He flipped the page to the one covering the weapons found in the lab. More nine millimeter pistols, another MAC-10, and a U. S. Army thermite grenade, issue one each.

Christ! They had a thermite grenade in there!

This was astounding. Just pulling the pin on that thing and releasing the spoon might have been enough to send the whole place up.

Come to think of it, maybe that's what it was for. Get surrounded, pull the pin, step outside to surrender, and then duck real quick as the evidence vaporizes in an explosion they would probably hear for a dozen miles. He flipped the page back and checked something.

They found the flare pistol, loaded, in a back corner bedroom on the second floor, along with several spare flares. He checked his rough sketch of the main house. Yes, they had a clear field of fire to the door of the lab from there. So one of the sentries had the job of sending the place to hell if the cops showed up.

They had been very lucky, JJ thought. It would not have been a good thing to have an ether-filled lab explode in their faces. He still didn't have a good grasp of the explosive power of such a place but from what he had heard from Davidson and learned from his courses it would have been something to see.

Say, from about three miles away.

JJ turned back to his terminal, doing a little cut and pasting from the electronic files of the agents' reports. After a few minutes he was satisfied that he had everything in it he needed at this time. He knew Davidson would be sending his own report to Columbus and would send a copy to the Sheriff's Office as well.

One of the outcomes of the drug lab raid was a lifting of the need for secrecy. The news media, bless their black hearts, would be clamoring to get this on the evening news at five in – he glanced at the clock on the wall – just about two hours.

The inevitable interview and press briefing would be handled by Davidson. That's how it was when the feds ran things. One spokesperson and that was it. They controlled the release of information to the media circus and they had long memories about people who tried end runs to get out their own stuff.

JJ wasn't worried. He had a good sense of Davidson. Cursed with having to operate within the Washington bureaucracy, he nonetheless played fair and JJ was confident he would ensure all hands would receive fair mention.

Besides, as the feds knew, eventually they would be gone and then anyone could say anything. So it was in their interest to make everyone look good so no one felt the need to get some coverage at the feds' expense.

JJ stacked the print-outs he examined – always easier to work with than looking at the same information on a computer screen – and put them in a folder. He slid it into the drawer of his desk and started to close it but paused. He reached down and pulled out two files.

One contained his notes on the Steel Rider leadership. The first page was the police summary of Jack Baker.

How're you feeling today, asshole? Just when you felt like you were winning, this place suddenly starts to feel a little small for you. Hang around. It's going to get a lot tighter.

The other contained his notes from the Friday morning presentation. He looked through it briefly, pausing at the slides of Thomas and John Parker.

Haven't forgotten you two.

Just then he heard his name called. He looked up; it was Anne. She was waving to him with a sheet of paper. He got up and went over to her.

"Sorry, deputy," she said, handing it over, "we got this fax while you were out and with everything going on I forgot to put it in your tray." She seemed genuinely worried and JJ took a moment to reassure her that everything was fine.

He went back to his desk and smoothed out the fax. It was from the Franklin, Indiana, Police Department. He glanced at the slides.

Talk about coincidence.

He turned over the cover page and read the brief announcement on the second page. JJ let out a low curse.

They were now able to provide an alibi for John Wesley Parker for two of the three original Steel Rider killings. University faculty thing for one, dinner with friends for the other. Sorry for any inconvenience, etcetera, etcetera.

He took a breath and let it out slowly. Well, that was too bad. He really thought John Parker was a prime contender for his little scenario. He tapped the fax with his fingertips.

That still left Thomas Parker. He slid the old man's slide free of the folder and looked at it. He studied the face intently, trying to find answers to questions in it, but there was nothing.

Are you killing people in my county, old man?

The level eyes of Thomas Luther Parker just looked back at him.

Chapter 40

Catherine, stationed on her building's front steps, saw her father's "town car" pull up to the curb and walked out to meet Ellen. She saw Ellen say something to her grandfather and then the young girl climbed out of the car. Her father waved to her and drove away.

"Hey, Big E," Catherine said, bending slightly to give Ellen a hug. She was a little surprised at the strength with which it was returned.

"Hey," was all Ellen said and clung to her for a moment longer.

When they finally separated, Catherine looked at her closely and saw Ellen's face rippling with emotion.

"Come on, let's go up to my office," she said, and held out her hand, which Ellen took with as little conscious thought as she might have when she was half her age.

The building was largely deserted, for which Catherine was grateful. She had an ancient couch across one wall of her office, jammed in among the bookshelves and she led Ellen to it and sat next to her. There was a moment of silence.

Catherine studied her in the silence. Ellen was getting older and Catherine saw the lines which would define her as an adult. She had a clean, firm jaw and a strong, typical Parker nose. Her eyes looked out from a face that would probably be described as handsome rather than pretty as she got older, but would probably serve her well through her life.

Though thin, Catherine thought she saw her own mother's carriage in Ellen. Her shoulders were a little wide and, if she went that way, would serve as a strong support for the kinds of muscles which marked her mother and, for that matter, her brothers. She had her grandfather's erect stance when she walked, and Catherine suspected it was a conscious copying.

There are worse adults she could model herself after.

"Well, you want to tell me what's going on?" she asked quietly. Ellen had her eyes down, not looking at her, as if she was ashamed of something. Catherine let the silence build. All she did was reach across and take one of her niece's hands.

It was enough. Ellen started crying and then made herself stop. Catherine watched the muscles in her jaw work, but she stopped the tears.

She's got some strength.

"Aunt Catherine, I need you to promise me that you won't tell anyone what I need to talk to you about." Ellen was blinking back a few last tears but she was looking straight into Catherine's eyes. "Ever."

Oh, Christ, she's pregnant!

Catherine took a moment, carefully choosing her words.

"Ellen, I can't write you a blank check like that." She saw the disappointment clouding the young girl's face and hurried on. "If you are in any kind of trouble, if you were in danger, for instance, I might need to call on some other people for help. But I will say this: if I don't have to tell anyone, if your life and safety doesn't depend upon it, I won't tell anyone without your permission. And Ellen," she squeezed her hand firmly, "you have my word about that."

Ellen said nothing and looked down at her lap.

I've blown it. Damn, damn, damn! Why did I have to act like an academic now of all times?

Catherine was about to open her mouth, to make whatever promise Ellen needed, when the young girl spoke.

"All right," Ellen said, nodding slightly. She looked up. "I guess that's about the best anyone could do." She settled back into the couch and began her story.

"Have you been following the news, about the motorcycle gang war going on?"

Catherine nodded; she had secretly rejoiced every time the television announced another one of the bastards face down on the concrete dead somewhere and had felt shame at the primal joy. But she remembered Eileen.

"Do you remember before this past weekend that there were two of the Steel Riders killed over in Middletown? Well, both times, and at a lot of other times, Grandpa Tom was gone from the farm." Catherine's eyes widened silently but she remained silent.

"I don't know," Ellen said, "I was wondering where he was going all those nights. I remembered that when he had trouble sleeping some nights he would go for a ride sometimes." Catherine nodded. "It seemed like too much a coincidence after I found some things in the attic." Here she paused and Catherine saw she was embarrassed as she dropped her gaze.

"I got into Grandpa Tom's old Army chest. It was an accident," she added hurriedly. "It had all kinds of stuff in it, from the war and everything. There were medals and papers and things. I found a citation," she pronounced the word carefully, as if this was the first time she had spoken it aloud, which might, Catherine realized, be the case. "It was about him killing some enemy soldiers in a battle. They gave him a medal. He killed five of them." She looked around the office.

"Then I found a big knife, an Army knife. On the back of the blade there were five lines, cut right into the metal. I knew right away what they meant." She stopped and swallowed and Catherine wondered at what that must have been like for her, while part of her mind realized that this part of her father's life was largely unknown to her.

He never said. We never asked.

"But I told myself that I had figured everything out wrong, that just because he was gone those nights that those two men were killed didn't mean anything, even though they were two of the men who killed Eileen, two of the guys the court let go, remember?"

Catherine nodded. Ellen's eyes were dry now and her voice was clear.

"So I decided I had made a mistake. I mean, I'm just a kid, what do I know?" Ellen gave a little shrug and looked back down at her hands. "And everything was okay." She looked up. "I mean, really, it was okay. Then Grandpa Tom said we could go for an overnight trip down to the river and that was great and everything so we went down Friday and came home Sunday." She shook her head.

"He was out late Thursday night; I saw him come back and saw him take something long, wrapped in a blanket, into the work shed, see, that's where he keeps the guns locked up when we kids are at the farm." She stopped.

"I know," Catherine said, "When I was a girl he locked them in the basement and had a lock on the basement door, but when the basement was remodeled he moved everything out to the work shed." Ellen nodded.

"So on Sunday I heard on the news while he was fixing dinner that another one, one of the five who killed Eileen, was killed Thursday night, the night he was late getting home." She paused, and again Catherine noticed her embarrassment.

"A while before this, after the first two were killed, I found the work shed lock hadn't been set right. Grandpa was gone so I went in. I know," she said hurriedly, "that we kids were forbidden to go in there without permission, but I was upset over him being gone, and was bored, and anyway I went in."

"I found a notebook he was keeping. It had pages of information on the five guys who killed Eileen. Stuff clipped from the newspapers, mostly, and some notes he had added. The two who were dead had big 'X's' across their pages. Well, anyway, that and finding the knife and everything, I sort of panicked but, like I said, I figured it was my mistake." She paused again and took a deep breath.

"The one guy who was killed on Thursday night, that was part of a big shoot-out and everything, but the thing was, it wasn't on the news Thursday night. I know 'cause I saw the late news, right after MST3K, and Grandpa wasn't home until around midnight. And when we left Friday we didn't hear about it, and we didn't listen to the news the whole time we were gone." She smiled weakly.

"Grandpa Tom put me in charge of the radio while he was in charge of the driving, so we listened to music the whole time. If anything like the news came on, I'd dial in a new station." Her smile faded.

"So we got home, I was in the living room, watching TV, and he was fixing dinner," she said, repeating herself. "Then on the news they were covering the gang war that was going on over the weekend and they named the third man, Nicholas Christopher, they said he was killed late Thursday night along with some other guys from the other gang and that had set off the war. Well, I knew who he was and everything. I made up an excuse that I was looking for Redbone, who was acting really stuck up, you know? And Grandpa gave me the key to the work shed. I went out there and checked the notebook. Nicholas Christopher was crossed out, too."

"Aunt Catherine," Ellen said, looking into her aunt's eyes, "he couldn't have known about the guy, because I was with him the whole time, and he hadn't gone out to the shed after we got back. So he had to do it Thursday night, and the only way he would have known Thursday night is if he killed him, and if he killed him, then maybe he killed the other two."

She leaned back into the couch and closed her eyes for a second.

"Aunt   Catherine,"   she   said,   "what   do   we   do?"

Chapter 41

Tom made his way slowly through Oxford. Even though it was summer, there were still enough college students around to make his driving cautious. It was a feature of people of their age, he decided, that they either believed that everyone would make way for them as they walked the streets, or they believed that an encounter between their bodies and a ton or so of metal, plastic, and rubber would only result in a demonstration of their invulnerability.

Over the years, he had his share of the irritation experienced by the local people with the "town and gown" division. He realized, somewhat wryly, that his tendency to be irritated with college students decreased as his own children approached and then entered that sub classification between adult and child.

Tom also realized some of his feelings came from jealousy. Despite his satisfaction with the course his life finally took, there was always the question of what might have been. As he looked back, he sometimes felt he had little choice about the way things had gone, that dealing with things as they arose closed off his chances for something different. Seeing people, the students, with all their choices in front of them, he found it tempting to think that he might make better use of the chances to choose they had.

He shrugged and waited while three young men chasing a softball raced out into the street in front of him.

Sarah said we always choose, even when we don't want to.

She was given, he remembered, to saying such things. Well, she took some college courses, off and on, over the years. He always said he thought it a waste of time, but when no one was looking, he would read some of her text books and never let her sell them back to the bookstores.

It wasn't about a degree. What did letters behind your name have to do with being a farmer, or being a man, for that matter? What it was about was education. When he looked around him, he saw a world filled with things to know, like lakes of cool water seen by a thirsty man.

He envied Ellen. She seemed to know so much, far more than he did when her age. More importantly, he thought, she could get to information, to learning, far more readily than he.

Tom smiled. He had agreed to Charlie's suggestion to get a computer not to help him with his books – he still entered everything in his notebooks before copying them to the electronic spreadsheets – but as a way of getting to learning. He had read articles in the newspapers and seen the discussions on television and saw the computer as a tool to get to the learning he hungered for.

So, quietly, without much talking about it except with Ellen, he had gotten a modem for the computer and a CD-ROM player and plugged them in.

Thank God for Macs. Don't think I could have done it if I'd had to learn the damned machine first.

He carefully read reviews of software, especially the education variety. His growing collection of CD-ROMs included several on art, one on aviation, and a large number on animals. By going online, he tapped into electronic encyclopedia and found others who shared his interests. There was a small group of reloaders, for example, he routinely compared notes with.

He haunted the local public library and all the bookstores in town, including the one run by the university. He had long since lost his feeling of being conspicuous while looking through the popular paperbacks on history, psychology or whatever had fired up his curiosity that month.

He knew he would never catch up to where he might have been. Indeed, he would never catch up with Ellen, whose learning seemed to be accelerating every year. He was amazed at times, listening her talk about what she knew, like birds, or computers, or stars, or whatever. Amazed, yes, proud even.

And a little jealous. He smiled. It seemed to be a little funny to have such a childish emotion at such an age as his.

Tom turned the car into the parking lot of the sporting goods store on the west side of town. It was called "Oxford Sports Equipment" but all the locals just called it "Jamison's," inasmuch as it had been run by the Jamison family since the end of World War Two.

The white building was graced by a particularly bad painting of a deer standing in what appeared to be a blue lava flow – Tom had never seen a stream behave in the way depicted in the picture but he figured that's what "artistic license" was all about.

The front of the store was filled with a variety of team sports gear. There were racks of jerseys of various professional and college teams as well as mannequins draped in sweatshirts and shorts bearing the Miami University logo. Field hockey sticks, basketballs, baseball gloves, and dozens of other items filled the shelves, row upon row.

In back, he encountered a maze of fishing gear, with nets hanging on pegboard, waders spread across shelves, and poles racked into a veritable wall, as if separating the front of the store from the back.

The fishing equipment formed a demarcation line. Past it, one tended to see only few college students, and they were mostly interested in the archery gear. Tom suspected it was here mostly because Pete Jamison had been on Miami's team years before and still was active in the yearly competition sponsored by the school that attracted international-class archers.

Across the back were the guns. On the wall were the rifles and shotguns while pistols were in a glass case before them. Over to one side was an assortment of cleaning gear, targets, and reloading equipment. On the other side was a set of wooden shelves with ammunition, though most was kept in back.

Jack Jamison, the third Jamison to manage the place, was talking over the counter with a man in jeans and a work shirt and a blue Dillon ball cap. They looked up as he approached and smiled.

"How's it going, Mr. Parker?" asked the man with the blue hat.

"Pretty well, Smitty," Tom replied. Bob Schmidt ran a garage that did contract work for both the town and the university and was also a member of the Sportsmen's Club where Tom went to target shoot.

Jack was a young man who was probably trying to look older by growing a mustache, but its scrawny nature just made him look younger. In addition to managing the store, he was in the National Guard and drove heavy equipment on weekend drills.

"Hey, Mr. Parker," he said, holding out his hand.

"Hey, Jack," Tom said back, quietly amused, and shook his hand. Since Jack initiated the gesture, it naturally followed that Tom and Smitty would shake hands, which they did.

"Say, Mr. Parker, my dad gave me something to pass on to you, if you want it." He scurried into the back room and rummaged around, occasionally sending out a muffled report of his progress.

In the meantime, Tom and Smitty talked about the weather and plans for improving the club's ranges. There was a lot of interest in adding some more skeet positions and the pistol people wanted to add an IPSC-style fast fire course, now that they had generated some enthusiasm for fast shooting with the bowling pin competitions.

Jack came out, a small, narrow, cardboard box in his hands. He opened one end of the tan box.

"Take a look, Mr. Parker."

Tom opened the ammunition box. It held twenty brass cartridges. All were identical, gleaming in their similarity. He pulled one free, studied it for a moment and then looked at the box again.

"Tracers," he said.

"That's right," Jack replied, nodding in agreement. "In seven point six two NATO, just like what you shoot with your Remington, dad said. He said they're yours if you want them; he doesn't figure to sell them to anyone. Not a whole lot of call for tracer rounds." He took a breath. "They're legal in Ohio but they are full-metal jackets, so.."

"Unethical for hunting," Smitty said and Jack nodded.

"And probably illegal for hunting, too," Jack said. "Dad said they are good for teaching people about ballistics, just make sure there's no grass growing on the target berm or you might get a fire."

"Do a little educating," Smitty added, "about ricochets if one catches a rock."

Tom wasn't enthused about the idea of shooting a bunch of tracer bullets down the barrel of his rifle, having the idea that they might leave more than the average residue behind, but then he thought Ellen might be amused at seeing a couple go down range.

"Well, tell him thanks for me, but I can pay for them."

Jack refused and they spent a few moments going back and forth over it with Smitty looking on before Tom finally accepted.

"There's something you may be able to sell me," he said. "You all still renting out plinkers?"

Jack raised his eyebrows. "Sure, we've got a couple of pistols and rifles that can be rented. What are you looking for?

"I'd like to get a .22 rifle, bolt action if you have it. Want to teach my granddaughter a little shooting."

Jack turned towards the gun racks, rubbing his chin. "Don't have any renters in .22 that are bolt action. How tall is she?"

Tom held out a hand parallel with the ground. Jack nodded.

"If you don't mind a semi-auto, I got this Ruger. Short barreled and everything easy to get to." He reached up and pulled down a short rifle with a green plastic stock. He pushed the operating rod handle back, checked the breech, and then freed the plastic clip before handing it over.

"It's got a nice trigger pull, though a little heavy," he said, "and you can have her load the clip one round at a time."

Tom sighted down the barrel. The rear sights were fairly far forward but they were at least a V-notch. He squeezed the trigger. It was heavy, all right, but broke clean. There was a sharp click. He opened the breech and turned the rifle and squinted down the barrel. Dissatisfied with the light, he put his thumb in the breech and used his nail as a mirror. The barrel was clean with no pits. It would do.

He handed it back to Jack. "I'd like to use it for three days. How about some ammo?"

Tom eventually bought four boxes of .22 caliber long rifle ammunition, along with a set of blue Sonic ear protectors and cleaning gear for the .22.

Smitty invited him to bring Ellen out the following afternoon as there was going to be some black powder shooters having a meet. Tom thought she might like that and said they would probably be there.

As he drove away, he thought about women and guns. He was always a little surprised that more women didn't know how to use them.

Fast cure for rape.

Sarah could shoot and had even done a little hunting, though she didn't like handguns. All of his children were exposed to guns but none had stayed with it that he knew of. Maybe it was a generational thing.

Hell, maybe they just had better things to do with their money. Tom smiled as he thought of the money he had sunk into his hobby over the years.

His father had taught him how to shoot back when Tom was a boy in grade school. Back then his mother would tell his father how many rabbits she wanted for dinner and he would take that many shells for the old Remington .22 out into the late afternoon light.

His uncle had been a tremendous shot. He still remembered the soup cans sent flying and being hit in the air as Uncle Dave would smoothly work the pump of the tube-fed rifle. Uncle Dave had told him the best shots in the world were Americans, and the best shots among Americans, as history plainly showed, were Ohioans. "Kentucky and Pennsylvania," he would explain with that south Ohio accent somewhere between a Southern drawl and a West Virginia twang, "are rightly famous for making rifles; we're the people who shoot'em." And, he would point out in all modesty, he was the best shot in Ohio, a statement which usually brought laughter from the other men gathered around.

Tom had been a good shot in the Army, but combat wasn't about rifle range accuracy, he discovered in Korea. It was about intent and he had discovered he had all he needed.

He resumed shooting after his marriage for no other reason than he liked it, liked the discipline, the concentration you had to maintain when trying to develop the smallest possible group of hits with rounds you loaded yourself. He liked meeting with other men, talking about shooting, watching each other, getting into a little competition now and then. It was fun and he never had thought he was ever going to do it with intent again.

Now here he was. Tom shook his head. Well, it was almost over.

Three   down,   two   to   go.

Chapter 42

Catherine looked at the clock. It was nearly time for her father to come back for Ellen.

"Look, E, I need some time to think about all this, you know?" Ellen nodded her head. "Let me check out a few things and then you and I will get back together and we will decide what we're going to do." She squeezed Ellen's hand.

"In the meantime, you relax." Ellen looked up at her, her head tilted to one side, questioning. "You're not in this alone any more, understand? We'll do this together, whatever has to be done. All right?"

Ellen nodded and then slowly smiled. Not much, but it was better than she had looked since walking into Catherine's office. Catherine put her arms around the young girl and hugged her close.

God protect the little ones.

They spent some time talking about other things. Catherine showed Ellen around her office and how her computer terminal worked. Ellen was impressed by the ease with which her aunt accessed the internet and spent some time bouncing from home page to home page.

Suddenly Tom was at the door.

I had forgotten how quietly he moves.

Catherine had a second of concern about Ellen's reaction but the girl seemed relaxed, as if sharing her worry had somehow lessened the burden. There was a brief exchange of pleasantries and then the two were off.

Catherine sat in her office, looking out over the loading dock. So now what?

She had no doubt that Ellen believed she was telling the truth. There could be no question of that. She knew how much the girl loved her grandfather. Coming forward with such a story must have nearly torn her in two.

Could Ellen be wrong? Was there something she missed, some explanation for everything?

What about the notebook? Maybe it was just a scorecard. A macabre one, to be sure, but she knew her father had been terribly hurt by Eileen's death, no matter what Chucky said. Maybe it was his way of pushing the pain out of himself.

Catherine shook her head. When her mother, Sarah, died, she had not seen her father shed a single tear. He was the steady one everyone else leaned on, the one who reassured everyone they had done everything that they could, the one who told them she had known they loved her even when they hadn't said it, and she loved each of them back.

Only someone as dense as Chucky would think he was unaffected by Mom's death. She saw his fingers on the back of the pew at church during the service, saw the muscles knot in the back of his old man's hands as he gripped it so hard she thought the thick oak would shatter.

There were those silences, when he would stare out the window, oblivious to the conversation going on around him. It was easy to confuse what he was letting show with his normal quiet. All you had to do was look and you could tell.

And Eileen's death was, in some ways, worse. Mom had been sick, they knew it was coming. But Eileen was like lightning on a clear summer day, and she knew that Eileen and Ellen had managed to secure a special place in his heart even before Mom's death.

She suspected he had, in some strange male way, blamed himself for Eileen's death. He attended every day of the hearing, the only member of the family to do so. She remembered the last day, when the judge came back with her ruling that dropped the case.

They were separated by the crowd, but as she was swept out of the courtroom by the press of reporters and observers, she had a split second glimpse of her father. The image was frozen in her mind's eye.

He was standing, one hand resting on the seat in front of him. His face was calm, he said nothing. All he was doing was looking towards the defendants, most of whom were pounding each other on the back and shaking hands with their lawyers. He just looked at them with eyes as still as stones.

She shuddered with the memory.

Maybe Ellen is right.

Chapter 43

The raid on the lab was highly successful for three reasons, as Davidson described it.

First, they closed down a speed lab before it ever had a chance to export its product. The task force agents were still grinning about that, talking about the amount of money and effort that must have gone into setting it up, only to have it snatched away from the outlaws.

Second, the lab and its equipment generated a truck full of leads. From the processing equipment to the chemicals, they had a dozen possible connections to the main lab, wherever it was, to follow. JJ shook his head as he read through one of the reports; they had found ether containers still in their manufacturers cardboard boxes, complete with distribution numbers and bar codes, ephedrine boxes with Mexican labels, a variety of tanks containing anhydrous ammonia (part of the stink JJ had noticed), and just to keep things colorful, red phosphorous.

Third, everyone had come back alive. There was no doubt the lab was rigged to be blown, and not only with the flare gun and the thermite grenade. They had found a small block of C-4 tapped to the back of the shelves holding the phosphorous containers. An electrical detonator had wires running off to the barn where a switch and battery trigger was rigged.

The firepower they found suggested the Steel Riders were prepared to fight it out for at least long enough to blow the place to its component molecules. They had additional automatic weapons scattered in caches about the property as well as warning flares and noisemakers trip-wired.

"It may not have just been for us," Davidson commented during the Tuesday morning briefing. "As you know, sometimes labs are targets of rivals and these people are not in a position to make use of their local 911." There were a few small laughs from the assembled agents.

"All in all, troops, a good job. We moved fast, got solid cooperation from the state and local folks, and got very lucky. If the three watchdogs had been there, I think things might have gotten a whole lot more interesting and damned quickly."

He pushed his notes around. "Now, we are working on having the recovered material traced. Of course, much of it was stolen. The anhydrous ammonia looks like it was bled off storage tanks, what are they called?" He looked at JJ.

"Nurse tanks," JJ said. "Farmers will have a big one that the distributor will fill. Then, when they want to fertilize the fields, they'll take some from the nurse tank. We've been working on getting farmers to lock up their nurse tanks and report any signs someone has tampered them."

"Thanks," Davidson said, nodding. He turned back to the group. "Discounting the stuff stolen, I think we're looking at two possibilities. Either their other equipment came from the main lab and our trace of it may take us to it, or it was ordered separately. If so, there may not be a direct connection to the main lab as such, but I think if we can find the trail we have a good chance of identifying the people who've been handling it, which in turn may take us to the main lab." He paused.

"Remember, busting the lab was a good thing, but labs can be rebuilt. What we really want to do is bust these guys, make them serve some hard time, put them flat out of business, now and forever." Someone in the group added, "Amen," and Davidson grinned. "You got that right, brothers and sisters. So don't lose sight of the fact that we want to find the lab to find the people."

He looked over at Steve, who was standing to one side. "Steve, what do we have from our three rocket scientists?" Steve walked up beside Davidson.

"Well, as things stand now their cooperation has at least temporarily faded. The law firm of Laucher, Brown, and Brown," there was a groan from the back of the room, "yeah, the Riders' first team, whose charming acquaintance we all made during the hearings on the Eileen Parker homicide charges, and who manage to spring from underneath some rock every time we bust a mule. Anyway, they've gotten to the lab workers and mum is now the word."

"But to be quite truthful, I'm not so sure they had a lot more to tell us. Before they zipped their lips, they told us that they were hired to run the lab. Every time we said 'Steel Riders' they went blank. I think there's a good chance they were compartmentalized and didn't really know who they were working for." He flipped the papers on his clipboard.

"The weapons and explosives are all being worked up by those friendly paranoids from ATF." There was an undecipherable catcall from the ATF agent present and Steve grinned. "We've already gotten a trace on several of the AKs; they were part of a pile of guns stolen from a business in Kentucky last fall. We're liaising with the Kentucky people and hope to pop some things loose from their end." He looked up. "That's about it for the update. Any questions?" There weren't any and he moved over to an open chair.

"OK, one last piece of business," Davidson said. "We've all been holding our breath but I can now say that John Paulson, AKA 'Johnny Ringo,' has surfaced. He came in from the cold," he paused, interrupted by applause and whistles. Holding up a hand, he continued. "He got away from the last Dragons he was with in Cleveland and got to the FBI office. He's being cleaned up and, our FBI liaison assures us, being provided with the best damned steak dinner they can find on the Lake Erie coast. He will be back with us tomorrow." He patted his papers into a neat pile.

"As many of you know, Johnny was our inside man with the Dragons for the past year, and was deep with them the past six months, all during their move against the Riders. He's given us info that not only has helped to shut down Dragon drug operations in the north part of the state, including a big gun smuggling operation into Canada, but has helped keep us on track with the Riders. The evidence he has provided will ensure that we'll be jailing damned near every Dragon that the Riders haven't killed. And he's picked up one more thing." He made eye contact with JJ for a second.

"Paulson says that our guess about the meeting at the Mail Boxx was right on target. The Dragons were organizing a major hit on the Riders' leadership." He paused. "In fact, he thinks that it might have already begun before the ambush. He bases that on some odds and ends of things he picked up, so he can't be absolutely certain, but he thinks it's a good possibility. That puts of few of the puzzle pieces into place, if it's true. So give'm an 'attaboy' when he gets back here. Now, any questions? No? All right, you all know what you're supposed to be doing. Go earn your paychecks." There was a small wave of laughter and the group straggled out.

Davidson caught JJ's eye and motioned him to follow. It took a few minutes to get to the DEA agent's office as a number of people wanted to stop and ask or tell him something. Mostly, JJ saw, it was just the natural "up" from the sudden success of the drug lab raid. There was a definite change in the atmosphere of the task force compared to just a week ago. They were winning and they knew it.

Once they were in the office Davidson closed the door and took his seat and gestured to the chair in front of his desk.

"OK, JJ," he said without preamble, "out with it. What's on your mind?"

JJ was taken by surprise. "Ah, out with what, boss? I don't have anything on my mind."

"Bullshit." Davidson leaned back in his chair, gesturing with one hand. "You've just had a hand in squashing a drug lab in your county. From your attitude towards these scumbags and the impact this will have on your career, I figured you'd be doing cartwheels all along the length of Ohio 73, but you've barely gotten a smile on your face. You're about as subtle as a dropped brick. So, Deputy Jeffers, what gives?"

JJ studied his hands for a moment and finally nodded.

"Carl, don't get me wrong. I am delighted that we've taken the Riders down a notch or three, and I'm really hoping we can follow through on all this and really nail these bastards. As for the career impact stuff, that is bullshit. I want these people down for the count. It's just..." He paused, groping for words.

"You're still stuck on the original three dead Riders, aren't you?" Davidson asked. "I remember your briefing. Well," he said, brushing back his nonexistent hair, "the question is fairly academic as far as the task force is concerned. It's officially a local matter is one thing. I really don't want to get in the way of your guys in Middletown or the Sheriff's Office. Some folks get a little antsy when feds offer to help." He smiled and continued. "The second thing, of course, is that it's not what we're here for. While I'd be happy to see various and sundry Riders thrown into prison for any reason, from illegal parking to income tax evasion, what we are being paid for is to bust their butts for manufacture, distribution, and sales of illegal substances."

He leaned back in his chair and held up a hand. "On the other hand, I'm not a local. This isn't my county, it's yours, and I figure unsolved murders in your jurisdiction probably gnaw at you, being a good cop, the way they would for anyone." He brought his hands together and tapped his fingers on his desk.

"Have you talked with the Middletown cops or your own guy about your ideas as to who might have hand in the killing of the three?"

"No," JJ said, shaking his head. "I was intending to, but then I got word that one of my possibles was now accounted for during two of the killings. That only leaves one, and, frankly, while it still pushes some of my buttons, I don't think anyone is going to buy him as a suspect."

Davidson nodded, looking at his hands. "And you don't like to say anything unless it's solid." He looked up and smiled. "I noticed that about you around here. If you want to take a little advice, it's okay to speak up even when you don't have absolute proof. You're right enough of the time that people will forgive the occasional error."

JJ smiled, slightly embarrassed.

"Well, here's the other shoe," Davidson continued, now taking a turn at looking slightly embarrassed. "It seems your man Phillips has been doing some of his own checking along the Parker family line and has encountered a few people who have already been talked to by you. He was a bit miffed and gave me a call." Davidson shrugged.

"I explained things, that you were doing the task force a favor by trying to rule out other explanations, that you weren't part of a wedge to drive in the way of their local investigation. He wasn't crazy about my explanation but he said he didn't figure you to be trying to pull anything on his own people." Davidson looked up and smiled slightly. "I guess you have a reputation within your own department."

"To get to the bottom line, I told him we would leave the possibility of local, non-Rider shooters in his hands and that you would personally turn over to him anything you had which shed light on the situation." Davidson held up a hand as JJ opened his mouth. "It's theirs, JJ, and we have to cooperate. One more reason for you to be talking to them – you have to."

"I gave him a briefing on what you had uncovered. He cooled down and admitted they had most of it and they, like us, didn't think it was anyone other than Dragons, especially when I shared the lead we got from Paulson." He paused, smiling slightly. "Your man Phillips is very sensitive about turf."

JJ nodded and kept silent.

"So what do you say, deputy?"

"I screwed up," JJ said, slowly. "Phillips is right; I should have been coordinating with him from the get-go." He sighed. "I'll send him my stuff, but it's not much, just background material. I never did get around to talking to any of the Parkers directly. Figure now I better not."

"That's probably a good decision," Davidson said. "Keeps me from having to order you to stay away from them. Well, I don't figure you're going to be worth a damn around here until you work this out. Just kidding," he said, holding up his hand. "I'll tell you what. Right now all we have going is running down the leads from the lab; a lot of that will be handled by people outside this office, so until we get some feedback useful, we're mostly going to be compiling data and pushing paper around. All you'll be doing is taking word on over to the Sheriff's Office as things develop, which will leave you with too much time on your hands. Do you have any independent projects you could follow up on, maybe something you've been thinking about that you haven't dropped on the rest of us out-of-towners?"

JJ grinned. "Well, I've been fooling around with some contour maps, playing a little game of, where would I be if I was a drug lab?"

"How far have you gotten with it?" Davidson asked, leaning forward.

"I've been able to eliminate chunks of the county based on what can be seen and some assumptions like that they wouldn't have it in any of the towns. My idea is that the reason they came to Butler County is because it both is rural with a fair amount of hills and woods to hide and is close to three interstates."

"Makes sense," Davidson said. "And it's near the junction of three states."

"But I was limited in understanding what these labs were like. I've attended the classes and read the literature, even seen the pictures, but I got a couple of ideas about where one might be after seeing the one we busted. I'd like to get out into the field and start checking on some possible sites. I got some encouragement from the fact the lab was in one of my possible areas."

"OK," Davidson said, patting his desktop for emphasis. "Then here's the deal. You're off the leash. Come and go as you need to try out your idea. Hell, you may be on to something. Check in with Anne daily for messages and keep abreast of what's going on here. Make sure we know where you are going and keep me updated on your progress. And make sure anything we need to pass onto the Sheriff goes. If we need you in a hurry for anything serious, we can page you. I don't know how long this pause will last so make the most of it." He looked intently at JJ.

"And if you are able to come across anything that helps with the murders, fine, pass it on to Phillips, though I think all you're going to see are Dragons. In any case, let him run with the local end of that part. How's that sound?"

"Sounds great, boss," JJ replied, standing up. "I'll keep you up to date on what I'm doing. Thanks, Carl." He held out his hand, which the DEA agent shook. JJ walked to the door.

"Now, remember, Cinderella," Davidson said before he left, "the clock is going to strike midnight eventually and you'll have to turn into a pumpkin again like the rest of us, so have fun while you can."

JJ grinned and stepped out into the hallway. Well, maybe he was too invested in the Parkers. The information from Paulson didn't seem to fit into his scenario. On the other hand, he was off the leash now, and who knew what the hell might be turned up?

He had his chance and he was going to run with it.

Chapter 44

Catherine spent a restless night after returning home and was out of the house at dawn, walking up and down the hills of Oxford, her mind unable to settle on a course of action. For a time, as the small town stirred to life, she sat on a bench in the main square and watched the birds fly on and off the water tower. They had no answers for her uncertain questions and she left them for a cup of coffee in the McDonald's.

Catherine considered going out to the farm but finally rejected the idea. In the first place, she had no need to check Ellen's story. The girl told the truth as she knew it, so undoubtedly there was a notebook with information on the five men involved in the killing of her niece.

Beyond that, the only other thing she might do would be to confront her father. She considered this carefully, moving around the idea gently but drawn to it, like to a healed wound one feels a need to test. But despite going over and over it, she couldn't see what would be gained by doing so.

How do you walk up to your father and say, "Hi, Dad. Been killing people?" She shook her head in exasperation with herself. There had to be a way of finding out what was really going on, and then stopping it if it was as Ellen believed.

About this last point, stopping it, Catherine found herself alternating between grasping it firmly and feeling it slip from her grasp.

What if he was killing those people who were responsible for the death of Eileen? He was, after all, her father. Would she turn him in to the police? She knew she could not do that, not even to keep the remaining two alive, not even to keep her father safe.

And by safe, when she used that word to herself, she meant more than his physical safety, though that was a powerful concern. She also meant the safety of his heart, of his soul.

Catherine had found two sources of stability when she was going through the storm of her reconciliation with herself and her family in years past. One was her cousin, John Wesley. He seemed incapable of becoming alienated from her, no matter what kind of convulsions were rippling through the family.

The other was her faith. Her mother opened the possibility to her and her siblings, though in a gentle way. Her father acquiesced, cooperated, but it was always clear he was following Sarah's lead.

Her mother ensured part of all the children's moral compass was exposure to religion. It was a relatively undemanding exposure, to be sure, but it helped to provide an additional frame of reference.

Now, of course, few of the Parker children were particularly engaged in formal religion, though most took their families to church on Sunday. For Catherine the early exposure left her open to the possibilities.

She was not born again, whatever the phrase meant. Her faith offered no fundamental absolutes, no guaranteed paths of certain belief. What it did give her was, if not a path, at least a direction.

Jesus, for example, had become important to her because of the example of his life. No matter what values others tried to put on it, no matter how others tried to interpret it, what she found when she read the story of that carpenter turned prophet was a story of the importance of love.

Love, unconditional, undistracted by behavior, seemed to answer so many of the questions she faced. The courage to love. When she felt the chasm between her and her family was becoming so great that no bridge might ever span it, she held onto love and refused to allow herself the self-indulgence of striking back from her own pain and confusion. The chasm closed, for the most part, and with most, and the love endured.

Did she love her father enough to do what might be needed to keep him from destroying himself? Catherine didn't know how to answer the question and wasn't sure it was the right question.

Walking back to her house, she realized that part of the problem of deciding what was the right action was that she was having difficulty seeing things from her father's point of view. Of course, she had been angry in her life and she could recall more than once having an impulse for revenge. Like the others, she was bitterly disappointed when the charges against Eileen's killers were dropped.

But taking it that next step, of converting that anger to violence, especially methodical violence, was a move she had difficulty understanding.

That her father could do it she had no doubt. He was a man capable of doing whatever he set out to do, and perhaps there was the problem for her understanding him. He was a man. Despite how well she thought she knew him, she would never have imagined him doing anything like this. Before she could determine what she should do, she needed to understand, as far as that was possible, the why of his behavior. She needed someone to help her gain that understanding, and there was only one person she could think of asking.

As she walked up her house's steps, she decided on her first move. She would talk to John Wesley.

Chapter 45

Ellen found talking with Catherine reassuring, though she understood nothing was finally accomplished. Still, sharing her fears eased the burden. She found it easier, during the ride back to the farm, to relax with her grandfather.

As they followed the winding road north out of Oxford, she occasionally pointed out things catching her eye, just as she had in the past, and, just as in the past, was content to share Grandpa Tom's silences.

Summer was almost gone and school was just over the horizon. More significantly, she would return to her parents in a few weeks. In spite of the recent crisis, she really wasn't eager to leave her grandfather.

The farm was interesting, in a way her house, in its prime location in a development, would never be for a child. She liked seeing the stars at night, unobstructed by streetlights, and hearing the hooted conversations of owls.

The animals all seemed, despite her continued exposure to them, fascinating, especially the birds. She still remembered the first time she saw and recognized an osprey flying over the farm. Not appreciating the rareness of the event, she sat on the back steps for hours afterward, expecting to see another at any moment.

The greatest treasure the farm offered was time with her grandfather. Her parents, she began recently to understand, were trying to meet her needs. Ellen overheard them talking about spending more quality time with her. She didn't fully understand what "quality time" was, but she was very clear that what she wanted, needed, from them, from someone, was time, period.

Ellen felt, at times, as if cast adrift from her parents. Not that they didn't care; she knew, despite everything, they loved her. Nonetheless, it seemed as if they didn't know what to do with her, as if being involved in her life was some sort of negative thing they needed to avoid.

It was true of her friends' parents as well. For many parents, it seemed as if they weren't supposed to be entangled in their children's lives. Maybe, as Ellen heard discussed on television, it was true they all were concerned with stunting their children's development. But often it felt like they just weren't interested and didn't want to be distracted from their own pursuits.

"As long as I'm not pregnant or arrested," one of Ellen's classmates said, "they don't care what I do."

Ellen's parents cared but they remained distant, and the distance lengthened as their undefined conflict surfaced and fell. While she liked the freedom, there were times – and these increased in frequency and duration – when she wanted them around more, to let her know that she really mattered to them. It wasn't about "quality"; it was about time.

Time made the farm, and her grandfather who it represented, so precious. Tom always had time for her. For a young girl in the craziness of the world, that kind of commitment and availability was a solid rock on which she stood and, when necessary, use for shelter.

That is why, she knew, she was so close to panic when she understood what he was doing. Riding in the car through the midday Ohio farmland, she knew her fears were not about the danger he might be in but what she might lose if anything happened to him.

Ellen looked over at the quiet figure beside her as they turned onto the gravel lane leading to the farm. Losing him would be the worst thing that could ever happen. Ellen felt the small surge of fear begin deep inside her.

Then came that pulse of strength she first felt on the riverbank. Something pushed back at the fear, shoved it down with a firm grasp. She even felt her jaw clench in response to it. Washing over her came warmth and a sense of determination almost exciting in its power and newness.

I'm not going to lose him. I'm not going to let that happen.

Chapter 46

Off the leash was a good phrase, JJ decided. There was a sense of satisfaction in following his own project, rather than waiting for whatever assignment the task force might give him. The need to strike at the outlaws, and that was the word he tended to use in his own mind, was always strong. That was why he volunteered for the assignment of liaison in the first place.

Since the raid on the drug lab, it had grown even stronger. As satisfying as it was to see it all go down, and go down so smoothly, he was a passive observer.

At least, that was how he saw himself. Doing liaison, no matter how glowingly Davidson described it in the letter to the department, was still just being a spear-carrier. More than anything, JJ wanted to be the spear point.

Spread across his desk were his maps and colored pens. With permission to try out his own idea, he didn't feel the need to hide his work from others. A few agents swung by to take a look. The most positive comment was an expression of admiration for his persistence. No one so far thought it had much of a chance to turn up anything. After all, there were still a number of leads coming out of the seized lab. All they needed was one connection to the main lab or to the Riders' leadership and it was payday.

He accepted the analyses with good humor, knowing they were probably right. He also knew, while the leads could turn out to be dead ends – it had happened before - and the odds were against him, nonetheless it was his project.

And by God I'm going to follow it through.

He blinked in surprise at the strength of feeling behind the sudden thought.

Whoa, partner. Got a little ego involved here, do we?

JJ grinned in embarrassment, recognizing the truth of his own insight. Well, that wasn't necessarily bad. A little investment in his work always led him to try to do the best he could, to try a little harder.

Steve Johnson walked over with some paperwork and stayed to get an explanation of the project.

"Yeah, Carl asked me to touch base with you about it," the FBI agent said. "I'm getting together some of the aerial stuff we have."

"Aerial photographs?"

"Some of it's Air Force, pictures they've taken during training, that kind of thing. It's not too old and I think it will update your maps, at least in terms of current structures and foliage coverage. We could get you some infrared scans, if you had a hot prospect, but that would only let you know what structures were in significant use within, say, the previous six to eight hours."

JJ nodded. "Well, current pictures would be a help. Even if I couldn't eliminate a building, I could do a little prioritizing. I would guess the lab is going pretty much around the clock."

It was Steve's turn to nod. "I think you're right. With the Kentucky lab burned down and our grabbing the other, they're probably running the big one 24 hours a day."

"And I can use the updates. I appreciate it, J. Edgar."

"No sweat, Deputy Dawg," Steve said, grinning. "I think the deck is really stacked against you on this but maybe our luck is turning now." His expression turned more serious. "The other thing is, I want you to check with us prior to visiting each area. Make sure we know where you are and check in when you arrive there and leave."

JJ looked at him. "It's great to be thought after."

"You can't imagine," Steve said, shaking his head, "the amount of paperwork involved every time we get our liaison officer shot. It's absolutely unbelievable."

He walked away, smiling. JJ found himself recalling the visit an hour later. He liked Special Agent Steve Johnson, even if he was a fed.

"Are you smiling at something funny or have you finally gone insane working around here?" Karen Deevers' voice cut into his internal monologue and he looked up. She stood next to his desk holding several computer printouts, a wry smile on her face.

"I am not," JJ said with mock seriousness, "authorized to go insane as my paperwork has not yet cleared the boss's desk." He relaxed and smiled back. "No, I was just thinking over some stuff. What're you up to?"

"Just going over some of the traces on the lab gear," she said, gently wiggling the printouts. She gestured at the maps. "What's all this?"

For some reason, he found himself momentarily silenced, which he tried to cover by pulling some of his notes together. He suddenly realized he didn't want to look foolish to her.

"I, ah, this is a thing I've been working on for a while," he began, his voice hesitating. She didn't seem to notice as she bent over, one hand resting on the edge of his desk, and studied the maps. "The boss told me to go ahead with it," he added hurriedly, as if trying to legitimize his work, "and Steve's going to get me some imagery to update foliage and structures, and some infrared..." His voice trailed off as he found himself studying the curve of her neck.

I am sounding like a jerk.

Starting over, JJ explained what he was doing. She seemed to be following him carefully, looking from him to the maps, tracing the colored zones with her fingertips. After showing her what he had accomplished before the raid, he described where he was taking the project.

"The thing to remember is," JJ said, his voice now steady, "I don't think they moved operations up here by accident. Between the ability to establish the lab in an isolated location and it being close to the major interstates, Butler County was an obvious choice. Plus, too, it was relatively close to their old center of operations in the Cincinnati-Covington area."

"And they didn't go into Indiana," Karen said, studying the map showing the Ohio-Indiana-Kentucky junction, "even though there were places where they could have hid the lab at least as easily as here, because the traffic flow there doesn't connect as readily to their markets."

"Right, right. I'm guessing they did consider Indiana, down here in the southeast corner, close by Cincinnati, but they probably passed on it because they had the growing connection to Columbus and Cleveland to service or maybe they couldn't find what they needed."

He pulled his laminated map free and spread it on top of the others.

"Now, the thing that I'm adding which I really didn't understand before is the matter of how badly these labs can smell. That seems to be a major problem for them." Karen nodded in agreement. "So I'm figuring that, even with an elaborate ventilation system, they would locate in a position where it would be unlikely that a neighbor might notice. Thing is, farmers pay attention to what's going on around them. They have to, even if it's something happening on a neighbor's farm."

"This translates, I'm guessing, to more than simple privacy from observation, which is what I was working on before. Now what I'm doing is trying to figure how isolated the lab would have to be from neighboring property, even if out of sight, so it wouldn't be smelled."

"That's a problem," Karen said. "A lot of speed freaks who make their own in the kitchen sink don't worry about the problem mostly because they're in places where people don't ask questions. Or they are too fried to care."

"So I've gathered."

"There are two main styles of ventilation for bigger places. One is like the lab we busted. One vent but distant from the lab and surfacing where people aren't likely to go. The other is multiple vents designed to disburse the odor." JJ nodded; he had gotten similar comments from some of the DEA agents and it matched what he had picked up from his reading.

"You're right. But both systems require room, and that's the key. Let me show you." He turned the laminated contour map around so Karen could see it better.

"Now here's what I mean. This area is an active farm, most of which is visible from this state route. Hidden from view is this area," his finger traced a path on the map, "which would have been a possibility before, but when you take into account the need for ventilation, take another look. See, there are these farms, including some of the actual houses, immediately adjacent, though out of sight. In fact, just a little east is this intersection, where you can find a gas station with one of those 24-hour stores, a bar, a garage, and a salvage yard. If there was something in this area giving off a stink, there's a damned good chance it would be noticed." He sat back in his chair.

"The lab we busted was located in a well thought-out position. They hid everything, and their vent was not only invisible, it was unsmellable. No one lived within a quarter of a mile of it, which was plenty of room. I think they gave the main lab just as careful consideration. So," he picked up a pink felt-tip and began coloring in the area, "I figure it is unlikely that the lab is here."

Karen looked at the map and smiled, shaking her head. For a moment, JJ felt his stomach drop.

"This is really good," she said, her fingers moving over the varied colored swaths. "You've accounted for more than half of the map already."

JJ grinned. "Some of it's easy. Just find an inhabited area and mark off anything to the west and north to take into account the prevailing wind. But to do it right is going to take going out and actually looking over the area. The map," he waved his hand over it, "isn't totally up to date in terms of buildings or foliage. That stuff can change every year. Steve is getting me some aerial photos, but I think I'm still going to have to check it out on the ground."

Karen nodded in agreement, still studying the map. Then she looked up. "This is really neat work, JJ. Even if you don't find the lab with it, it may pay off just in terms of narrowing our search area. I can see why Carl is letting you run with it."

JJ felt no temptation to tell her that Carl's motivation for letting him pursue his project had little to do with his expectation of results.

"Well, it's a long shot," he replied, "but I figure it's worth the effort." He tried to hide his pleasure at her approval.

"Listen, keep me posted on this. If I get anything that might help you narrow the field, I'll give a yell."

"Deal," he said. She gave him a smile and walked away.

He found himself noticing that she was wearing slacks that were snug across her butt. Chagrined, he deliberately shifted his eyes back to his map and didn't allow himself to look back up until he was sure she was back at her own desk.

Idiot. She treats you like a professional and you act like a pimple faced, teenaged jerk.

He glanced around the room, trying to distract himself, and met the eyes of Steve Johnson, who was leaning back in his chair, smiling at him. Embarrassed, he looked away.

Great. Now everyone knows I'm a jerk.

He forced his attention back to his maps. Whatever was going on with him about Karen Deevers, it would have to go on the back burner, he decided with less than firm emphasis. He had work to do.

JJ picked up the pink pen and began coloring again.

Chapter 47

John Wesley Parker took the stairs to the front door of his house two at a time in spite of his leg's arthritis, but he failed to get to the telephone before it stopped ringing. He tossed his book bag onto the chair in frustration.

His dog Pupper, a mongrel mix of Border collie, terrier, and probably something else, walked over to him grinning, happy to see him again and utterly indifferent to telephones. The dog sat next to him and cocked his head to one side.

John smiled back and sat down to scratch Pupper's ears, which got his hand licked.

I think one of us has the proper perspective on these things.

He stretched and rose. Pupper immediately got to his feet, his tail wagging, anticipating going outside. John motioned towards the back of the house and the dog raced to the door. As John passed through the small kitchen, he slipped off his sport jacket and hung it over a chair.

The backyard merged into a wooded area, beyond which were Indiana farm fields stretching to the horizon. After taking care of his immediate needs, Pupper ran around the yard, his nose held low, seeking out one of his toys. Finding an ancient tennis ball – its original green now a particularly unhealthy-looking gray – he ran back to John and dropped it at his feet.

Pupper had trained his human well; almost without thinking John picked up the ball and, after a few mandatory feints, threw it to the edge of the woods, about twenty yards away. Pupper raced after the ball which, having almost none of its original elasticity, barely bounced and seemed reluctant even to roll. He leapt on the ball, gave it a savage rat-killing shake, and ran back to John. He circled the human twice, just to let him see his accomplishment, and then dropped the ball at his feet. The process was repeated for about fifteen minutes before John raised both hands in surrender and walked back to the house. Pupper immediately followed, the ball having lost its significance.

John went to his bedroom near front of the small house and changed into jeans and an old work shirt. He paused when scooping the loose change from the top of his chest of drawers to look at the pictures flanking a small jewelry box.

On one side were his parents in a posed portrait, blue wall behind them back-lit; they only vaguely looked as he remembered them. They were dressed in their church-going clothes that, while neat and clean, were of an older style.

On the other side was a black and white photograph of a group of eight men, the ones in front kneeling, the ones in back standing. They were all clad in tiger-striped camouflaged uniforms with a wide variety of military equipment and weapons hanging off them. With the exception of two in the front row, they all had weapons in their hands, loosely but naturally held, as if so familiar with them the weapons had become natural extensions of their selves.

The two in front were holding a two-tone flag, gray above in the photo, darker gray below, with a lighter star in the middle. Most of the men were smiling, but with few exceptions they were the artificial smiles of his parents, generated by the command of the camera.

He touched the picture, briefly, and then walked out of the room, Pupper close behind.

Walking back outside, he crossed the yard and entered the woods. Pupper took this as a signal to race ahead, alternating running about with careful, nose-first investigations of various artifacts. John kept walking, knowing that the dog would keep circling back to him.

Eventually, he came upon the creek which marked the edge of the woods and the start of the cultivated area. He followed the stream as it gently curved and made its way eastward. There was little slope to the land here in the middle of the state so the stream's movement was relatively slow; at times, where it backed up and formed a pool, it gave the impression it had stopped.

John finally paused after a half mile and sat down on a fallen tree. Pupper took the opportunity to pause for a drink from the stream after walking into it until his belly touched the surface. Eventually John took off his shoes and socks and sat on the bank and tangled his feet in the water. The stream was never more than a few feet deep at best so the water was fairly warm. Pupper apparently regarded it as quite refreshing and continued to stand in it, occasionally raising his head and sniffing at something in the slow wind.

"Well, today really sucked," John said to Pupper, who looked back at him, perhaps picking up on his human's tone of frustration. "I finally got all that junk into the review committee, cleared my schedule for the meeting, and at the last minute McPeters canceled it." John threw a rock into the creek and Pupper immediately investigated the splash, sticking his snout into the water to see what might lurk there.

"Asshole. That makes three cancellations; this time he didn't even give a reason, just left it on email. If I hadn't checked, I would have walked into the room and no one else would have shown up. Asshole," he said, repeating himself. Pupper came wading over and looked up at him.

"Not your fault, old boy," John said reassuringly, stroking the dog's head. He used his thumb to rub the inside of a floppy ear and Pupper leaned into it. "Hell, it doesn't really matter. It's just the graduate chair. Doesn't actually mean anything." He got up and went back to his seat on the tree and wiped off his feet with his hands and then a bandanna.

Though his feet were still damp, he pulled on his socks and shoes. Pupper climbed up the bank, walked over to him, and violently shook the water from his coat. John had seen it coming and stepped back as the dog went into its corkscrewing motion and was spared most of the spray.

They went home. Pupper happily engaged in mini-explorations of ground he had been over several hundred times before but which he investigated as if it was a newly discovered continent. John, distracted, was almost surprised to find himself walking up the steps to his backdoor.

He checked Pupper's water and food bowls and reheated a container of stew for himself. While it was turning inside the microwave, he went to the living room and retrieved his book bag.

John was halfway back to the kitchen when he realized he hadn't checked his mail in his rush to get to the telephone. He grimaced and walked outside to the big, black mailbox perched on a post beside the street. He found a cardboard box from a book club and a stack of mail, mostly junk.

Returning to the kitchen, he checked the timer and began to sort through his mail. Most went unopened onto a chair. The book, David Herbert Donald's Lincoln, brought a smile to his face. Even though his primary area was Twentieth Century American history, Lincoln was one of his heroes. He had read a friend's review copy and had ordered the book the first time he saw it in the History Book Club catalog.

He put the book aside to be shelved later. At some point, he would reread it, just as soon as he got through the two-foot high stack of unread books which sat on the bottom shelf of the big wooden bookshelves in his study.

Bills went into another pile. There were several catalogs, most of which went into the junk pile.

There was only one letter. John deliberately kept it for last. He held it in his hands, turning it over slowly. It was thicker than he thought it would be, heavy with several pages. The imprinted return address identified the Naval Institute Press. Finally, he opened it.

It was not what he was expecting. The Naval Institute, which published a range of literature on naval topics from biographies to fiction was extremely well regarded as a source for books on naval policy. While some academics sniffed at the Institute, those who were knowledgeable about naval matters knew that it published only topflight material, rigorously reviewed. Hence, his surprise.

His book manuscript, Fire from the Sea: The Evolution of U. S. Naval Policy in the Twentieth Century, was accepted for publication. An initial contract was enclosed and he was to regard this letter as a commitment on the Institute's part to publish. If he agreed, they had a number of editorial suggestions they would like to see implemented (see enclosed list) and the name, number, and email address of an editor who would work with him. They admired the scholarship of his analysis and enjoyed his writing style.

John read and reread the letter and then put it down and just looked at it. He didn't move until the microwave beeped. He got his food and poured himself a glass of cider and sat back down.

Well, how do you feel, Dorothy?

The book would, of course, take his application for the graduate chair further into certainty. He already had more than all the minimum requirements, from article publications, to teaching load, to student, peer, and department evaluations, to serving on committees, to being involved in community activities, he had done it all, almost compulsively, keeping careful score.

But all the time John was filled with a barely suppressed sense of futility. He was doing a lot but it didn't mean anything. Yes, he enjoyed studying history, and it was satisfying to have a light bulb go off in a student's head, and writing was fun. Most of his work in the university was enjoyable, and the part that wasn't was insignificant, he knew, even when he allowed himself to feel frustrated.

If it isn't green tracer, it just doesn't matter.

But it didn't feel that it had any real value. Oh, he knew, intellectually, what he did was worthwhile at some level to somebody at least some of the time. Studying and teaching history were important.

But...

John sighed and folded the letter. He knew he was good at what he did, better than many of his peers in the department. He had a steadily growing reputation within his field as a result of publications and presentations.

For a time, he had sought recognition as a way of proving to himself that he was of value, that what he did mattered. Rapidly he discovered that those were actually two issues. About his competency he had no doubts. He pushed himself as hard as he could to be as good at what he did as he could be and, while recognizing he still could improve, he knew he was excellent as a university teacher.

That left the value of the work itself. He was unable to accept that it had value because he enjoyed it, as some of the other instructors did. He needed to believe that it mattered in the scale of things.

The problem was his scale. John got up and put his glass in the sink. The bowl went on the floor for Pupper to have last licks. John walked to the spare bedroom he had converted into his study. It was getting dark and he flipped on a light.

A large black desk, a computer resting on it, was up against one wall. A cheap stereo system was in a corner with CDs scattered across its top. One wall was almost entirely hidden by a single wooden set of bookshelves; smaller bookshelves of various dimensions and material, looking like children following their larger parent, were scattered about. There was little in the way of empty shelf space and several grocery bags contained books to be hauled away and donated to the Franklin public library hinted at his ongoing struggle with space.

John sat at the desk and fired up the computer. It blinked into life and he wrote a letter in reply to the Naval Institute, agreeing to their offer. He faxed a copy of the letter to the editor and printed out two copies of it. One he signed and put in an envelope to be mailed to the Institute; the other he attached to the Institute's letter and put in his book bag to be added to his chair application materials.

John logged onto the university's email system and messaged the members of the selection committee, requesting they change the notation for *Fire From the Sea* from "Submitted" to "In Press." Dean McPeters, always hungry for faculty to get published and, more importantly, be recognized so as to serve as a draw for students, would enjoy seeing that.

He pulled up his resume and scrolled through until he got to his publications section. He cut the entry for *Fire From the Sea* from beneath the submitted listings and pasted it under the publications section, adding the notation that it was in press with the Naval Institute.

He slowly scrolled backwards, looking at the list of papers, presentations, and honors and distinctions. Then there were the entries under "Other Employment." They read:

1968-1971 Officer of Marines, United States Marine Corps

1973-1977 Secondary School Teacher, Indianapolis Public Schools

He hadn't bothered to list his part time jobs held while going to college, either as an undergrad or as a graduate student.

Only the first entry stirred anything in him. It seemed like that was the last time in his life he had really meant anything, really mattered. Things then were clear with sharp black and white contrast; since then everything was fog-bank gray, a little fuzzy and out of focus. How important could things be now on that scale? What he did then, the decisions he made, meant life and death. It mattered.

He mattered.

John felt anger with himself. Why couldn't he appreciate what he was doing now, why did he drag around this stuff from more than twenty years ago? He shook his head.

Idiot.

Pupper came in and curled up on a throw rug in front of the stereo. He would want to go outside soon so John shut down his computer and turned off the light. He went to the backdoor and attached the long lead, anchored at one end to a hook on the house, to Pupper's collar. Pupper sat waiting patiently. He never let the dog out off the lead unless he was with him. While the road out front was not frequently traveled, he didn't want to find the dog on it some day because he was too lazy to snap on his line.

He had just sat down in front of the living room television when the telephone rang. He picked up the receiver.

"Hey, hi, Cathy!"

Chapter 48

JJ understood his map project was based on a number of assumptions, two of which were critical. First, and this was his idea since he began studying the maps, he felt it unlikely that the speed lab was in a town or city. If the Riders were willing to run the risks associated with operating in such an area, then why bother to locate in Butler County? Why not in one of the cities where the interstates met, like Dayton or Columbus?

The second assumption, that they would want distance from any areas people might be in, used his experience at the captured lab. Whatever ventilation system they might use for disbursing the smell and clearing the air, they would want, he believed, some distancing between themselves and anyone else. The system could always fail. Why risk it?

It was, he admitted to himself, a hell of a set of assumptions. On the other hand, by making them he had given himself at least a manageable workload. He colored in areas of public places like businesses, roads, and housing developments. Then he extended from those areas and colored in the map any area close enough to be noticed by odor.

He was tempted to reduce the size of the map by coloring in areas of farms, believing that the lab would not be in a position where its smell might be noticeable by someone tilling a field. Unfortunately, he was unable to account for all country properties in the county. While he knew many were actively working farms, he did not know if others were active, fallow, or even in the hands of the outlaws. Farms could fold up due to death or the market place and he had no magical way of knowing them all. On top of that, even on land belonging to an active farm there could be large areas allowed to become wooded or otherwise unused.

Accounting for potential odor narrowed the unmarked portions of his map to twenty-seven, some of which were quite large. What he needed to do was verify his map and see if the assumptions meant anything.

Which was why he was walking slowly through a patch of woods in the eastern portion of the county, cautiously approaching a low rise. According to his map, beyond the rise, well out of sight of any road or farm, and sufficiently isolated that the prevailing winds would not carry a drug lab's odor to any area where people might be, were several unidentified structures.

As he moved quietly among the trees, JJ remembered as a boy meeting his great-grandfather; the man's image was dim in his mind, conflicting with several old black and white photographs held in an album somewhere. The old man had joked that, at one time, a squirrel could have run from Lake Erie to the Ohio River without ever touching the ground. Well, the rodent would have a hell of a time doing that nowadays.

But Ohio, JJ thought, remembered. It remembered what had been, back in those days of forests and wilderness. You could be trying to get through a tree line bordering a farmer's field and bust through to the other side into another field that was only a few yards away but totally invisible. And sometimes you'd come out two days later. There were in Ohio still wild places, places once cleared by farmers that Ohio quietly had closed back in on and captured.

Sometimes, when going through the forests, the trees would seem to press in a little too close as if to remind you, these forests were once wild, were once dangerous. Then, having made their point, the tress would spread a little and let in the light.

Ohio remembered.

JJ had changed into old jeans and a cotton shirt that he wore loose so as to cover his .45. He carried a pair of binoculars and a radio dialed into the task force's frequency in a fanny pack.

From time to time, JJ paused and listened to the noises of the forest. Moving as slowly as he could with frequent stops encouraged the birds and insects to maintain their conversations; he was listening for pauses which might suggest someone else was in the woods with him.

JJ paid close attention where he put his feet. He remembered the detection device rigged on the lane of the other farm. From reports of other labs he knew the Riders could have all kinds of intruder detectors, even lethal booby-traps, scattered around. Thus far, all he had seen was an old wire fence tangled in the leaves as its wooden fence had rotted and given way.

The trees were thinning out as he approached the broad crest of the ridge so he got down on his stomach and crawled forward. He took up a position beside a tree trunk and studied the ground below.

The view illustrated the problem JJ had with his maps. The topographical maps were accurate insofar as they represented the terrain; hills didn't move much, unless a developer's bulldozer wandered by. However, the indications of foliage, especially in a farming area like Butler County, could change radically in between map updates. The same was true of buildings and other structures.

Instead of three buildings below him, there were four. Three were old structures, while the fourth, a pole barn made of aluminum, could have been assembled last week. JJ pulled out his binoculars and studied them.

It was soon apparent that none of the buildings housed an illegal drug lab. One was so old and decrepit he could actually see through its wooden sides where boards had fallen off the frame. The roof was partially caved in as well. The other two wooden buildings were small and open on one side, exposing their interiors. He guessed that they were used for equipment storage in the past. Now several cows were using them for shade, placidly chewing their cuds in the afternoon heat.

The aluminum building had sliding doors on either end and, from his angle, he saw the light of the open far door through the door closest to him. In the shadows, he could just make out the shape of a tractor wagon.

JJ sighed and lowered the binoculars. Well, so far today that made three down, twenty-four to go. He glanced at his watch. There was still a chance he could check out another site or two before getting back to the office. He smiled slightly as he got up and walked back to his car.

A jay scolded him as he thought about why he wanted to get back; he had decided to ask Karen Deevers out for a date.

He was nervous about it, but kept telling himself that if nothing was ventured, then nothing was gained. The thought didn't help much, just occupied his thinking.

The occupation of his thoughts explained why he wasn't watching what he was doing and managed to trip in the old wire fence he had crossed earlier. The jay greeted his fall with a harsh cry of triumph and flew off. JJ stood up, brushing off his clothes, feeling a little embarrassed and glad no one was with him.

You really have that woman on your mind.

Which is why, he told himself, he wanted to date Karen. It was time he did something to sort out his feelings and just running around in his own mind wasn't getting it done. After all, if she said no, then at least it was resolved and he could stop thinking about what might be.

What if she says yes?

Then an array of possibilities opened up. And with the possibilities came anxiety.

JJ wished it was just simple lust. He knew what that was like, it was quantifiable, containable, and didn't have any other baggage associated with it. That, however, wasn't the only thing which attracted him to Karen, though it was certainly part of it.

There was a security, for a man, in staying focused only on sex. With Karen, it felt like he might be taking a step into deep water, into currents which had never been plotted. He had been married before, very briefly; his wife had had little tolerance for the requirements on his time that the job brought. After two years, it was over. Then there was only the job.

JJ couldn't understand his fears, for it was unclear what he was risking. Nonetheless, he felt that, even as he prepared himself to find a thing, he was potentially losing a thing.

He wondered if it was the same for women, but he doubted it. They seemed self-assured, able to move with certainty.

His ex-wife had seemed damned certain when she asked him for the divorce. He felt like he never really understood what was going on and could not make himself angry at her. He assumed it was his fault in some undefined way and agreed to her request. She remarried and, by all accounts, was happy with her husband of the past eight years.

Women seemed, at least as he pictured them, knowledgeable when it came to relationships. Was this part of their upbringing? Did their mothers impart special education to them or did they suddenly gain access to genetically stored data when their hormones fired up in puberty?

JJ shook his head as he got into his car. It wasn't that women were a mystery; it was that being a man was so confusing. As he drove away, he suddenly wondered:

Did   women   know   that?

Chapter 49

Catherine hung up the telephone. She had not said much to John Wesley (she always thought of him with his first and middle names, a habit from childhood) except to say that something had come up that she needed to talk to him about. He was reluctant, distracted by, she thought, his going through the Mickey Mouse of the chairperson application.

He became more attentive when she said she thought her father, his uncle, might have a serious problem. John Wesley's loyalty to his family was fierce, a feature of his which she discovered years before when it looked like at least some family members were going to split her off. She had tried to talk to them about what she was finally accepting about herself.

Her brother Charles had reacted as she expected; his anger was carried around like scalding liquid in a cup with too shallow a brim and it was easily slopped onto people nearby. Her other siblings seemed, in varying degrees, hurt and confused, uncertain as to how to respond. Even her own father was hesitant.

Only two people were unconditional in their acceptance. One, of course, was her mother. She remembered her in the kitchen as she fought to speak, to try to explain what she was only barely able to understand herself, and how her mother reached out to her and, in so doing, rallied her father. Or, at least, begin to rally him. It took him a while to come around.

With John Wesley there was no hesitation. Friends since childhood, sharers of secrets, they offered each other a kind of sanctuary over the years. When she told him, filled with fears and trembling with emotion, he looked at her with level eyes and just said,

"So?"

Then John Wesley Parker reached over and took her in a hug and held her until she stopped crying. He always seemed to do the right thing by her.

They had their secrets, of course, parts of their lives they never shared even with one another. He had never talked much about Vietnam to her, and there were things she never discussed with him. On her part, the little she held back was because she didn't want to look bad in his eyes, though she had surprised herself over the years at the number of things she finally had talked to him about.

Catherine wondered at his silences, not sure if there were things left unspoken for that reason or because he thought there were things she could not understand. On the other hand, in some ways he was more like her father than his. His father Richard was fairly gregarious, quick to laugh and express himself. Hers...

Well, Dad took a little reading at times which was why she wanted to talk to John Wesley. He always had a good sense of his uncle, something she saw most clearly during her mother's illness and death.

She heard Terri's car in the driveway and walked into the kitchen to put on coffee. Terri worked as an emergency room nurse in a hospital in Middletown and she often needed to sit and talk after what were termed "tough days."

They had met because of a particularly tough day. Terri was at the hospital only a few months when a pickup truck, overloaded with teenagers celebrating a football victory, tried to run a fast changing light. They hadn't made it and were slammed into by a pizza delivery van. The impact tore the cap off the truck's bed and young people went flying across the intersection. The truck rolled and the cab roof was crushed, pinning four more kids inside.

The county activated, as part of its emergency protocol, a Critical Incident Stress Debriefing team. Catherine, trained by the former paramedic and firefighter turned psychologist, Jeff Mitchell, who originated CISD, was part of the team.

They worked with everyone – police, fire, dispatchers, and ER personnel – who was a part of the emergency response. So many people were immediately involved that several debriefings were set up. Catherine didn't meet Terri until later in the week when she checked in at the emergency room to see if anyone needed any follow-up.

Terri was shorter than Catherine, with close-cropped dark hair and serious eyes, as if waiting for a challenge. But she was quick to smile and had a fine sense of humor. They started talking during Terri's break and both cautiously looked for the private signal flags indicating it was all right to proceed.

They arranged to meet at an art museum in Cincinnati, followed by dinner. Catherine thought she was reading Terri correctly but to check it out suggested stopping off for a drink at a bar known for a particular clientele downtown. Terri's eyes slightly widened and she smiled, cocked her head to one side, and said,

"I thought you would never ask."

They never made it to the bar, not that night. Terri moved in with her a few weeks later. That was almost four years ago; they had an anniversary coming up in October.

Terri came in and yelled a hello from the front door as she dropped her keys and purse on a stand. Catherine yelled back and heard Terri jog up the stairs. Soon she heard the water of the shower running. She waited; Terri's use of the shower after her shift was usually a sign of heavy work, part of a process to clean herself psychologically rather than physically – the ER staff could shower at the hospital – and she sometimes needed a few moments alone while the water pounded on her.

After a while Catherine took two cups of coffee and went upstairs. Terri was just shutting the shower down and stepping out when she entered the bathroom.

"I shall nominate you for sainthood," Terri said, grabbing a cup of coffee and a thick terrycloth towel at the same time. Her voice had vestiges of a Kentucky twang, which came pronounced when her emotions flared, good or bad. She took a sip and sighed. "Or possibly statehood."

Catherine grimaced and took the towel. Terri sat on the edge of the tub while Catherine dried her back.

"Tough day?" Catherine asked. She often watched the news in order to anticipate what Terri might have encountered during the day but she had missed it while talking to John Wesley.

"Tough enough," Terri said, taking a sip. "We had a couple of kids come in DOA but the EMTs had started resuscitation so we had to keep it going 'til the doc called it." She shook her head. "Wasn't their fault, the medics had responded to a TA with an extrication but after pulling two dead out they thought they had got something when there probably wasn't a line at all." She sighed.

"The rescue folks were just desperate for a save, is all. But it meant we had to keep going even though we knew it was going nowhere." She lowered her head for a moment while Catherine kept rubbing her now dry back. She continued to do it until Terri's head came back up, then Catherine threw the towel over her head.

"Dry your own self," Catherine said with a mocking tone as she got up. "I've got work to do."

She went downstairs. It was important to give Terri both a chance to talk and some room to process whatever she had to deal with, and part of the challenge was in finding the balance. She didn't do therapy with Terri; she didn't have objectivity and, besides, inflicting the kind of pain therapy could cause wasn't something she ever wanted to do.

Catherine busied herself at her computer. Logging onto the university system, she checked for email. There were the usual campus and faculty announcements that would be replicated by memos and fliers in her mailbox back at the department. She shook her head while ordering her Performa to delete message after message. Outside of helping her writing, she didn't believe the computer revolution had resulted in any time being saved. Certainly not her time, anyway.

There was one email message from a psychologist at a VA hospital in Pennsylvania responding to her recent comments about treating trauma. She saved it to be re-read later.

And there was one final message, this one from Ellen, a reply to a message Catherine had posted earlier in the day.

Dear Aunt Catherine,

I'm at the farm (but you know that–I must be very forgetful. Can you be senile at 13?). <G> Anyway, thanks for talking to me. It's OK to talk with John about this stuff. Hope you can figure things out. ;-}

Love you,

Ellen

Beam me up, Scotty; there's no intelligent life down here.

Catherine breathed a sigh of relief. She hadn't told John Wesley what she needed to talk to him about, other than it involved her father, which he must have found mysterious. She didn't think she could violate Ellen's confidence and had wondered how she might talk around the specifics of the girl's fears.

Catherine was glad to see the grin indicator and the "smiley" at the end, though her automatic tag line was ancient. Maybe the girl was feeling better. She typed out a quick reply that she would be seeing her soon and transmitted it back to Ellen's CompuServe account.

Catherine was shutting everything down when Terri came down the stairs. Besides tight jeans, she had put on a black t-shirt showing a wolf in the woods and a Harley-Davidson motorcycle with the caption, "Survivors."

"What's for dinner?" she asked, plopping down in a comfortable chair in the living room.

"I picked up a pizza from Alfredo's on the way home."

"Sicilian vegetarian?" Terri toweled her hair.

"Yep. It's warming in the oven."

"I accept your premise that there is a god." Terri finished with her hair after giving it a shake. "Let's eat."

"It'll be ready in a minute," Catherine said.

Terri folded the towel neatly, carefully, as if it was important. She was pausing, Catherine knew, getting herself ready to ask or say something important but afraid she might offend.

"Did your niece call again?"

Catherine shook her head. "No, but she left me some email. She seems to be OK."

Terri looked at her. "And how are you doing?"

Catherine sighed. "I don't know. I feel like I'm caught between two speeding trains. On the one hand, there's my family. I never thought anything would ever cause me to reconsider my loyalty to any member of it. On the other, I feel like some of the things I value most are being called into question."

"You mean your faith."

"Yes," Catherine said. "It's been like an anchor for me. Something solid that's kept me from being cast adrift and running aground. But my faith is telling me one thing while my feelings about my family are telling me something else."

"You've spent too much time sailing this summer," Terri said, grinning. "Too many nautical metaphors. But I get your meaning." Her voice turned serious. "I wish I had your faith. I envy it. I guess I had such a hassle with the church that I couldn't hold onto it." Her smile returned. "I'm not fallen away; I leapt."

"You have more faith than most people I see in church, old girl," Catherine said firmly. "You show it every time you walk into that emergency room."

"Yeah, well, maybe," Terri said. "But how do you find the balance between your faith and your loyalty?"

"I don't know," Catherine said slowly. "But there's part of all this I don't understand. That's why I'm going to talk to John Wesley."

"You need the point of view of a historian?"

"No," she said, shaking her head, "I need the view of a man, of a particular kind of man with particular experiences."

Terri was slow to respond and Catherine saw her thoughts turning. Terri was many things but a hider of her thoughts and feelings she was not.

"Well, your cousin's a good person." Then she grinned. "For a man, of course." Her voice went serious again. "And, of course, it's a family thing so..."

"That's not it," Catherine interrupted. "Ellen asked me to keep to keep it secret. You know that."

Terri held up her hand. "I know, I know. Really, I do. It's just that I can see you're bothered and I wish I could just do something about it."

"Old girl, you do that just by being here."

"You do have a way with words," Terri replied, smiling. She ran her fingers through her hair in a half-hearted attempt at restoring order to the chaos. "It probably does her some good to have someone to share her problem with."

"I think you're right." Catherine hesitated. "I appreciate your not pressing me for details about what it was all about."

"No problem, Cath," the dark haired woman replied. "I wished I'd had an adult I could have confided in while growing up. Might have kept me out of some craziness." She shook her head. "Has it ever seemed to you that there's something wrong with a species where the young can't learn from the old when they need it?"

"Well," Catherine said carefully, "she has someone; her grandfather has always been there for her. The problem has to do with him, unfortunately."

Terri's eyes went wide. "Wait a second, Cath. Forgive me for asking, but she isn't in any kind of danger or anything?"

"No, no," Catherine said quickly, shaking her head, "nothing like that. Her grandfather would never hurt her. In fact, he would..." her voice trailed off.

In   fact,   he   would   kill   for   her.

Chapter 50

Sometimes things happen so smoothly they give the impression, at least in retrospect, that they were foreordained, or at least so naturally obvious that there could have been no reason for ever doubting their occurrence.

Asking Karen for a date was a lot like that. All the way back to the office JJ managed to keep his stomach in a spin with nervousness. He had been in high-speed pursuits where he had felt calmer. Hell, he helped deliver a baby in a thunderstorm at a car wreck in the middle of the night and felt calmer. He kept thinking of experiences in which he felt calmer until he parked his car, a little surprised to find himself back.

JJ learned a long time before the best way to deal with things that had you nervous was to go do them immediately. So he strode up to Karen as if a soldier on parade. She looked up from her paperwork and smiled, a little surprised.

"Karen, I was wondering if you'd like to go out to dinner with me?" His voice unconsciously settle into the tone he used when issuing citations or reading someone their Miranda rights.

"That would be fine," Karen replied, smiling. "Nice of you to ask."

"Yes, it was," JJ replied without thinking, still fixated on his mental script. "How about tonight?"

"I can be ready by six," she said, working hard not to laugh.

"Fine," JJ said. Then he turned and marched towards his desk. He went about six steps before he realized what he had said.

Idiot.

He visibly slumped and his march almost became a shuffle. He didn't dare look at her for fear of what he might see. He pretended he was studying his files and just sank lower into miserable embarrassment.

Just before everyone left for the day, Karen walked over to him. She had seen his embarrassment and finally decided to take him off the hook if she could.

"Listen, JJ," she said, "I forgot to ask. How should I dress?"

He looked up, an expression of surprise on his face, as if he had thought he would never see her again.

Karen looked into his eyes and felt the electricity she had come to know whenever he looked at her.

How can a guy with eyes like that ever be uncertain? And how come it took him so long to ask me out? What did I forget to do?

"Ah, it'll be fairly casual." He gestured with a thumb. "There's a nice steak house I thought we would try. Family kind of place. If that's okay," he added hurriedly.

"That would be great," she said, turning on her best smile. "I'm looking forward to it." She upped the amperage of the smile and turned and walked back to her desk. She had just started to sit when she wondered if she had come on too strong.

Idiot.

With the anxiety both were feeling, a reasonable projection of the coming evening would have been for a social disaster in a scale comparable to that of the Titanic, or at least the Hindenburg. But once the two were in JJ's car the stiffness and the tension melted away, evaporated by mysterious forces which couples, if they are at all lucky, discover.

The food was excellent, though neither noticed. The service was a bit slow; neither noticed. It was raining when they left the restaurant; they noticed, but they didn't care. Being together seemed, from the very beginning, as natural as a stream flowing downhill.

And when Karen invited JJ into her room at the motel where the agents were staying, it seemed as natural as that stream merging with a river.

When he was driving home several hours later, JJ rolled the window down and let the cool night air sweep in and cover him. Ohio farmland had a scent at night he had never noticed any place he had ever been. It was sweet, warm with promise, with a heavy, almost erotic, earthy smell.

It was a good night, he decided, remembering the past several hours, for sweet odors.

What about tomorrow? Tomorrow, JJ decided, was a time for possibilities. Amazingly, his anxiety about the uncertainty of possibilities involving Karen was gone. What would be, would be, and he wouldn't lose it for lack of trying.

Karen lay in her bed, watching the red numerals of the clock slowly change. Now what? JJ was a source of excitement, of arousal, almost from the first day she met him. His quiet competence, his self-assured manner, without the heavy-handed male competitiveness she encountered so often, and, she admitted, his strong hands and eyes that seemed to draw her inside him, all of it had triggered her interest.

But this had happened before and she had always been able to keep a distance. Desires could be satisfied, but she had stayed away from anything like a commitment. For most men, that was fine.

JJ, she was rapidly discovering, was different. She was feeling like she a part of her she never knew was missing had just been discovered. That was a little scary. Could she give a commitment? Could he? Part of her wanted to just let it go, to let it just be "one of those things" which she let slip into her past.

Or maybe she should hold onto him with everything she had. Maybe he was the one, she grinned in the dark, remembering a discussion and phrase from junior high.

At least, maybe he was one worth fighting for. Her sigh seemed to fill the dark room.

Maybe.

Chapter 51

Tom was up at dawn, as usual. He reheated the "day-before" coffee in the microwave and had a slow cup, considering what he had to do during the day.

As usual, there wasn't much, not when compared to when the farm was being worked by him. He did want to check on the acreage being used for his neighbor's dairy cows; the stream that went through was susceptible to erosion on its banks and he was thinking of putting up a wire fence to keep the cows back. He wanted to change the oil and filter on the tractor, maybe do the plugs at the same time.

And, of course, he needed to clean the guns. Today was the surprise visit to the sportsmen's club range for Ellen and he wanted to be sure everything was ready.

The cows were in the field and a few looked up when he arrived in his pickup. The stream formed the southern boundary and was fenced on its far bank. He opened the gate made of wooden boards and walked through, being careful to close it behind him.

Tom amused himself while walking by trying to see his breath in the cool air. It was almost cold, especially for an August morning, but not cool enough.

As he walked to the stream, he heard a rustle behind him and, looking over his shoulder, saw that a large number of cows were slowly ambling behind him, playing the cow version of follow-the-leader. They were surprisingly silent and he could still remember the first time, as a boy, a herd had done that to him. He had been almost frightened.

The cows, on the other hand, were, well, cows. Who knew what they were thinking?

The stream bank was in fairly good shape. The cows tended to use the same place for drinking, a portion with a particularly gentle slope. While bare of grass, it didn't look like it was eroded. He turned back to the cows, who were standing silently, patiently watching and waiting.

"Happy to see you all haven't messed things up," Tom reported to the cows, who continued to be silent. He shook his head; it was definitely time for breakfast. He walked through the herd, which slowly stepped aside for him and then followed him in a parade back to the gate.

Ellen was up and fixing breakfast. She was a little distracted of late, he noticed, but he was reluctant to push her to talk about it, assuming it had something to do with her parents.

He looked at the calendar. It was Wednesday, an egg day. Sure enough, she was poaching him one. It wasn't his favorite way to have an egg, much preferring frying, but the doc was pretty emphatic about the restrictions on his cholesterol and fat intake.

That's why she was cooking up some turkey sausage patties to go with it. He shook his head. Turkeys were to be eaten, preferably stuffed, two times a year and never for breakfast.

What's the world coming to?

Ellen just about had everything done, and all at the same time, when she heard the car in the drive. Her grandfather was already at the back door.

"It's your Aunt Catherine," Tom said, and a few moments later Catherine was climbing up the back steps. Grandpa Tom opened the door for her and held it as she came in, giving him a kiss on the cheek as she did.

"Hey, Big E," she said.

"Hey, Aunt Catherine," Ellen replied. "Want some breakfast?"

"Just coffee," Catherine replied. "I ate before leaving home."

Ellen noticed that her grandfather didn't ask why his daughter was there. He never asked when any family came by, just sort of accepted it.

Eventually, after Ellen finished shuffling pans, pots, plates, and cups – she didn't care for the taste of coffee and liked an herbal tea called "Bengal Spice" because of its taste and a really neat picture of a tiger on the box – they were all sitting at the kitchen table.

"What's up, Aunt Catherine?" Ellen asked around her food. Unlike her grandfather, she almost always asked about what might be going on.

Except for one thing.

"Not much," Catherine said. "The term is finally over and we have a couple of weeks before classes begin again." Ellen felt a cold pang; she would be leaving the farm in a couple of weeks. How had time gone by so fast? It wasn't fair. She forced herself to listen.

"...just a few papers to grade, so I thought I'd slip out here and see you guys before you had to go on back home." There was that pang again.

"John Wesley is coming out for the weekend," she was looking at Grandpa Tom, "and I thought we might have you all for dinner, maybe on Saturday."

"Who else will be there?" her grandfather asked, his voice flat, almost emotionless. Ellen sensed a rise in tension but had no idea what was causing it.

"Well, you two," Catherine said, "and John Wesley, and Terri, of course." Her voice trailed off a little but she kept her eyes steady on her father's. Ellen sat silent, switching her gaze back and forth between the two adults, trying to understand what was happening.

Her grandfather wiped his mouth with his napkin and then pulled out a handkerchief and blew his nose. He carefully folded it and put it away. No one said anything.

"That would be," Tom finally said, "fine." Suddenly, Ellen found that the room was lighter, as if the sun had been hidden by gathering clouds but was now emerging.

"I think I've met Terri once or twice," he continued. "At the school."

"Yes, last year," Catherine said, nodding, "She was there for the awards ceremony during graduation. I don't think the two of you had a chance to talk much."

"No," her father said, "It was pretty busy." They were talking about the award Aunt Catherine had received for her work in trauma, which was given in a little ceremony during a big graduation. She had only seen Catherine from a distance, clad in a cap and gown and looking very formal. Her friend Terri and she had shaken hands when the dark haired woman walked up to the family members present and introduced herself.

Was she the only one who had shaken hands with her? She couldn't remember. Terri was a nurse, she remembered from somewhere, and at one time she had wanted to be a nurse herself. Then she had wanted to be a farmer like Grandpa Tom. But now she wanted to be a Professor, like Aunt Catherine or "Uncle-in-law" John Wesley – she used the slightly teasing title she and Eileen had invented years before.

"I need to go feed Redbone," Ellen announced, and she went out to collect the cat's bowls. As the screen door banged shut, Catherine looked over at her father.

"Looks like Ellen's had a good time this summer on the farm," Catherine said.

"She's managed to keep us both busy," her father replied. "She's got enough energy for three or four people."

"I'm glad you're going to come over, Dad," she said, changing the subject abruptly. "I appreciate it."

Tom shifted in his chair, uncomfortable. "Sometimes," he said slowly, "you need to remember what your priorities are."

"What do you mean?"

"Taking care of your own," he said less slowly, as if on familiar ground, "can mean doing things that you might not do otherwise."

Catherine felled a stir of unease. "Do you mean because of love?"

Tom shook his head. "That's just the start, sometimes. What I mean is duty. Fulfilling your responsibilities, no matter what. That can be even if there is no love, I suppose, but..."

Catherine suddenly looked alarmed and Tom quickly shifted.

"I love you, Cathy. Never doubt that." He reached his hand across and put it on hers. "I was just talking about what you have to do sometimes. Yes, Terri and all that is something that I still try to figure out." He smiled slightly. "I'm a little behind the times, I reckon. So I get a little uncomfortable. My problem, not yours. You two love each other, that's the key. Your mother taught me that and she was right."

Catherine nodded and blinked back tears. "I know, Dad. I guess sometimes I get a little scared. So much has happened, it plays on my imagination and I worry about losing you." She squeezed his hand.

"Never worry about that," her father said, squeezing back.

"I don't mean your love," Catherine gently corrected. "I mean you." She looked into his eyes. "Sometimes, the things in your life, in someone's life, can hurt them, maybe even destroy them, from the inside out."

Her father looked at her, his head slightly tilted to one side, and he paused before saying anything.

"On the other hand, there are times when if you didn't do what your obligations required, that failure would destroy you. You wouldn't be able to live with yourself." He fell silent.

"I guess," Catherine said slowly, as if her words were a minefield she had to walk carefully through. "That's something I'm still trying to get a handle on, the idea that there are things you have to do which, if you don't do, would mark you as some kind of failure, but if you do them, might affect you in terrible ways."

Her father moved his napkin around on the table, quiet for a moment.

"I suppose," Tom said finally, "that's the nature of duty; you don't assume it unless you can live with it." His words were certain but he didn't look at Catherine. "It can cost you a lot, even doing what you're supposed to." He raised his eyes to hers. "I think that's something your mother and I wanted to be sure you and the other kids understood. Doing right can be very hard."

"But when things, when values, conflict, how do you know which is right?"

Before Tom could respond, Ellen came running in.

"I hosed off his bowls outside and filled the water one," she announced. "Just have to get him some food." She plopped the steel bowl on the counter top and poured food from a bag. "He's stretched out on top of your car, Grandpa. Do cats try to get a tan?"

"I don't believe so," Tom said, smiling slightly.

"If they did," Catherine added, "I would think they would all move to Florida."

"That makes sense," Ellen replied seriously, closing the bag, a smile playing on the corners of her lips the only indication that she knew the adult was fooling. She picked up the bowl, ran back outside and was back almost instantly.

"Aunt Catherine, do you want to see my garden? My watermelons are just about ready to be picked."

Catherine looked at her father and then her niece.

"Sure, E. Let's see what you got."

Tom watched the two leave. He took the breakfast dishes over to the sink and cleaned them. He frowned slightly. What did Catherine know? He shook his head. It was impossible for her to know what he was doing to the men who had killed Eileen.

Catherine was not a stupid woman, and she might have put some clues together. Maybe something Ellen said, though he was certain he had kept his movements and plans hidden from her.

He had tried to reassure her without saying too much but he wasn't at all certain he had done so. More than any of his other children, she had her mother's religious sense, a concern with the spiritual. She wasn't a blind zealot, he knew. On the other hand, she found strength in faith that he had never known.

All you can ever depend on is yourself and, if you are lucky, your family.

If Catherine knew, or even suspected, what would she do? Tom shook his head, knowing the answer as soon as the question appeared in his head.

She would do what she thought was right, just as she had done with everything else in her life. He would live with that, he decided. He couldn't try to force her to do anything else.

Her struggle would be hers and whichever way it went, he would stand by her. That part, at least, came easy.

Chapter 52

JJ eased the government car into the parking lot and got out slowly. He had forced himself to get up early to check out one more location on his map; his jeans' wet knees suggested it had not been an easy job, but there had been no discovery.

Eight down, nineteen to go.

Davidson caught up to him at the coffee urn, where he was fixing himself some blood substitute.

"Good morning," Davidson said, adding a little more coffee to his cup. He glanced at JJ's jeans and beat-up old Army jacket. "Been doing a little field work this morning?"

JJ nodded. "Place just below Hamilton. Map showed it being covered by woods but they've mostly been cleared since it was made." He shrugged. "Couple of spots were still pretty much out of sight and I ended up following a stream to get to them. Nothing there, though. The aerial pictures didn't cover the spot so I had to do it the old fashioned way."

"When you get a chance," Davidson said between sips, "get me a copy of your map with an update on the places you've already covered. I've got Peter running down some info which may give us a lead on how far away the main lab is from the one we busted. It's a thin lead," the DEA agent admitted, "but your stuff might fit in."

JJ said he would and Davidson turned to go. He paused and looked back.

"Almost forgot. We're going to do a press conference on Monday to give them info about what we've done so far. It'll be at the Sheriff's Office in Hamilton and I'd like you there." At JJ's startled look, he raised his free hand. "Don't panic. We're going to have me, Steve Johnson, Karen, and you there from the task force, and Sheriff Joseph Donald Pippen, and representatives from Hamilton and Middletown PDs and the County Prosecutor's office. Probably some federal prosecutors as well. You don't have to say anything, I just want you there."

Davidson swirled the plastic stick in his coffee cup. "You've missed it, but during the past couple of days the media got a whiff of our busting the lab and they were setting up camp in our parking lot. We finally got them to withdraw by agreeing to the conference. Figure we can dole out some political points to the locals at the same time. Sheriff Pippen and everyone else has agreed to let me do the talking; the prosecutors on all levels have been very supportive of that. But they'll be up there with me and be introduced."

JJ nodded. That was important. While all the cops were fully invested in busting these assholes, they also lived in the real world of budget fights and, in the case of the Sheriff, elections. Sometimes it took some delicate tightrope walking and it was a stupid federal agent who didn't take into account the needs of local cops. Davidson was not stupid.

"So wear your uniform and be prepared to do introductions all around if anyone doesn't know everyone, that sort of thing." Davidson walked off.

Back to being a spear-carrier and no longer the spear point.

JJ turned back to his coffee. Well, Davidson hadn't said the leash was being hauled in so he still was on his own. He walked back to his desk to get his map. Maybe, if he worked through the weekend, he could get a few more sites checked out before Monday, just in case.

He was at the copier getting duplicates of his map when Steve Johnson walked up. Like everyone else this morning, he was carrying a cup of coffee.

"Hey, Deputy Dawg," Steve said. "How's it going?"

"Not bad, J. Edgar," JJ replied, studying the copies and making notations with a felt tip pen.

Johnson looked around. "Listen, you got a minute?" JJ looked up and saw Steve's expression was serious. He nodded and they walked down the hall to a small conference room. JJ closed the door behind them after they entered. Johnson put his coffee cup down and turned, putting his hands in his pockets.

"I might be way out of line here," Steve said slowly, "but I need to ask you. What's going on between you and Karen?"

"That's none of your business," JJ snapped.

Steve held up his hands. "I know, I know; you're right most of the way." He paused. "Look, here's the thing. I've known Karen for a long time. Years. She's close to my wife and I. Hell, she was at my daughter Elisa's christening. We know her family. I've been like the big brother she never had. And I know she's taken more than a few hits in her life, you know?" He paused, looking a little miserable.

"Christ, I know I don't have any right to intervene. But I think you're a pretty decent man. I'm hoping that what you two are putting together is something that will go for the long term; she deserves it. On the other hand, if this is just something for the moment, then I want you to know that she might be a little vulnerable."

JJ remained silent for a moment, letting his flash of anger subside. Finally, he let himself speak.

"Look," JJ said, "I know you're trying to do the right thing by her. But so am I, all right? All I can tell you is that I wouldn't do a thing to hurt her. As for what's going on between us, that's still our business. I will say that, as far as I'm concerned, this is not a one night stand."

Steve nodded. "Thanks, JJ. I know I've crossed some boundary lines here, but, again, please understand that I'm a friend of hers and that's where I'm coming from."

JJ thought for a moment and then held out his hand, which Johnson took quickly.

"No harm done, J. Edgar," JJ said. "She's lucky to have a 'big brother' around."

The two men smiled at one another and walked out of the room. Johnson walked with JJ back to his desk.

"Hey, you know that news conference on Monday?" JJ nodded. "Carl wants me to bring some displays for the presentation. You know, some charts and maps for the easel. But Karen and I are going with him so we can get our notes together. If you're going over in your own vehicle, could you take them? I'm afraid we're going to be a little tight for room and they might get messed up."

"No problem. I was going to check in here before driving down to Hamilton, anyway. Just leave them with Anne if you have to take off before I get here and I'll get them to you."

Steve grinned. "Thanks, Deputy Dawg." He made a shooting gesture with his hand and walked off.

Not a spear-carrier but a poster carrier.

JJ shook his head. Oh, well, what the hell. He grinned. So he wasn't interested in a one night stand, was he? Well, it was nice to discover that about himself, even if it was by accident.

There was a lot to do between now and then, he thought as he stacked his copied maps together and stapled them for Davidson.

Still   time   to   get   some   hunting   in.

Chapter 53

Tom and Ellen were in his truck, making their way north into Preble County. He had carefully loaded the guns and ammunition behind the seat and covered them with a blanket. Ellen, told only that she was going to have a surprise, had fixed a lunch of sandwiches and apples.

The gravel road into the sportsmen's club was well graded. It curved around rising terrain but they didn't have to follow it very far before they came to the 100 yard range. As it was the middle of the day, there were few other shooters around.

Two middle-aged men were using the twenty-five yard pistol range adjacent to theirs. They had placed bowling pins on a table made of railroad ties and, one at a time, they were firing rapidly with automatic pistols, trying to knock them off the table.

Her grandfather showed her how to use the earplugs, squeezing them down before putting them in their ears. As they expanded, the world around Ellen went quiet and she felt a heaviness in her ears. It was a little weird but possibly cool. Then he showed her how to wear the ear protectors. His were an old, beige colored set, while hers were still in the cardboard and plastic package. They were slimmer than his and were blue. Definitely cool, she thought.

Her grandfather let her watch the speed shooters for a while. They were wearing golf shirts and baseball caps and she saw when they turned that they had on yellow sunglasses. They waved and she waved back.

She raised one ear protector as her grandfather explained.

"What they're trying to do is not only hit all the pins but to hit them in just the right way so that they're knocked off the table. You can see that their guns have been modified for the competition." Ellen nodded, though she wasn't at all certain how they were modified, except that each gun had what looked like a big tubular sight and she knew that handguns didn't usually have such things.

Ellen watched some more and then went over to help her grandfather unload the things in the truck. She had seen his guns before, of course, though she had never handled them. The dark blue long case carried the rifle, she figured. He had a big fishing tackle-like box and she carried that. He also carried something shorter than the rifle case wrapped in a blanket.

They walked over to the other range. It had places to sit at tables. There was no one else there and Tom used one of them to set up their stuff. He opened the case and removed the long, black rifle. This was the closest she had ever been to it.

Its stock seemed to be made of a dark gray fiberglass-like material, not wood. The barrel and trigger were black, as was the forward folded bipod. Mounted on top was a black telescopic sight. Her grandfather dropped the bipod legs and extended them, rotated the bolt to the rear and left it there, and examined the breech, ensuring there were no loaded rounds in the rifle. Satisfied, he let the rifle rest on its butt and bipod and went over to the case she had carried.

She stared at the rifle. It seemed to be a black finger, pointing at something she could not see. It looked as dangerous as it was, lean and dark, capable of a kind of controlled savagery she could only guess at. And yet, even with all of its menace, there was something else present as well.

There was a kind of dark beauty to the Remington. It was built as a precision instrument; it reminded her in some ways of the microscopes and medical instruments of her favorite television shows, though its purpose was very clearly not about healing. In its sharp lines, it also conveyed a sense of grace, like a beautifully wrought sword. She wondered if the people who made it thought of themselves as similar to the artisans she read about who made the swords of ancient Japan and Europe.

She found herself both drawn and repelled by the rifle. Her hand lifted from the benchtop and reached out tentatively. She ran her fingertips down the underside of the synthetic stock. It was cool to the touch and hard, as if self-contained, complete in itself, needing nothing from the outside.

That was not true, Ellen knew. It was meaningless, useless, without someone to use it. Its meaning, she knew, was found not in it but in its user. Without a person to use it, it was just so much pointless weight.

She turned and saw her grandfather looking at her, pausing over the opened case. She smiled nervously, wondering if she had done something wrong by touching the rifle, but he only smiled back. He pulled some paper targets from the case and closed it. He motioned downrange with his head.

He was talking to her but she heard almost nothing until he smiled and lifted her protectors and positioned them under her chin.

"You can put them back on in a minute," he said. "Let's put up some targets."

There were target butts set to one side of the range made of cheap fiberboard and six by six's at twenty-five feet and fifty yards. A longer set crossed the sixty foot width of the range all the way down at its end, a hundred yards away. A few riddled targets of various types were still up on the fiberboard.

They stapled their targets, four in all, in a neat line with about a foot separating each. On the way back her grandfather stopped at the twenty-five foot butts and put one target up. They walked back to their gear.

"I have something to show you." He unwrapped the blanket and a short rifle emerged. Ellen just looked at it for a moment and suddenly realized that it was for her to use. She missed what her grandfather was saying, but it wasn't because her ears were covered.

He wants me to shoot?

For a moment, Ellen felt her heart pounding and a sense of panic swept over her. Her fears of what her grandfather might be doing, the killing he might be doing, the danger he might be in, all carefully held down since she talked with Catherine, threatened in that moment to overwhelm her.

Her grandfather's voice came to her like a lifeline in a hurricane. She looked into his calm face and found herself, maybe because she was used to doing so, maybe because she wanted to, pulling herself away from her fears and towards him.

"This is a rifle," he was saying, hefting the semiautomatic carbine in one hand, sitting next to her. "It can be a lot of fun to use or it can be a deadly weapon, dangerous even to the person using it. It all depends on how it is used, and that means you've got to be willing to take on the responsibility of that use." He looked at the short rifle with its green, plastic stock.

"When you pick this up you make a decision, whether you intend to or not." He looked into her eyes. "You've got to decide, before you ever put a hand on it, what you're about. You've got to make a commitment."

He was talking about rifle safety, she knew, but in that moment, on a rifle range under the Ohio late summer sun, she made her decision without quite knowing it. She would trust in him, in her Grandpa Tom, and she would live with that commitment. The fear washed away, leaving only a stain behind, almost just a memory of what she felt before.

Ellen would not be able, then or later, to explain because she did not understand how standing next to him while he explained how to shoot a rifle would resolve her concerns. It had something to do with his quiet competency, yes, but there was more than that. The tension building in her could not be sustained indefinitely, of course; having to talk to someone else about it was a sign it had been held too long for her to endure.

Her need to hold on to him was greater than her fear of what might happen and what it all meant. A child, still, she needed what an adult could offer but which few adults in her experience would. Her fear had not been about his actions, not in terms of right or wrong, but whether they might cost her him.

In one of those flashes of approaching adulthood, she suddenly grasped the idea that the only way she would lose him was by death or by letting go herself. He would never abandon her; the stars would fall before that. The choice, then, was hers, to hold on to him or to let go, to run away, to flee the fear of loss by losing.

Choosing what to do may have tapped into all the hours of hearing him, both in words and silence, and into a decision a young girl made standing on the Ohio River shoreline. There was a sense of strength, not desperation, in her realization and decision. She would stand by him, whatever it took.

He saw a change in her face, as if her attention was off him, and Tom felt a surge of irritation.

Kids.

Then she was back and her head lowered slightly, her eyes locked onto his, there was a small smile, perhaps a little grim around the edges, and she suddenly looked ten years older for a moment. He did not know what she was thinking but he knew without any doubt that she was with him as completely as she could ever be.

Perplexed, Tom continued talking about the rifle. He explained its functions, how it was loaded, cocked, how the safety worked. He demonstrated how to aim it and described what a sight picture was. He passed the rifle to Ellen and watched as she demonstrated her understanding of it.

All that time Tom wondered what was going on with her, not quite realizing that she had shed, for the second time under his gaze, another piece of her childhood.

He had her load one round at a time and fire at the nearest target, just to get used to it. He offered suggestions and she tried them out. The little black holes in the white of the target began to appear closer to the black bull's eye. Eventually, they were all in the black.

He had her sight the rifle and then close her eyes and pause. When she reopened her eyes he had her adjust her whole body to reposition the sights back onto the target. She seemed delighted at the improvement.

Then he directed her to fire at one of the targets all the way down at the one hundred yard butts. She squinted, looking at the distant targets. He expected to see some hesitation, perhaps some anxiety, but there was none. She looked, nodded slightly, and folded herself into her shooting position, elbows on the bench, and carefully squeezed off her shots.

He let her fire three from the clip. Using the telescopic sight of the Remington, he saw she had fired about a five inch group well below and to the right of the black bull's eye, which was remarkable shooting for the rifle she was using and her lack of experience. He showed her how to adjust the sights and had her reload the clip with five rounds.

She was a natural, he decided. He watched her breathing change as she fired, how she slowly squeezed the trigger with its heavy pull, how she didn't flinch in anticipation of the .22's flat crack.

The five shot group was in the black, though still slightly right and low. He let her estimate how much of a correction should be applied to the sights after diagramming how much movement her shot group got from the last correction. Then she loaded her clip with five more rounds, jacked one into the chamber, and began firing again.

The rifle and ammunition she was using wouldn't permit extreme accuracy, of course, and the four inch group she was getting was probably about as good as could be done with the combination. On the other hand, she grasped the principles in manipulating the sights perfectly. Ellen's group was centered on the middle of the target.

Tom had her shift fire to another target and shoot out the rest of the box, offering small suggestions and comments as she went. When she was done they went down and retrieved her targets.

The twenty-five foot target brought a frown from her and she studied it all the way down to the hundred yard butts.

When they got to the furthest butts, she looked at her first hundred yard target and saw the three clusters of holes. Her grandfather used a pencil to circle each group and numbered it. She fingered the holes, contemplating them.

"I didn't do very well," she announced. "I got hardly any in the X ring."

Tom blinked in surprise and then smiled. She didn't understand what she had accomplished.

"Well," he said, his voice dry, "you have to understand it was your first time." He smiled more broadly as he saw her nod, her expression serious.

The second target was a sieve of holes clustered around the center. Again she frowned.

"I don't seem to be getting any better."

"Ellen," he said seriously, "that is very good shooting for that rifle and that ammunition."

"You mean for a beginner," Ellen said, looking up at him and squinting in the sunlight. He shook his head slowly.

"No," he said it slowly so she would be sure to hear him, "that is very good shooting for anyone with that rifle and ammunition. Period."

She studied his face for a moment and then smiled.

"Cool."

They retrieved her targets and walked back to the shooter's bench. He talked about the difference in rifles, their quality and workmanship, and a little about ammunition. She seemed to be listening and finally nodded.

"So that's why you load your own," she said.

"That's right," he said as opened the case and took out a plastic box of his hand loaded ammunition for the Remington, "That, and it's cheaper if you do a lot of shooting."

He set up the Remington, placing the butt against his shoulder, his left hand in a fist underneath it, holding it against him and supporting it at the same time. His right hand was gripping the stock lightly. He positioned himself and then closed his eyes, using the trick he had taught Ellen. When he saw how much the target had strayed from underneath the Leupold's crosshairs, he shifted his position again slightly and tried once more. Eventually he was satisfied. He loaded one round.

"This may be a little loud," Tom said, peering into the sight. He took a breath and let it out slowly. At the same time his finger lightly made contact with the trigger and gently pulled it towards him.

Ellen stood behind her grandfather, watching him, when the rifle fired. The Remington slammed the air around her in a sharp explosion that came through her ear protectors and plugs. If the .22 was like the irritated snap of a small dog, the .308 Remington spoke with the angry authority of a wolf. She stood still, her eyes wide, the blue-white smoke drifting away.

"Six o'clock, touching the X ring," her grandfather announced, picking another round from the case. He fired again.

"Six o'clock, in the X ring." He loaded another round, hunched over the rifle, and fired a final time.

"Dead center."

He opened the bolt and left it all the way to the rear.

"Let's go down and see the damage," he said, pulling his ear protectors down around his neck. She did the same and followed.

"There are two schools of thought about precision shooting," Tom explained as they walked. "They're both about how to keep the barrel at the same temperature for every shot. Some people like to let it cool down between every shot. You know, shoot once, have a cup of coffee, maybe read the paper, then take another shot." Ellen smiled at the picture in her mind of a bunch of shooters with their feet up, reading the morning newspaper, while she went around selling cups of coffee to them.

"The other approach is to get the rifle barrel warm by firing a few throw away rounds and then doing your serious shooting."

"How do you do it?" she asked.

"I like to keep the barrel warm," Tom said, "but that may be because I get impatient."

They walked up to his target. As he had called them, the three bullets had made a small path starting just to the outside of the innermost ring. The first hole overlapped the ring. The second was inside the ring and was just touching one of the feet of the X. The third round hole was just a little high and a little to the right of the middle of the X. He shook his head.

"Got a little sloppy," Tom said, "and rushed them. Must have been," he added, showing no smile, "shook up by all that dead-on shooting I saw earlier." He peeled the target down but maintained his serious expression until he saw her smile and he returned it.

They walked back to the bench, one target left behind.

"Can I try it?" she asked. He looked at her and nodded.

He crouched behind her and adjusted the bipod for her. He helped her position her arms around the rifle and had her dry fire a couple of times.

He placed a folded cloth under her right elbow and another behind the rifle's butt. He noticed that she closed her eyes and checked her position without being told.

Tom slipped one round into the breech and let her push the bolt forward and lock it into position. Then he stood back.

Ellen was impressed by the weight of the black rifle. Her left hand was open, the fingers extended to grip her right shoulder and forming a V with her thumb. The base of the rifle's butt rested in the V. Her right hand was a little small for the grip but she was managing it.

The view through the Leupold telescopic sight had been a problem; initially she had attempted to put her eye up against it. That resulted in being unable to see anything. Under her grandfather's gentle instruction she had positioned her head back until she got the maximum view through the lens. The thin crosshairs rose and fell with her breathing. When she tried to stop breathing, it was only a few seconds before they started bouncing in a regular rhythm.

That's my heartbeat!

It seemed strange that the rifle was so responsive to her that it was affected by her heartbeat.

She took a breath and slowly let it out. At the end of her breath, with the crosshairs hovering around the center of the bull's eye, she started to pull on the trigger.

The Remington fired almost immediately, the front part lightly bouncing on the bipod. It was a lot louder being this close to it but didn't shock her.

That's just how it talks.

Where her cheek had rested on the stock felt like she had been lightly slapped, probably because she was unable to press against it as firmly as an adult while still seeing through the telescopic sight. Much to her surprise, while her shoulder had been jarred, it didn't feel like she was hurt by the recoil, though she was glad for the cloth under her elbow.

Her grandfather reached over her, worked the bolt and ejected the empty brass casing.

"Not bad," Tom said as she disengaged herself from the .308. "Want to go see how you did?"

She had hit the black, putting her round inside the 8 ring at about the nine o'clock position. She carefully freed the target, intending to keep it with her other targets.

After they got back to the bench, her grandfather pulled a cardboard box of bullets out of the case.

"Let's see how these work," he said, loading one into the rifle. He sighted carefully at an old target someone had left on the hundred yard butts. Ellen watched carefully.

The rifle fired and for an instant there was like a laser, like something from Star Wars, lancing from the rifle towards the target. She blinked, trying to figure out what she had seen. It had glowed bright red, and seemed to have been a meteor, which raced from the rifle to the target almost faster than she could see it.

Tom pulled the bolt to the rear, sending the empty case dancing across the bench to fall to the ground.

"Well," he said, "I don't believe I'll be firing a lot of those through my barrel, but it was pretty."

"What was it?" Ellen asked, still trying to figure it out.

"A tracer," Tom told her. "They're not really accurate, not like a regular round, but soldiers use them to see where their bullets are hitting so they can adjust."

"Don't they know?"

Tom paused and looked at her. "The good ones usually do."

They gathered up their gear and began repacking. Ellen found all the empty cases for the Remington and carefully placed them in the empty slots of the plastic case holding the unused rounds.

Ellen looked back at the rifle range as they drove off and then over at her grandfather.

I   didn't   know   how   easy   it   was   to   do.

Chapter 54

Ohio can fool you when it comes to weather, Tom thought, though most of the time it played fairly straight. So far, August had been pretty hot and muggy. As the sun rose, it seemed to bake the moisture out of the ground and plants and leave it in the air.

But this morning came up crisp and clear as a day in fall. He went back into the house for his windbreaker, knowing he would probably be putting it on a fence at some point later in the day.

The sun had cleared the eastern tree line by less than a finger's width by the time he came walking back to the house from the barn where he had changed the tractor's oil and filter. The barn held the night cold and his hands seemed to draw the chill in, seeping it into his fingers like some slow moving disease. He rubbed them together and, cupping them, breathed on them.

His doctor had told him about some over the counter medication for his arthritis but he disliked using it, feeling that the more he used the more he would eventually need.

Maybe just being stubborn about getting old.

He was just short of the back door when it flew open and Ellen came jumping out. He never was able to figure out a teenager's need for sleep; they could sleep until noon or be up with, he paused as he heard a call from a neighboring farm in the cold, still air, the cock's crow.

"G'morning, Grandpa," Ellen said, landing at his feet. "Want me to fix breakfast?"

"Well, I'd promised to pick up a couple of boxes of old clothes from church this morning and take them over to the town counseling center. How about we get something in town after I take care of that?"

"Great!" She ran ahead to the truck and was seated, seatbelt fastened, before he was half way to it.

As they drove down the almost deserted road towards Oxford, he noticed that she seemed more animated, more energetic, than she had in the past few weeks. She was looking around at the morning scene, interested in what was going on, pointing out an early morning hawk, waving to a horse standing next to the road, and humming some song to herself.

Tom turned on the heater and alternated putting his hands in front of the panel vents. The cold seemed to be deep inside, as if ice had formed within the bones and collected around the joints.

By the time they got to the church, his hands felt better and he had no trouble putting the cardboard boxes, bound with a motley assortment of tape and string, into the bed of the pickup. He shook hands with the deacon heading up the clothing project and was glad to find it only hurt a little.

The counseling center mostly handled crisis intervention work but, since it was available and willing, also served as a general community support system. Whenever someone came up with a project like this, the center could be counted on to provide help. It was also an advantage that it was open twenty-four hours. A sleepy college student, one of the hotline counselors, showed him where the boxes were stored and he and Ellen stacked them.

The restaurant was on the west end of town, on the road which went up to College Corner on the Indiana border. Being on the side of town away from the university, it tended to be frequented primarily by locals. This early in the morning, it was mostly farmers and people who worked with them who came in.

Several of the men and women sitting around their cups of coffee said hello as Tom and Ellen came in and he returned their greetings with a nod while Ellen smiled and said hello back.

Ellen was working on her stack of pancakes, reading the movie reviews from the Oxford Press, while her grandfather ate his way through a slice of melon and a bowl of oatmeal. There wasn't a movie theater in town – hadn't been one since the old Miami-Western closed years ago – but there was a big one near Middletown she sometimes was able to talk her grandfather into going to if there was something really good on.

"Hey, E."

She looked up in surprise to see Aunt Catherine and her friend Terri standing beside their booth. She smiled in welcome and scooted over to make room.

"Hey, Aunt Catherine. How you doing?" Catherine made no move to sit down.

"Just fine, E." She turned to her father. "'Morning, Dad."

Tom looked up at Catherine and Terri and paused before answering.

"Good morning, Catherine." He paused and then slid over. "Good morning, Terri," he added.

Catherine grinned and sat beside him while Terri sat beside Ellen.

"Good morning, Mr. Parker," Terri said. She had a funny lopsided smile, Ellen noticed.

"How you doing, Terri?" Grandpa Tom replied.

"Just fine, sir."

Grandpa Tom wiped his mouth carefully with his napkin before replying.

"I think, Terri," he said finally, "that you can call me by name, if you'd prefer."

"Thank you, Tom," Terri said.

Ellen though she saw Terri's eyes glisten for a moment, though she had no idea why. But suddenly everything seemed more relaxed, though she had not noticed any tension before. She shrugged.

Adults.

They talked about the farm, mostly, before the waitress took Terri and Catherine's order, and then the conversation turned to Ellen's summer. She talked about all she had done and finally got to the trip to the rifle range the day before.

"You fired Dad's big rifle?" Catherine asked, a little surprised.

"You bet," Ellen said proudly. "And Grandpa said I did real well."

"I've always been a little afraid of guns," Terri said. "You must be very brave."

Ellen blushed a little in response, and more so when she heard her Grandfather's response.

"She is. It runs in the family." When Terri looked over at him, he added, "All the women in the Parker family have been special."

"I agree with that," Terri said quietly, holding his gaze. He nodded, though what he meant was not clear.

"Well, if you want," Ellen piped in, "Grandpa Tom could teach you to shoot." Catherine smiled and looked out the diner window. Terri looked a little perplexed for a moment, not sure exactly how to respond. Tom spoke into the silence.

"Yes, we could do that, Ellen and I." Ellen grinned. "I think all women should know how to shoot."

"I don't know," Terri said, feeling like she might be walking across a minefield. "I really don't like violence. I see so much of it on the job."

"I don't like it, either," Tom said, nodding in agreement. "Women tend to be targets of it, though, and it might be a useful tool to know how to use."

"But I don't know if I could ever actually shoot and kill someone," Terri said. "I mean, it might be fun to learn target shooting. My brother used to shoot skeet and I thought that looked pretty challenging. But I don't know if I could shoot someone else, even to protect myself."

Tom nodded. "Some folks are like that. They respect life so much they would be willing to sacrifice their own before taking another person's. My own point of view," he said, shrugging, "would be that those people are more worthy of preserving than their assailants, but that's not a decision we get much chance to make. But let me put it another way. You might not kill to save yourself. All right. Would you to save someone you love?"

Terri frowned in concentration. "I don't..."

"Would you kill to save Catherine?"

Terri's eyes widened slightly.

"In a heartbeat."

There was silence at the table for a moment. Ellen sensed something had been said, something was acknowledged which was more than the old argument about guns and stuff she had heard people debating all her life. It was something about her grandfather and Terri and Catherine, but she couldn't make all the pieces fit, so she just looked from face to face. It was probably something really complex, and really boring, and really stupid.

Adults.

Chapter 55

John Wesley Parker opened the passenger door of his Ford Ranger and let Pupper leap up onto the seat. Blocking the exit, he then snapped off the lead. It wasn't that he didn't trust the dog, but he didn't want to lose him to carelessness.

He had lost enough in his life to carelessness, he thought.

Driving across Indiana, he had time to wonder what Catherine was concerned about. She was a fast, clear thinker, one he suspected was actually more intelligent than he.

Though they had known each other since childhood, it was only after they became adults that he had truly come to appreciate her. Her friendship was steady and unflinching; he had put it to the test after his return from Vietnam.

He had thought about staying in the Marines but the thought of returning to Vietnam was an idea that both attracted and repelled him. Something inside him wanted to go back to Vietnam as the place where he had felt a sense of purpose. There was the acceptance of other fighting men, which was a thing never to be experienced anywhere else but in an army at war. And Vietnam was a place to take rage, the fury, the sense of no longer being a part of things, and he had all that, and more.

The more was the sense that his future was gone, slipped away from his hand in the upper reaches of the Hoi An valley, as he felt a friend slip away from him while he held him in his arms. In part, he had felt that he had no right to be alive when so many good men weren't.

Catherine was there to fight those feelings, even when it felt like she had to fight him. She had grabbed a hold of him from the first, fierce hug when she met him at the airport, a hug he flinched from, confused, uncertain how to respond, not sure what he would be responding to. She never let go of him from then on. She saw, better than he did, the wounds of heart and soul which don't show to those who don't look.

No wonder she became a shrink.

He eventually saw his anger, that cold blooded rage, as a dragon which he could chain and, after a great deal of painful practice, control. But the chains were, at best, loose, and others often sensed that and backed away from him. John Wesley did not have many friends, but those he had he was fiercely loyal to. Catherine was one of the precious few.

When Catherine struggled with her own feelings, she had kept it to herself, as if she thought her burden would be too great for him to bear. He suspected what was going on, of course, long before she spoke to him. While visiting her apartment at school he saw certain books on her shelves, noticed the lack of any reference to any male dates, and other clues. It didn't take a genius to guess.

It made absolutely no difference to him, which slightly surprised him. She had been, was, and would always be Catherine; everything else was incidental to his love for her. Feminists would be, he knew, appalled that he had so little regard for what they would consider so significant a portion of her identity.

He could give a rat's ass, he decided, what anyone thought about his feelings for her. To be perfectly honest, he was a little self-satisfied with his reaction. It was nice to find his cynicism could be moved to one side for something so important.

John Wesley held his breath when she said she was going to tell her parents. He knew her mother to be a caring and compassionate woman. But her father Tom was, from his perspective, a fairly rigid, strait-laced man with some pretty old fashioned ideas about what was right and wrong. He figured she was in for some tough sledding.

On the other hand, there was a side to Tom suggesting deeper feelings. When he was getting ready to join First Force Recon in Vietnam, there was an obligatory family gathering for dinner at his uncle's farm. It was an uncomfortable affair with the tension in the air typical of thousands of other families in America in the most painful decade of the Twentieth Century. Some in the crowd of Parkers and in-laws were supporters of the war, some opponents, most confused, all caught up in the anguish of one of their own going into harm's way.

He hated the solicitation from the others, even though he understood they meant well. Finally he ducked out back and went behind the barn. He sat on a low bench where he had played as a boy. In the dark, Tom Parker walked out to him. Though John was regarded by his peers as fairly alert, he still remembered being surprised at the older man's silent movements.

Tom sat beside him for a while, not saying anything, just watching the stars in the Ohio night. Finally, he spoke.

"You may be in for a hard time," Uncle Tom said, "and when you get back you may find that you've got a need to talk about it but no one who can understand what you've got to say." He let the silence roll over them for a few moments before continuing.

"When you feel that you've got to talk, I'm here. I've had a taste of what you're going to run into and I can listen real well." John knew Tom had been in Korea but didn't know any details. "Maybe we'll get a couple of sleeping bags and a bottle and go on out to the woods and you can talk about it."

John mumbled his thanks, believing he would never need it. He never took his uncle up on the offer, even after he realized he did need someone to talk to.

He shook his head as his truck crossed into Ohio. Stupid not to, he supposed, but at the time he felt like there was no one to whom he could turn.

Except Catherine. He hadn't talked to her about the war, not the most important parts of it; he hadn't done that with anyone. But she was like an anchor for him during those hard times, and he would never forget it.

He eased the truck onto the east bound road heading into Oxford. A lot of traffic, maybe from the frosh coming in for orientation.

He didn't know what was going on, but if Catherine needed his help, he would be there for her, he thought while scratching Pupper's chin. He would be there come hell or high water.

Especially   if   come   hell.

Chapter 56

Tom eased his way through the brush, moving slowly, pausing to listen. In the early evening twilight, there was still a faint glow to the west from the escaping sun, though little of it was penetrating to the forest floor. He was following, more by feel than by sight, an animal path, using it to guide him around patches of thorn bushes and other obstacles.

It helped that Tom had been here before. He reconnoitered the route by day and night several times. He knew he would eventually come to the border of the woods. Then there would be a clear, sloping field, cut by several wire fences. At the edge of the field, about three hundred yards away would be an isolated house, a run down and neglected place with its yard pockmarked with scattered piles of mechanical junk.

Next to the house was a barn converted into a garage of sorts. It was highly probable Tom would find Bobby Baker, warlord of the Steel Riders, brother of Jack Baker, working in the garage.

And Bobby Baker was on his list.

Tom paused in the increasing darkness, listening. For a moment, the insect noises around him stopped, perhaps in response to his passing. Or maybe someone else's. He waited as the chirping and chattering returned. He waited longer, moving his head very slowly, using the edges of his sight to see in the dark.

After ten minutes, Tom decided there was no one else. He moved again, but very slowly, with his feet lowered heel first and then feeling for any twigs beneath before he rolled his weight forward.

At the edge of the woods, he saw the yellow lights of the house and garage. He thought Bobby Baker lived alone but waited to see if there was any movement in the house. Nothing moved behind the one lit window after fifteen minutes. He heard, faintly, rock music coming from the garage. He checked the safety on his shotgun and slipped through the wire fence and walked toward the garage.

Tom walked upright, the shotgun carried across his chest. Every few yards he stopped and listened, but all he heard was the steadily increasing volume of the music.

There was no moon, only a few stars out in the night sky glow. The wind was from the south and west, and it came up gently with warmth carrying a hint of possible rain by morning. An owl announced itself behind him and somewhere far off to the right a farm dog could barely be heard barking an urgent communication about something of importance to at least dogs.

Tom stood outside of the barn, to one side from the wide opening. He waited in the darkness, and listened. He heard the music. No commercials, probably a cassette. From time to time, he could hear mechanical sounds, metal on metal, and once what sounded like a can falling to the ground followed by a low curse. The same voice occasionally tried to sing parts of the various songs but was not very successful at it.

There was no window to look through, only the barn door slid to one side. He thumbed off the safety and stepped into the light.

Baker was on his back, under a Toyota four-wheel drive pickup truck, one of those with hyper-extended shocks. The truck was a garish display of metal flake paint and chrome. Tools were scattered around the concrete floor in a haphazard fashion. The music was very loud and came from a boom box sitting on a low table near the door.

Tom measured the distance. Baker's upper torso was mostly under the truck. He was considering shooting him where he lay when the cassette player clicked off. There was a pause and then Baker rolled out from underneath the truck.

He was a well-muscled, short man who wore his hair in a ponytail. At the hearing, he was clean shaven. Now he had a neatly trimmed, downward turning mustache that gave him a vaguely piratical appearance, or maybe that was just how Tom saw him. He was in jeans and a black t-shirt and his eyes were wide with surprise as he saw the man standing before him.

"Who the fuck are you?" he asked in a quavering tone, which might have been from fear or anger, though his expression left little doubt. He was trying to frown but his bunched up face resembled that of a little boy about to cry.

"I'm Tom Parker," Tom replied almost automatically, surprising himself a little for he had not intended on having a conversation with the man. "You killed my granddaughter." He tightened his grip on the shotgun. Baker must have seen the slight movement, or perhaps was responding to the flat, dead tone in Tom's voice.

The biker had not gotten to his feet and, still on his knees, raised his hands. The look on his face was one of terror.

"Look, look, old man, you got it wrong, all wrong," Baker pleaded, the words pouring out of him like blood from a wound. "I wasn't doing the shooting. That was my brother. The fucker is crazy, he just started shooting, I didn't know he was going to do it." Tears were running down his face. Tom saw a stain spreading in his crotch.

"Christ, man, I'll give him to you. He doesn't mean shit to me. The prick is always getting me into trouble. Just don't kill me, please don't kill me." He burst into tears.

"Your brother?" Tom spoke more in amazement than anything else.

"He's out at Rader's place, the old farm." Baker pulled himself together for a moment. "Shit, man, I'll draw you a map, just don't kill me." His voice became shaky again and he started to cry. No, Tom thought, he was weeping, a crying so pitiful that only weeping could describe it.

Tom hesitated in the face of the man's behavior. For a moment, he found Baker embarrassing, even a little disgusting. Baker saw the hesitation and threw himself to one side with startling speed, lunging towards a toolbox.

Tom snapped the shotgun towards the leaping figure instinctively and fired. Within the confines of the barn the explosion was deafening but he didn't notice as he worked the slide and pumped another shell into the chamber.

The empty shell arced to one side and clicked off the concrete floor with surprising loudness in the silence following the blast. There was no other sound as the shell rattled to a halt a few feet away. Tom looked at Baker.

Baker lay on his side facing Tom, frozen in a fetal position, his knees almost up to his chest, his hands gripping at something hidden by his legs. His face was pinched shut and as still as if it was carved in stone. It was several seconds before Tom realized that the man was breathing. He walked closer.

Baker moaned. Blood emerged from beneath him in an increasing puddle. He started shivering. Suddenly his eyes opened. His mouth moved like a fish ashore, gasping for its breath, but for a moment, he said nothing.

His aimless gaze found Tom's face and he squinted, trying to focus. His mouth kept working and finally he spoke in a shaking, gasping voice.

"You fucker," Baker said slowly, "I hope..." He fell silent, the puddle suddenly expanded and, along with whatever he hoped for, he died. The smell of feces slowly rose into the air.

Tom stepped around the puddle and with the shotgun aimed at Baker's head, toed the now limp body. Baker unwound, his arms and legs spreading as he rolled onto his back. The bloody hole in his abdomen, slightly left of center and above his navel, was still oozing blood and tissue. Tom waited for another minute, then reached down to Baker's neck for a pulse but there wasn't one.

He stepped back and glanced around. He saw the empty shell and picked it up.

Then he stepped out of the light and into the darkness.

Chapter 57

Catherine was looking out the window when John's car pulled up. Though he had come into Oxford the afternoon before, he elected to use one of the motels on the edge of town. When he called to tell her of his arrival he mumbled something about not imposing but she knew it was really about his own need for privacy. They agreed to get together early and have breakfast.

Terri was at the hospital, covering for another nurse's shift. Just as well. While Terri and John got along well, Catherine felt awkward talking about what she termed "family business" in front of her because of her promise to Ellen.

It was hard not confiding in Terri; she often served as Catherine's sounding board, someone who was objective, even challenging, as she tried to sort things out. On the other hand, John was able to do much the same thing, though he tended, at times, to be a bit less diplomatic.

She remembered attending the end of one of John's lectures when he was an invited presenter to a seminar at her own school. A pompous graduate student, full of self-importance, attempted to twist what John had said. John responded none too gently, and she overheard two professors sitting in front of her lean towards one another and one say, "He does not suffer fools gladly." The other nodded slowly, as if hearing an important academic pronouncement.

John and Pupper got out of the car together, the dog leaping about on the end of his leash, delighted to be out of the car. John paused long enough to squat beside the animal and, scratching its ears with both hands, touched foreheads with him.

Are they communicating via osmosis?

She opened the door.

"Hey, Johnny!" she said, smiling broadly.

"Hey, yourself," he replied, and then gave her a big hug while Pupper sat looking on. After the hug, the dog stepped forward, tail wagging, a look of expectancy on its face. She squatted before it and carefully scratched its chest. For her efforts, she got several delicate licks of her chin.

"Good to see you again," she said to the dog. She looked up at John, who was watching with a smile matching her own. "You, on the other hand..." John only smiled more broadly. "All right," she said to Pupper, "come on in and I'll feed you. And bring that human with you."

The two of them set to work on fixing breakfast. Like many men, John enjoyed cooking, though he tended towards foods that Catherine would ordinarily avoid, such as fried bacon and eggs. They compromised with poached eggs and home fries. She opened the box of dog food she had gotten for Pupper and poured him a bowl, though the dog was clearly more interested in human fare than his own.

They finished and were sitting back and watching Pupper lick up their plates they carefully placed on the floor. A small portable television sat on a kitchen counter, providing background noise in the form of a morning news show.

"I swear that dog keeps count," Catherine observed, shaking her head.

"I think you're right," John said, taking a sip of coffee. He paused, watching the dog, then swung his eyes towards his cousin. "Now, what's come up with Tom?"

Catherine bit her lower lip for a moment. She had thought about this, about how to approach the subject, and she had found no answer. In the clear morning light it seemed incredible to even be talking about it. Finally, she sighed and looked at John.

"I think there's a good chance my father has been killing the men who killed Eileen."

John said nothing, just looked at her. Her words seemed to lie on the table between them, like something large, dark, and dangerous. He pushed himself back in his chair and finally spoke.

"Are you out of your fucking mind?"

She took no offense and grimaced in response.

"I wish." She sighed again and explained. "Look, Ellen came to me with this. My Dad has been gone at night, a lot of nights, over the summer while Ellen has been there. Including the times when several of those bastards have gotten themselves killed."

"Wait a minute," John interrupted. "I thought there was some sort of gang war going on between them and another gang, what were they, the Dragons?"

"I did a little checking," Catherine said. "The little group that killed Eileen started dying before the gang war started. Now, the newspapers put it all on the doorstep of those Dragons, and maybe so, but it was a hell of a coincidence that the first three deaths in the war were three of the five who were there when Eileen was killed." She paused for a second. "But there's more."

"Ellen got into Dad's work shed; you know, where he keeps his reloading gear and where he locks up his guns when kids are visiting the farm." John nodded. "She said she found a notebook with all five of the bikers in it. Newspaper clippings, pictures of them, small notes, that sort of thing."

"And..."

"And she found that two of them were crossed off. They were both dead by the time she got to the notebook."

"But, hell, that just means he was paying attention to the bastards who killed Eileen," he said, frowning. "Probably began to collect clippings during the arrest and hearing and then, when he heard about a couple of them being killed, he was happy to 'X' them out."

She shook her head. "That's not all of it. He and Ellen went on a short trip over the weekend. Ellen says they were together the whole time. When they got back, she heard on the news for the first time that another of the five was dead, number three. She got into the shed and looked. Sure enough, he had also been crossed off the list."

"Maybe he did it before they left."

"That's the point. He was out the night before they left. The man was killed that night. But his name wasn't announced until after they left the farm and they didn't hear it until they got back. The only way he could have crossed him off the list before they left is if he already knew, and the only way he could have known is if he had done it."

Catherine fell silent, listening to her own words. For the first time, she realized that she believed Ellen's story and understood that her father was killing people.

Murdering people?

The question was tentative. Was this murder or something else?

"Is there any chance at all that Ellen is mistaken?" John said, interrupting her thoughts.

"I don't think so," Catherine replied, shaking her head slowly. "She's being as honest as she can be. It's really put her through the wringer." She looked over at John for a moment. "I think I not only believe she's telling the truth as she knows it, I believe it's happening."

It was John's turn to shake his head. "If you do, why are we talking?"

"Well," she replied, drawing out her answer, "when I was trying to come to grips with this, I found that I kept having trouble making the leap in understanding it. Even now, now that I've spelled it out to you, and I know that Dad is killing those people, even now I have trouble understanding it. I'm having trouble..." Her voice trailed off.

"What you want to know is how can someone kill?" His voice was very calm. "So you wanted to ask me about that so you could maybe understand what was happening with your father?"

"God, John," she said quickly, "I didn't mean to make it sound like..." Again, she lost her words.

He shrugged. "It's all right. It's something you don't know about. Who else would you ask, seeing as how it's not exactly something you can take to your Dad, not under these circumstances?" He leaned back in his chair, folded his arms and studied his empty coffee cup.

"The thing you need to understand is that there are many reasons why people kill. I suspect that, given the right circumstances, anyone, and I mean anyone, could kill. Maybe to save their own life, maybe to protect the life of another, maybe without thinking about it."

"How could you not think about it?"

"It's a defense; if you stop and think you might be so overwhelmed by the horror that you would become dysfunctional. So what you do is you change how you look at it, how you think about it." He shifted in his chair. "I knew men who concentrated on the job, on the technical aspects of it, so that they would not see what was happening in human terms. Other guys treated it like a big, competitive game, and killing someone was like tagging them. Others got into it..." He stopped, avoiding her eyes, and looked over at the television, which was displaying various weather maps.

"Treating it like a game? I don't understand."

"It's just a way of distancing yourself from the reality. For most men, it's hard to stay with the reality that you're killing people. You've got to find a way to stand back from it, otherwise you may not be able to handle it, maybe freeze up."

"What about Dad? How is he handling this?"

John shook his head. "I'm not totally convinced he's doing what you think he is." He held up a hand, cutting off her interruption. "I believe you

281

when you say Ellen is telling the truth, but maybe she simply doesn't have all the facts, maybe there's something that she's overlooked. As for your Dad, remember, he was a soldier, once, and in a nasty little war. He already knows how to cope. But that isn't the issue."

"Then what is?" Catherine had a puzzled look on her face.

"Look, someone like your Dad, he isn't facing any mystery about killing people, there's no great unknown for him to confront and deal with. He's been there and done it, you know?" Catherine nodded. "The real question is why he is doing it. If he is," he added quickly.

"Well," Catherine said, thinking for a moment while the television cheerfully announced a new product from Dodge, "I thought he was doing it in revenge for Eileen's death." John shook his head.

"I doubt it; I don't think that's what's going through his mind." John Wesley leaned forward in his chair and put his elbows on the table. "Revenge would mean putting his butt on the line to take care of old business, and that could be a part of his motivation, but it's a small part. See, Tom knows the position he occupies in the family, how important he is to the family. If he's doing these killings, he's putting himself at risk. In other words, he would be putting the family at risk of losing him. And, while revenge might light his fuse, that would not be sufficient to keep him going."

"So what else could there be? I mean, I see where you're going with this. If he's doing it and we want to get him to stop, we need to understand his reasons. So what else could there be?"

But John Wesley didn't answer. He was staring intently at the television and the picture of a news reader who had a graphic of a chalk outline of a body suspended behind him. She leaned forward and began listening.

."..death is the latest in what appears to be an ongoing war among rival gangs for control of the illegal amphetamine drug trade in the tri-state area. Baker was charged in the killing of a young Butler County girl this past fall, though those charges were later dropped. In other news, the Drug Enforcement Agency Task Force operating in our area announced it would have a major press briefing on Monday to..."

John looked at Catherine and was silent for a moment.

"'So what else could there be?' I don't know. Let's go ask him."

Chapter 58

If Jack Baker, official President of the Steel Riders Motorcycle Club, was seen by an observer with a literary flair, he might have been described as looking knife-like, or perhaps like a black snake whip. The descriptions would tend towards implied violence as well as reflecting his thin, almost gaunt, physique.

There was no such observer at his brother's home. Instead, there was his brother's current woman (a featureless creature who was willing, as the late Bobby Baker had put it, to fuck the Sixth Fleet in exchange for a little speed) who sat on the ground next to the house listlessly smoking a cigarette and watching the paramedics and cops clustered around the barn.

She found Bobby Baker lying in a dried pool of his own blood. With one of the strongest displays of will power in her life, she refrained from immediately jumping back into her own car and taking off for some place where the day old smell of old blood, feces, and human guts, and where the swarming buzzing of early morning flies, would not be. Pausing only to vomit twice, she made her way into Baker's house and found the kitchen telephone.

Instinctively she dialed 911 and, thanks to Butler County's recent addition of call tracing, they were able to identify her whereabouts even after she hung up the telephone. She terminated the call because she realized that the thing she needed to do first was call Jack Baker.

One thing she learned very early on in her relationship with Bobby Baker and the Steel Riders was that it was a very bad idea to piss off Jack Baker. The problem was, of course, she was never quite sure what might do that. It seemed, as she caught her breath after a bout of dry heaves, that not telling him his brother was dead might fall into the category of Things Which Will Piss Off Jack.

Her call to Jack was almost as incoherent as her 911 call. Nonetheless, Jack finally, after struggling through a miserable hangover, made some sort of sense of what she was babbling about. He ran down the stairs of the old Rader farmhouse, collecting other Riders as he went. Disheveled, blinking the morning sun out of their eyes, pulling on bits and pieces of their clothes, they crowded into a station wagon and finally raced down the gravel-covered lane, fishtailing and spraying stones in all directions.

By the time Jack and the other Riders arrived, the ambulance crew and a police car, soon joined by several others, were already there, their lights flashing in bright competition to the sunlight. Not too long after Jack's arrival, the first of several news vans showed up. It was turning into a circus.

Various cops were by to take statements. The Riders followed Jack's lead and cooperated. There was no reason not to and Jack knew this was not the time to generate any antagonism from the heat.

Anyone watching Jack would have been impressed with his stoic endurance of his brother's passing. Not a ripple of emotion crossed his sharp, dark figures. What only the other Riders knew was that Jack was incapable of mourning inasmuch as he was incapable of emotional attachment.

It was, Jack thought, a decided advantage, and a gift he would have given daily thanks for if there was any deity around with sufficient power to impress him. Where others entered into entangling alliances with people, he remained cold and aloof, always figuring out what was best for him without the distraction of considering the needs and feelings of others.

He discovered this gift at a very young age when he found that he could kill his neighbors' and his own pets and have no feeling about it other than a small enjoyment at the sense of power it gave him to kill and, in the case of the neighbors, to hurt.

With a natural ability like that, coupled with an above average intelligence, he became a superb manipulator of others. The best tool for that was feigned emotional attachment. By the time others discovered the truth he was through with them.

The Riders admired his cruelty, mistaking it for strength. He was a superb organizer, knowing almost instinctively how to use people to get tasks accomplished. The most important task was always, of course, getting more power for Jack Baker. That this meant getting power, money, weapons, drugs, and sex for the Riders was simply the cost of the freight that mattered.

But no organization like the Riders was politically stable for long. They attracted various kinds of members, including other walking versions of Jack's personality. While there were few overt challenges since he used a chainsaw on the body of William "Jack-Snake" Faulkner (the device had the advantage of killing his rival, making disposal easier, and, most importantly, shocking the hell out of the few Riders present as witnesses), time stood still for no man or outlaw motorcycle gang.

There were grumbles, and they were heard again as Jack and the others stood beside the station wagon.

"Jack, this really sucks," opined Paul Peterson, a short but powerfully built man with a shaved head and arms almost totally covered with tattoos.

"Yeah, man," said one of the others, not quite understanding what Peterson, one of the upwardly mobile members of the gang, was referring to. "Too bad about Bobby."

"Yeah, right," Peterson said abruptly. "Look, Jack, you said if we took the Dragons down after they started hitting our people that would be the end of it. You said they'd all run back to Buffalo. You said we had cleared them all out. Now they've blown away Bobby. And that's not all. You said..."

"What the fuck?" Baker enquired. "You know the Dragons had to be taken out or our whole business would have been down the shitter. Christ, they had begun to cut into our distribution in Columbus. In Columbus, for Christ's sake! And were we supposed to stand around with our dicks in our hands while they killed us one at a time?" Baker's voice never rose above a harsh whisper, but several Riders instinctively stepped back as if he was shouting.

"Hell," Peterson said, his mouth grinning while his eyes remained cold and hard, "I'm not arguing against wasting the Dragons, but even a moron could see our little war has been half-assed. We should have hit them all at the same time. We were slow getting to those pricks up in Dayton and the ones in Columbus scattered like greased pigs before our people got there." He winked at the others. "I'm betting one of those guys decided to come back and leave a little parting gift in exchange for the Mail Boxx."

"Yeah, maybe," Jack replied, eyeing the arrival of yet another police vehicle, this one a dark van with Sheriff's markings. "If so, he's probably out of the state now. If he's still around we'll find him. And when we do I'll take care of him. Myself."

The Riders glanced at one another and then found things to stare at. Peterson, however, was not showing that he was impressed.

"Yeah, maybe," he said, his tone faintly mocking. "But we got other problems. The cops took out the other lab even before it got into

285

distribution. We've got deliveries that are overdue. Hell, you had us shut down our main lab during our little war with the Dragons. The cops have been laughing like hell at us. The pricks are even going to have a big TV dog and pony show on Monday to brag about it." He shook his head. "We fought the Dragons to maintain our power but the cops are going to make us look like fuckin' wimps." His arm muscles twitched, making it clear that at least he didn't regard himself as a wimp.

Jack turned his black eyes towards Peterson, eyes that Ellen had found as flat as those of a shark. Few men could return Baker's stare. Peterson was one of them, which Baker noted and used to make a decision.

"You think I'm getting soft, is that it?" Baker's voice carried just a trace of amusement. "Well, I've got a little plan to demonstrate to anyone concerned that the Riders are still here and still strong." He reached out with a thin finger and tapped Peterson's broad chest. "And you can come along, if you think you can hack it."

Chapter 59

JJ was still in bed when his telephone rang. He threw an arm in the general direction of the nightstand, still mostly asleep, and surprised himself when he encountered a blanket covered body.

"Hey, sailor," came a muffled voice. "Watch it."

Karen.

Now fully awake, and feeling a little pleased with himself, he levered himself over her body and picked up the receiver.

"Jeffers," he said quietly.

"JJ, this is Davidson. Hate to disturb you on your day off but we just got a courtesy call from your department. Bobby Baker's been whacked."

Number four.

The thought was spontaneous and was accompanied by a memory flash of Tom Parker's picture.

"Can you swing by Baker's place and touch base with your people?" Davidson asked, interrupting his thoughts. "Paulson and Steve are already there but I'd like to have you along. You know how nervous some folks get with feds peering over their shoulders." Davidson gave a small chuckle.

"Right, no problem, boss. I can be there in about thirty minutes." JJ started getting out of bed, the receiver still in his hand.

"Okay, good. I'll let them know you're coming." Davidson hung up and JJ did an awkward dance over Karen to the nightstand and put the receiver down.

He dressed as fast as he could, not bothering to shave or otherwise clean up except for taking a swig of mouthwash which, in his hurry, he inadvertently swallowed some. It burned all the way down.

The perfect start to a perfect day.

On top of his chest of drawers he looked for his pistol. Karen had put both of hers up there and in the dark he fumbled a bit before he found his and his keys.

"What's up?" Karen had barely surfaced her head from beneath the covers and was looking at him bleary eyed, her short hair spiked out in all directions. She looked a mess and she looked beautiful.

"Looks like Bobby Baker's got himself killed. Carl wants me there to liaison. Steve and Johnny Ringo are already there."

"Any Riders around," Karen said, "they might see Ringo and realize he was under cover if they had eyes on him when he was a Dragon."

"At this point, I figure no one gives a damn."

She gave a grunt and dropped her face to the pillow.

"Have a good time," she said, her voice again muffled. "Don't stay out too late."

"I'll be back as soon as I can." He paused. "You be here?"

She raised her head and looked at him steadily for a moment. "Where else, sailor?"

He grinned, gave her a quick kiss on top of her head, and hurried to his car.

JJ got to Baker's faster than he had told Davidson. The back road Saturday morning traffic was very light and his flashing blue light gained the cooperation of what little he did encounter.

Paulson, aka "Johnny Ringo," and Steve were standing near the back of the Sheriff's forensic van. While Steve was wearing the standard coat and tie of a federal agent, Paulson was in jeans. He did have on a sport coat. His hair was longer than usually seen on a government agent and he sported a short goatee. An earring dangled from one ear. He was tall and well built, with a strong jaw and dark eyes that were almost always in a narrow squint. A small smile played around his lips but never seemed to stay.

JJ sized him up as a man who was still transitioning back to the real world after many months with the Dragons. Steve made the introductions and JJ saw Paulson studying him closely.

"Morning, deputy. This is DEA agent John Paulson." Steve's tone was semiformal, so JJ came on the same way.

"Good morning," he said, shaking hands with Paulson. "Deputy Sheriff Jim Jeffers." Paulson's handshake was dry and firm but without any attempt to demonstrate his strength. JJ turned back to Steve.

"What's the situation?"

"We got a quick brief from one of your people." He looked down at his notepad. "Bobby Baker was shot and killed last night, exact time to be determined, by a shotgun at close range. The body was discovered by his girlfriend." He motioned towards the house, where JJ saw a small cluster of people. "She called 911 and then his brother. He and his friends got here right after the ambulance and patrol car."

JJ took a long look at the group of people. The woman was a stranger, sitting slouched against the wall of the house. He could identify several of the men, all members of the Steel Riders' inner circle. He saw the thin form of Jack Baker standing slightly apart from the others and wondered what he thought of all this.

He doubted Baker was in mourning, but maybe he was worried.

Wonder if he's been counting and knows he's number five?

"What's your take on this?" he asked, turning to Paulson.

Paulson had a large voice with a country flavor, reminding JJ of the singer Hoyt Axton, but he kept it low and quiet.

"Steve told me that you thought there was a possibility that some of the hits on the Riders might be coming from people other than the Dragons." JJ nodded in reply. "Well, from what I picked up, I can tell you that if the Dragons didn't waste those Riders, they intended to. I know they had imported at least one shooter from New York." He shrugged. "I don't know if that guy ever got into the act before the Riders dropped the hammer at the Mail Boxx, and I don't know why he would have hit that kid, Larson. He was nothing in the hierarchy of the Riders and I never heard his name mentioned."

He looked over at Baker. "But old Jack, there, he figured prominently in the Dragons' thinking, as did Bobby and Hollingsworth. I didn't know anything about Christopher, but I've read the intel you all had and he was Bobby's right hand man, so maybe he was a target for them as well." He looked back at JJ. "If Jack hadn't ordered up a state-wide massacre, the Dragons were intending to do the same thing to him."

He looked over at the barn as the ambulance crew wheeled a gurney out with a black body bag on it. "I don't know, maybe the shooter is still around fulfilling his contract." His voice was dubious, but JJ understood the possibility did exist.

He didn't buy it, though. He felt certain that Tom Parker would be unable to account for his whereabouts at the time of the killing. Unfortunately, it looked like there was no other evidence pinning the crime on the old man. Nonetheless, there was no doubt in his mind as to who had blown Bobby Baker away.

Bob Phillips emerged from the barn, talking to two other men, one in uniform. He looked up and caught JJ's eye and nodded. He continued talking to the others for a moment and, when they left, motioned JJ over.

"Well, let me see what I can learn," JJ said to Paulson and Steve.

Phillips shook hands with JJ as he approached.

"What can you tell me?" JJ asked after saying hello.

"I gave the prelim to those two." He motioned with his head towards the federal agents. "Say, is that one guy really a fed?"

JJ smiled. "For sure, Bob. He's spent most of the past year undercover with the Dragons. Barely got out alive when it hit the fan."

Phillips nodded. "Still decompressing, I gather. Sure doesn't look like a fed." He looked at JJ. "Hell, Jim, he can probably tell us more about what happened here then we can. Baker was apparently taken by surprise while working. We found a handgun a few feet from the body. He was hit by a shotgun. Looks like a twelve gauge, double-ought, same as the one that hit Hollingsworth and Larson."

He rubbed his unshaven jaw.

Guess we all got up in a hurry this morning.

"I read the summary you sent about the amphetamine lab. Those bastards were pretty heavily armed. You said that there were 12-gauge guns recovered at the scene."

JJ nodded. "Right. One was brand new, right out of the box. Never been fired. The other was chopped. Looked like something a stagecoach guard would carry."

"Yeah, but the thing that caught my eye was that it was even there. From what intel we have, these assholes tend towards automatic weapons, Uzis, MAC-10s, AKs, that sort of thing. It just caught my eye to see shotguns there. Maybe it's a more common weapon than we thought."

"Maybe so," JJ said. "Paulson said that the Dragons were planning to decapitate the Riders and may have brought in an outsider, maybe from New York, to do a little selective killing. He thinks there's a chance the guy, if he came in, may still be in the area fulfilling his contract."

"Now there's an interesting thought," Phillips said. "Wonder how that sits with Jack Baker?" He looked over at the gang leader. "Hope it keeps him up at night." He turned back to JJ. "Got anything else I can use?"

"Not really. Davidson said yesterday that Paulson's summary on the Dragons would be released to you on Monday. I figure they'll be running down the lead of the New York shooter. Anything we get on that I'll forward immediately."

"Thanks, appreciate it." Phillips looked around. "Hell of a way to start a weekend. My boy's got a game this afternoon. Semifinals. Hate to miss it." He paused and looked back into the dark opening of the barn. "Well, back to work. Maybe I can catch at least some of it. See you later." He started to walk away and then stopped.

"You going to be at the conference on Monday?"

JJ nodded. "Yeah. The Sheriff will be there, too. It'll be a big shindig. Davidson figures it will get the TV people out of our parking lot for a while."

"Yeah, they kind of blew your cover," Phillips said, smiling. "I'd guess everybody and his uncle knows the DEA has set up housekeeping in that foreclosed savings and loan."

"You know the feds," JJ said, grinning back, "they probably leaked the location themselves just to get a little more press."

Phillips gave a short laugh and walked away. JJ went back to Paulson and Steve.

"Didn't get a whole lot," JJ said without preamble, "mostly because they don't have a whole lot. Anything we can get on that possible New York shooter would be a real help."

Steve nodded. "The New York office is already on it, based on John's report. NYPD is cooperating, but so far all they got is zilch." He squinted in the morning light and looked at JJ. "You going on back to breakfast, Deputy Dawg?" JJ understood that whatever had led Steve to be formal with him when he first arrived was dealt with; maybe he had needed a chance to talk to Paulson a little, or Paulson needed a chance to size him up.

"Absolutely, J. Edgar." He smiled. "We local yokels need food to survive, unlike you children of Hoover who can go on indefinitely on a diet of newspaper clippings and television air time."

"Please, please," Steve said, "it's not that we're greedy for publicity, it's that we fervently support the public's right to know."

"Uh, huh. Sure. I believe you. Of course. Absolutely." JJ turned to Paulson. "Nice meeting you, Agent Paulson."

Paulson reached out his hand. "Call me John," he said. "Nice meeting you." He looked over at Steve. "I appreciate you're not holding it against me that I came here with a Fee-Bee."

JJ grinned while Steve rolled his eyes. "Call me JJ," he replied. "Well, we can't always help our fate." They broke up and went to their cars.

As JJ slowly backed his car away from the others he had to stop to allow the ambulance, its strobe lights pulsing but its siren off, and its escorting police car leave. He reached up to adjust the rearview mirror and it flashed the image of Jack Baker, still standing with his small group.

So what are you going to do, Mr. Baker? Do you hear a clock ticking?

Chapter 60

Ellen enjoyed the breeze coming in the truck window as she and her grandfather wandered the back roads. Behind the seats were two paper grocery bags stuffed with the makings of a picnic lunch, most of which Ellen had made herself. The deviled eggs were her grandfather's contribution.

"I believe I can boil an egg," Tom said with a smile the night before as they prepared things. Actually, he made great eggs, using a brown mustard with the hard yolks and topping all of the egg halves with a light coating of red paprika. More than anything Ellen liked the colors of the deviled eggs, the scattered red of the paprika contrasting nicely with the white of the eggs and the yellow-brown of the filling.

She made ham sandwiches, using a favorite rye, slices of sharp cheddar, and more of the brown mustard for her grandfather's sandwiches and mayonnaise for herself. He had cocked an eyebrow at her sandwich and then shook his head.

"I believe that may be illegal in some states," he said in a mock serious tone.

With the morning work done, they elected to wander a bit before settling down on a place to have their picnic. A small cooler held ice and several soda cans and both of them had an open one in their hands as they drove along and enjoyed the day. Cool for an August day, it seemed to be heating up fairly quickly.

She noticed her grandfather had his county map out, carefully folded into a square which he had attached to a beat-up old clipboard. It didn't seem to be showing anything special, just a portion of the area north of Hamilton, along the county line. She saw roads snaking out of Middletown on their way west, cutting through green areas. She thought he might have in mind stopping in one of the green areas, some of which were bordered by wandering blue lines.

They traveled north for a while, paralleling the Indiana border, and then turned east, just beneath the county line. She saw they were in the area of the map. To their southwest lay Oxford; she saw a sign indicating Hueston Woods State Park to the north. Ahead the ground became hilly and soon they were on old roads born when the farms they bordered were settled.

They would travel in a straight line for a half mile or less and then go due south or north for sometimes only a hundred yards or so, and then do a ninety degree turn east again. Before too long they would come to another farm and the road would go through its series of right angle turns to go around the farm. She decided the county engineers had never heard of eminent domain and gave the farmers the right of way. Which was nice, of course, but made for slow driving unless you went over to one of the main state routes.

They encountered streams that fed into one another and the ground became hillier. They even encountered curves. Her grandfather was looking around as much as she was, almost as if he was a stranger to pastures. Maybe he was just getting into the spirit of the day. Ellen gave him a smile, but he didn't seem to notice it.

At one point, he did a curious thing. They were going down the narrow road with only wire fences and a few cows around when he slowed the truck, studying a black mailbox on the other side of the road. A dirt road led over a hill from the mailbox. He looked at the road and then his map.

A little later, they came to an intersection and he turned left, north. He followed this road, which was straighter than the one they had been on. At the next intersection, he turned west. All along this road his attention was split between his map and looking south. There wasn't much to see. The hills blocked most of the view and what they didn't large patches of woods did. At the next intersection, he turned south. This road did a lot of twisting as it followed a major stream before it intersected their original road, which he turned onto and continued on past the black mail box again.

He put the clipboard behind his seat and drove on. Ellen noticed the loop they drove and thought he might have been lost for a moment, or maybe he was just looking for a place for their picnic. If so, he missed a couple of nice places along the stream, but maybe it was too early to eat, anyway, so she didn't say anything.

Besides, Ellen already knew that men hated to get advice when they were lost and would never ask anyone for directions. So she sat back and enjoyed the ride.

Eventually they swung way to the west, close to the state border, and slipped into the north part of Hueston Woods State Park. Tom stopped at a set of picnic tables overlooking Acton Lake.

They set up their food on a cloth Ellen spread across one of the picnic tables. At a nearby table, a family gathered, sharing their food with one another and their dog. Ellen guessed the dog was eating a bit more than any of the humans.

They had finished their sandwiches and she had made a sizeable dent in the number of deviled eggs – Tom had restricted himself to one – when she heard a rumble like distant thunder coming from the road looping around the lake. She looked up and saw a group of motorcycles coming, flashing bright paint and chrome in the sun.

Ellen couldn't help herself; for a moment she felt a flash of fear and froze in place, watching the approaching motorcycles. Then she felt her grandfather's hand on her shoulder and it was all right again.

She saw they were all big bikes in a wide variety of colors. Most had two people on them, and several had big fairings and luggage racks. A few even had antennas sticking up in the air. The bikers were a mixed crew but none looked like outlaws.

They pulled into the picnic area and went down to the end where there were several unoccupied tables and a barbecue pit. One of the passengers, a woman, waved to her as they passed, but she didn't wave back. Grandfather's reassurance or no, these people rode motorcycles. They were bikers.

And bikers, she knew, killed Eileen.

"They bother you." Her grandfather was making a statement, not asking a question.

Ellen nodded in reply silently. She didn't want to talk about it but he let the silence stretch on. Finally, she spoke.

"They scare me." Her voice was small, even to her ears.

Tom looked at her for a moment. He had seen her draw on her strength, had seen her find courage along the Ohio not too many days ago. He was tempted to help her pack everything up and leave, to alleviate her distress by taking her away from it.

After all, Tom knew something about reacting to the sight of motorcycles, remembering the night at the roadhouse. On the other hand, he thought of fear as an acid, which, unless dealt with, would continue to eat away until it weakened, maybe even destroyed, you.

"I know what you mean," Tom said finally. "A lot of bad memories are attached to people who ride motorcycles. So what do you want to do about it?"

She sighed inside herself; she recognized what he was doing. The first time she could remember him saying something like that was when she was trying to learn to swim and having a terrible time of it. She knew what he expected and she was mature enough to know he was right.

Well, then, let's do it.

"I reckon we ought to go over there and take a look at them," Ellen said reluctantly, her Ohio twang revealing itself.

"I reckon you're right," Tom replied, hiding his smile.

They walked the short distance to where the bikes stood. The riders were shedding various jackets. Black leather seemed to be a common uniform, but there were lots of other colors as well. People were running around, unpacking lunches, throwing a Frisbee, opening cans of soda and beer, and igniting a fire with entirely too much starter fluid.

In the middle of the group, like an island in a chaotic sea, stood a tall, heavy man with a beard. He was gesturing broadly, an open can of soda in one hand, and laughing at some story he was telling to several other people clustered around him. He wore a brown leather vest and a black t-shirt beneath with a Harley-Davidson logo. There was a phrase over it. "If I have to explain you wouldn't understand." Ellen didn't get it.

The man looked over at them and paused for a moment. Then his smile became even larger.

"Hey, is that Tom Parker?" he yelled.

She looked up at her grandfather and saw that he was smiling.

Grandpa Tom knows bikers? But I thought he was killing them.

Both men shook hands and suddenly she was being introduced to people whose names she couldn't remember. They were all friendly and very talkative, though a bit loud, and soon she was standing there with a cold can of soda in her hand and not quite sure how it got there.

"Yeah, we did an early morning run up to the Air Force Museum at Wright-Pat and then came back down here for lunch," Joe Bernelli was explaining. "Some of the group went on to Columbus for a bike show, but most of us are going to go tomorrow and take our kids."

She was looking at the motorcycles. They were pretty, once you got close enough to really look at them. They were all big bikes and she wandered around to look at them. Joe and Tom followed her, mostly talking about some highway construction going on over on the interstate.

"What you're looking at," Joe said to her as she examined a big maroon bike that had a passenger seat perched high like the aft deck of a Spanish galleon, "is a Honda Gold Wing. It's got a CB, cassette deck, electric reverse, radar detector, AM-FM, automatic leveling, and enough cargo capacity to pack in the Queen Mary." He leaned forward. "It's a nice beginner's bike and only lacks training wheels to be perfect." This last was said with a wink.

"Now over here," he said with a sweeping gesture, "we have a real motorcycle. An American motorcycle. It's got a windscreen, to be sure, but none of your effete electronic doo-dads. It is a creature of the road, designed to do one thing, and one thing perfectly: to lope great distances like a ranging wolf."

"I like wolves," Ellen allowed, eyeing the low slung red and pearl gray machine, "but what do you mean this is a real motorcycle?"

"Young lady," Joe said with a smile, "thank you for the opportunity. Allow me to demonstrate." He turned toward the other bikers. "Hey, Jules, come here for a second."

An older man with white hair came over. He wore leather pants dyed the same maroon color as his motorcycle and a short-sleeved knit shirt with a Honda emblem on the pocket. He was accompanied by an equally white-haired woman wearing the same uniform, including the knit shirt, but with the addition of a green scarf and dark sunglasses.

"Jules and his wife went down to Daytona and back on their bike this past March," Joe said. "He's also the club Ride Captain. Jules, would you do the lady a favor and fire up your bike for her? She hasn't been close to motorcycles before."

"Oh, we can do better than that," Jules' wife interrupted. "Here, dear, why don't you get up in the passenger seat?" She took Ellen by the arm and before she quite knew how she did it, she was perched up on the passenger seat, her forearms laying on the arm rests.

The seat was very comfortable and she was surprised at how high off the ground she was. Jules, who had held the handlebars while his wife had put Ellen on board, got onto the front seat with familiar grace. He inserted an ignition key and did some things with the controls.

The Honda started smoothly and settled into a low hum. Jules revved the engine a couple of times but little vibration came through the thick seat. It sounded very much like a car, though a little louder. Ellen decided it was very nice, kind of like sitting on top of a big, purring cat. Jules shut off the engine and helped her to the ground.

Ellen thanked Jules and his wife and they returned to the picnic. Joe gave Ellen another wink.

"Now, want to try the Harley?"

The other bike sat its passenger closer to the ground, though she could not reach it with her foot. Instead of a throne-like chair complete with armrests, the seat was relatively narrow with a low, padded sissy bar; at least, that's what Joe called it. Studded saddlebags lay below the passenger seat and the handlebar sported leather fringes on its hand levers. Joe slid into the seat, reached down to do something near the engine, pulled in the lever on the left hand grip, gave the right one a few quick turns, punched a couple of buttons, and there was a burst of sound.

The Harley did not purr; it seemed to laugh, a loud but warm bubbling laughter, which settled into a contented rumbling chuckle. It was deeper and more distinct than the Honda. There was more vibration, but it wasn't uncomfortable. It was like she imagined a horse might act who wanted to be off and running. Joe looked back at her over his shoulder and smiled. She saw his right hand twist the handgrip and suddenly the Harley wasn't laughing as thunder exploded from beneath her.

Her eyes widened and she instinctively held onto Joe. Her grandfather was beside her and she looked towards him with a smile. This was exciting! Joe quickly rolled the power off and the big bike settled back into its deep-throated rumble. When he switched it off, she was disappointed.

After she got off, Joe, still sitting on the Harley, cocked his head and asked, "Well, what do you think?"

"It was," she said, excitement in her voice and her eyes still wide, "cool."

Joe chuckled and agreed with her. He got off the bike and walked with them back to their table. After everything was packed, he and her grandfather shook hands and he gave Ellen a wave as they drove away.

Ellen's excitement was still so high that she didn't notice that they went slightly out of their way to go back the road with the black mailbox. And she was busy talking to her grandfather when they passed it so she didn't see the name on it, pasted there with plastic, reflective letters.

Rader

Chapter 61

John Wesley was playing catch with Pupper beside the barn when Ellen and Tom came driving home. Ellen bounced out of the truck and was greeted by Pupper who displayed an equal degree of bounce and tried to lick her while holding a tennis ball in his jaws. The dog finally released it long enough to give her a good chin cleaning, at which point she grabbed the ball. Pupper immediately sat down, his ears alert, watching her, waiting for the toss.

"Hey, Ellen," John called, walking around the corner of the barn. "How goes it?"

"Hi, John," Ellen said, her eyes not leaving Pupper's as she started to feint with the ball. "We were on a picnic and I sat on a motorcycle. Two motorcycles and one was a Harley." She tossed the ball in a great arc and Pupper was off and running after it. She crouched down and waited for his return.

"Afternoon, John," Tom said, folding up the county map. "How are you doing?"

"Not bad, Uncle Tom," John replied. "You got a couple of minutes?" John was smiling but there was a serious look about his eyes and he was looking intently at Tom.

Tom made a motion with his hand and the two men started down the lane going past the barn. John looked over at Ellen.

"I think Redbone is hiding out in the barn. You can take Pupper on in the house in a bit if you want and give him some water."

Ellen shouted an acknowledgement and she and Pupper went running off in the other direction, the dog leaping up beside her, trying to reach the ball she held above her head.

Tom and John walked in silence for a while, their feet making soft sounds in the weeds growing in the lane. Finally, they stopped at a gate. Tom leaned against it while John put a foot up on a lower rail.

"So what do you need to talk about?" Tom asked.

John looked across the pasture, collecting his thoughts. He shook his head and turned to face his uncle.

"I don't think there's any easy way to get into this, Tom. I got a question for you and I need an answer." He paused, looking into his uncle's eyes.

"What I want to know is, have you been killing the men who killed Eileen?"

The question seemed to drift in the warm Ohio air, like a dandelion seed, and for a moment John could not tell where it was going to land. His uncle said nothing, just stared at him.

"Where the hell is that question coming from?" Tom finally said.

"That doesn't matter," John replied, returning his intense gaze. "I need to know if that's what's happening."

"And if I say it isn't?" There was an angry edge to Tom's voice.

"Then I'll ask you to clear up a few things." John's voice was calm but the tension in it was clear.

Tom looked at his nephew for another minute and then studied the fence gate. It was clear to him that he had made a mistake of some sort and someone, someone in the family, had learned what he was doing.

Ellen? Damn, I thought I kept her out of this.

Tom realized that he had been deluding himself in believing he could be doing all the searching out, all the planning, and the killing, without Ellen learning of it, or at least suspecting. All those nights, prowling the county, checking out locations, surely she was bright enough to begin adding things up.

But was it only suspicions, or did she have stronger proof? Maybe she and John were just reacting to coincidence. After all, John had asked if he was killing those bastards. What real evidence did they have?

He sighed. The other thing, he began to realize, was a part of him wanted to talk about it with someone. Not looking for absolution or forgiveness, he told himself, just...

It's been a lot to carry alone.

He looked back at his nephew and thought for a moment. No, Ellen would not have gone to John with this, not first. Who, then? Her parents? That was very doubtful. He knew that Charles had made himself semi-unapproachable to his child, and her mother, well, if Ellen was looking for strength, for support, he doubted that her mother would be the first name to come into her mind. Who else?

Catherine. Of course. He saw the looks between the two of them and knew something in their relationship had grown during the collapse of the hearing.

And Catherine would go to John. Those two were peas in a pod since childhood. Hell, John was a better support to her than anyone else in the family when she came out with her "trouble." Tom nodded; better than he had been.

So it all went back to Ellen and something she had picked up on, or at least suspected. Maybe there was still room for maneuver. Dragging the rest of the family in on this was not the way to go.

But he was stuck on actually lying to a member of the family. He tried to choose his words carefully, to work around having to lie.

"I don't know what you think you know or where you got it, but you need to think about the fact that there may be a number of other explanations."

But John wasn't buying it. "Tom, that may be the first time I've heard you be other than perfectly straight in answering a question." He shook his head. "If I had any doubts before, I think you just took care of them."

"If it was true," Tom said, inwardly wincing at John's statement, "what would you do about it? Tell the police? Make me stop?"

The silence grew while John studied his hands for a moment, thinking. Finally, he looked up at his uncle.

"No," John Wesley said, shaking his head, "I wouldn't make you stop. I could never turn you into the police, you know that. And I don't think I could make you do anything you didn't want to do." He looked out across the pasture. "You always were one stubborn son of a bitch," he added quietly.

"No, I wouldn't do any of those things." He looked back into Tom's eyes. "Because I want to come along." Before Tom could reply, John went on.

"Look, let's cut the bullshit. You've been killing the men who killed Eileen. You're four for five at this point. There's only one left. If we go back into your work shed and pull out your notebook, we'll find four names crossed off, right?"

So that's how she figured it out. Idiot – why didn't I get rid of that thing when all this started?

Because I didn't trust my old man's memory...

"I want to go along, Tom. You've been lucky so far. But face it. You could use someone watching your back. And you know me. I can do it."

Oh, yes, he could do it, Tom realized. He knew from his own experience there were some things that you never forgot how to do, like riding a bicycle.

Or killing people.

And Johnny was very, very good at it, if the brief notes in the newspapers were any guide.

He takes after me.

"Why do you think I'm doing it?" Tom said.

"Revenge," John replied. "These pricks killed Eileen. And something else."

Tom shook his head. "No, not revenge. Maybe that's how it was when I started," he said, finally admitting what he was doing, "but that's not all of it." He searched for words but none came. "And why do you want to get involved? It isn't revenge for you, either."

"No, it's not," John admitted. "It's a bunch of things." He ran his hand through his thinning hair. "A big piece of it is simply that I want to cover you. I don't think I can stand back and know you're out there somewhere in danger and I'm not doing anything about it."

"I can understand that," Tom said. "What else?"

"You remember when I was getting ready to go 'Nam and you told me that when I got back I should look you up and we'd go up in the woods and you'd let me talk about it?" Tom nodded, remembering.

"I never took you up on the offer. Didn't figure I needed to, didn't figure anyone else would understand." He shrugged. "I was wrong. But the thing is, everything since 'Nam has been like in shades of gray. As awful as that was, and it got real bad at times, I felt like I was doing something that mattered, you know?" Tom nodded.

"I'm not talking about the adrenaline rush. Hell, if that was all it was about I could go out racing cars or skydiving or some damned thing. No, it was being responsible, having peoples' lives in your hands, being competent in a time and place where you knew immediately whether or not you were any good at what you were doing." He looked towards the horizon, silent for a moment, his thoughts somewhere else.

"I was an officer of Marines," John Wesley said softly, "and it didn't matter what the politics were, or the arguments. I knew I was good at what I did, which meant bringing my people home alive."

He shook his head and grimaced. "I like what I'm doing now but it's not the same. Sometimes it doesn't feel like it means anything. It's like I need to put it on the line one more time, to just show myself that I matter, that I can do something that matters. Watching your back, getting you out of all this alive, that matters." He paused and smiled, looking slightly embarrassed. "Sound like a full blown idiot, don't I?"

"Not entirely," Tom conceded. "After I got back from the war, my war, that is, it was real hard for me to take anything, or anybody, seriously. I was something of a wild man for a while, worse than you were. Had some trouble with the law, was drinking myself to death, going right over the edge. Then along came Sarah." He stopped and looked across the fields.

John nodded. "For me it was the work, teaching, and learning. I threw myself into it, trying to keep myself focused away from what felt like an empty hole in my soul. It was never enough. Never did find anyone like Sarah. Think I drove most of the possible candidates away. Whatever." He fell silent and both men stood next to the gate and felt the warm breeze.

"There's only one left," Tom finally said.

"That's enough," John replied.

"All right," Tom said. "You're in." Both men shook hands. "There are some rules to this. It's Jack Baker we're after, no one else, and we don't do anything that might endanger a civilian. So the other Riders walk."

"Unless they try to stop us?" John asked.

"We fight them only in self-defense, only if we have to," Tom said emphatically. "They may all be bastards but only Baker and the other four crossed the line. Only those people slipped past the law. We're not taking over for the system."

"I understand," John said. "We stop him and avoid the abyss, if we can." Tom looked at him questioningly.

"A man once wrote that when you stare into the abyss, the abyss stares into you. You run the risk of becoming it, the thing in the dark." He looked over at Tom. "So what we want to do is get this done without becoming Jack Baker."

"That's it, we just want to get it done." Tom nodded and pushed the gate open. The two men stepped through and walked across the pasture's uncertain   footing.

Chapter 62

Karen always went with JJ back to his place rather than taking him to her motel room after the first night they spent together. The Federal Bureau of Investigation had loosened up from the days of Hoover – her own presence was evidence of that – but there was still a conservative bent to how agents' conduct was viewed, especially by supervisors, so the two of them tried to be discrete.

Every other agent in the task force knew, of course. Cops, more than psychologists, are trained observers of human behavior and it would have taken a blind and deaf one to miss the subtle changes in the interaction of the two. That, and cops are just as gossipy as anybody else. From the men's point of view, Karen Deevers was an attractive woman and most had the biologically-generated response of appreciating her. Only a few had ever tried to go beyond that aesthetic sense and they had all gone down in flames, albeit gracefully. None had pushed very hard. Cops dating cops was a complication on the job that most preferred to avoid.

The task force women agents liked JJ and his almost old-fashioned southern Ohio politeness. It wasn't coupled with any trace of condescension so they were happy to accept it and didn't feel they were giving up anything in the socio-political arena. Besides, he had a nice smile, great hands, and a good ass, depending on which female agent was polled.

Since it was Saturday and Karen didn't have the watch, they were spending the day together. While they had no definite plans, JJ thought to show her the area a little and then go out to dinner and then, if all went well, the two of them would fuck their eyes out.

Where does that come from? How come one moment I feel like a goddamned 18th Century romantic and the next it's all testosterone and gonads?

JJ would have been astounded to know that Karen experienced much the same swings in her thinking. What the two of them also had in common was the sense of uncertainty about what would happen when the task force left town.

JJ tried to shut the thought from his mind with no success. He knew Karen was subject to the vagaries of the federal assignment system. Besides, she was definitely on the fast track; everyone on the task force said so. She had an impressive record and was being groomed for promotion. In fact, her assignment to the DEA-run task force was to get her interagency cooperation ticket punched. She could find herself going to the top, if she wanted. What would lead her to stay?

Karen wrestled with the same question, though in a different form. Would JJ go with her, would he be willing to leave behind his job, his career? And do what? The man was a cop, a county-mountie. She had gotten into his record. It was impressive. With his training – he looked to have taken every training course offered to locals by the state and federal governments – and years of experience he could easily have moved on to a higher paying job in law enforcement. But he stayed here, in Butler County. This was his home, she understood. Born and raised here.

It was an alien concept for Karen. A military brat, she spent her entire life on the move. The longest she had ever been any place was the four years she spent in college. The idea of having one place that you thought of as "home" seemed exotic.

She guessed that's how it was for him. He would never leave Butler County.

And she couldn't stay. There were things she wanted to do, still. Settling down was not one of them. She didn't care about making her way up the ladder. Right now, she was happy being a Special Agent of the Federal Bureau of Investigation. Being a supervisor or, worse, an administrator didn't attract her. She just liked being a cop.

JJ was following Route 73 as it curved east and south of Middletown. While he didn't care much for the city, seeing it as an extension of the ever growing mass of Dayton, there were some good places to eat there and he had in mind a family-run Italian place on the outskirts.

There wasn't much of a lunch crowd for a Saturday and they got a nice table near the back. It turned out Karen was an authority on Italian cooking and even had a good knowledge of the language. The older man taking their order was delighted to slide into Italian as the two of them went over the menu and selected lunch.

"Where did that come from?" JJ asked.

"Oh, we were stationed overseas a lot when I was a kid and we spent some time in Italy. Had to take the language in school so when I was in high school and college I went for it to fulfill the foreign language requirement. Haven't had much use for it in the Bureau."

"I'm impressed," JJ said. "I struggled through high school Spanish. I use a little of it on the job. We have a growing Hispanic community here. But I'm really crude at it."

She smiled. "I'm sure you do your best communicating nonverbally, just with body language."

He grinned back. "You do a fair to middlin' job of that yourself, Agent Deevers."

She found herself actually blushing, something she thought she gave up in grade school. Oh, well, the man did have something going for him. And for her, too, for that matter.

As they worked their way through wet and delicious antipasto, Karen looked over at JJ.

"What's your plan, J?" she said, using the one initial that had become her mode of address when they were alone. "Do you figure to stay a county-mountie?" The question was asked nonchalantly and she avoided eye contact as her fork hunted through the food.

"Actually," JJ replied, "what I'd really like to do is go to law school." He surprised himself with the quickness of his own response.

What are you talking about? You've only played with the idea, never been serious. What's the deal now?

But his mouth was working on its own, with little input from his mind.

"There's a program at the University of Cincinnati which looks pretty good. I could take the LSATs this fall for enrollment in the spring semester." Suddenly, he discovered that his runaway mouth was actually describing what he wanted to do. It was a little amazing to have these thoughts, which were simmering on the back burner of his mind, out in front of him. "I'm pretty much as far as I can go in the Sheriff's Office, not being interested in politics as such. What I'd really like to do is get into the prosecutor end of things, or maybe even work my way into being a judge."

Surprise, surprise; you've never been able to bring this idea out into daylight and actually say it to yourself, much less talk about it to anyone else.

Ain't love grand?

Karen had stopped eating and was looking at him intently. "So you're not pinned to the ground here, then."

JJ wiped his mouth carefully and looked at her, sensing what she was asking about.

"No, not really. I love the county and the people, mostly the people. They're damned fine; solid, reliable, decent people, and I'm glad I was born and raised here. I feel like I've been giving them something back for what I was given. It's just," he shrugged, "I want to do more than being a deputy will let me. And the law, it's always been a fascinating thing to me."

"I think I know what you mean," Karen said. "I'm doing what I do because of the same kind of feeling, though it's not about one place. It's more of a payback to the whole country." She grinned. "It's a cliché, I know, but I'm one of those military brats who learned to love their country by spending so much time out of it. I learned to feel very lucky." She looked down at her food, still smiling. "It's not a word used in public any more, but it feels like patriotism."

JJ nodded, his expression serious. "Some nights I watch the news and, as screwed up as things are here, I feel like somehow I've lucked out in being born here instead of somewhere else."

"So you want to be a prosecutor or a judge?"

"Yep," he said firmly. "The administration of the law is where I'd like to try my hand next. I've done the enforcement thing for a while and I've really enjoyed it, especially working with the other officers. I've got to say, though, actually delivering justice, what the prosecutors and judges do, I think that would be really interesting. Fascinating." He felt like he was beginning to repeat himself and paused for a second, collecting his thoughts.

"See, what we do on our level," JJ said, making a horizontal gesture with his fork, "we enforce the law. We don't dispense justice. Our hands are pretty well tied by the system." He leaned back in his chair. "Course, that's the way it has to be. Can't have the cop on the beat, or the occasional Fee-Bee, deciding what justice is. Then you start getting South American death squads and shit like that."

"Yes, but how much freedom do you think you'd have as a prosecutor? How much," Karen asked, "do you think what you did would have to do with justice?"

"I know, I know," he replied, "the court has to do what it has to do. They've got restrictions, too. But my point is they have greater freedom than we do and because of that can get closer to the ideal of bringing justice to the law."

"We need both," Karen said, "and people don't always understand that they're not the same thing."

"That's right. Without the law, our attempts at justice degenerate into simple revenge and retribution. You end up with Bosnia or Ireland or some other messed up situation."

The waiter brought their main course, whose name JJ hadn't caught, but it involved chicken. Their conversation paused for a moment.

"So you're looking to balance law and justice; that can be a real juggling act," Karen said, smiling as she cut up her food.

JJ reached for the bread. "I know, but I think it's worth the effort. If we don't try, then all we have left is the work of..." he paused, and the picture of Tom Parker floated up into his mind.

"All we have left," he finally continued, "is the work of vigilantes."

Chapter 63

John Parker sat in Catherine's kitchen as night fell, sipping on a cup of tea. She was busy over the stove, fixing something with a lot of vegetables in it. In the living room, Terri was working with the computer, wired into the internet, doing research for an article she wanted to write for one of the trauma medicine journals.

"Well," said Catherine, not turning around. "You've been sitting there silent for the better part of an hour. What did he say?"

John glanced in the direction of the living room. Terri had the stereo on and he heard a John Stewart compact disc. The singer-songwriter, whose stuff he learned of through Catherine, was singing something about "angels with guns"; he didn't catch the rest, but it was loud enough to shroud their conversation.

"I talked to him about it," he said.

"And..."

"And he admitted it. He's after all five of the bastards who killed Eileen."

Catherine froze at the stove, not moving, her head down. Finally, she spoke.

"Dear God," she said, and it sounded like a real prayer. "Doesn't he understand what could happen?"

John studied his cup. "I think he knows, maybe better than you, as far as that goes. He's not the kind of man to have illusions about violence and what it means."

Catherine turned to face him, her arms folded, her expression hard, almost angry. "I'm talking about consequences to the family. What will it do to Ellen if her grandfather gets killed, or arrested, playing this stupid game?"

"I don't think you understand him on this one," John said, folding his hands. "It's not a stupid game to him."

Catherine looked for a moment like she was going to say something angry but caught herself. She stared at John for a moment and then covered her eyes with a hand.

"You're right, you're right, I don't understand." She dropped her hand. "That's why I turned to you in the first place. I couldn't get a handle on this and I hoped that you could and explain it to me. So what is it? Is it revenge?"

John shook his head. "He says it's not all or even mostly that and I believe him. What I think it is, is duty." Catherine looked at him and the anger faded, replaced by puzzlement. "Look, he's a man with old fashioned values and beliefs. One of them is that a man's job is to protect his family. So when Eileen was killed he felt he let her down, he wasn't there for her, he didn't protect her."

"But nobody could have," Catherine protested. "There was nothing anyone could have done. It wasn't his fault."

John held up a hand. "You're right, of course, but that's reasoning. For Tom, and for people like him, duty is a commitment you make that goes beyond what is reasonable. It's a matter of devotion."

"You make it sound like faith," Catherine said dubiously.

"That's exactly right," John replied. "It's on the same plane as religion. It's not a matter of reason, of logic, but of faith." He picked up his cup and gestured with it. "When I went into the Corps I took an oath to uphold and defend the Constitution of the United States – there was no phrase about doing it when it was reasonable to do so. Come whatever, hell or high water, it was to be done. Your dad never took an oath to take care of his family or to defend them, but he might as well have."

"But aren't you still talking about retribution?"

"No," John said. "That's there for him, I'm certain, but he sees himself as protecting his family from those bastards ever doing it again."

"That's not too likely," Catherine pointed out.

"Of course it isn't," John conceded, "but on the level that your father is feeling those men have become a threat. Their past action proves it. Rather than wait for lightning to strike again he's stopping them where they are. He's protecting his people."

"You don't think he's just playing out some sort of soldier fantasy, some sort of death trip, trying to get himself killed, now that Mom's gone?"

"No." John shook his head emphatically. "If he wanted to be a kamikaze he would have gone in like Jesse James and gotten himself blown away a long time ago. No," he repeated, "he is intent on killing these people because they represent a clear and present danger to his people, to his family."

Catherine brought over a kettle from the stove and poured John some more hot water. He took a tea bag from a bowl in the middle of the table.

"You know what he reminds me of?" he asked as he dunked the bag. "A woman I know of."

"What do you mean?"

"Oh, not present company," he said, looking up and smiling. "This is out of history, but it might give you an idea of what this 'duty' thing is to him."

"It's a story one of my guys told me in Vietnam. During the last century, there was a cavalry engagement between the Cheyenne and the U.S. Army. Took place along the Rosebud River. On a hill nearby were the Cheyenne old people, women, children, watching their young men fight the whites and their Crow and Shoshone scouts. A Cheyenne fell off his horse."

"Now that's about the worst place to be in a cavalry firefight," he said. "The cavalry troopers tried to shoot him where he stood while the scouts tried to ride him down and count coup on him to steal his heart and soul."

"His sister, her name was Buffalo Calf Road Woman, saw her brother go down. Without any thought to her own safety, she rode into the middle of the battle to get him. Somehow, she got to him and pulled him up on the horse behind her. Then she turned the pony around and rode the hell out of there."

John leaned forward, folding his arms on the table while the tea steeped. "I've looked it up. It actually happened. She and her brother made it out of the battle. And as they made their escape the Indian scouts and the Army troopers stood in their stirrups and cheered her courage." He twirled the bag around the cup.

"The Cheyenne know a little about war and warriors and duty. The Army calls the fight the 'Battle of the Rosebud'. The Cheyenne, who understand that a warrior's duty is to take care of one's people, call it 'The Battle Where the Woman Saved Her Brother.' Because that is what is important to remember."

"I think I see," Catherine said, her expression serious and nodding her head. "He's doing this because he feels he has an obligation to the rest of us."

"Right," John said, "that's a big part of it."

"But what if we don't want him to take on that obligation?"

John shook his head. "That's the other part. Like your faith, duty isn't about the opinions of others. That's all secondary. Duty is about keeping the faith, not only with others but with yourself. It doesn't matter, in the long run, what others want you to do. It's what you know you have to do."

He leaned back in the chair and stretched. "That Cheyenne Marine I was telling you about, the one who told me the story of Buffalo Calf Road Woman, I met him on his second tour. He said the honor of a warrior was in the offering of the gift; if you treated the gift with contempt you only dishonored yourself, not the giver. That thought got me through a lot after I got back to the world. But it's what your father is doing. He's giving a gift by taking it upon himself to get rid of this threat to his family that no one else has dealt with. Telling him you don't want it won't stop him."

"It's not some simple minded macho thing." Catherine's comment was a statement, not a question.

"No," John said, "that kind of thing is for the weak. Your Dad's got nothing left to prove in that area, if he ever did. This he's doing for Eileen, and you, and Ellen, and all the rest of his family."

Catherine shook her head. "I think I get it, at least a little. But I'm so afraid of what might happen to him." Tears welled up in her eyes.

"Well," John said, moving in his seat, "if it helps any, he's going to have an extra pair of eyes watching his back."

Catherine looked at him, puzzled. Then her eyes went wide.

"You don't mean..."

"It's the only thing I could do," John said, holding up a hand to cut her off. "Like I've been saying, he's intent on finishing this off, and will whether or not I go along. I got him to agree to take me with him. I can watch his back and pull him out if he starts to put himself in a dangerous position."

"Wait, wait, wait," Catherine said, holding up her own hand. "You're going along with him when he goes after Jack Baker? Both of you are going to be in danger?"

"No, no," John said, "I'm going along to keep the odds on his side. He's not going to be doing any kind of O. K. Corral scenario. I'll be there to keep him from doing that in case he gets tempted, which I doubt. I can be that other pair of eyes. Remember, I used to do this kind of thing for a living and I know how to handle myself."

"But, God, John! I only wanted you to help me find out what was going on." She shook her head emphatically, tears beginning to work their way down her face. "I didn't want you to risk your life, I didn't want you endangered."

He got out of his chair and walked over to her. He put his arms around her and she returned the hug.

"Don't worry, kid," John said, "I'm not in this to take any chances. Remember, I'm a professional coward, given any choice at all."

She pushed at his chest and began wiping her eyes.

"You idiot," she said, "what am I supposed to do now?"

He stepped back. "Just hang on for a while. It's almost over. Maybe it'll turn out that it's impossible to get Jack Baker. And I'll be there to keep him as safe as possible. That's all I'm there for."

She looked at him. "Is that all it is for you? You're not on some sort of duty-thing yourself, or trying to finish old business, trying to get back into the war one more time?" They heard a knock at the front door.

"Absolutely not," he said. Terri was calling that it was Tom and Ellen.

It was the first time John Wesley had ever lied to Catherine.

Chapter 64

It was, JJ decided, a zoo. The news conference was held in the County Courthouse in Hamilton, the only public building large enough to accommodate the crowd of news people and their equipment. He was astounded to see local television news people from not only Cincinnati and Dayton, which were expected, but Columbus and even Cleveland. But what was surprising was to see two national broadcast services as well.

Davidson was everywhere in the hours before the conference, talking with the local police representatives, mostly the top people, setting up how the conference would go, who would be on when. He was careful to make it clear that this was a federal show, most particularly a DEA show, and everyone else would participate to the extent they stayed on good behavior, which meant following Davidson's script.

That part, the presentation, was disciplined. The media were anything but. People were everywhere and confusion among the news people was rampant. JJ helped by handing out summary and background statements, but there were many more hands grasping for the stapled papers than there were papers. Apparently some of the media were taking multiple copies. JJ suspected it was a tactic to keep the information out of the hands of rivals but he kept back the last copy and had an officer run down to the local quick copy service. An extra thirty copies soon had the problem taken care of, though he wasn't sure what the county was going to say when the bill was presented.

All the reporters from whatever source vied to get seats close to the front. Some of the brighter ones had their seats held by people who arrived earlier in the day and simply occupied them and read magazines until the rest of their group arrived.

He set up the easel and poster boards. Most had enlarged pictures of the seized drug lab. One had lists of drugs, chemicals, and weapons captured. He double checked with Davidson to make sure the sequence was right.

A table was set up for Steve, representing the FBI, Davidson, representing the task force and the DEA, the chiefs of the Hamilton and Middletown police, and the county Sheriff, each with a name card with letters large enough to be read by the video cameras in the back of the room. A podium, carefully decorated with the DEA seal (JJ hadn't seen it brought in but admired Davidson's thoroughness), stood to one side.

Shortly before the scheduled start, Davidson and the others came into the room. Steve caught JJ's eye and gave him a thumb's up. JJ half waved and moved to the rear of the room but he was in the way of the television cameras and found that he was gradually shuffled to one side until he was out of the room.

Well, that was fine. He didn't need to stand around and hear Davidson and the others recount old news. He looked around. There were many people out in the hallway, mostly the technical support people for the television crews in the conference room. There were power cables everywhere and he felt clumsy stumbling over them and looked for the exit to the parking lot.

It wasn't much better being outside. All the television crews had vans, some of which were in live link to satellites. Engines and generators were running and the warm air felt hard to breathe. He kept on walking.

Karen was at the edge of the parking lot where a few trees stood on the divider. It was already getting hot and she was taking advantage of the shade. She had a can of soda and waved to him as he emerged from the herd of vehicles. He walked on over to her.

She was dressed in a blue blazer and light colored shirt and slacks. Her identification hung from her coat pocket. JJ was in gray Deputy's uniform, complete with narrow-brimmed Stetson-style hat, which he desperately wanted to take off as it seemed to hold the heat but wouldn't while in public.

"I thought you had to go back early to take the duty watch," he said as she passed the can over to him.

"Did. Switched with Janet; she had to finish up a report for ATF and figured it was going to be quiet in the office with all the media over here. And hello." She grinned.

"Hello yourself," JJ said, taking a long swallow. "I think she made the right call. They got every news person in there who exists. Hell, I thought I saw Edward R. Murrow hanging around."

Karen took the can back. "Well, this is big news. People are getting alarmed about the speed trade. Back in Phoenix where my mother lives, they've had a two hundred per cent increase in the number of fatal speed

ODs in the past two years. Up the road, Columbus says they've had it even worse. And down in Cincy..."

"Whoa, whoa," JJ said, holding up his hands, "I'm already sold. I read the same reports." He dropped his hands and reached for the soda can but Karen kept it out of his reach. "So if you're going to be hanging around here, what does Davidson have you doing?"

"I got the job of hand-holding with some of the visiting congressional staff, but after their briefing they all took off. Some flight to Mexico to investigate patent infringement on the Yucatan peninsula where a bunch of Mayan ruins are basking in the sun. Couldn't miss it."

"Gotcha. Junket express." He finally reached the soda can, but discovered it was empty. He walked over to a nearby trash can and dropped it in.

As he walked back to her he glanced down at her handbag which lay at her feet.

"Damn, that thing is big enough to carry a small car."

"A girl has to have plenty of space for her things," Karen replied. "Like stuff for nose powdering, a tape recorder, note pad, blank tapes, a couple of spare clips of ammunition, handcuffs, wallet, ID case, ratchet wrench, toothpick..."

"And a partridge in a pear tree," JJ said, interrupting. "You really carry all that stuff?"

"Nah," Karen replied. "I lied about the toothpick."

"So what're you doing after the dog and pony show?"

"Got to go back to the office. Carl wants Steve and me to get the reports together for the Senate subcommittee meeting in two weeks. DEA wants our stuff to be a part of their briefing on the national scene." She shrugged. "Probably turn out to be nothing more than a footnote, but most of the labs we've been discovering of late have been from fires, not busts. This is one of the few intact labs we've grabbed in Ohio, so, since the committee chair is from Ohio..." She grinned.

"Gotcha again. You all are sweating the budget negotiations coming up this fall. Wouldn't hurt to look good."

"You got that right, Deputy Dawg."

"Which reminds me." JJ looked back at the courthouse. "Did you know I got a big brother type talk from Steve?"

"Really?" She sounded amused. "How gallant of him."

"I didn't think you needed protecting," he said with a little irritation. "Is there a history here I should know about?"

"Not really," she said, cocking her head to one side, her face becoming serious, "but I'm not sure how much of it's your business."

He was silent for a moment, just stared across the parking lot. He felt a surge of anger but bit down hard on it before he let himself say anything.

"Your past," JJ said finally, "is your past, and it doesn't matter to me. I just wanted to be sure that I wasn't stepping on any toes or getting in the way of something in progress."

Karen looked at him. "Listen, honey," she said, "there's nothing in progress and there are no other toes to be stepped on. I wouldn't set you up like that."

"I know," he said. He grinned awkwardly. "I guess I was feeling a little..." He fell silent.

"Jealous?"

He remained silent for a moment, and finally shook his head.

"Damn, I don't know why it's so hard to admit, but, yeah, I was worried that I might be sharing you with someone else." He looked over at her. "It's a man thing, I guess, worrying about the competition."

"Woman thing, too," Karen said, reaching for his hand. "But there isn't any."

"Not for you, either," he said.

They held hands silently for a minute, and JJ remembered a scene like this from the eighth grade. He struggled for the girl's name, but it didn't come. But he did remember the warm feeling of that day so many years ago and it gave him a scale from which to measure what he was feeling now; for that he sent a silent wish of thanks to that nameless girl. What he was feeling now was off the scale.

And he liked it.

"By the way," Karen said, interrupting his thinking, "Steve is married to a former agent who was my best friend at the academy. He's decided he's the older brother I never had ever since I outshot him on the combat course. I think he admires women who enjoy using assault rifles."

"He and I have something in common," JJ said, grinning. "Of course, I admire other things some women use even more."

"Don't you ever get your mind out of the gutter?"

JJ thought for a moment. "Nope."

"Good. It's about your only redeeming quality."

Eventually the news conference was over. JJ went over with Karen to catch up with Davidson and Steve. There was a swirl of people around them but Davidson seemed like an island of calm.

"Look," Davidson said, "I've got to hang here for a while with a couple of the locals to clear up a few things. No big deal, but with everything going on," he jerked a thumb over his shoulder where a camera crew was doing an interview with the Hamilton chief of police, "it'll take some time. Let me hang onto the car, Steve." Steve fished out the keys and passed them over.

"JJ, the Sheriff is going to supply Steve and Karen a ride over to the office. A deputy named Black. Do you know him?"

JJ nodded. "Yeah, he's working traffic and patrol."

"Okay, help Karen and Steve find him in this mad house. I think he's supposed to be over in the county reserved parking area. Oh, and please make sure the posters go back with you guys."

"Already got them, boss," Steve said. "One of our guys is holding onto them over on the steps."

"Great. Well, I think it went real well. All the locals seemed happy and I think the people in DC will be satisfied." He started to turn away and paused. "By the way, JJ, the Sheriff is very happy with your work. He was worried that we might be trying to steal you away from the department." Davidson smiled. "I told him we're not allowed to steal. Against the law and all that."

JJ smiled back and Davidson walked off to conduct his political schmoozing.

He found Deputy Black, who happened to be black, standing beside an unmarked county patrol car, though he was in regulation summer uniform. He made the introductions and Steve and Karen climbed into the car.

"Let me take the back," Steve said, "so I don't have to put the posters in the trunk." He loaded the large three by four foot placards into the back seat.

"Great," Karen said, "I like riding shotgun." She got into the front seat and fished for her seat belt.

JJ checked that Black knew where the task force offices were.

"No problem, JJ," Black said with an easy smile. "That place has been on the evening news so much since the lab bust, I think I could find it with my eyes closed."

JJ grinned. "Yeah. Feds seem to attract TV cameras like flies..."

318

"Come to shit," Black said, completing the sentence and laughed. He got into the car and buckled himself in. JJ leaned over and waved to Karen beside him and then tapped the car roof as Black backed the car from its slot.

JJ turned away to go back to the main parking lot to find his car, hoping that the news vehicles would have cleared out enough that he would be able to get out. He didn't watch the county car pull out onto the road, so he didn't see the pickup truck across the street with the two men in it pull out of its parking space and follow.

And he didn't see the passenger talking into a cellular telephone.

Chapter 65

Karen still hadn't gotten to the tab of her seat belt as they pulled out onto the street. Black caught her struggle out of the corner of his eye.

"It's up near your shoulder," he said.

"Thanks," Karen replied. She located it and then removed her Wesson 10-mm. from her right hand hip holster and put it into the holster in her bag, which was secured to an inner divider by a spring-loaded clip. Then she pulled the lap and shoulder belt combination across her body and secured it.

"Is that the FBI issue ten?" Black asked, his eyes watching the road.

"Sort of," Karen said. "I've had some work done on it and I don't carry standard loads."

"Yeah, I heard they depowered the original loads. Too much penetration."

She nodded her head. "I use Federal HydraShoks. I don't like the idea of the round going through."

"We're mostly carrying nines," Black said. He was just making conversation as he drove. "Used to be the old police special .38s, I'm told, but that was before I joined up. I like all the ammo you can carry in a nine."

"Absolutely," Steve said from the backseat as he finished pushing the posters around. "Lots and lots of bullets, all headed away from me. That's the way I like it."

Black gave a quick snort. "You and me both, partner. You from around here?"

Karen noticed that the deputy had shifted his conversation over to Steve, another male. It was a subtle thing, but one which was fairly constant in her experience. Whenever she was with a male agent, both men and women generally directed their comments to him unless she stayed in their face. It was a minor irritation, at most, but she noticed.

Karen listened only partially to the conversation between Steve and Deputy Black, whose first name was Robert. The two men had somehow begun talking about football (In August?) and discovered they had something in common – they were for any team playing against Dallas. She tried to listen and occasionally throw in a word or two, but she didn't follow football much, especially in the summer, and soon gave up and watched the farmland roll on past.

Black said at one point he was taking the most direct route back to the office and then noted it also happened to be the only route back, unless you wanted to do a big, loop-around detour. The car's air conditioner was working, the conference was over, and it was nice to sit back and relax a little, so Karen didn't mind.

She thought they were about half way to the office and crossing some railroad tracks when she heard Steve, his head resting on his arms on the back of Robert's seat, lament the departure of Joe Montana from the game; Robert joined in and it began to sound like a gridiron Greek chorus. She smiled to herself and opened her travel bag.

Karen was looking for the rough notes she had already put together for their subcommittee report. She pushed her automatic pistol aside and found the small, spiral notebook and pulled it free.

Really need to do some serious excavating of this damned bag.

They were rounding a curve to the left with a three foot embankment on the right and a weed covered ditch on the left. She happened to glance up and saw a white, windowless van sitting in a lane just ahead on the left where the curve ended.

Suddenly, the van lurched forward onto the road, spraying dirt and gravel from its rear wheels. Black slammed on the brakes and the patrol car, equipped with ABS, nosed down sharply and went forward in a straight line. They were just coming to a halt fifteen feet short of the van, Steve muttering a muffled curse directed towards the other driver and his now visible passenger, when the van door slid back.

Karen saw two men in the back of the van, a bald one sitting on the floor, another crouched behind him. The passenger was looking directly at her. The driver was a dark silhouette beyond him. All were holding guns and all the guns were aimed at the patrol car.

Black jerked the transmission into reverse while Karen sat momentarily frozen. As he hit the accelerator, he screamed for everyone to get down. At that instant, the men fired.

The windshield exploded as bullets slammed through it. Karen instinctively ducked; but her shoulder strap wouldn't let her go forward and she found herself with her head almost in Black's lap while she tried to pull her gun free of her bag. The gunfire was an almost unbroken roar from the front.

The car suddenly lurched in a sharp turn to the left and then slammed into something, its back end dropping well below the front. Bullets were still slamming into the car from ahead. Karen felt the butt of her pistol and pulled it free while her other hand struggled to find the belt release.

She heard a choking noise above her and felt something wet and warm spray the side of her face. Black was hit but she didn't know how bad. He slumped over on her and was still. Steve yelled something about getting out and for an instant there was no shooting. Part of her mind realized the ambushers must have run out of ammunition and were probably changing magazines.

Her frantic fingers finally found the belt release and she pulled herself over to the door, a move made awkward by the unusual position of the car and Black bent over her. The left rear of the car was in the ditch. She heard Steve's door open. Her own seemed to be almost impossibly heavy. Just as she got it moving the firing began again.

As her door opened she saw its glass shatter and felt shards rake her face. But the front of the car was partially covering the door and she managed to get out without being hit. She heard Steve firing and brought up her weapon between the door and its frame, shouldering the door to one side as it tried to swing shut.

With both hands on the automatic, she aimed at the open van, at the mass of the two men, and fired. As fast as she could bring her pistol back down on her target from the recoil she fired. She saw both men fall backwards and swung her pistol towards the passenger, who ducked beneath the door sill. She fired a round at the driver beyond him but saw no effect. The man was firing back with a pistol.

She made herself concentrate and was deliberately aiming at the driver when she heard shots from behind. Karen turned and looked over the car roof.

Rounding the curve forty feet away was a pickup truck. A man was standing in the bed, firing an automatic weapon as he came. She saw the driver hunched over the steering wheel, wearing a baseball cap.

Have to lead him, and go for the flat of the windshield so it doesn't deflect.

As if on a firing range she saw the front post sight come up into the square notch of the rear sight, and the combination led the driver by half a foot. She fired once and the windshield in front of the driver went opaque from the impact. She tried to fire again but she was out of ammunition.

As she dropped beside the car and pulled a spare clip from her coat pocket, she heard the firing from the van resume. Something like a jackhammer was working over the patrol car's front grill and fender. The car settled as the right front tire was blown out. She slammed the clip in and released the slide. She wondered for a second where Steve was and then the pickup was less than ten feet away, almost alongside, and sliding into the embankment.

The man in the bed bounced off the back of the cab and fell out of sight beneath the side panel. She saw the driver lying against the steering wheel, blood covering the side of his face, his baseball cap still in place. She aimed just above the panel and the passenger got up in a crouch, his automatic rifle in his hands. She fired twice, once low, once high as she brought the sights down from the recoil.

The man spun around and fell over the other side of the truck bed. Karen lay flat on the ground and looked around the front tire towards the van. There was broken glass everywhere but it didn't matter.

The van passenger was back up, firing a pistol at the car. In the back, one man was still firing a submachine gun. The other was on the road, collapsed in a pile. The man with the automatic weapon saw her and swung his fire towards her.

His rounds were sprayed, not aimed, and she forced herself to concentrate and returned his fire. She saw one of her rounds hit beside his head and he began screaming at the front of the van. The van suddenly backed up, throwing off her next shot, and then shot forward, turning sharply away.

Karen braced her elbows on the pavement and kept firing at the van as it sped away. She kept squeezing the trigger on the weapon even after her gun was empty.

Then it was very quiet. Karen heard a crow in the distance and some metallic ticking coming from the car. For a moment she lay on the road and it felt like it was everything she could do to breathe. She slowly got up and looked around her.

The patrol car was riddled; it looked like some gigantic sewing machine had chewed away at the front of it. To one side, the pickup, its engine stalled out, was immobile, its front end pressed against the embankment. The driver had not moved but the passenger could not be seen.

Her left hand felt in her coat for her second spare clip. She knew she had one but could not remember where she put it. Her hand seemed to be searching on its own, as if separate from her, and began to tremble. It found the clip and, on the second try, drove it into the bottom of the grip.

Black was slumped over on her side of the seat. He was unconscious, his lower jaw a chewed up bloody mass that she had trouble recognizing. It was a moment before she realized it was partially gone. His breathing was ragged. Karen could not see Steve. She tried to call his name but nothing came; her throat was dry and constricted.

Her left hand, now noticeably shaking, reached across the dash to the microphone. She keyed the mike and saw a light go on the radio panel. She wasn't sure what she said and after a while she dropped the mike.

Then, with her legs uncertain and gripping the still empty pistol with both   hands,   she   went   to   look   for   Steve.

Chapter 66

JJ was just turning onto Route 73, heading towards Oxford, when his car radio came to life.

"All stations stand by."

That was unusual. The last time there was an all stations call, an alert to all vehicles monitoring the county's common frequency, was back when Eileen Parker was murdered and they were trying to block the escapes of the perpetrators. He turned up the volume.

"All stations, officer down, officers down," the dispatcher said, correcting herself with emphasis. "Grant Road, west of Hamilton, probably west of Louisville Road. Report incomplete. All responding units report in."

JJ pressed down the gas pedal and the Pontiac fishtailed as the rear tires slid with the sudden acceleration.

Jesus, no!

He fought for control with one hand while the other pulled out the blue strobe light from beneath the radio and put it on top of the dash. He heard other cars responding to the call. There was confusion as they were not certain of the location.

He saw Louisville Road coming up on the right and spun the big car around the corner. He keyed the microphone.

"Dispatch, Sheriff 46. I am responding. Do you have any further information on the officers down?"

"Negative, 4-6. No further contact since the initial call."

He cursed to himself and gunned the engine as he hit a straight stretch. Grant Road was four miles away but it seemed to take hours to get to it. When it finally came into view he saw a State Trooper car, its lights and sirens full on, race across Louisville Road heading west. He made the turn and tried to follow as best he could.

The front end of his car left the ground as he crossed some railroad tracks and there was a curve up ahead. Like sparkling islands, he saw blue and red emergency lights flashing above the farm field. Flares burned on the road surface approaching the curve and a police officer from one of the local towns held up his hands to stop him.

"Anyone behind you?"

JJ blinked, not understanding what the man meant.

"What..?" he began.

"Ambulance. Is there an ambulance behind you?" The officer was impatient and sounded angry.

JJ shook his head in the negative. "No, I didn't see anything behind me." He gripped his steering wheel so hard his knuckles almost glowed white. "Look, I may know those people."

"Go ahead," the officer said, and waved him through.

As JJ rounded the turn he saw the back of the county car and the pickup truck at about the same time. The state trooper he had followed was pulled off the road behind the truck. Beyond he saw another police car and, just pulling up behind it, an ambulance coming to a halt, followed by another highway patrol car.

There was a cluster of officers just on the other side of the county car, gathered around the driver's side. Partially hidden, he couldn't make out what they were doing. A trooper was on the right hand side of the truck, looking underneath it.

And Karen was standing next to the county car, leaning against the front fender. Her head was down but he could see blood on her face. He stopped his car and threw the shift forward into park. He tried to hurry but it was like his hands had gotten extra fingers not entirely under his control.

JJ half ran to her, calling her name. She didn't look up. He saw she had her gun in her hands, pointed down at her feet. The hammer was back and the slide was forward, safety off. It looked like her finger was on the trigger. He slowed down as he approached her. She was shaking like a puppy caught out in an ice storm.

"Karen?"

She looked up. There was blood all over the right side of her face, matting her hair, in which he saw bits of windshield glass. She blinked her eyes several times, as if trying to focus.

"I found it," she said in a quiet voice. "It was in my inside pocket. I don't know why I put it there, but I found it."

JJ slowly reached over with both hands and took her pistol.

"Let me take care of that, honey." He eased the gun away from her and slipped the safety on. She just looked at him.

"JJ, I'm sorry. I really tried." She shook her head. "There were so many of them." He saw lacerations on her neck and face as she made small, pointless gestures. The fabric of her pants was torn over her knees and he saw blood oozing down them.

"Are you okay, Karen?"

"I think Steve got the one in the van, the one on the road," she said. "I might have wounded another one, I don't know. The truck." Karen looked around, blinking as if surprised. "The truck came from behind. I got the driver I think but Steve was already down. I was too slow turning around. I was too slow." She shook her head as she dropped it.

JJ slipped her pistol into his belt. He held her by the shoulders and quickly looked her over for signs of serious wounds. The blood on her face could have been from a scalp laceration but he didn't find a wound. She looked up at him.

"Hey, J." Her voice was trembling. "Your guy, Robert Black, he's hurt real bad. Facial wound. And they got Steve. I'm really sorry, J; I really tried. I was just too slow turning around." She began shaking and he pulled her to him.

"Jesus, Karen, Jesus." JJ found himself saying it over and over again.

He saw two EMTs, guided by a trooper, running with a stretcher to the other side of the car. Suddenly there was another pair next to him, he didn't know where they had come from until he looked over his shoulder and saw a second ambulance.

"Let us take over," the taller one said, and for a moment JJ felt a surge of irrational anger. Then they gently pried him away from her and began checking her over. She looked up at him, blinking, tears in her eyes.

"I'm okay, J. Could you see to Steve?" He let go of her hand as the EMTs guided her away. One of them gave him a thumb's up signal but he didn't know whether or not to believe it.

JJ walked around the front of the car. It was totally shot out. Raw metal and primer surrounded what looked to be dozens of holes. The windshield was a sieve. He couldn't imagine how anyone in the car had gotten out alive.

On the driver's side the EMTs, with the help of three officers, were easing Black onto the stretcher. Someone was holding an IV bag over him as they positioned him on his side. Slowly they worked their way out of the ditch. JJ stood to one side as they passed.

A state trooper stood by the rear tire. The passenger door was half open, blocking his view. He stepped into the ditch and worked his way back. As he did he saw a yellow blanket covering a body lying across the ditch. As he approached, the trooper motioned with her hand to move away from the car and he saw she was trying to get him to get out of the ditch. Probably trying to preserve the crime scene, or maybe just avoid walking on the body.

The footing was poor on the sloping side of the ditch but he braced himself as best he could when he reached down to lift the blanket.

Steve lay on his back, his eyes and mouth half open, as if he was about to explain something. The back of his head was a sodden, bloody mass. There was a bloodstain under his right arm and another on his left side. The weeds cradling him were dark with his blood. JJ shook his head.

You took a lot of killing, J. Edgar.

He lay the blanket gently back down, covering Steve's face.

He made his way around the back of the car and stood in the road, feeling bits of glass under his feet. He looked over to the second ambulance. Karen was out of sight and he assumed she was in back being attended to. He started to walk towards it when the trooper who was checking the truck stepped up to him.

"You're Deputy Jeffers, aren't you?" The trooper was a broad shouldered black man with a leathered face reflecting many years of patrolling the state's roads. JJ nodded.

"We were in a seminar together up in Columbus last year on hostage negotiations. I'm Jack Bingham." His voice was very deep and it seemed somehow reassuring.

"Right, right," JJ said, vaguely remembering. "How're you doing?"

"Fine, but here's the thing." He motioned towards the truck. "I was checking out the truck. The lady wasn't too clear when I got here but she seemed to be saying there was another person in the truck. I found the driver, like you see, and in the truck bed I found some blood." He looked at JJ. "There's a blood trail going up the embankment there. You up to coming along? There's some heavy woods a couple of hundred yards in that direction and if we've got a rabbit I'd like to head him off before he gets into that stuff."

"Hold on," JJ said. He walked over to his car and opened the trunk. Under a blanket was a 12-gauge shotgun. He grabbed a handful of shells from a box and stuffed them into his pocket and started feeding others into the shotgun. He jacked the slide and fed another round into the weapon. He walked back to the trooper.

"Let's go," JJ said, his voice tense.

The trooper led the way around to the other side of the truck. He silently waved at blood smears on the side of the truck and in the crushed brush. He squatted down and pointed at an AK-47 assault rifle. The stamped metal of the receiver had several drops of blood on it.

The two men climbed up the steep embankment, keeping to one side from the path taken by the fugitive. As he got to the top, JJ took a quick look and then crawled over. Whoever they were after might still have a weapon and he didn't want to silhouette himself.

The field beyond was a planted with corn. The stalks, taller than either man, effectively blocked vision beyond a few yards. The earth looked dry and was cracked in places. JJ thought it might be drier than the rest of the field because of its closeness to the road and drainage.

The blood trail was very easy to follow. There was an almost continual line of blood drops. Here and there the ground was crumbled where the fugitive must have fallen; there the blood lay in heavy, sticky clumps. JJ wasn't surprised a few minutes later when they saw the feet of the man a few yards ahead.

They approached cautiously. JJ kept the shotgun to his shoulder, the barrel pointed at the chest of the man as he walked forward. The trooper had moved to one side and was crabbing forward, using one hand to push aside the leaves and stalks while the other held his black automatic in a steady aim at the man.

The man lay on his back. He wore blue jeans and a dungaree shirt with a black vest. He had long hair and a full beard which obscured his face. A bloody wound on his right side was slowly dribbling blood; there was another in his left forearm. His legs were slowly moving in a crawling motion and his breathing was labored.

JJ stood over him, the shotgun aimed at the man's face and watched as his eyelids fluttered and then opened. His eyes were unfocused and he didn't seem to be aware that JJ was there. His mouth worked but he said nothing as he lay in the dirt between the corn rows.

JJ felt his heart beating. It translated into microscopic movements at the end of the shotgun barrel. Everything else seemed to have gone very still and he felt as though he was all alone with the man who had tried to kill Karen. The silence was the kind of silence you hear in the instant before the flat roar of an explosion comes, as if nature itself was reflexively holding its breath, waiting for a blow to fall.

He was, he realized, anticipating the sound the shotgun would make when he fired it into the man's face. He wanted to see and hear it happen. More, he wanted to make it happen. He could visualize what would happen, how the 12-gauge would explode the man's skull like a watermelon, and his finger tightened on the trigger.

"Deputy?" The trooper was beside him. "Deputy?" His voice was quiet, soft spoken, but it came clearly. JJ held the slack he had pulled on the trigger for a moment more, and then slowly released it.

"Stay with him," JJ said, lowering the shotgun, "I'll go get the EMTs."

"That's a good idea," the trooper said, his voice carefully neutral.

JJ made his way back through the corn and clambered down the embankment. The scene was now crowded with police cars and other emergency vehicles. The ambulance they had taken Karen to was still there and he ran over to it. On the way he signaled to another state trooper.

Karen was sitting on a jump seat in the back of the ambulance, a yellow blanket wrapped around her shoulders. JJ turned to the EMTs and the trooper.

"We found another perp, right over the embankment, maybe thirty yards into the corn field. He's in bad shape; you'll need a stretcher to get him out. There's a trooper with him. I'll show you the way."

The EMTs gathered up their gear, including a collapsible stretcher. JJ and the trooper grabbed some of their orange colored chests and he led the way back to the wounded man. The trooper was steadily talking on his handheld radio and soon there were several more officers with them. JJ leaned over to Bingham.

"I'm going back to the ambulance and check on Agent Deevers." Bingham nodded, his eyes on the wounded man. JJ started to turn away and then leaned back. "By the way, thanks."

"Don't know what you mean, man," Bingham said. "I didn't see a damn thing my damn self." He held out his hand and as JJ took it he added quietly, "You did the right thing, deputy."

"Maybe," JJ replied, and then he was running back through the corn.

Karen was still huddled in the ambulance. A police woman stood nearby and she nodded to JJ and left. A medic had cleaned her up a little and he saw the remaining dried blood in her hair was not hers. She had numerous small lacerations on her face, neck, and hands, and they had cut off her pant legs to get at her knees, which were now covered with bandages.

She was looking at her hands, which lay listlessly in her lap.

"Hey," JJ said quietly. She looked up.

"How's Robert?" Her voice was small, as if she needed to hide it.

For a moment JJ went blank, then he remembered.

"He's alive," JJ said, "They took him away," he glanced at his watch and was surprised at what he saw, "twenty-five minutes ago. He's in surgery by now." He squatted in front of her and gently put his hand under her chin and lifted her face.

"How are you doing?"

"I'm okay," Karen said, shrugging. "A few scrapes, nothing serious. They want me to go in and get a more thorough check, but I'm all right." Her voice was flat and toneless.

Still shocky.

"One of the guys you hit is still alive. They'll be taking him to the hospital. How about if I take you to get checked out?"

She nodded. Karen got to her feet and climbed out of the back of the ambulance. She took off the blanket, folded it neatly, and carefully laid it in the ambulance bay. JJ guided her over to his car.

He started to open the passenger door for her but she put her hand on his and stopped him.

"J, I..." She looked around, her face pinched, fighting back tears. "God, J, I couldn't save him. I didn't even know he was hit."

"You did all anyone could do, kid," JJ said. "It's a miracle you're still alive."

She shook her head. "That doesn't feel good enough."

He couldn't think of anything to say as she got into the car. He was going around the front of the car when he saw Phillips coming over.

"Taking her to the ER?" JJ nodded and Phillips went on. "Something weird here." He motioned up the road where there were a cluster of officers. "There's a perp down. He's got two holes in his front. One's kind of small and came out small. Was one of the agents using a nine millimeter?"

JJ shook his head. "Don't know, maybe. You can check."

"Yeah, I was just on my way over. And the lady fed, what was she shooting?"

331

JJ reached into his belt and pulled out the ten millimeter Wesson. "It's Karen's."

"Pop open the clip for me," Phillips said. JJ was puzzled but complied with the request.

"Thought so," Phillips said, looking at the bullets in the clip. "See, she loaded it with Federal Hydra-Shoks. There's one hole through and through his right torso. Didn't look like there was any bullet expansion. The perp had a second entry wound in his front – upper left torso hit. Came out inside his left shoulder blade and made a hole you could park your car in. That one was Karen's. Looks like both she and the other agent scored a hit on him. I'm not sure how serious the other hit was but hers would have been fatal, I think, but it didn't kill him."

JJ looked up in surprise as Phillips handed the clip back.

"What do you mean?"

"You might want to take a look at this," was all Phillips said.

JJ studied Phillips silently and then went around and talked to Karen for a minute. He followed Phillips as he made his way through the crowd.

The dead man was lying in an awkward heap, his arms and legs sprawled out; empty shell casings, each one already circled in white chalk, lay around him. A small stream of blood led away from him across the road. People were trying to avoid it but JJ saw someone had miss-stepped and now there was a set of bloody footprints, gradually fading in clarity, going down the road.

The dead man looked like he was relatively short, though JJ had difficulty estimating his height with his arms and legs folded like they were. His well-muscled arms were covered with tattoos. His most obvious feature, a smoothly shaved skull, was marred by a gunshot wound in the back of his head. The bullet had exited through his eye. His face appeared slightly bloated and his remaining eye was discolored red.

"Yep," Phillips said. "Your people nailed his ass, but whoever was with him finished the job." Phillips looked around at the scene. "Three dead, two wounded, that we know of, maybe more."

He walked with JJ back to his car. "The Fee-Bees will be moving in on this, along with the staties. This will get real hot, real fast." Phillips stuck his hands in his pockets. "That guy back there, you recognize him?"

"He looked familiar, but..." JJ shrugged.

"Yeah, that head wound kind of distorted his otherwise charming features. One of my guys made him. His name is Peterson. He's a Steel Rider. Some kind of big wheel."

JJ turned and looked at Phillips.

"Yeah, JJ," Phillips said, "Jack Baker has declared war."

Chapter 67

Right after Tom and Ellen arrived at the apartment, Terri was paged by the hospital and left hurriedly.

"Anything wrong?" John asked.

"No way of telling." Catherine shrugged. "They've been chronically short of nurses, so when things get busy they sometimes have to call people in."

Ellen and Catherine took control of the kitchen and chased Tom and John into the living room. The men talked of making chili but Catherine vetoed the attempt, pointing out that John Wesley's version of chili was banned in three states. He had ungallantly thrown the gauntlet at her feet and demanded that she demonstrate her ability to produce a meal, if she wasn't willing to accept his efforts.

Catherine had a moment of near panic. She regarded herself as what she called a "survival cook" – this meant that she usually survived her own cooking – and was happy that Terri liked to do the cooking in their household. But she felt confident when Ellen grinned and gave her an exaggerated wink.

After the men were out of the kitchen the two examined what was in the refrigerator.

"Wish I'd had a chance to go shopping," Catherine said ruefully.

"I think," Ellen said, "it's lasagna."

"I'll grate, you slice," Catherine replied.

Tom and John sat down in the living room. The television was on, but they had muted the sound off. John looked towards the kitchen.

"So when do you want to go?" John asked.

"I think we'd be better off going sooner than later," Tom replied, his voice low.

"You said Baker's on a farm near the county line, and we can approach from the north or the west."

"Yes," Tom replied, "but I think the best way is from the west. I had a chance to do a quick look yesterday after hauling some junk to the landfill for the church, and there's a good place to park. I walked a little way in, not too far, didn't have much time. I'd guess the woods get within a couple of hundred yards of where I'd estimate the house is."

John nodded. "We can go in and take a look. If the opportunity is there, we can take it. But if it doesn't look right, we pull out."

Tom nodded. "I don't have a problem with that. I was lucky in the past, and I don't want to rely on that again."

"So when?"

"I figured we could give it a try on Thursday. Catherine is going to take Ellen over to the mall in Middletown. We can do a daylight recon. Get a good look at things, at least. Then maybe come back at night."

John nodded. "Makes sense to check it out before trying anything."

"We'll play it safe," Tom added. "We'll take the guns."

Both men were silent, thinking about what was coming. The television silently shifted meaningless scenes in a variety of colors. Finally, John spoke.

"That may have been the shortest combat briefing I ever got."

Tom grimaced. "It's been a little bit like that," he said.

"Shame we can't call in an air strike," John said, smiling slightly.

"That would make things easier."

"What would be easier?" Catherine asked from the doorway. Ellen stood beside her, wiping her hands with a dish towel.

"Waiting for our dinner, which never seems to come," John said smoothly.

"Well, it's going to be ready as soon as it finishes baking," Ellen announced. "But in the meantime there's enough time for a game of hearts."

"And do I hear a challenge?"

Ellen grinned. "Girls against the boys. Losers wash dishes."

"Seems fair," Tom said, getting up.

Catherine led the way into the kitchen. "You might not think so after you see what we've been cooking," she said with a smile.

In the living room the muted television picture changed from a commercial about trucks to a talking head. The woman silently moved her lips and then the picture changed to a shot of ambulances and police cars on a county road. An orange blanket covered a human form in the middle of the road. The picture moved up and a late model pickup truck, its nose firmly pressed against the road embankment, came into view. Then the picture panned to the right and in the stark glare of the video lights a car, its front lacerated by gunfire, could be seen.

The picture suddenly changed and a reporter's byline appeared at the bottom of the screen along with a "5 Alive" logo. Someone in a coat and tie was holding a microphone in front of an emergency room entrance. Again the picture suddenly changed. The logo was replaced by a caption reading "Live." The camera was apparently hand held and bounced as EMTs and police came into view and vanished.

The picture zoomed onto a woman sitting in a blood-spattered suit and hair matted by dried blood. Suddenly a man in gray Sheriff's uniform was in the way. The picture shifted to his face, held it for a second, and then quickly shifted away.

The viewers couldn't tell what caused the camera operator to turn away. Perhaps, if they thought about it, it was the authority of the badge. A naive handful might have thought it was compassion for the shocked FBI agent sitting in silence.

What they couldn't know, what the camera operator would never admit, not even to the director screaming into his microphone, was that none of those things caused him to back up and turn the camera away.

It was the eyes of the man who stood in the way. They were eyes which promised   death.

Chapter 69

Karen had undergone preliminary questioning at the scene, of course. They needed information if they were to have any chance of apprehending the ambushers. The questions were brief and to the point and, while abrupt, were made as gently as possible under the circumstances.

A second, more thorough interrogation took place at the hospital. The questioning officers were representatives of the county, state, and federal agencies – final jurisdiction was still being negotiated, but the defining of political boundary lines was of more concern to politicians than to the cops, at least for the moment.

Half a dozen people, including JJ, were crammed into a small office with Karen. She kept her head down, her gaze on her hands which lay in her lap unmoving. She recited the sequence of events of the ambush in a low monotone, pausing only when interrupted by a question.

She was thorough, JJ thought. She was giving every detail she could. The other cops were impressed, he could see that, but they were also aware she was a still out of it. From time to time, an officer would glance at another and raise an eyebrow.

The best cops were always the compassionate ones, though that made them the vulnerable ones. To protect themselves they built emotional walls that became thicker with time, sometimes so thick that nothing got in or out, including the rest of their lives. That was why so few of them had successful long term relationships. Some of the best cops around were in the room with Karen and their hearts went out to her.

But there was a job to do, and one cop was dead and another lay in surgery one floor away from where they sat and stood, so the questioning, much of it repetitive, went on. Karen kept responding, passively following the questions.

As they started to wind down the cops tried to help her. She was a woman and they were all men, that was part of it. But the main thing was she was a cop who had just been through a few acres of hell and most of them knew what that was like. They wanted to help one of their own.

So they gave her the latest information on Robert Black's surgery. He would make it, they said. She nodded her head. His lower jaw would be rebuilt, over time. His tongue muscles were largely intact. He would be all right. Eventually. She nodded.

They told her the truck driver was dead and congratulated her. She said nothing. They said the other man was still in intensive care but the doctors didn't think he would make it. One of them said something about nice shooting. Her hands moved. She said nothing.

When one of them thanked God she had made it, she began to cry. Softly she began to drop tears, so softly at first only JJ, who felt like he was wearing her nerves, knew it. The other cops finally noticed and looked at one another, embarrassed. JJ raised a hand, heads nodded, and the others left.

He crouched beside her and put his arms around her. She said nothing, but the crying continued. Every so often her body would shake, briefly, and the tears continued.

"Let me take you home," JJ said after many minutes and the crying had eased.

`He went into the small bathroom off the office and brought back a damp washcloth and a dry towel. She wiped her face and gave him a grim smile. One of the nurses had helped her clean some of the blood out of her hair but brown, matted streaks still marred her appearance.

JJ guided her out one of the hospital back exits to avoid the press camped out at the main entrance. When they stepped outside they found it was dark and had begun to rain in a steady, slow drizzle. JJ welcomed the refreshing feel of the rain after the day's heat.

Karen didn't say anything until they were in the car. As he started the engine, she reached over and put her hand on his.

"Take me back to my room," she said quietly. He looked at her.

"Are you sure?"

She shook her head. "I need to stay alone for a while."

"You're not going to help yourself by stewing in all this," JJ said. "You did the best you could. I don't know anyone who could have done better." He felt frustrated by the inadequacy of his words.

She was silent for a moment, just looking out through the rain smeared windshield.

"I know," Karen said, her voice barely a whisper. "It doesn't seem to help."

He squeezed her hand because he couldn't think of anything else to do and then started the car. She said nothing else all the way back to the motel. He got out of the car with her and walked her to her door. She turned to him.

"You have my gun?"

He shook his head. "They needed it for the lab. I have your back-up."

"I'd like it, please."

He went back to the car and picked up the automatic. He ejected the clip and made sure the chamber was clear. He hefted it as he walked back to her.

"Are you sure you want this around tonight?"

"The only way I could sleep tonight is to have every gun I own next to me," she replied, taking it from him.

As she unlocked her door he put his hand on her shoulder.

"You going to be okay?" JJ felt stupid asking, but couldn't think of anything else to say. Karen looked up at him and gave a half smile and then was gone, her door closing with a soft click. He heard the deadbolt click into place and then started to walk back to his car.

The door to the room next to Karen's opened and Janet came out, her arms folded in front of her.

"How is she, JJ?"

"Pretty messed up," he said, fumbling with his keys. "Blames herself for Steve. I tried talking to her but she's not hearing much. Not yet."

Janet motioned with her head toward Karen's room. The lights were narrowly emerging from behind the pulled curtains. "I'll keep an eye on her tonight."

"Good, thanks," JJ said. "I'll be by in the morning."

Janet touched his arm and went back to her room. JJ stood beside his car, alone in the dark, staring at his keys as if he had forgotten what they were. Finally he got in and drove away.

JJ didn't sleep much through the night. He was awake well before dawn, which was obscured by low hanging clouds. He cleaned himself up and drove to a nearby diner for breakfast, though he had little appetite. He kept an eye on the time and shortly after seven was pulling into Karen's motel parking lot.

As he got out of his car, Janet emerged from Karen's room. She walked up to the car, a sweater pulled across her shoulders to ward off the morning coolness.

"'Morning, JJ," she said, leaning in the driver's side window.

"'Morning, Janet," JJ replied. "Where's Karen?" He was unable to keep the concern out of his voice.

"They came by just a few minutes ago to pick her up. They called last night. They need her to walk through the shooting scene. She's going to be tied up there all morning. She asked me to tell you to meet her at the office." Janet's face was pinched with concern.

"All right," JJ finally said. "How's she doing?"

"She didn't get a lot of sleep last night," Janet replied. "Mostly tossed and turned. Steve, well, she was pretty close to him and his wife. I don't know, she didn't say much. I think you're right, she's blaming herself."

JJ nodded. "Yeah, she was talking that way yesterday." He looked up at Janet's drawn face. "And how are you doing?"

"Feel like shit," Janet said calmly. "I tried to reassure her but I don't think I made much of an impact. Hadn't known Steve long, myself, but..." She let it hang.

JJ nodded again. "Know what you mean. It's family." He looked at his wristwatch. "You need a ride to work?"

"No," Janet said smiling ruefully. "I just got off the horn with Davidson and he told me to sleep in a couple of hours before coming in. I'll be there around ten."

"Okay. Thanks for looking after her."

Janet straightened up. "No big deal." She patted the window frame and went back to her room.

JJ swung through a MacDonald's on the way to the task force headquarters and picked up a large, hot coffee. He still didn't have an appetite but there was a creature comfort in sipping on the hot drink.

Despite his side trip, he was still in to the office well before the normal start time of eight. Nonetheless, almost everyone was already there.

Anne raised her hand as he came in, her eyes red and puffy. The conversations in the room, coming from small clusters of agents, were low, subdued, and stopped for a second as he entered before resuming.

JJ kept glancing at Steve's desk, irrationally expecting, hoping, to see him there. But the space remained empty. He tried to work on preparing his report. It was hard, getting his mind to focus. He kept thinking about Karen, back out on that road with its white outlines, walking through the shootings again and again.

Around ten Davidson came into the room. Again the conversation died down for a moment as people looked towards him, waiting to hear whatever news there might be. He looked towards JJ and motioned him over.

They went into Davidson's office.

"How was Karen yesterday?"

JJ shrugged. "About what you'd expect. She was pretty much in shock when I got to the scene. She was better by the time I dropped her off at the motel. She's blaming herself."

Davidson nodded. "Reason I ask, I just got called from the shooting team. They were just wrapping up and she lost it. They're bringing her back here. She's insisting on it. But they wanted us to know and maybe have some people available. You available?"

"Of course." JJ looked at his hands and then at Davidson. "I just don't know what to say."

"Sometimes there's nothing to say. Just be here." He motioned to a fax on his desk. "DC is getting us a critical incident debriefer. He'll be here tomorrow. I know the guy – name is Roger Studervan. He's OK, for a shrink. Does debriefings for us, ATF, FBI, and a couple of state police organizations. Contractor. He'll do an all hands critical incident debriefing in the next couple of days. He can follow-up if anyone needs something more."

"Yeah," JJ said, "I know about these debriefings. We have a county team for EMS and police services."

"Good," Davidson replied. "I'd like everyone involved in this. He'll probably bring in your county team. Anyway, what I'd like you to do is let all the local folks know what we're going to have, time TBA. The feds know it's part of the program, standard issue."

"It pretty much is for us, too," JJ said. "But I'll talk to anyone who's unfamiliar with it."

"Good," Davidson repeated. He leaned back in his chair. "I got a look at the prelim from your man Phillips. He says it looks like it's a miracle Karen got out alive. He said she doesn't remember packing Black's wound but apparently she positioned him while he was unconscious and kept him from drowning in his own blood. He said she killed one outright and wounded at least two, one fatally, and maybe more – they found a couple of blood drops on the road away from the guy from the van. Maybe from the passenger. He also said he thinks the guy in the road was dead from her shot before his own people put a bullet in his head." He shook his head. "She was some kind of hero out there."

"She doesn't feel like a hero."

"Hell, maybe that's how you feel when you are heroic. Did you know that was her first shooting incident?"

JJ shook his head. "When are they getting here with her?"

Davidson glanced at his wristwatch. "Be another fifteen minutes." He looked up at JJ. "This is the second time I've lost a member of my team. It doesn't seem to be getting any easier."

"Steve was a good man," was all JJ could say, feeling a hard lump rising in his throat.

Davidson nodded and moved the papers around on his desk. JJ took it as a opportunity and cue to leave. He thought he had seen the DEA agent's eyes tear up – *Hell, I'm not so dry eyed myself!* – and understood that such feelings among men were generally kept private.

He tried to return to work. From time to time other members of the task force would come by and ask after Karen. He told them what he knew. The clock moved, but slowly.

Karen's arrival was subdued. JJ looked up and she was standing next to Anne's desk, talking quietly. He got up and walked over. Her eyes were red but she smiled at him.

"Hey."

"Hey, yourself." Anne was smiling up at the two of them, her eyes full of tears. JJ touched Karen's elbow and guided her towards her desk. The other people in the room were trying not to watch.

"How're you doing?"

"Not great," she said with a grim smile. "After the fifth time of walking through the ambush I had had it. Got the shakes and couldn't stop. Kept seeing that truck coming at us from behind." She shook her head. "It has not been a good day."

Karen was silent for a moment. JJ could think of nothing to say and just lay his hand on top of hers. She didn't seem to notice.

"I've got to make a phone call," she said unexpectedly.

"Well, if you've got work to do, why not pass it off and take some time to stand down?"

"No," she said, shaking her head. "No one else can make this call."

He stood beside her as she punched the numbers on the telephone's panel. She held the handset against her ear while her other hand shielded her eyes.

"Jackie? Hi, this is Karen. Yeah, honey, I heard. I'm really sorry. Is your mom there? Thanks." There was a pause. "Barb? It's Karen." She waited. JJ heard the murmur of another voice. "No, no, I'm fine. Just some scraped knees and a little whiplash. Nothing, really. How are you doing?" There was silence. Finally Karen spoke, her voice a whisper.

"God, Barb. I'm so sorry." JJ could hear little from the other end. "I don't know, I couldn't see. He was on the other side of the car and I couldn't see him. I don't think he suffered. He was gone when I got to him." There was another pause. "No, it's all right. Whatever you need, kiddo." Her hand on the receiver opened and closed, the fingers rippling. JJ saw a tear hit her desktop.

"It was an ambush, yes. We think we know who was behind it. I'll let you know what we learn. You're going to be okay?" She paused again, and her hand did its ripple once more. "Yeah, she's a trip. Okay, I'll call again latter. Give the kids a hug for me. You take care. Yeah. 'Bye."

She hung up.

"Her sister is arriving today. They didn't give her a lot of details. But she's got friends in the Bureau, and Steve's friends, they're already there and helping out." She rubbed her forehead. "I should be there."

"All you can do is all you can do," JJ said. "We need you here to get those bastards."

"If I'd been better, we would have gotten them yesterday."

"That's not..." He was interrupted by an agent, waving for his attention holding a telephone. "I'll be right back."

He walked over. The agent was Jocelyn Chalmers, one of the DEA people. She kept her hand over the receiver.

"JJ, just got a call in. The guy Karen hit just died. You want to tell her?"

"Probably ought to," he replied. "Thanks."

He walked back to Karen. One of the other FBI agents, Larry Smythe, was talking to Karen. He looked up as JJ arrived.

"I was just telling Karen that, if it's okay with Davidson, the Bureau will give her some time off." Smythe was a thin but good looking man with dark hair. JJ knew him as one of the team of data analyzers who periodically gave the team briefings, though he hadn't worked with him directly himself.

"Might be a good idea," he said to Karen.

"No, I want to be here," she said. "I want to see this through." She pulled a file over from a stack. "What was your call about? Anything new?"

"Well," JJ glanced at Smythe, "the wounded perp just died."

"Sorry, Karen," Smythe said quickly. "It can be tough knowing, but you did what you had to do. It was you or him." His assurances sounded as if made of plastic.

"Sorry?" Karen's voice was as sharp edged as a razor. "Sorry? I'm not sorry. I wish I'd killed all those bastards." She half rose from her chair and Smythe took a step backwards. "I hope he spent his whole time in agony, and I hope his friends burn in hell alongside him forever." She was speaking through clenched teeth and fire burned in her eyes.

"Uh, yeah," Smythe said. "Well, okay, I got to go." His last words were said as he retreated. Karen sat back down in her chair.

"I think you scared him," JJ said after a minute. She looked up in the general direction of Smythe's retreat.

"Not used to women being angry." It was a flat statement.

"Probably not," JJ agreed. "Men tend not to be familiar with women full of rage."

"What about you?" Karen looked up at him, the fire still slightly flickering in her eyes.

"Whatever you need, I can handle," JJ said, looking back at her steadily. "Believe me. I won't cut and run."

"I believe you, J. Just," the fire died down and she looked around, "just hang in there with me."

"No problem." His voice carried calm reassurance.

"You know," she said, "this isn't how it is in the movies. I mean, the ambush was tough, but it was like all adrenalin or something. The hard part, the part that really hurts, is the afterwards. That's the part you never see in the movies." JJ nodded in agreement. "And I got a feeling it's going to hurt a lot more before it ever begins to feel better."

Chapter 70

Terri called near midnight to let Catherine know she was going to be held over a shift at the hospital. She didn't talk about what was happening in the Emergency Room that brought her in; she only talked about her work when she was face to face. They shared their disappointments and talked a little about how dinner went. Then Catherine heard the ER chimes in the background and Terri was gone.

Catherine sighed and went to bed. She half expected to be up all night but was surprised to find herself waking up late. It was almost nine.

With a cup of hot tea beside her, she logged onto the university network with her computer and pursued the various messages and files having to do with the upcoming school year. It was the part of being a teacher she disliked most but being able to do it from home did make it easier. At least there were no telephones ringing.

On the other hand, she could see email kept being added to her electronic mailbox, even as she tried to catch up with the long list already existing. She felt like every time she got one done another was added. Apparently, a lot of other people were at home catching up on their work as well.

Terri came in a little before lunch. Her face was drawn and sagging and she had little energy in her step.

"Bad night?" Catherine said, looking up from her screen.

"It sucked," Terri said, patting her on the shoulder as she walked on to the kitchen. Catherine heard her putting water on and waited a few minutes before logging off and walking out to join her.

She saw the hair on Terri's neck was still damp. She showered before coming home, something she did occasionally. But when it was very bad in the emergency room she would want to take another when she got home. She used the shower like a cleansing ceremony, Catherine thought, as if shampoo and soap would erase from her mind whatever horror she encountered as it cleansed her body.

Terri poured her cup of tea and sat down in silence. Catherine stood behind her and massaged her shoulders. The muscles felt like iron and she finally felt a tiny shrug from Terri and stopped. She poured herself another cup and sat down across from her.

"What happened?" Catherine was enough of a therapist to know not to ask if Terri wanted to talk about it. People who went through high intensity situations and were bothered by them almost never wanted to talk about them. On the other hand, talking about it was often an important first step toward some kind of resolution.

"There was a shooting." She looked up. "It was probably on the news. An FBI agent was killed and a county deputy was pretty badly wounded but he'll make it. Two others were killed and one was wounded. He died this morning."

"Sounds rough."

"We were pretty busy on the deputy. The other guy was expectant from the time he hit the ER. He was just too torn up. His kidneys went last night. Put him on the machine but everything else began to go this morning."

"Is that what's bothering you?"

"No." Terri shook her head. "We did some nice work on the deputy. They've already begun prepping him for some graft work. Going to use a plastic mold for reconstruction." She paused and studied her tea.

"I felt real good about the deputy. And the guy who died is one of the people who hurt him. Him and the FBI agent. He was killed. Did I say that?" Seeing Catherine's nod she went on. "The other two DOAs were some of the other bad guys." She stopped and blew on her tea and then put it down without taking a sip.

"Last night one of the people they brought in was another FBI agent. She had some abrasions, minor stuff, whiplash from the crash. Nothing serious. She was just sitting there, stunned, not moving." She looked up at Catherine. "Kind of like that 'thousand meter stare in a ten meter room' combat vets talk about. I tried to talk to her after we got her cleaned up but she just wasn't really there. She had a county cop with her who was hovering around her like some kind of guardian angel. He really wanted to hurt someone. You could see it." Terri finally took a sip of tea.

"I did manage to get her hair cleaned up a little. It was all matted with blood and stuff. But that didn't bother me." She leaned forward, resting her forearms on the tabletop. "Here's this woman, this FBI agent, and another agent has been killed and one of our guys has had the front of his lower jaw blown away, and she's just killed two, maybe three, of the people who did it and all I could think was, 'Good for you, girl!'"

"And that bothers you?"

"Hell, yes!" Terri's anger quickly faded. "Cathy, I'm a nurse. All my life I've felt there was nothing more precious than human life. It's why I do what I do. And here I was taking satisfaction from some people getting blown away. I felt like I was betraying something."

Catherine sat silently, waiting. Terri wasn't looking for interpretation or even absolution, not yet. She needed to feel her own way for a while. Besides, Catherine never did therapy with her family, friends, or Terri. In addition to the issue of objectivity, there was the reality that no one ever listened, anyway.

"Was that all there was to it?" Catherine's question was softly asked.

"No, not really." She looked up and grinned. "You know, that FBI agent was kind of cute. Thing was," the grin faded, "she's about my age, and when I looked at her I tried to imagine doing what she did. The thing was, for a moment I actually could see myself doing it, killing someone."

She took another sip of tea. "You remember that breakfast we had with your dad? Remember what he asked me? Well, I said, sure, I would kill to protect someone I loved, but that was like an intellectual exercise. But last night it became real to me. If someone hurt you or someone I loved, I really could kill them."

"And that's the problem." Catherine offered the statement.

Terri nodded. "It's not just that I was taking some satisfaction in seeing one of our guys avenged. That was there. But the big thing was finally seeing how it could happen. How you could do it. It like sank into me, down into my feelings, not just my head."

"And that means that how I thought about myself was wrong."

Catherine nodded.

"I need to think it through, a little." Terri finished her tea in a few quick swallows and put her cup down. "You know, there's never been violence in my family, much less in my own life. I've always assumed that I was above all that. This has been a real wake-up call."

"Welcome to the human race," Catherine said with a smile.

Terri returned her smile with a touch of ruefulness. "I've been working ER for three years now, and I swear I spend more time straightening myself out than my patients."

"Maybe the patients are easier. You just work on their bodies. When you work on you, you're talking about head, heart, and soul stuff. That can be harder."

"Maybe I ought to go into your line of work."

"Don't. Too much competition as it is."

"Want to scrub my back?"

"Thought you'd never ask."

As they walked upstairs, Terri said, almost to herself, "I hope she's all right."

"Who?"

"That FBI agent," Terri said a little louder. "Her name's Karen. She went through a lot, and has more to go through. I hope she can handle it." She paused at the top of the stairs. "But how do you handle hell?"

"As best you can," Catherine said, taking her hand, "as best you can."

Chapter 71

Davidson came out of the critical incident debriefing and went straight to the coffee room. Listening to the other members of his group go through the experience of learning of Steve's death was rough and it left him with a lump in his throat. A hot cup of coffee, he thought, would make it easier to swallow.

He wasn't the only one, of course. About a third of his group of fifteen joined him. Most of the others went to the bathroom while a few went outside for a cigarette. Talking was subdued but they were talking, which he took as a positive sign.

These debriefings weren't therapy, of course. They were exactly what the firefighter-turned-paramedic-turned-psychologist designed them to be, a support service which helped carry people through traumatic experiences – "critical incidents" – and break down the isolation and withdrawal so common a reaction to those experiences.

Having the group leave rank at the door was hard but it could be done. What was harder was getting everyone to speak up and describe individually what they were thinking and feeling as it all went down. It was voluntary but most of the task force members were well enough educated in the psychology of traumatic events that they willingly stepped forward when the groups were offered.

Nonetheless, it could be rough, and this one was. The recurrent theme of helplessness was a tough one for cops to confront. It was most decidedly not how they saw themselves. But when they began to get the pieces of the ambush over the radio and telephone that was exactly what they all were.

All but one, of course. Davidson looked down the hall where the second group was meeting. That was Karen's group. When the debriefings were being set up he had talked to Dr. Studervan and let him know about Karen. The doc had ensured that she was in his group. They were still going.

He went back into the coffee room. Most of his group was there. He watched the interactions and saw the conversations were at a more normal tone, with less of the near whispered guardedness. A few jokes floated about. A good sign, he decided.

After a few minutes, Davidson went back to his office. Might as well work on some of the eternal federal paperwork while waiting for the remaining task force members to get out of their group.

Pinned to the wall over his desk was a copy of JJ's map, searched areas carefully colored. Davidson hadn't thought much of the deputy's project when he first looked at it. Too damned time consuming. Besides, there was no guarantee the Steel Rider lab wasn't in one of the towns and out of JJ's consideration. He had let him run with it for a while because there wasn't all that much for JJ to do and it was politically smart to let the local representatives feel like they were full blown members of the team.

Of course they weren't, but that fact had to remain unspoken. If there was something sour going down in the county, then it was possible local law enforcement was compromised. So there were things which weren't shared with all the various locals.

JJ was one of the exceptions. He was, Davidson decided, one of the original straight arrows, someone who followed the letter of the law, who lived with it in lieu of a wife. Or a life, for that matter.

So when JJ brought up the idea, Davidson thought there might not be much to it but, what the hell, let him have his run. He made sure any additional intel which might help JJ was fed to him. Mostly it was negative information, in the sense that it was data which ruled out various locations. That made the map's open areas a bit smaller.

What had really sold him on JJ's map idea was the simple fact that the lab they busted was in one of the uncolored areas. So maybe Deputy Dawg – that was Steve's nickname for JJ, he realized with a start – was onto something.

And JJ's map project might find more than the lab. Davidson suspected Jack Baker wouldn't be too far from it. He looked at it for a moment and then reached for a stack of papers.

He was deep into a budget report when there was a knock at the door. He looked up and saw Dr. Studervan leaning in.

"Got a minute?"

"Come on in, doc," Davidson said, motioning to a chair.

Studervan came in and sat and let out a breath. He was a tall man, a few inches above six feet, with dark, curly hair and a ready smile. Definitely high energy, which was a trait Davidson figured he developed while dealing with cops. They weren't into low profile types.

"How did it go?" Davidson asked.

"Went pretty well," Studervan said, nodding to his own statement. "You got some good people here."

"Damn straight."

"Piece of information I didn't have which was asked about. Where will the funeral be?"

Davidson raised his eyebrows. "Hadn't even thought about that. Steve isn't from around here. I think he and his wife live in northern Virginia, somewhere near DC. Suppose it will be there."

Studervan nodded. "Wherever it is, you might see about letting people go who want to."

"Right." Davidson scribbled himself a note to check on the funeral. "Anything else? Everyone okay?"

"It went all right, I can't be specific. I've set up a one-to-one with one of the people in my group. I'll talk to the debriefer who ran your group and see what I might need to do there. And I'll do a follow-up in two or three days to see if anyone needs some additional assistance."

Davidson resisted the temptation to ask who would be getting the individual attention. He would know soon enough and, besides, Studervan played by the rules and wouldn't say.

"Okay, Roger," he said, getting up, "I appreciate your doing this."

"Glad to help out," he said. "I posted my phone number on the bulletin board where I can be reached at the motel I'm staying." He walked with Davidson down the hall to the entrance.

"You still traveling around the world teaching that eye treatment therapy stuff?"

Studervan raised an eyebrow. "Are you federales keeping tabs on me, Carl?" The question was asked with a smile. "Yeah, I was in Kiev a little while ago. Nice people."

"Third world stuff. That can get rough," Davidson said as they got to the door.

Studervan laughed. "Not as bad as it could be. I got a couple of friends going into Sarajevo to do the same thing."

Davidson shook his head in wonderment and shook hands with Studervan. He watched as the big man walked out into the parking lot and got into his rental car and drove away. He shook his head again.

There have got to be easier ways of making a living than helping people deal with trauma.

He was walking back down the hall when he saw JJ.

"How you doing, JJ?"

"All right. Nice to get that shit off my chest." The deputy had a mug of coffee in his hand.

"How's Karen?" Davidson asked, his voice lower.

"She seemed okay," JJ said. "She's going to see Studervan later for a follow-up session. It was her idea."

Bingo.

"Yeah, I thought that might be the case. Good idea. Give her a chance to talk about it to someone who's not a cop. Different point of view, maybe more objective."

JJ nodded, though he didn't look happy about the idea. Davidson suddenly had a realization and it was all he could do to keep from slapping himself in the head.

Oh, hell! JJ's in love with her.

"Step in my office for a second," he said.

As JJ followed him he gestured at the map.

"You've got a chunk of this done," Davidson said. "Maybe a dozen areas yet to go."

"Fifteen," JJ corrected.

"Fifteen. Well, I'd like you to concentrate on checking them out. I appreciate that all this is nothing more than a surveillance. We don't have warrants and couldn't get them for something like this. But I think it's worth the effort." He looked at JJ. "And it will keep you out from underfoot for a few days."

"Well, I sure as hell would like to be doing something to find these bastards, and sitting on my ass making liaison phone calls is definitely not where it's at." The sharpness of JJ's tone was unusual and it corroborated Davidson's decision to get the deputy out of the office and burning off some of his energy.

"Okay, keep me posted. Remember to check in each morning to let us know which areas you'll be taking a look at that day and get your message traffic. I'll let you know if there's any reason to come in otherwise. Stay in touch by radio and update me daily on your mapping. Anything else?"

"Just one thing," JJ said. He paused.

"Well?"

"If you guys get ready to bust Jack Baker and his people, I want to be in on it." JJ's voice was calm enough, but there was anger barely beneath the surface.

"You got it, JJ. We'll all go on that one." Davidson shook hands with him and JJ left the office. Davidson shook his head.

If Baker is lucky we'll get to him before JJ Jeffers.

Chapter 72

Tom reached down and scratched Pupper's chin as Catherine and Ellen drove away. He straightened up, slowly, and gave a wave in response to Ellen's thin arm held out from the passenger window. What women saw in shopping, of walking around in malls with crowds of other people doing the same thing, was a mystery to him.

But it got Ellen out of the way for the day, and that was the important thing. He glanced at his watch. John Wesley had left earlier that morning to return to his place and would be back in maybe an hour.

Then they would go searching for Jack Baker and see about coming back that night.

What if he's not there? What if he's gone?

Too many people knew, Tom realized. Catherine, John, and, worst of all, Ellen. He had seriously underestimated her. His need to act, his obligation to act, had influenced his judgment of her.

Should have waited until she went home after the summer or sent her home myself. Thought I was so smart. Thought she was just a kid, even though I was seeing she was more than that. Didn't want to see it. Didn't want my plans blocked, and didn't want to see her getting older.

Tom unlocked the work shed and went in. His notebook, with the information on the five Steel Riders, was in its usual place. He took it down from the shelf and walked back out into the sunshine.

There was a rusting 55 gallon drum resting on cinder blocks off to one side of the barn. It had numerous holes in it for ventilation and was scorched from the occasional fires used to take care of trash. As he approached the drum he tore the pages out of the notebook.

He started a fire with a couple of pages and dropped them into the drum. The fire was a small one but it was thorough. He carefully fed the sheets of paper to it a few at a time. He watched as the fire consumed the pages of notes and pictures. Hollingsworth, Larson, Christopher, Bobby Baker, the newsprint pictures were eaten away to ash and vanished. He kept adding pages to the fire, even the blank ones.

So if he's not there and he's gone, what then?

There was no dodging the answer. Too many people knew. It couldn't continue.

If he's not there, then it's over.

He held onto the page with Jack Baker's picture for last and threw in the remainder of the notebook. He studied the gray-toned photograph and then dropped it into the flames. It burned from the edges inward, and the last of it Tom saw were the eyes encircled with eating fire.

Chapter 73

The air conditioner in JJ's car wasn't working so he had the window down to allow in the cool morning air. If asked, he would have admitted he preferred to drive without air conditioning and would explain it was an old habit from his days of driving traffic patrol. Getting in and out of an icy car in the Ohio summer heat could be rough.

In reality, one he would not admit to easily, he preferred to drive without air conditioning because it gave him an opportunity to smell the air, even if, as it was this morning, it carried the threat of a baking, humid day. The farms and woods around him had their own smells, like signatures signed onto the wind, and their familiarity was comforting.

Part of him was looking for comfort. The suffering from the ambush was still taking place and he wanted to do something about it. There was Steve's family, out in Virginia, who would be enduring his loss for the rest of their lives. Robert Black, looking ahead to months, maybe years, of physical suffering as they went about the business of rebuilding his face. Everybody on the task force had taken a hit, one which added its own weight of pain to the scales all cops carried.

And Karen, of course.

He wanted to stay with her but she had taken him aside and told him to get back to work, just as she was trying to do. She would fly back with Steve's body and attend the funeral as soon as transportation was worked out. She left what would happen after that blank.

How could any punishment inflicted on Jack Baker and his followers possibly balance, much less negate, the pain others would live with? So many people, so much suffering. He shook his head.

It was a feature of him that he did not add his own name to the list as he totaled up the cost in prolonged suffering of a few minutes of violence. Another part of him overruled personal considerations. He never mentioned it, but he thought of himself as a "lawman," a part of him which took its strength from his concept of his manhood and his belief in the law. He had enough experience as a cop to know that, at best, the law was simply an instrument for attaining some approximation of justice, and sometimes a very blunt instrument. Nonetheless, working on behalf of that instrument, accepting its discipline in a manner not unlike that of a monk, always seemed to him to be the best hope for the struggle for justice.

He looked for a second at his map on the seat beside him to check the route to the next place he wanted to check out, a small farm located in the northern part of the county.

The map, with its variously colored patches, reminded him of a quilt. *Crazy quilt.*

JJ pulled himself away from disparaging his work. He knew the odds were against success; they always were for any particular lead a cop might follow. The law worked because of persistence. Like the quilt making old women he had known as a boy, he reminded himself, everything depended upon persistence.

And maybe all the people he knew were like threads in the quilt. There was Jack Baker, a dark, twisted thread, one which needed to be plucked from the weave. Karen's thread, stained by guilt and sorrow, ran close to his own. He wondered if it would wander away after all this.

There was Davidson and the task force and Phillips and all the other cops. Bright, blue threads, holding the whole thing together.

And there was Tom Parker. What color thread was he?

Were all these threads coming together, forming a pattern he could not see? You only appreciated the beauty of a quilt from a distance, and that was one thing he did not have.

He checked his map again and glanced ahead. There it was, the entrance to the farm, marked by a large mailbox next to a gravel filled lane which went over a rise and then disappeared. It looked like he could approach the property from the rear, from the north. According to his map and the updated imagery of the county, there should be some woods there which would allow him to get into the small valley which took up most of the farm's property.

He sighed as he came abreast of the lane. Probably come to zip, as usual, but it was better than sitting around the office. He glanced at the black mailbox and noticed the white-painted name, which meant nothing to him.

Rader

Chapter 74

John Wesley turned his truck onto the lane for his uncle's farm. He saw the old man playing with Pupper as he drove up. Tom had changed out of his denims and into a faded green work shirt and pants.

The day, even in the last of its morning, carried the threat of one of those muggy, Midwest days marked with the heavy, hot hand of August. He wished, not for the first time, that his truck had air conditioning. But a university professor's salary, even a tenured one up for a prestigious position, was not as lavish as it might be.

The graduate chair position. He had downloaded his email when he got home almost reflexively. There were messages of congratulations from, as expected, his department chair and some of the other teachers logging in over the summer. Unexpectedly, there was a long message from the chairperson of the selection committee.

The man's message was almost florid with praise. He had even, and John had made himself reread the message to ensure he was reading it correctly, described John's application as being "in the bag," a remarkable change from the cold, almost disdainful manner with which he had treated John before.

John saved the message but did not reply to it. It didn't seem important. Maybe later.

Maybe after we take care of Jack Baker.

He parked his truck beside Tom's. As he got out, the older man walked over.

"Got your things?"

John nodded and pulled a gym bag from behind the driver's seat.

"I've got an old cammie shirt, which I thought would be better for snooping and pooping than this polo shirt. Couple of other things."

"Well, come on over." Tom led the way to the work shed and went in.

Tom opened the steel doors to the gun locker. He pulled out his pump shotgun and Remington rifle and placed them on the work table. Then he reached back into the locker and brought out a handgun. John saw it was an older model Colt .45 automatic. Tom closed and locked the doors.

John put his bag on the table and pulled out a shirt marked in a camouflage pattern, which he put on. He stuffed his old shirt into the bag and then brought out a black baseball cap. Finally he pulled out a Smith and Wesson .357 Magnum revolver. It was already in a brown leather holster, which he quickly attached to his belt. The baggy shirt hid it from view. He put several speed loaders into one of the shirt's side pockets.

Tom lifted a green, plastic utility box with a carrying handle from below the table. Resembling a fishing tackle box, he flipped the lid open. Inside were several plastic boxes of his hand loaded ammunition and a couple of commercial boxes. There were several clips for the .45, already loaded, one of which he put into the pistol. The others went into a pocket. He jacked a round into the chamber and slipped the safety on. He put the pistol into the box and took out a small pair of binoculars.

"Why don't you take the shotgun?" Tom said, and handed John a box of shells from the utility box. John loaded the shotgun, worked the slide, and put another shell in. He checked the safety and then looked at Tom.

"I think we're ready."

Tom closed the lid of the utility box and hefted the long rifle.

"Not quite. Let's load this stuff."

After putting everything into Tom's truck and locking up the shed, he took Pupper into the house. A few minutes later he emerged with an empty, plastic milk jug. He paused by the outside tap and filled it. He handed it to John, already in the truck, who put it between his feet.

"Figured it's going to be a hot day," Tom said and walked around the truck, selecting the ignition key as he went.

"Hotter   than   hell,"   John   said   quietly.

Chapter 75

Catherine and Ellen drove to the mall in silence. Ellen seemed distracted and most of the time stared ahead, not paying attention to the scene outside the car.

They parked near the main entrance. Though it was early and a Thursday, there were already many other cars present. Catherine looked over at Ellen, who made no effort to get out of the car.

"What's up, Big E?"

"You haven't said anything to me about it, so I guess what I thought about Grandpa Tom was true."

Catherine almost flinched. She nearly had forgotten about Ellen in her own wrestling with the problem. She reached over and put her hand on the young girl's shoulder.

"Ellen, there's no proof that your grandfather has done any of those things," she said carefully. Ellen looked at her sharply.

"It's not about proof and you know it."

Catherine nodded and sighed.

"You're right, Big E, you're right."

"See, what I don't understand is why he's doing it. It's not going to bring back Eileen, and it's putting him in danger." Her eyes began to fill with tears.

"He knows that, honey. He's not about revenge, not really."

"Then what?" Her voice was small and shaky. Catherine though for a moment.

"You know that picture over the fireplace?"

"The one with the big wolf standing over the little wolf in the snow? It's called 'Watcher in the Woods.'" Her voice was suddenly calm and matter of fact, changing with a child's abruptness. "It's by Bob Travers. He does a lot of neat wolf pictures. I have his catalog."

"Right, that's the one," Catherine said. "Your grandfather is like the older wolf in the picture. He wants to protect his family and will do whatever he must to keep them safe."

Ellen thought for a moment as she gazed at the parking lot.

"I saw this show on TDC about wolves," she finally said. "They showed a pack and even the wolves that didn't have children would protect the young ones, even at the risk of their own lives. It's kind of automatic. You know, a natural part of them."

"That's what I mean," Catherine replied. "That's how it is with your grandfather. Like those wolves, it's a natural part of him. He would not let his family be threatened. And once Eileen died, those people were forever identified to him as a threat to his family."

Ellen nodded while she considered what Catherine said.

"Wolves are pretty sociable and they're good hunters. They can be very ferocious." Ellen paused and looked at Catherine. "But if Grandpa Tom is like a wolf, doesn't that mean we are, too?"

Catherine was silent as she looked into Ellen's steady, clear eyes, which, for this moment, were not the eyes of a child.

"It's not all we are, Ellen," she finally said, "But we are of him, and I guess that means, yes, if we have to be."

Chapter 76

JJ was particularly pissed off, as he would put it if there had been anyone to talk to. He parked north of the Rader farm and, after climbing over a wire fence, entered a thick patch of woods. Movement was not particularly difficult until the trees abruptly came to an end.

Apparently, a narrow strip of forest had been cleared for farming but then abandoned several years ago. Now it was almost totally overgrown with thorn-laden berry bushes. His jeans did not offer much protection and after several painful attempts to go forward, he was forced to retreat. Angling to the east, he finally found a meager animal trail headed in the general direction of where he thought the farm was. It was rough going, with frequent stops to unhook himself from thorns and, at one point, a rusting line of collapsed barbed wire fencing.

Then he was back in the woods. The thorns were gone but the ground was cut by shallow ravines and, with the humidity and heat of the day beginning to make themselves felt, it became a physical struggle. Part of him welcomed it as something he could fight that was real, something to take his frustrations out on.

JJ arrived at the edge of the woods overlooking the farm two hours later than he thought he would. His shirt was matted to his back with sweat and there was a cut on his thigh from the fencing, deep enough that he wondered if his tetanus booster was up to date. He found a log he could sit on and study the area while remaining relatively concealed. He checked the sun and made sure he kept his binoculars within the shade.

His position was on a gentle hillside. Sloping away from him was a soybean field, its crops turning a bright shade of yellow. It had not been maintained since being planted, however, and numerous weeds sprouted up between the rows. To his right, to the west, he saw the wood line made a right angle turn south. It went in that direction for a couple of hundred yards before again proceeding east. That portion appeared to be largely made up of the remains of the trees that had once occupied the soybean field. Dead, bleached tree trunks were bulldozed against the living trees and formed an almost solid barrier.

The barrier line ended almost opposite him on the other side of the soybeans. Fortunately, the farm buildings themselves were open to his view. He saw, just on the other side of the tree line, the front of a large work shed. Then came a two-story, white frame house. He was directly opposite its screened-in back porch. To the left of the house was a parking area in which sat a car facing away from him, its trunk open. A motorcycle was also parked there.

To the left of the parking area was a tall barn with a fenced-in area extending away from it, but there were no animals in it and through his binoculars he saw there were weeds growing in the enclosed paddock. The barn doors were open and he saw another motorcycle, partially dismantled and resting on a small, wheeled platform right in the entrance. Another one was parked just outside the barn. There was something, maybe gray, behind it, further into the barn, but there wasn't enough light to make it out.

To the left of the barn was a big Quonset hut made of curved, aluminum sheets, what the locals would call a pole barn. On the end he could see were large, closed, sliding doors, maybe ten feet high. One of them had a regular door in it. What attracted his attention was an exceptionally large external air conditioner, about the size of a small car, attached to the side of the building. Wide, aluminum piping ran from the unit to the building. Similar piping formed a tall, wire-braced chimney, almost twice as high as the top of what was very likely the drug lab he had been searching for. His heart pounded and he licked his lips.

Hold on, partner. This might be someone's drying shed.

JJ pulled his handheld radio from its belt sheath but didn't call in. He wanted to be sure. Besides, he doubted that a warrant could be obtained for what he had seen thus far. He put the radio back into its sheath.

There was movement around the car. Someone came out of the house's side door and got into the driver's seat. He faintly heard music begin as the radio was switched on. The driver left his door open. The side door opened again and was held there. He saw an arm but the figure came no further.

And then Jack Baker stepped into view. He stopped, looking back into the house, saying something. He had a large, dark blue gym bag hanging by a strap over his shoulder and after a moment, his conversation over, he walked on over to the car and put it into the trunk. He left it opened and returned to the house.

Gotcha, you son of a bitch.

He knew that technically Baker was only wanted for questioning. The dead men from the ambush were Steel Riders, but that was all they had. While JJ held his binoculars with one hand, the other dipped towards his radio, paused, and then rose back to the binoculars to steady them. He thought there was something in the barn...

Someone turned on a bank of fluorescent lights. Behind the motorcycle he saw the back of a vehicle. In the shadows before, it had been indistinct and he had ignored it. He saw a figure approach the motorcycle and squat down behind it. He ignored the man and concentrated on the vehicle. Another bank of lights flickered to life and he could see better.

It was the back of a windowless, white van. The man at the motorcycle half rose and looked over to one side and said something. Another bank of lights came to life. JJ focused on the back of the van.

There were small, black dots on the white paint. Around some of the dots he thought he saw gray primer or bare metal.

Bullet holes. Karen's bullet holes.

He reached for his radio again. Then his hand froze, hovering above it.

To his right, hidden from the farm buildings by the tree line, he saw two men. They were slowly and carefully making their way down the edge of the soybean field. The one in front wore a camouflaged military shirt and carried a shotgun. The second, clad in faded green work clothes, had a pistol.

He could see them clearly when they paused to listen, half crouched next to the piles of dead tree limbs and trunks. While he had never met them, he knew their faces well.

Thomas Luther Parker and John Wesley Parker were coming.

JJ's   hand   did   not   move.

Chapter 77

Tom had no trouble parking his truck off the road and out of sight. The bushes were very tall next to the road and there was a narrow lane which turned off the road and then jogged parallel to it. A small, abandoned camping trailer stood at the end, its windows and doors gone, the ground in front of it strewn with empty beer cans and bottles.

He and John climbed out of the truck and paused for a moment, both men listening. Somewhere in the distance was the drone of an airplane and as they stood in silence the sounds of the woods came slowly back, though subdued in the increasing heat.

"As I said," Tom spoke softly, "I went a piece into the woods. It's fairly dense but easy walking. I stopped short of a soybean field. I couldn't see it, but as best as I could figure, I was probably a few hundred yards short of the farm house."

"Okay, then, let's take our time and see what we can see." John's voice was as quiet as Tom's. His eyes kept sweeping the woods in the direction of Rader's farm. "If he's there, then we'll come back tonight or some other time. No need to press it today. Agreed?"

Tom nodded. "I'll take us as far as I went before. Then you take the lead." He paused and grinned. "Your ears may be a bit keener than mine."

"All right," John said. He picked up the shotgun while Tom slung his rifle. They had agreed earlier that their cover story, if anyone asked, was they were looking for a place to shoot their guns; Tom's utility box held cleaning gear, a few boxes of ammunition, and some paper targets, which would corroborate their story.

Tom led them deeper into the woods. The older man was right. While the trees were close together, their canopy cut the light and discouraged bushes from growing. At first they moved fairly quickly, pausing every so often to listen. They had travelled for about a half hour, perhaps something less than four hundred yards by John's estimate, when Tom stopped and raised his hand. John froze, listening.

Tom turned slowly and made a "come here" motion with his finger. John carefully moved up to him. Tom pointed ahead.

"See the field?" he whispered. John nodded, seeing the flare of yellow through the trees ahead. "Take the lead."

John nodded and stepped around him. John found his old skills coming back and he moved quietly, putting his foot down gently, heel first, feeling for branches and leaves which might make a sound. He approached the edge of the field carefully.

He stopped just short of the field. Tom came up slowly beside him. From their position they saw the field was bordered on the north by more woods which extended out of sight over the hill to their left. On the right, the south side of the field likewise was bordered by a tree line; this one marked by piles of logs and limbs, pushed up against the growing trees and forming what looked to be an impenetrable barrier.

Tom put the utility box down and slowly opened it. He took out the small binoculars and passed them to John, who examined the area. He put the pistol in his belt. Tom closed the lid and sat on the box. He unslung his rifle and popped open the plastic lens covers on the Leupold sight. He brought the rifle up and looked around.

The tree line ran to the west about two hundred yards. From their position near the northeastern corner of the field, they saw buildings beyond the tree line. Most exposed to view was a large, aluminum-covered building with a curved roof reaching the ground. Just around the corner of the building they saw the edge of another, smaller metal structure, which appeared to be attached to it by large air ducts. The building, which Tom thought might be used for drying tobacco or other crops, had large, closed sliding doors facing them. A smaller, normal door was built into one of the sliding doors, but was also closed. Just visible beyond the tree line was the edge of a barn and a fenced in area, overgrown with weeds.

John motioned towards the tree line with his hand and then moved his hand parallel to it. Then he pointed at his eyes. Tom understood and nodded. He put the rifle down, laying it across the box, and pulled out his pistol. They would have to follow the tree line to get close enough to see who might be at the farm houses.

Again John led the way, moving very slowly towards the tree line, staying within the woods. He paused every few feet, listening. He carried the shotgun with the butt against his shoulder, his left hand holding it low but moving it so it was kept pointed in the direction he was looking.

When they got to the corner formed by the tree line and woods, John waited before stepping out from cover. If this was where Jack Baker was, he expected to see some sort of security around. Thus far there was none. Maybe it was all on the side facing the main entrance, which seemed too foolish to be counted on. He looked back at Tom. His uncle was keeping his head moving, looking and listening. The older man nodded to him and John started to step out of the woods.

Old sensitivities saved them. As his leg went forward slowly, he felt something touch his shin. It might have just been a twig but he froze in place. Looking down, he saw a black string. It was taut across his leg. He raised one hand to halt Tom from coming forward. Without adding or lessening the tension on the string, he held his leg still and carefully followed it with his eyes.

To his left, about five feet away, he saw a wooden stake had been driven into the ground just behind a soybean plant, making it virtually invisible from the woods. The string was tied off on it. He looked to the right. The string disappeared into the pile of shattered tree limbs. Judging the position of where the string disappeared and where it tied to the stake suggested to him that the string had been slack when his leg encountered it.

He slowly moved backwards. The string went limp as his shin withdrew, sagging to a position about three inches off the ground. He slowly followed the string into the pile of branches. By changing his angle he saw it went to a small, green-painted device securely taped to a log. It was probably, he decided, some kind of alarm rather than a mine, since it was so small. Maybe a flare or whistle. He cut the string with a pocket knife and carefully rolled it up and lay it beside the device.

He moved back to the stake, gathering up the thin string as he went. He saw another string leading from the stake and disappearing into the foliage beyond it. He laid the loose string beside the stake and returned to his position next to the tree line. He looked back at Tom and gave him a thumb's up. Then he started forward again.

This close to the tree line he saw it never got very thick, more of a windbreak than anything. What concealed them from the farm buildings were the remains of the cleared trees. On their left it was all soybeans for about two hundred yards, and then the woods began again. The dirt underfoot was dry and cracked, covered with weeds. He didn't like the feeling of being exposed, especially to the north, but there was little to be done for it. The tree line was too thin to walk in without being visible.

They were half way down the tree line when they heard music from up ahead. It was faint and faded in and out. John stopped and squatted. Between the weeds and the broad leaves of the soybean plants, he couldn't see very far, even down the edge of the tree line, but he waited and listened. The music did not sound like it was coming closer and after a few minutes he rose from his crouch. He looked around slowly.

For a moment, he thought he saw movement in the woods to the north but finally decided it was nothing, maybe a deer. If a person was there, they would have been seen ever since they stepped out of the cover of the woods behind them and the alarm would have already been sounded.

Silence implies consent.

John began moving. He didn't bother to look behind him for Tom; he knew his uncle was there.

Near the end of the tree line, just before the cleared area holding the farm buildings, John stopped and squatted again. He had gotten a glimpse of the barn through the foliage. He looked back at Tom and pointed at his eyes, touched his chest, and then made a curving motion in the direction of the tree line's edge. Tom slowly raised and lowered his head. John handed back the shotgun and slowly pulled his pistol. He rose slowly and, keeping his body close to the tops of the weeds, walked forward.

Chapter 78

Jack Baker rubbed his slowly returning goatee in frustration, an emotion he seldom experienced. It was bad enough the ambush did not go as well as he planned. Losing the two men other than Peterson, who he personally shot through the back of the head after he tumbled to the road, had not been anticipated. Worse, they now had a van with a lot of bullet holes in it. He wanted it dumped somewhere and burned but that was still not done. Everyone was too afraid to be out on the road in it, even at night. He would probably have to do it himself after dark.

Bunch of chickenshits. Everyone was walking around with a gun handy, sometimes more than one. An Uzi and an AK leaned against the kitchen wall, left there by the two working on packaging the speed. He was carrying a pistol himself, though it was mostly for appearance. There was no way the police could have trailed them here and their operation was as secure as it had ever been, he believed.

In part, the drug lab's security was based on the fact that damned few people in the Riders' organization knew of its existence, much less of where it was located. Only a few people actually worked in the lab or provided it with its guards.

The other source of frustration was that the Riders were behind in their deliveries. The intermediate distributor in Indianapolis, who passed product on to Chicago and other Midwest cities, was climbing the walls, and the Dayton contact was going ballistic. So now they were trying put together a load to be driven to the distributors. There was no lack of volunteers to drive the car, since the driver got a cash reward for delivery.

But the circuit breakers in the lab had blown while he was away setting up the ambush, thoroughly shutting it down and, while the cause was being investigated, they had to take the stuff into the kitchen to weigh and pack it.

He had the lab workers taken away last night, along with some of the security to keep an eye on them. With the lab down until the electrical problem was cleared up, there wasn't anything for them to do. He wouldn't allow anyone to work in the lab until ventilation was restored – too much chance of an explosion with subsequent permanent loss of production, not to mention most of the surrounding farm.

Besides, Jack hated looking at them. The workers tended to resemble gaunt, red eyed ghouls, sitting around twitching, like their skins were trying to crawl off them. Far better to have them crammed into an RV and taken on down to Covington. *Keep'em drunk in a whorehouse until it was time to put them back to work.*

On the other hand, with the shortage of people, the work of packaging the already produced speed and repairing the electrical system was going slowly. Kerosene on the fire of his frustration. He knew that his standing over the two weighing and packaging didn't help at all, but he couldn't stay away.

Even if it did, fuck'em.

One man, red-haired Les Coulter, didn't seem to mind, grinning as he carefully added yellow-white powder to the measuring cup. The other man, his brother Mike, clearly did. He scowled behind his heavy, black beard and mustache. Baker noticed he had not worn his hair in its usual pony tail and was letting it hang over his ears. Probably trying to cover the bandage wrapped around the lower part of his left ear. He had been in the passenger seat of the van and a cop bullet had taken away his ear lobe.

They were carefully measuring the methamphetamine on electronic scales. They would then dump the contents of the measuring cups into large, plastic bags. When a bag had the proper amount, they inserted its open end into a sealer, which used heat to close the bag. The weight was written on the bag with a felt pen. Some bags, destined for particular locations, had colored dots or large initials drawn on them. When enough bags were collected, they were loaded into a gym bag and taken out to the car.

So far, exactly one loaded bag had been taken out. Jack had done it himself, pausing only to tell the others to keep working. It was going slowly and he suspected the whole load would not be ready for another hour.

He stepped back outside. The car driver, Charlie Dawson, was lounging behind the wheel, listening to some top-40 station out of Cincinnati. He had an M-16 slung on the open car door. Idiot. Probably draining the battery. The only reason Baker let him take the run was he had been the driver of the van and done a hell of a job getting them out of there. One of those cops nearly took Baker's head off and that was close enough.

Beyond the car he saw Smitty Toreson working on his bike. The fat, heavily bearded man was a natural with tools, kind of like that kid Larson. Behind him, looking over Smitty's shoulder, was Dale Menken, who straightened up when he noticed Baker looking at him and rested his hand on his belt buckle, not far from the automatic pistol he carried. Menken had been a friend of Peterson's and Baker was keeping an eye on him. It looked like Menken was returning the favor.

Two men emerged from behind Menken and walked towards the lab. Jimmy Eisley, the taller of the two, had blond hair partially hidden by a bandanna. He had a tool chest in one hand and a plastic bag in the other while a length of heavy duty electrical cable was looped over a shoulder. His companion, a short, stocky biker wearing glasses and the improbable name of Jay Hoover, likewise carried a toolkit. Jimmy saw Baker.

"Just about done. Be about an hour," he yelled. "We found the short. Got everything we need."

Baker nodded.

An hour. Great. Another fucking delay. Everything around this fucking place takes a fucking hour.

He watched as Hoover handed his toolkit to Eisley and motioned toward the tree line. Jimmy grinned as Hoover grabbed his crotch and began hopping away, his MAC-10 flopping around his neck like a talisman. Jimmy continued towards the lab. Baker shook his head in disgust and went back into the house.

Bunch of damned clowns.

Then   he   heard   gunfire.

Chapter 79

John Wesley only intended to look around the tree line to see what lay beyond it. He took two crouched steps to the edge and was getting ready to lower himself to the ground to go the rest of the way when Jay Hoover walked around the corner, his fingers already fumbling with his pants zipper.

Hoover froze but John didn't. The former Marine immediately slammed his pistol into the side of Hoover's head. Hoover fell backward, stunned, and then began groping for his submachine gun. It was a fatal mistake.

John brought his pistol to bear and fired twice. The .357 Magnum Silvertips operated as designed, blossoming into metal flowers which kept the high velocity bullets from exiting Hoover's body. The first tore into his liver, essentially destroying it, while the second tore apart the wall separating two chambers of his heart and went on to fracture his spinal column. The shredded heart spastically pumped blood out the entry holes but John was not watching.

Someone ahead of him yelled as he fired the second time and John threw himself to one side and forward, clear of the soybean field but out from the cover of the tree line. He saw a red-haired man running toward him from twenty yards away, pulling a pistol out of his belt, with what looked like a bunch of electrical cable looped around one arm. John raised his pistol and formed a sight picture, the front post between the notches of the rear sight.

The other man fired as he ran, holding his gun straight out in front of him. John concentrated on his sights, putting them in the middle of the running figure. He squeezed the trigger and the .357 fired again.

Jimmy Eisley saw Hoover down and a man crouching beside him. Beyond the two, a man rose from a crouch, a shotgun in his hands. As he ran forward, he pointed the gun and fired repeatedly. He couldn't understand why he was missing.

He did not feel the impact of the bullet. Suddenly, it was very hard to breathe. He needed to stop, catch his breath, and take better aim. Before he could make himself do any of those things, he was looking up at the sky. It was a second before he realized he was on his back. Then the pain came.

John Wesley heard shouts from within the now revealed house and there were two men coming out of the barn and another man was getting out of the car. He had a clear shot at one of the men from the barn and he fired twice, then reached for a speed loader.

Smitty heard the shooting and grabbed the shotgun just inside the barn door. He ran forward but couldn't see anything. Someone hit him in the stomach with a ball peen hammer and he slid to a halt while starting to fold over the pain. He looked around, trying to see who was hitting him. The second bullet crashed into his skull, blowing away his forehead, and he was dead. His body fell forward and struck the ground. Bits of white bone and pink brain mixed in blood dribbled out of the ugly cavity.

John extracted his empty cases and pushed the speed loader in and twisted it free. He slapped the chamber closed. The man running from the barn was down. He couldn't see the other man who had been with him but the one from the car was straightening up and closer so he aimed at him.

Charlie Dawson loved, insofar as he could feel the emotion, his M-16 rifle. His was the military version, capable of three-round burst firing, and he kept it loaded with a 30-round magazine. It just looked cool, a slick piece of black plastic and metal. He liked to stand with the weapon, holding the pistol grip with the butt resting on his hip. He thought he looked like those guys in the Vietnam war movies. He had always imagined what it would be to be like Sly Stallone, firing his rifle on rock and roll, watching the enemy drop like flies. He had always wanted to be Rambo.

When Dawson heard the firing behind him he almost peed himself. Then he grabbed the rifle and stood out of the car, turning to see what was going on.

As he turned, he saw Toreson skid to a halt while Menken ducked for cover behind several empty cardboard packing boxes. Toreson was bent over, a look of confusion on his face. Then his face was gone as his head erupted in a spray of red and white. Dawson turned toward the source of the shots. He saw Hoover's body and a man lying beside it reloading his pistol. From around the corner of the tree line another man was emerging. Dawson thumbed the selector switch and raised the rifle to his shoulder. He anticipated laying bullets over the two men like using a garden hose.

But his rifle was the newest issue of the military version of the M-16. It could not fire fully automatically for more than a quick burst of three rounds. Dawson's burst was low, spraying dirt into the face of the man on the ground, but not hitting him. In his excitement, he didn't release the trigger and when the burst ended his continued squeezing accomplished nothing except generating a sudden sense of panic in himself.

John had started to fire at Dawson when the rounds impacted in front of him. Immediately he was blinded by the spray of dirt. He rolled to one side, trying to wipe his eyes clear.

Tom stepped over his nephew, the shotgun already up to his shoulder. He leaned forward slightly and fired. The 12-gauge, loaded with Remington "Double-ought buck" rounds, let loose nine buckshot, each one almost the size of a 32-caliber bullet. In the twenty yards to Dawson, they had spread less than a foot and a half – nearly all took him in his torso. Dawson, dropping his rifle, fell backwards and tried to hold himself up by grabbing at the car roof and door frame. Tom jacked another round and fired a second time. Dawson's face, struck by six buckshot, exploded in a spray of red and he collapsed.

Tom had seen one man duck behind some boxes between the barn and the Quonset hut. He did not recognize the man but was sure it was not Jack Baker. He started to swing the shotgun towards the stranger's position but suddenly the doors to the house burst open. Someone was firing from the porch and he felt John move behind him.

"Hold still!" Tom yelled, and fired into the open doorway.

When the firing started the Coulter brothers looked to Jack Baker for guidance. But Jack was in no hurry to stick his head out the door. He went to the back window and looked out through the screened porch. He saw Hoover and a stranger, who was firing, on the ground and a man coming up behind the shooter, an old fart with a white mustache. He turned to the Coulters, who had retrieved their weapons. He pulled his own pistol free and chambered a round.

"It's not cops," he said, though he wasn't sure of that. "Two guys, coming out of the field. You," he looked at Les Coulter, who was nervously fingering his Uzi, "cover us from here. Mike and I will go out the side and nail these bastards."

Les went to the back door and whipped it open and quickly stuck his head around the corner and then pulled it back.

"One of them is down!" he shouted.

374

"Let's go!" Baker yelled and pushed the other Coulter brother in front of him. Mike wasn't in a hurry to be the first out the door but he heard his brother's Uzi firing on full automatic so he jumped through the doorway.

Les Coulter saw an old man with a shotgun standing over a man on the ground. The old guy was pointing off to one side. The man on the ground wasn't dead, he realized. He saw him wiping at his eyes with one hand, the other still holding a pistol. If he wasn't dead he was about to be. Coulter stepped into the open doorway, the Uzi at his waist, and opened fire.

His rounds were high, he realized immediately, and he brought the shaking barrel down. He saw dirt clods kicking into the air beyond and to one side of the old man, who was swinging his weapon towards him. Desperately, he moved the Uzi back and forth, trying to cut the old man in two.

The shotgun fired and he felt the impact low in his abdomen. He collapsed and fell into a well of pain, pain so awful he couldn't see for a moment. He lay on his back, trying to push himself away from the doorway and that terrible shotgun. He heard other shots fired but they didn't mean anything. Somehow he pushed himself against a wall. He forced himself up into a sitting position and looked down upon himself.

His lap was a pool of blood. Weakly he pulled at his clothing. The impacting buckshot centered just below his belt buckle. His shirt and pants were ripped and bloody. It was impossible to tell which was which. He kept pulling at his clothing, dragging the tatters from what felt like a pool of fire from his thighs to his stomach. He pushed his jeans aside, looking at his crotch.

Because of what he saw, when death finally came, he was the only man at the farm to die happily.

Tom swung the shotgun back towards the side door of the house. Two men were out. One was facing him, raising a military-style rifle, while the other, carrying a pistol, was trying to get around to the front of the car. Tom snapped a shot towards the man with the rifle. The buckshot must have missed him, but the man beyond fell down. Tom worked the slide and fired again. Incredibly, the man with the rifle hadn't fired. Tom's round caught him full in the chest and he fell.

Mike Coulter had a burst of anger when he felt Baker's hand on his back, pushing him forward through the side doorway. He came out so suddenly he almost fell down and barely skidded to a halt before hitting the car. He looked towards the back and saw an old man firing at the house. He started to raise his Kalashnikov but saw the old man fire at him.

The buckshot passed him to the left. Two pellets punched through his pant leg and his bladder voided but he didn't notice. It was the ambush all over again, with that woman cop firing at him, at him, over and over again, not ever stopping, not even when they raced away, hearing the slam of her bullets into their backdoors. Part of him tried to raise the AK, but his muscles weren't responding. The second blast from the shotgun was like being hit with a board and he dropped his rifle and fell down. He was still afraid when he died.

Tom looked around, the shotgun to his shoulder. The two men who came out of the house were down. Neither was moving. There was still the man behind the boxes. He crouched beside John and reached down and held his nephew's hand.

"It's okay, John," he said. "Leave your eyes alone. I need shells."

John Wesley stopped trying to wipe his eyes clear. He looked up at his uncle. He kept one eye shut, the other pinched almost completely closed. He reached with his free hand and pulled shells from his shirt pocket. He handed them up to Tom, who fed them into the shotgun. John barely saw Tom's form but he kept handing him shells. He heard the slide work and he gave Tom one more.

"That's it for now," Tom said. "I've got to go check out one of them."

"Watch your ass," John replied.

Tom started towards the boxes. He could see to either side of them and beyond; if the man behind them started to run he had him. Suddenly a stranger's head popped up and immediately disappeared. Well, if he wants to run away he can go, he decided.

Dale Menken had not intended to be there at all. When he heard Peterson was dead he immediately suspected Jack Baker had a hand in it. It was time, he decided, to get the hell out of Dodge. If Baker thought he was part of any rival faction, Menken figured it was just a question of time before he, too, was dead.

Instinctively, he had turned toward the shooting but then had realized that it wasn't any of his business any longer. Let the other dumb bastards deal with it. He ducked behind the boxes, which he realized were empty only after he was crouched out of sight of the gunfight.

Menken stayed where he was, listening to the shooting. He saw Toreson go down, and then Dawson. There was a lot more shooting, but the last shots were from a shotgun, and he didn't think any of the others had one. Then there was silence.

He waited but heard nothing. He finally decided to sneak a look over the top. An old man with a shotgun was coming towards him; there was a man on the ground behind him. Menken ducked his head back down. He hadn't seen enough of either man to identify them.

Who the hell were they? What was going on? Must be Dragons, coming for bloody revenge. Christ, now what do you do? He rubbed his chin with the top of his pistol. He had no faith in his ability with a handgun. There was only one thing to do.

Tom paused after seeing the man behind the box take his look. Approaching head on did not seem to be a great idea. He started to slide to his left, trying to get an angle which would allow him to see behind the boxes. He had moved a few yards when suddenly the stranger dashed from behind the boxes and ran towards the barn.

Tom tracked him with his shotgun, leading him, but didn't fire. The man ran to the motorcycle in front of the barn and jumped on it. There was a very long pause while he fumbled with his keys. He dropped his pistol but made no effort to pick it up.

The big Harley roared into life, and the biker twisted the throttle on as he slammed it into gear. He tore a circle, spraying gravel nearly as far as Tom. Then he was racing down the lane, up shifting as fast as he could, swerving the big bike from side to side, almost losing it.

Tom watched as the bike disappeared over the hill. He heard its roar decrease as it reached the road, and then the sound was moving off to the west, the gears rapidly worked through. He shook his head.

Tom decided he ought to check the other buildings. He opened the door to the Quonset hut. It was dark inside, though a portable electric light was set up near an open electrical junction box near the door. He picked up the light and shined it around. Inside it was like a laboratory. There were rows of glass piping and beakers on a long table running down the center of the building.

The smell was almost overwhelming. It had a strong, medicine overtone to it, along with a chemical odor and something that smelled like cat urine. There were several large mixing tubs with yellow and white substances in them. Near the base of the roof were bags of chemicals of different sizes. In the back were cardboard boxes, dozens of them. Their lids were all slit open and he raised one.

Each box held four brown, plastic, wide-mouthed bottles. Tom put the light down and pulled one up and tried to read the label and realized he needed his reading glasses. He unscrewed the cap and immediately smelled ether. He put the lid back on. That was the medicine smell he had noticed.

He looked around, the light playing on the equipment, the bags and boxes, the vats and mixers. His eyes kept watering but he had no problem figuring out what the place was. It was a drug lab. It belonged to Jack Baker.

But where was Jack Baker?

Once outside he went to the barn. It had been converted to a garage, complete with a poured concrete floor. Several banks of lights glowed brightly overhead. Pegboard was nailed to the walls and a variety of tools hung there. There was a large, rolling tool chest and a five gallon gas can. He nudged the can with his foot; it appeared to be full. In the corner a white van was parked.

Tom approached it with the shotgun leveled. He saw several bullet holes in the back and a couple of exit holes on the left side. It proved to be empty.

He stepped outside and checked the bodies. There was a man down with part of his head shot away. The car driver was dead, his face and chest covered with blood. He went around the car. One of the men from the house lay there, also dead. He heard John call him.

"You all right?" Tom asked as he approached his nephew.

John was on his feet. He had one eye opened, though it appeared he was having trouble focusing it.

"I heard a motorcycle."

"One got away."

"Damn. Was it Baker?"

"No, I had a good look at him. Some other guy who didn't want to play. I let him go."

"You let him go?"

"Those were the rules. Baker's the one we're after. He was no threat."

"Maybe not," John replied, "but if he can identify either of us we are in deep trouble."

"And things were going so well," Tom said with a rare try at humor.

John snorted and shook his head. "Anything else?"

Tom looked around, alert. "I found what looks to be a drug lab."

John nodded. "Sounds like Baker's kind of place. He was supposed to be involved in drugs. Did you find any trace of him?"

"I'm still checking," Tom said. "You see well enough to shoot?"

"One eye working. It's enough." John motioned with his pistol. "Go ahead and get this wrapped up so we can get out of here."

Tom turned and walked up to the back of the house. He moved slowly up to the porch and cautiously entered. He found another dead man, blood covering almost half the floor. He carefully stepped around it and checked the rest of the ground floor but found nothing. He made his way upstairs. The place was deserted.

He was in a front bedroom when he looked out a window. He saw a man crawling across the ground in front of the house. Tom quickly went down the stairs, trying to make as little noise as possible. He went to the front door and slowly opened it.

Jack Baker was fifteen feet away, crawling on his elbows. His right leg was bloody behind the knee. Tom silently stepped out of the house and walked towards him.

When Baker and Coulter came out of the house Baker immediately made for the front of the car, intending to put it between him and whoever was attacking them. He heard the shotgun and felt a wasp sting behind his knee.

His leg folded up and he fell on his face, his gun skidding away. For a moment, his breath was gone. He heard a second shot and Coulter's grunt as he fell. Baker played dead, trying to see his gun through half-closed eyes. When there were no more shots he tried to get up to go back and get Coulter's gun, but his leg refused to support him. The wasp sting was beginning to feel like a piece of iron stuck into the joint.

After the motorcycle sped off, Baker heard movement off to his left towards the barn and decided this was a good time to get away. Crawling, he thought, had the advantage that it kept him low and out of sight. But the pain was increasing with every move and he found he had to stop and let the hammering in his leg subside before he could proceed.

A few minutes later, he heard movement in the house and realized it was probably being searched. It motivated him to keep going in spite of the pain. His target was a woodpile on the other side of the front yard.

Suddenly he felt a foot in the small of his back, pressing down, not too hard. He stopped.

"You want to roll over very slowly," a voice said.

The guy hadn't killed him, Baker realized, which meant he wanted something, which meant there was still a chance. He tried to roll away from the man but the lifting of his right leg was too painful. He went the other way and managed it, though he had to grit his teeth to keep from calling out. He looked up into the muzzle of a shotgun. He squinted at the man holding it, some old guy with a white mustache wearing a farmer's cap.

"You're Jack Baker," the old man said.

"So what do you want?" Baker demanded. "What's the deal?"

The old man cocked his head to one side. "What do you mean?"

"I mean," Baker said through clenched teeth as another wave of pain swept up from his leg, "what do you want? What's an old bastard like you doing here? What did you come for?"

"Do you remember Eileen Parker?" The old man's voice was soft and calm.

"Who?" Baker squinted up, trying to place the face. It was somehow familiar, but he was sure he had never met the man before. "Ah, yeah," he went on, remembering. "She was that girl who got accidentally shot. So what about her?"

"She was my granddaughter."

Baker pushed himself up on his elbows. "Your granddaughter. Is that what this is all about? Who the fuck do you think you are, some kind of Dirty Harry? You came here for some kind of revenge thing?"

The old man shook his head.

"No. I just came for you."

Then   Baker   was   dead.

Chapter 80

JJ watched the Parkers moving down the tree line and still did not use his radio. His powerful binoculars made it possible to focus in clearly on the two men's faces. They were alert, serious.

He knew they were coming for Jack Baker and part of him knew he could not allow it, could not allow these men to take the law into their own hands.

Even as he saw them, he saw the picture of Karen leaning against the shredded patrol car, Robert Black's blood matting her hair, her body trembling, her hands still gripping her gun.

Those people tried to kill Karen. They killed Steve Johnson. They mangled Robert Black. They killed Eileen Parker. They make and sell poison.

He swept his binoculars back to the farm. The two men coming from the barn had separated. He finally recognized one, a Rider named Hoover. The other one walked towards the Quonset hut, but Hoover, clowning as he went, headed towards the edge of the tree line and the Parkers.

If he called for help, what would happen? In the time it would take for a response, the Parkers would be gone, if this was just some sort of recon. If it was more than that, then what? If they were really coming after Jack Baker, by the time reinforcements showed up they would be dead.

After all, this was an old farmer and his nephew, a college professor. Forget about their backgrounds. That was ancient history. They weren't soldiers any more. They were out of their league.

JJ swept his binoculars back to the Parkers. Tom Parker was kneeling down, holding the shotgun. John Parker, a few feet ahead, was slowly stepping forward to the edge of the tree line, both hands holding a pistol low. JJ saw Hoover approaching and, rising, started to shout a warning.

Then the shooting, the killing, began.

Hoover was down and John was above him, firing downward. Then John dove to the ground and out of sight behind the soybeans. JJ saw men running towards John's position even as Tom Parker got up and stepped forward. Men were hit, falling, then the man from the car fired a burst where JJ thought John was. There was no return fire from John.

JJ put his hand on his pistol while his other hand kept the binoculars to his eyes. He was too far away for a shot at the man trying to kill John Parker but... Without realizing he was doing it, he walked forward, his hand pulling his pistol free.

Tom Parker stepped from behind the tree line. He was firing as he came, looking like some wrathful figure from the Old Testament. The man from the car went down but firing started from the house, a burst from an assault weapon. Parker spun and fired.

Then two men spilled from the house side door. Parker fired twice and they were both down.

It seemed to be over. In seconds. JJ had taken no more than four steps and now stood at the border of the soybean field, a collapsed wire fence gently touching his shins. He saw John Parker handing additional shells to Tom who then moved slowly towards the barn. A man suddenly emerged from behind a pile of boxes and ran away. Incredibly, Parker let him go. The fading thunder of the motorcycle was the only sound JJ heard.

JJ holstered his pistol – too little, too late to intervene, he thought. He brought his hand up to the binoculars and slowly crouched. It looked like it was over. Now what was he going to do?

He saw Tom Parker checking the buildings but there did not appear to be any other people left. The old man was gone for a fairly long time in the Quonset hut. He came out waving his hand in front of his face and pausing to take several breaths. Leaving the door open behind him, he walked over to the barn. After a moment, he re-emerged and walked back to where John Parker lay. John rose from the soy beans, apparently all right, and the two talked for a moment.

Tom Parker went to the house and up the steps to the screened porch. He disappeared into the house. Several minutes passed. JJ noticed that a breeze had come up and a line of low, dark gray clouds was appearing above the trees to the west.

There was a sudden boom from the shotgun, followed by more silence. Tom Parker came around from the front of the house and passed the car. He returned to John, helped him stand up, and said something to John. He gave John the shotgun.

John handed him something small back and Tom studied it for a moment. JJ caught a glimpse of what the old man was holding – a shotgun shell. Then Tom was looking at the ground and slowly doing a walk around John, pausing to bend over and pick things up off the ground.

Policing up his brass.

Then he walked John over to a water tap on the side of the house. He turned the water on and John washed off his eyes. Tom turned and went into the barn.

After a minute he came out. He had a large, red gas can, one of the heavy duty five gallon models. From the way Parker was walking it was probably full. In his other hand he was carrying what appeared to be a long-shafted screw driver.

Parker went into the Quonset hut, leaving the gas can in the doorway. He disappeared into the darkness for several minutes. He emerged briefly, wiping his face with a bandanna. He was taking deep breaths.

That's definitely the drug lab.

Parker tied the bandanna around his face and went back in. He was out a few minutes later. He picked up the gas can and stepped back in. JJ saw he was doing something with the top of it. Then he dragged a chair over into the doorway. He took a moment to position it, looking across the field, and then put the gas can on it. He tilted the can over so its base was facing the doorway. Then he left.

JJ studied the lab for a moment. The gas can's bottom, elevated a couple of feet off the floor by the chair, was clearly visible. JJ saw an intermittent stream of fuel dribbling down. It would start, run for a while, then stop, replaced by a few drops. Then it would start up again. It wasn't very heavy, so it wasn't the case that the cap was removed. JJ suddenly realized that the smaller vent cap was open. Fuel would come out until the air pressure inside dropped, at which point it would have to stop while air bubbled into the can. The stream would resume until the pressure dropped.

What the hell?

Tom returned to John. John had the shotgun while Tom held his arm, though John seemed to be able to walk without difficulty. They cut across the soybean field, not going back by their route alongside the tree line. They were aimed for a point about two hundred yards to JJ's right. He followed them with his binoculars until he could no longer track them without leaning out of his covered position.

After a few seconds there was a sudden, loud whistle, followed by a bang. He remembered the devices back at the first drug lab.

Must have tripped a noise-maker, not that there's anyone to notice it.

He put the binoculars down and looked at the radio. Now what? Did he call for help now? What was his story?

He realized he did not wish to do anything to harm either of the Parkers. They had come here, he believed, out of need to avenge Eileen Parker and it looked like they had done that, and then some. In the process they cleaned Butler County of some ugly people who JJ had been hunting for what seemed to be a very long time.

They had done, he finally realized, what he would have liked to do. He wanted revenge for what they had done to his county, his friends, his lover, and he felt no regret that the vengeance had come from outside the law.

After all these years, it seemed a little strange for him to let the law go in favor of justice.

Maybe it is time for you to stop being a cop. Maybe going to school, maybe working at this whole justice thing from another angle is what you need to be doing.

He looked up at the gathering storm. It looked like it would be a good one. There was the smell of rain in the air.

Suddenly there was the sharp report of a rifle and a streak of red ripped from his right, like a glowing iron bar twenty or thirty feet long, and lanced into the open doorway of the drug lab. JJ barely identified the thing as a tracer when there was an orange-white blossom of a fireball, almost immediately followed by a tremendous explosion from within the building.

A blue-white, expanding wave of fire engulfed the first fireball as the wall of the lab blew outward. The metal structure flew apart and the explosion erupted out of the building, instantly hiding it within a climbing, churning, flaming mass.

Instinctively he ducked and he felt the explosion in the earth beneath him. The shockwave and sound slapped the air around JJ and the trees shook.

Burning pieces of the lab came down everywhere; he heard them rippling across the soybean field. Larger torn sheets of metal came down next, striking the ground with metallic slaps. When he looked back up the lab had disintegrated. Its sloping metal cover was peeled back like a banana in places; the rest was gone. Fire burned, with ugly black and white smoke, virtually the entire length of the lab. The flame was of several different colors as it fed off the stored chemicals. Burning pieces of building and equipment were all over the place. The pile of boxes was burning and there were a couple of small fires on top of the barn's roof, and a blown-in window was emitting a slow tendril of smoke. Little islands of fire and smoking material were scattered on and beyond the house.

Well, that's sure to be noticed.

He could not see the Parkers. He picked up his radio and made his way back to his car. It was a lot easier going back, since he knew where to avoid the problems he encountered on the way in. Still, it took him a good half hour, even pushing himself as fast as he could. He heard sirens while he was still deep in the woods.

He got to his car and quickly turned it around. He tossed the handheld radio aside and got onto the car radio.

"This is Jeffers. Anyone there?"

"Ah, yeah, JJ. Pete Santiago here. What's up?"

"I just saw the drug lab we were looking for explode. Get everyone you can to come out to the Rader farm. It's on White Horse Road, just east of..." He paused as he got to the intersection and slued the car to the left. "East of Perryville Road. Got it?"

"That's a rog," Santiago said. "I'm scrambling everyone. What about locals?"

JJ laughed. "This thing went off like a nuke. You already got every volunteer firefighting company for ten miles on the way and they'll be bringing the local cops and they've probably called it in to county. Just hurry." He put the mike back and scanned the county frequencies. As he expected, there was a lot of excited chatter. He cut in.

"This is Deputy Sheriff James Jeffers. There has been a chemical explosion on the Rader farm on White Horse Road. Let the Ohio EPA people know and make sure incoming firefighters have masks and protective gear. It's a crime scene so secure it as best you can. There will probably be federal agents responding."

There were a series of acknowledgments. He saw numerous flashing lights in front of him and he slowed down. Another Sheriff's car was at the lane entrance for the farm. He raised his ID to the woman officer standing there and she waved him through.

When he crested the hill, he saw half a dozen emergency vehicles, including a police car and an ambulance. The barn was partially on fire and the firefighters were busy with it. The debris fires on the house appeared to have gone out on their own. He slid the car to a halt in front of the house.

He thought for a moment, then opened the glove compartment and took out the two old batteries there; they were the ones, he remembered, that had faded. He popped out the batteries from the handheld radio and replaced them with the two from the glove compartment. He stuffed the other two back into the compartment, shut it, and got out of the car.

It was a lot darker. Low clouds covered the sky, and they were a deep black. The smell of rain was greater. JJ went back to the trunk of the car and got out his rain gear, a heavy black slicker with "Sheriff" in tall, yellow letters on the back. He shrugged himself into it and walked towards the house.

There were two local police officers and an EMT standing over a body on its back on the yard. JJ joined them. It was Jack Baker.

"Deputy," one of the locals said, looking up. "Got any idea of what's going on here?"

"That's Jack Baker," JJ said, looking down at the dead man with a fist-sized hole in his chest. "He's wanted for questioning about the ambush of those officers a few days ago." The cop's eyes went wide. JJ pointed towards the barn. "There's a vehicle in there that was probably used in the commission of that felony. You might want to ask the firefighters to drag it out of there if it looks like they can't save the barn." The officer immediately ran off. The other officer and the EMT looked at JJ.

"Have a nice day," JJ said, and walked away.

More emergency vehicles were arriving, kicking up the driveway dust. He felt a heavy raindrop hit his shoulder. Other drops began to kick up little spurts of dust as they impacted the earth. Then it began to really pour, accompanied by an increase in the wind. He pulled an old Cincinnati Reds ball cap from a pocket of the slicker and pulled it on.

The drug lab was mostly foul smelling smoke and twisted wreckage. The barn was burning along one wall but the firefighters were attacking it from both inside and outside, using a tanker truck attached to two different pumpers. Police were arriving and more ambulances were showing up. Vehicles were parking on the shoulder of the lane and county deputies were directing traffic.

He walked over to the edge of the soybean field. Hoover's body had not been disturbed. The rain was coming down furiously now and it was hard to see very far. The firefighters were winning the battle for the barn;

the outside fire seemed to be completely out. He started to walk towards the house when he felt something under his foot.

He looked down. It was a red shotgun shell, partially covered by a clod of earth. He glanced around, but no one was looking in his direction. He reached down and picked it up. Remington 12-gauge, double-ought buckshot. He put it in his pocket.

Fifteen minutes later the rain had not let up at all. The fires were all completely out and many of the crews were being released, which was making for a bit of a traffic jam as they tried to get up the lane while other vehicles were still trying to get in.

Eventually a couple of officers using radios got it straightened out. Task force cars arrived and he saw Davidson's bald head on the other side of several police cars. He suddenly felt very tired and looked for a place to sit down.

JJ was sitting on the house's side door steps, watching everyone else work and letting the rain come down on him as if in penance, when Carl Davidson walked up. He had on a black ATF jacket and baseball cap with a federal emblem but it offered no protection for his lower legs, which were completely soaked.

"Let's get in your vehicle," he said, and led the way. JJ followed.

"Christ, what a mess," Davidson said, and blew his nose. "I think I'm developing pneumonia." He did an elaborate wiping maneuver on his nose and then stuffed his handkerchief away. "So what do you got?"

"I came up on the farm from behind, on the other side of the field. Wanted to get some eyes-on an area from my survey. I thought I saw Jack Baker and some other Steel Riders walking around. Could make out that big building out beyond the barn. Did you see it?"

Davidson nodded. "What's left of it."

"I could see that it had a big air conditioning unit attached to it, so I figured I'd hit pay dirt. Then all hell broke loose. I saw at least two people, there could have been more. Big firefight. The lab went up and the people took off. I tried to call for help, but my radio's batteries were too weak." He pulled it from its belt sheath and put it on the dash in front of him. "Had to get back to the car and use my radio."

"Yeah, Santiago took the call." Davidson sniffed. "Why didn't you use the telephone in the house?"

"Well," JJ said, "after the explosion I thought the house was going up as well. To be honest, I didn't think of it until I was deep in the woods and at that point I figured it was faster to get to my car then to try and go back."

Davidson nodded, though he looked a little disappointed. "Yeah, I ran into Bob Phillips. He said the phone and power lines were cut by the explosion." He began fishing for his handkerchief again. "Sorry we didn't get here earlier."

"No big deal," JJ replied. "Not much anyone could do about all this."

"You get a good look at the perps?"

"No, they were hooded, masked. Hit the place like pros. Seemed to know exactly where they were going. Who do you think they were?"

Davidson shrugged. "Santiago and Johnny Paulson think this was the hit team we heard the Dragons were importing to take care of the Steel Riders, that they were nibbling at the edges up to now and finally dropped the hammer."

"Sounds possible," JJ said carefully.

"Maybe." Davidson's voice was flat. "There's not much left of the Dragons. Hard to believe contract hit men would follow through when there was no one to pay them."

"Paid in advance?"

"Hitters with a sense of business integrity?" Davidson snorted. "Next thing, they'll be getting some sort of award from Forbes magazine. No, I figure if they had their money they would have just walked, at least after the Dragons were blown away. Why bother?"

"So...?"

"So shit," Davidson replied. "I don't know who the fuck did this. Christ, the place looks like it was hit by the Marines. Whoever did this was very, very pissed off."

There was a knock at the window. JJ rolled it down and another deputy was there.

"Hey, JJ," the woman said.

"Hey, Carol," he replied. "What can I do you for?"

"Bob Phillips needs you for a couple of minutes if you can get away."

JJ looked at Davidson, who said, "Go ahead. I'll wait here for a while."

JJ followed the deputy and got to Phillips, who was in the middle of a circle of police officers near the speed lab.

"Are we having fun yet?" he asked as JJ walked up.

"Every day and in every way," JJ replied. "What's up?"

"Can you do a walk around with me and give us a preliminary ID on these people?"

"Sure," JJ said. "The one out front is Jack Baker. Did you already get that?"

"Yeah, but I want to take a look. Let's go."

He and JJ did the circuit of the dead men, most of whom JJ knew from the task force's files and had no problem identifying them as he stood over them. The rain had cleaned up the bodies a little before they were covered, but it didn't help much. JJ found he had no reaction, even when looking at the head wounds, until they went into the house and saw Les Coulter.

"Jesus, that poor son of a bitch," one of the other officers said with a quavering voice. Phillips glanced at him and then at JJ, who was calmly looking into the dead man's open eyes.

"You know him?"

"Lester Coulter. Brother of the other Coulter we saw outside. County's going to have a Coulter shortage, it looks like." His voice was calm. The officer with the shaky voice suddenly left. They heard him vomiting outside. JJ looked down at the corpse.

"As you sew, asshole," he said quietly to himself.

"What?" Phillips asked.

"Nothing," JJ said, shaking his head. "We done?"

"Six dead and a drug lab blown to hell. We're either very done or we've only just begun." Phillips grinned. "Yeah, go ahead. I'll get you guys a prelim by the end of the day."

JJ nodded and went back to his car. Davidson was gone. He looked around. The rain had seemed lighter when he came out of the house. Now it was picking up again, along with the wind. The yellow and orange tarps over the scattered corpses were flapping in the wind; one blew away and he saw a police officer chase it down next to the barn and bring it back.

He walked into the barn. Santiago and a couple of others from the task force were looking over the shoulders of some forensic people who were carefully dusting the rear door with fingerprint powder. There was a heavy smell of burned wood in the air and firefighters were still inspecting the far wall. It was getting dark, but some emergency lights, running off their own generator, were just coming on line. He watched the forensic people, wearing blue windbreakers with big "FBI"'s in yellow on their backs, for a while.

Santiago turned around. "See the holes? From Karen's ten mike-mike. She done good, JJ."

JJ nodded. "I hope she understands that."

It was Santiago's turn to nod. "Sooner or later, she will."

JJ went back out into the rain, looking for Davidson. He finally found him near the destroyed lab. He was watching more forensic people, this time in hip wader boots and air masks, slowly walk through the wreckage. From time to time one of them would carefully crouch down and examine a piece of wreckage.

Davidson looked up. "They're looking for bodies. But they're not going to find any, are they?" It sounded vaguely like a challenge.

"I don't know," he said.

"Well, did you see anyone go in before the explosion?"

"One man went in and then came out. The explosion took place a little later. I figured it was a stray round."

"Uh-huh." Davidson's voice was noncommittal. "Stray round."

Something was going on with Davidson, but JJ didn't know what it was. He decided the safest thing was to keep silent.

He followed Davidson around for the rest of the day. The rain finally slacked off towards evening and more emergency lights were set up, filling the air with the sound of their generators. The firefighters left. With the identification of the white van as being from the ambush it became a federal investigation and the locals were released a few at a time, though a handful stayed to keep the site secure.

One of the fire companies brought a service truck with it. Run by volunteers, it dispensed hot coffee, sodas, and food. It stayed on after the emergency and fire vehicles left, for which the feds were grateful.

JJ and Davidson were working on cups of coffee and watching as more federal forensic people arrived. JJ was impressed by the numbers involved. Night was falling rapidly. The rain was gone but the low hanging clouds brought early darkness.

"Getting dark," he observed.

Davidson nodded. He blew his nose and then looked over at JJ.

"What do you think happened here?"

JJ paused. "Maybe Santiago is right, maybe it was a professional hit."

Davidson shook his head. "No." He took another sip of his coffee.

"Doesn't add up," Davidson finally said. "The money doesn't fit, and the style doesn't fit. Looks like someone used a shotgun and a pistol on these people. Kind of underpowered for professional hitters. There's several thousand dollars laying in plain view on a chest of drawers upstairs, untouched. And already packaged, highly sellable speed in the trunk of the car and in the kitchen, also untouched. Doesn't make any sense that pros would leave that shit behind. No, I think this was different."

He paused to blow his nose. "Damn summer colds are the worst," he observed. JJ waited in silence.

"You remember a long time ago, back when we got the word on Hollingsworth being blown away, and then Christopher, and we were all trying to figure out who was doing what to whom? And you suggested it might be someone other than the Dragons, a third party?"

JJ nodded, silently.

"What I think happened here," he said, making a sweeping gesture with his handkerchief, "is that a third party came along. This was not a professional hit. This was personal. I think."

He took another sip.

"And what do you think, Deputy Jeffers?"

"You could be right," JJ said.

Davidson nodded. "Well, we'll see." He stuffed his handkerchief in the pocket of his windbreaker and held his coffee with both hands, taking heat from it in the cooling evening breeze.

"Yeah," he said, looking around at the yellow tarps flapping in the wind,   "this   was   personal."

Chapter 81

JJ arrived at work early but the parking lot of the task force office building was almost full. Davidson had released him before the rain began again but he listened to it all night as he lay sleepless in bed. He tried to call Karen but there was no answer.

He went into the building. Anne was working away at her keyboard, earphones plugged into a cassette player, and she smiled up at him as she typed. He checked for messages but there weren't any.

"Karen in this morning?" he asked, leaning over to Anne. She suddenly looked concerned.

"Oh, JJ, she's gone." She took off her earphones. "She left this morning, to accompany Steve back to Virginia. I thought you knew."

"Must have slipped my mind," he said weakly and went to his desk.

Peter Santiago and John Paulson came over.

"Good morning," Paulson said. "Did you hear that you may finally be getting us all out of your hair?"

JJ looked up, puzzled. "What do you mean?"

"What he means is our work here is done," Santiago said. "There's no lab to find, except with tweezers, and there's no organization to investigate, except with a mop. It's over, finito, done. We're out of here."

Paulson nodded. "Yeah, Carl got the word last night when he talked to DEA-DC. Wants us to shift our ops to the Illinois thing. We got an investigation going on..." Santiago caught his eye and Paulson paused.

"Ah, shit, Pete, this is JJ, for Christ's sake!"

Before Santiago could say anything JJ held up a hand.

"I understand. The locals only need to know what they need to know." He paused. "No harm done, no offense taken." He made himself grin, though he didn't feel it.

Back to being a spear carrier. Maybe less.

"Besides," he continued, "I got enough paperwork of my own to take care of, without having to keep you feds out of trouble."

Santiago nodded and looked down, embarrassed by the situation. John Paulson, AKA Johnny Ringo, looked JJ in the eyes.

"Class, man." He lightly punched JJ in the arm and the two agents went back to their desks.

JJ turned on his computer. He had three messages. The first was a general memo to everyone saying that the task force would be shifting location within the next few days and that everyone would be getting their individual assignments. The second was a message from Karen. It just listed a telephone number and asked him to call after three PM. He looked at the clock. Seven hours to go. Great.

The third message was from Davidson and asked him to see him as soon as he could. He got up and straightened his tie. His stomach was contracting into a knot. He didn't know what was coming but he wasn't looking forward to it. How much did Davidson know? How much had he guessed?

He knocked on the open door of Davidson's office. The DEA agent was talking with another person, looking at an open folder, and held up one finger. JJ waited outside for a moment and then the other agent left. He took a breath and walked in.

"Close the door, would you, Deputy?" Davidson's eyes were on him but were unreadable. JJ closed the door and sat down in a chair Davidson gestured towards.

"A couple of things have come up," he said. "I want to bounce them off you." JJ nodded as Davidson paused. "You remember you said when you saw Baker's place attacked, you tried to call for help but your batteries were too weak to reach us, so you had to make your way back to your car?"

JJ nodded, his heart pounding. Davidson reached over and opened a desk drawer, He pulled out JJ's handheld radio and carefully laid it on the desk.

"You left this behind when you went to talk to Phillips last night. Forgot it, I guess. A lot of that going around, seems like. I forgot mine; left it in my car." His gaze was steady on JJ. "Didn't want to go out in the rain to get it, what with my cold. So I tried yours. Figured that even with weak batteries I could talk to our guys at the scene."

He picked up the radio and turned it on. There was an initial surge of static and it went silent. He keyed the transmit button and released it. There was another quick spasm of static, then silence again.

"So I turned it on just like that last night. Had no problem raising our guys, like I figured. Loud and clear. I was about to put it away when I got a call on it. It was the watch officer. She was here and had heard my transmission, so she responded. Loud and clear. She had no problem reading me." He thumbed the radio off and put it down.

"I was surprised. Couldn't figure it out. Then a couple of things fell into place. I remembered that when my radio died you gave me your good spare set of batteries. I left my shot batteries with you. Remember?" He proceeded without waiting for JJ to respond. "After you gave me your good set, I remembered and got a new set and replaced the dead ones when I went to lunch the next day. Your car door wasn't locked so I slipped the new ones in your glove compartment and threw away the old, dead ones. Meant to tell you, but got busy and forgot. Like I said, a lot of that going around."

"Having nothing else to do and a little curious, I popped open your radio and there they were, the two new batteries I left for you. I could tell they were the ones I left because, when I got them out of their damned plastic wrapping, I accidentally scratched them right across their fronts with my scissors." He shook his head. "Damned near took off my own finger getting those things out. Anyway, there it was, mystery explained. Your batteries had failed and you had reached for spares and used the ones I had left. Left your dead ones in the glove compartment. No problem. That the way it went?"

JJ could think of nothing else and nodded.

"Wrong answer. You make a lousy liar, deputy."

He folded his hands "Except what caught my eye was they have the same expiration date as the ones in your radio. Month and year, sitting there in plain sight. This morning I ran a quick test and the two batteries left in the glove compartment have turned out to be just as good as the new ones I left for you. To put it another way, despite what you told me, none of the batteries you had were bad."

JJ started to say something but Davidson held up his hand.

"I don't want to hear some dumb shit about sunspots. There's more. In the mess of the speed lab the forensic guys found the bottom of a heavy duty gas can. Nothing left of the rest of the can. Bullet hole in it. Doesn't look to match the caliber of any of the other weapons used in the gunfight. Almost as if someone had deliberately nailed it. Seems damned odd. One explanation could be that someone shot it up from a distance in order to blow the lab." Davidson unfolded his hands.

"See, the lab didn't just burn down. It blew up. From end to end. The forensic folks say it could only have happened if there was an explosive aerosol mixture. The building itself was a bomb, holding a mix of air and fuel. These places are time bombs, no question, but this was so thorough it suggested that the ether, the prime suspect for the aerosol explosive, must have been highly concentrated, very highly concentrated." He leaned forward.

"And so it was very interesting when we found, late last night, some of the metal caps to the ether bottles. The plastic bottles themselves were gone, of course, melted away. But a lot of the lids survived. Guess what? Each one had a hole punched in it, like if you had used a screwdriver. Do that to enough bottles, leave them on their sides and let them dribble out into an enclosed place, and then set the whole thing off by igniting a gas can."

He waved his hand. "The plastic ether jugs come four to a box. Easiest thing for a methodical man would be to open the top of the box, punch his holes, and put the box down on its side. All four bottles dribble away. On to the next box. There were probably ten or twelve such boxes in there, I would guess, maybe more. Throw in the gas can and the other chemicals lying around, including the gas line for the Bunsen burners, and it's Hiroshima."

"But all that means someone took some time to do it. Not the work of a pro. He would throw in a grenade, maybe some C-4, something quick and dirty. This guy wanted to blow this place to another universe. Not a pro," Davidson repeated.

"Strange goings on. So where does this leave me?" He looked at JJ. "I've been doing some thinking. I don't know if any of this is provable, and I know there are other explanations. Care to give me one?"

JJ remained silent.

"I didn't think so." Davidson sat back in his chair and put his hands behind his head. "Okay, let's build a scenario. Let's say we've got a dedicated county cop who's really pissed that a bunch of scumbags are polluting his territory. He's working hard, trying to apprehend said scumbags, but he's not having much luck. And the scumbags are real shit, as such people tend to be. They kill a young girl, total innocent. They get off on a technicality. Then they try to kill a woman in whom, how to put this, he has an interest. They mess her up psychologically. And they kill a friend of his, and badly wound a guy he works with, another cop."

"And let's say our cop begins to suspect somebody, maybe a relative of the young girl, is coming after the scumbags. At first, he played good cop and let everyone know his suspicions, but no one took them seriously. But after his lady friend is hurt and his friend is killed and his buddy is shot, he stops talking about his suspicions. He probably doesn't even notice, though maybe his boss does."

Davidson rested his elbows on his desk, his voice calm. "His boss is his boss because he is very good at being a cop himself and he notices things, like batteries' expiration dates, like bullet holes in gas cans that remind him of a dead biker named Christopher, like things people talk about and don't talk about."

JJ remained silent.

"Our cop is checking out the area and he succeeds where everyone else with their computers and data bases and informants has failed. He finds the scumbags. But so has the young girl's relative. And our cop has a dilemma. Does he try to stop the relative from extracting revenge? Maybe he really doesn't have a chance to, maybe it goes down too fast. The relative, maybe more than one, is something of a pro, it turns out. That's what our cop has been trying to tell everyone, but no one listened, no one took him seriously."

"Once it goes down, he has another choice. Turn the relative in, or keep his mouth shut. But he constructs some lousy story about bad batteries. He puts his ass on the line for the little girl's relative. So," Davidson leaned back in his chair again and folded his arms across his chest, "what's it going to be, deputy? Is our cop going to talk?"

JJ recognized, even in his nervousness, what Davidson was doing. He also knew Davidson had no real evidence. He remained silent. Davidson let the silence go on for a minute. He shook his head. Finally, he smiled.

"This isn't our investigation any longer. We're out of here by the end of the week. My speculations are my own and aren't going to be shared with anyone. You and the others may be home free."

Davidson paused and then continued. "Karen told me you were thinking about going to law school, getting out of being a cop. That may be a good idea. At our end, the law is a structure we've got to work with. Too much chance of causing too much damage if we step over the line. You know that. You've been too good a cop not to. Give it some thought. Maybe it's time for you to move on." He stood up.

"I'm seeing to it that a letter of commendation will come from DEA-DC to your superior." As JJ stood Davidson held out his hand. "You did good work with us," he said, "and Steve Johnson and Karen Deevers are friends of mine, too."

JJ got to his feet and took Davidson's hand.

"JJ, you southern Ohio boys play a little rough," Davidson said quietly. JJ said nothing and left the office.

Chapter 82

You live your life on a knife edge but seldom realize it. Each moment is a critical junction with the outcome of the path not taken forever unknown, only suspected. JJ spent the hours before making his call to Karen wondering on the choices he had made and wondering what would be found on the path now taken.

Davidson was right. He had crossed a line and he realized he could not go on being a deputy. He had exercised a power which he had no right to, not as long as he wore his uniform. He had passed judgment on the Parkers, one that he felt was the right one, the just one, but the very act of judgment was forbidden to him. It was time to move on.

Threads; the lives of the people around him were indeed like threads. Flimsy, they could end abruptly, as they did for the six men at Rader's farm. Or they could be pulled easily from the weave of his life. He looked around the room. These people would be leaving his life soon and he would never see most of them again.

What had he lost by the unsaid word, by the choice to turn left instead of right? What might have his friendship with Steve Johnson become? If he had offered to give him and Karen a ride, what would have changed? And Karen, what of her? Did he say the right thing, the wrong thing?

Like most honest men, he did not know what the right thing for a woman always was and most of the time had to work hard to keep his clumsiness, his fear, out of the way.

The clock crawled by as he tried to distract himself with paperwork. William Rader, after planting his last crop in the early spring, had died. His widow, angry at the very earth that had taken her husband's time and, eventually, life away from her, had fled to relatives. The farm was rented out. A multilayered front had taken it up and moved in the drug lab from its previous location below Covington. Evidence found in the house was providing leads to bank accounts, other front organizations, drug connections and suppliers.

None of the reports were real to JJ. Others would be following up the leads, doing the investigations.

He waited until three and then punched the numbers into the telephone. It was answered by a woman whose voice he didn't recognize.

"Hello." The voice sounded very tired.

"Hello, this is Deputy Sheriff James Jeffers calling for Karen Deevers." He waited a small eternity, maybe two seconds, until the woman responded.

"Just a minute." The receiver was put down. He heard voices in the distance. Then the phone was fumbled with.

"Hello?" It was Karen.

"Hello, it's me, JJ," he hastily added. "What's up? How're you doing?" *What should I be saying?*

"Hi, JJ." Karen's voice sounded very small and far away. "Sorry I couldn't see you before I left, but the arrangements were made kind of suddenly and they asked me if I would escort Steve back."

"No, no, no problem," he said quickly. "I understand. How're you doing?"

Karen paused. "It's been hard," she said finally. "Barb's hanging in there. I think it's a help that I'm here. I don't know."

"It sounds rough."

Karen made no reply.

"They're moving the task force," JJ said.

"I know," she said. "Carl called a little while ago."

JJ took a breath.

"Will you be going with them?" He paused and closed his eyes. "Or will you be coming back here?" There was silence. He heard bits of distant static and clicks, echoes from some other dimension.

"Oh, J. So much has happened. So much." She fell silent.

JJ understood. As much as he didn't want to, he understood. She had been through an avalanche, and he was associated with it. How could she ever look at him again without seeing all those other, terrible pictures? And because he loved her, he found that he was willing to let her go, to let her go easily, even while he hated himself for it.

"Yeah, that's true. Well, you take care of yourself, and if there's anything I can do to help out from here, just..."

"JJ, what are you saying?"

"I, ah," he fumbled for words, trying to end it cleanly, "I mean I understand. You've got to go on and..."

"JJ, would you please shut up?" He did, mostly because he had no idea what was happening. She came back on the line, her voice still small and distant.

"Do you love me?"

"God, yes!" he said, almost blurting it.

"Then I'm coming back," she said, her voice stronger, firmer. "What I was trying to say is a lot has happened but one thing that has helped me get through it has been loving you. Do you understand that?"

For a moment ,JJ couldn't speak and he silently nodded his assent.

"Yes," he said silently. "Yes, I understand."

"I'll be coming back. I have some leave saved. We'll talk, make plans, maybe I'll take that slot in Cincinnati."

"Whatever," he said. "I love you."

"I love you."

They hung up and JJ just looked at the telephone for a long time and thought about threads that intertwined and became as one.

Chapter 83

John Wesley Parker, a temporary patch over one eye, and Thomas Luther Parker sat on a hillside on the family farm and watched the sun slide down, a finger's width from touching the horizon. The doctor at the Oxford Community Hospital had insisted John continue to wear the patch for several more days, though there was no damage to the eyeball itself. The eyelid, painted in antiseptic, was badly cut and he wanted it to heal properly. He had then gone on a lecture about farm accidents and urged John to be more careful around dirt-moving machinery.

"A cheap pair of safety glasses are worth it," he said as they left the ER, and they agreed with him.

Between the two men was the jug of water Tom had packed before they left for Rader's farm. From time to time one or the other would unscrew the lid and take a short swallow and pass it to the other.

"I remember what you told me before I left for 'Nam," John said at one point, "about how when I got back we'd take a couple of sleeping bags and go off in the woods with a bottle."

Tom patted the top of the jug of water. "The bottle would have been for you. I can't touch the stuff anymore, myself."

"Just wanted you to know I never really forgot that offer." John took a swallow. "I should have taken you up on it." He passed the jug to Tom who also took a drink.

"Well, we all do what we can," Tom replied.

"I think I'm glad it's over," John said quietly. "I felt like I had to find out, one last time, if I still had it, if I could still unchain the dragon and do something that mattered."

Tom looked at him. "I know the feeling. Nothing worse than beginning to feel you're irrelevant. But I'll let you in on a little secret." He took a sip. "As long as your family lives, your life matters. They will always need your strength."

John took the jug and took a sip.

"Hey, what're you guys doing?" Ellen, Catherine and Terri in tow, was coming up the hill from the direction of the farm house.

"Just watching the sun go down," John said as Ellen flopped down beside him.

"It's very pretty," Ellen judged.

"Yes, it is," Tom agreed.

Catherine sat beside her father and Terri beside her.

"It's over," Tom said. She squeezed his arm.

"No, it's still going down," Ellen said. "See? Everything is turning orange."

"Is your eye okay?" Terri asked John.

"Oh, it'll be fine. But I'm keeping the patch on for my committee meeting next week. I think it makes me look like a pirate."

"It looks cool," Ellen said. "But don't make it a habit." John gave her a hug.

"I'll try not to."

"We have a visitor," Tom said, motioning towards a figure coming up the hill from the farm house. They all turned and looked. In the dimming light the figure, a tall man, was hard to identify, but they could see his dark uniform, complete with a narrow brimmed Stetson.

"Hello, folks," JJ said. "How're y'all doing?" He spoke with a southern Ohio twang.

"We're doing just fine, officer," Tom said, rising to his feet. "Admiring the view."

"It is pretty," JJ said. "I'm Deputy Sheriff James Jeffers. Most people call me 'JJ'." He held out his hand to Tom.

Tom took it and started to introduce himself.

"That's all right, Mr. Parker," JJ said, interrupting him. "I know you and your family." He shook his hand firmly and turned to the others, shaking their hands in turn.

"You're John Wesley Parker, I believe. Hope your eye's okay. And Ms. Catherine Parker, good to meet you, ma'am. Ms. Terri Stoneroad, Ms. Parker's friend; we've met a few times at your hospital, though you probably don't remember me. I appreciate the kindness you've shown my friends." Terri's eyes were wide with remembrance and she nodded to JJ. He stepped over in front of the young girl. "And you're Ellen Parker, Charles Parker's girl."

Ellen got up to shake his hand and noticed that he didn't act cute but took it and it shook if firmly. "Ellen," he said.

"What can we do for you, deputy?" Tom asked.

"Well, I just wanted to come by and meet you all face to face," JJ said. "As you know," he paused, "the business with those Steel Rider people is pretty much over." He glanced at Ellen.

"You mean the men who murdered Eileen," she said in a matter of fact tone. Her voice turned hard. "They're all dead." JJ looked at her for a moment.

Jesus, she sounds like she had a hand in it.

"That's right," JJ said. "There's still an investigation to find out who exactly did it, but no one's expecting to learn much. Figure it was the work of professionals. I just came by to check on you all, see if there was anything you needed."

"No," Tom replied, "we're fine, but I appreciate your asking after us."

"And I just wanted to make sure you understood it was over," JJ said, looking Tom Parker in the eye. "It's over."

Tom looked at him for a moment.

"I believe it is," he said finally.

"Good," JJ said. "Glad to hear it." He turned to the rest of the group. "Well, y'all have a good evening." He turned back to Tom and held out his hand a last time.

"You take care of these people, sir." It was said as an observation and statement, but not a command.

Tom nodded and took his hand.

"I intend to."

JJ nodded back and turned to go and then stopped. He fished in a pocket and pulled something out.

"This is yours," he said, and handed it to Tom Parker, his eyes flashing with the last of the light. Then he walked down the hill into the gathering dark. He was soon lost to sight.

Tom sat back down, looking at something in his hand.

"What did he give you?" Catherine asked.

"Just an old shotgun shell," he said, passing it to John. "An empty."

John's eye widened with surprise as he examined the shell. He looked down the hill towards the now vanished deputy.

"That," he said, "is some piece of work."

"What're you drinking?" Ellen asked.

"Not drinking," Tom said, slowly smiling. "Kind of making toasts."

"Cool. Let me make one." She took the jug and hefted it with both hands. "Here's to everyone here." She took a swallow and then got up and walked it over to Terri. "Ladies first," she said with a grin.

Terri hefted the jug while looking down the hill in the direction of the now vanished deputy sheriff. "Here's to those that take care of us," she said and took a sip. She wiped her mouth with her sleeve, grinned, and passed the jug to Catherine.

"Here's to love," Catherine said and took a sip. She reached over and gave it to John. She looked at her father out of the corner of her eye. "Beauty before age." The old man smiled but said nothing.

John looked off to the west, toward the sun almost out of sight, and maybe looked far beyond it. He raised the jug.

"Here's to everyone who didn't make the freedom bird," he said quietly, and took several large swallows. Then he poured a small amount on the ground. He wiped his mouth with the back of his hand and blinked several times. He passed the jug to his uncle.

Thomas Luther Price looked at the jug for a moment. He looked up. The sun was gone. He raised the jug in the descending darkness.

"For all my people."

They stayed on the hillside until they could see the stars. Ellen caught fireflies and brought them back to show off before releasing them again.

Then   they   went   down   the   hill   together.

Steven M. Silver

Cover by Eric Strehl
Blackheart Studios
http://www.ejstrehl.com

Other books by Steven M. Silver
  With Susan Rogers, Ph.D. *Light in the heart of darkness: EMDR and the treatment of war and terrorism survivors.*

Poetry

American Travelers
Hot Chrome, Smooth Leather, and a Red Bandanna
Victor Echo Zero Five

Fiction

The Wild Geese Saga
Mercenary's Heart
Mercenary's Honor
Mercenary's Code
Mercenary's Logic
Mercenary's Destiny
Mercenary's Soldiers
Mercenary's Redemption
Mercenary's Courage
Mercenary's Peace
Mercenary's Justice
Mercenary's Humanity
Mercenary's Promise

The Ellen Parker Series
A Dangerous Man
Killers
Woman on the Wire
Hidden Things
Child in the Dark

www.ingramcontent.com/pod-product-compliance
Lightning Source LLC
Chambersburg PA
CBHW070617260626
47161CB00007B/2465